D0170260

THE SPECULATIVE FICTION OF MARK TWAIN

DOVER THRIFT EDITIONS

Mark Twain

DOVER PUBLICATIONS, INC.
MINEOLA, NEW YORK

DOVER THRIFT EDITIONS

GENERAL EDITOR: SUSAN L. RATTINER
EDITOR OF THIS VOLUME: MICHAEL CROLAND

Bibliographical Note

This Dover edition, first published in 2018, is a new selection of eleven stories reprinted from standard texts. A new introductory note has been specially prepared for this volume. Readers should be forewarned that the text contains racial and cultural references of the era in which it was written and may be deemed offensive by today's standards.

Library of Congress Cataloging-in-Publication Data

Names: Twain, Mark, 1835–1910, author.
Title: The speculative fiction of Mark Twain / Mark Twain.
Description: Mineola, New York : Dover Publications, 2018. | Series: Dover thrift editions
Identifiers: LCCN 2018019467| ISBN 9780486826653 | ISBN 0486826651
Subjects: LCSH: Speculative fiction, American.
Classification: LCC PS1303 2018 | DDC 813/.4—dc23
LC record available at https://lccn.loc.gov/2018019467

Manufactured in the United States by LSC Communications
82665101   2018
www.doverpublications.com

Note

MARK TWAIN was born Samuel Langhorn Clemens in Florida, Missouri, in 1835. He was born two months prematurely and faced health complications for the first ten years of his life. Beginning at age eleven, he worked at a variety of jobs to support his family after his father died.

In 1863, Clemens began using the pen name Mark Twain, a river term for water just barely safe for navigation. He largely focused on humor writing. In 1865, he wrote a letter to his brother saying that he was not "proud" of his "'call' to literature of a low order—i.e. humorous," but it was his "strongest suit." His greatest books include *The Adventures of Tom Sawyer* (1876), *The Prince and the Pauper* (1881), *The Adventures of Huckleberry Finn* (1884), and *A Connecticut Yankee in King Arthur's Court* (1889).

The stories in this collection span Clemens's writing career, with the first predating his use of the pseudonym Mark Twain. The publication dates of the stories range a century, from 1862 to 1962, with two stories published posthumously. "Petrified Man" was originally published in the Virginia City *Territorial Enterprise* on October 4, 1862. "Earthquake Almanac" was originally published in the San Francisco *Dramatic Chronicle* on October 17, 1865. "From the 'London Times' of 1904" was originally published in *The Century Magazine* in November 1898. "The Loves of Alfonzo Fitz Clarence and Rosannah Ethelton" was originally published in the *Atlantic Monthly* in March 1878. "Mental Telegraphy" was originally published in *Harper's Magazine* in December 1891. "Mental Telegraphy Again" was originally published in *Harper's Magazine* in September 1895. "Extracts from Adam's Diary" was originally published by Harper & Brothers, New York, in 1906. "Eve's

Diary" was originally published by Harper & Brothers, New York, in 1906. "The Great Dark" was originally published by Harper & Row, New York, in 1962. "Captain Stormfield's Visit to Heaven" was originally published in *Harper's Magazine* in December 1907 and January 1908. "The Mysterious Stranger" was originally published by Harper & Brothers, New York, in 1916.

Clemens knew setbacks and hardship in his life, including the death of his son, Langdon, in 1872, and his later years were particularly difficult. He declared bankruptcy in 1894. His daughter Susy died of spinal meningitis in 1897. His wife, Olivia, died in 1904. His daughter Jean, who had suffered from epilepsy, died in 1909. Despite having to contend with so much loss, Clemens was appreciated in his final decade. He received honorary degrees from Yale University, the University of Missouri, and Oxford University. He passed away in 1910, survived by only his daughter Clara.

Mark Twain is remembered as one of the most important and funniest American writers. Owing to his clever sense of humor, his authentic representation of American characters, and his strong command of spoken language, Twain's novels, short stories, and other writing continue to be beloved and revered.

Contents

THE SPECULATIVE FICTION OF MARK TWAIN

PETRIFIED MAN

A PETRIFIED MAN was found some time ago in the mountains south of Gravelly Ford. Every limb and feature of the stony mummy was perfect, not even excepting the left leg, which has evidently been a wooden one during the lifetime of the owner—which lifetime, by the way, came to a close about a century ago, in the opinion of a savan who has examined the defunct. The body was in a sitting posture, and leaning against a huge mass of croppings; the attitude was pensive, the right thumb resting against the side of the nose; the left thumb partially supported the chin, the fore-finger pressing the inner corner of the left eye and drawing it partly open; the right eye was closed, and the fingers of the right hand spread apart. This strange freak of nature created a profound sensation in the vicinity, and our informant states that by request, Justice Sewell or Sowell, of Humboldt City, at once proceeded to the spot and held an inquest on the body. The verdict of the jury was that "deceased came to his death from protracted exposure," etc. The people of the neighborhood volunteered to bury the poor unfortunate, and were even anxious to do so; but it was discovered, when they attempted to remove him, that the water which had dripped upon him for ages from the crag above, had coursed down his back and deposited a limestone sediment under him which had glued him to the bed rock upon which he sat, as with a cement of adamant, and Judge S. refused to allow the charitable citizens to blast him from his position. The opinion expressed by his Honor that such a course would be little less than sacrilege, was eminently just and proper. Everybody goes to see the stone man, as many as three hundred having visited the hardened creature during the past five or six weeks.

EARTHQUAKE ALMANAC

EDS. CHRONICLE:—At the instance of several friends who feel a boding anxiety to know beforehand what sort of phenomena we may expect the elements to exhibit during the next month or two, and who have lost all confidence in the various patent medicine almanacs, because of the unaccountable reticence of those works concerning the extraordinary event of the 8th inst., I have compiled the following almanac expressly for this latitude:

Oct. 17.—Weather hazy; atmosphere murky and dense. An expression of profound melancholy will be observable upon most countenances.

Oct. 18.—Slight earthquake. Countenances grow more melancholy.

Oct. 19.—Look out for rain. It would be absurd to look in for it. The general depression of spirits increased.

Oct. 20.—More weather.

Oct. 21.—Same.

Oct. 22.—Light winds, perhaps. If they blow, it will be from the "east'ard, or the nor'ard, or the west'ard, or the suth'ard," or from some general direction approximating more or less to these points of the compass or otherwise. Winds are uncertain—more especially when they blow from whence they cometh and whither they listeth. N. B.—Such is the nature of winds.

Oct. 23.—Mild, balmy earthquakes.

Oct. 24.—Shaky.

Oct. 25.—Occasional shakes, followed by light showers of bricks and plastering. N. B.—Stand from under.

Oct. 26.—Considerable phenomenal atmospheric foolishness. About this time expect more earthquakes, but do not look out for them, on account of the bricks.

2

Oct. 27.—Universal despondency, indicative of approaching disaster. Abstain from smiling, or indulgence in humorous conversation, or exasperating jokes.

Oct. 28.—Misery, dismal forebodings and despair. Beware of all light discourse—a joke uttered at this time would produce a popular outbreak.

Oct. 29.—Beware!

Oct. 30.—Keep dark!

Oct. 31.—Go slow!

Nov. 1.—Terrific earthquake. This is the great earthquake month. More stars fall and more worlds are slathered around carelessly and destroyed in November than in any other month of the twelve.

Nov. 2.—Spasmodic but exhilarating earthquakes, accompanied by occasional showers of rain, and churches and things.

Nov. 3.—Make your will.

Nov. 4.—Sell out.

Nov. 5.—Select your "last words." Those of John Quincy Adams will do, with the addition of a syllable, thus: "This is the last of earth-quakes."

Nov. 6.—Prepare to shed this mortal coil.

Nov. 7.—Shed!

Nov. 8.—The sun will rise as usual, perhaps; but if he does he will doubtless be staggered some to find nothing but a large round hole eight thousand miles in diameter in the place where he saw this world serenely spinning the day before.

FROM THE "LONDON TIMES" OF 1904

I

Correspondence of the "London Times"

CHICAGO, APRIL 1, 1904

I resume by cable-telephone where I left off yesterday. For many hours, now, this vast city—along with the rest of the globe, of course—has talked of nothing but the extraordinary episode mentioned in my last report. In accordance with your instructions, I will now trace the romance from its beginnings down to the culmination of yesterday—or to-day; call it which you like. By an odd chance, I was a personal actor in a part of this drama myself. The opening scene plays in Vienna. Date, one o'clock in the morning, March 31, 1898. I had spent the evening at a social entertainment. About midnight I went away, in company with the military attachés of the British, Italian, and American embassies, to finish with a late smoke. This function had been appointed to take place in the house of Lieutenant Hillyer, the third attaché mentioned in the above list. When we arrived there we found several visitors in the room: young Szczepanik; Mr. K., his financial backer; Mr. W., the latter's secretary; and Lieutenant Clayton of the United States army. War was at that time threatening between Spain and our country, and Lieutenant Clayton had been sent to Europe on military business. I was well acquainted with young Szczepanik and his two friends, and I knew Mr. Clayton slightly. I had met him at West Point years before, when he was a cadet. It was when General Merritt was superintendent. He had the reputation of being an able officer, and also of being quick-tempered and plain-spoken.

4

This smoking-party had been gathered together partly for business. This business was to consider the availability of the telelectroscope for military service. It sounds oddly enough now, but it is nevertheless true that at that time the invention was not taken seriously by any one except its inventor. Even his financial supporter regarded it merely as a curious and interesting toy. Indeed, he was so convinced of this that he had actually postponed its use by the general world to the end of the dying century by granting a two years' exclusive lease of it to a syndicate, whose intent was to exploit it at the Paris World's Fair.

When we entered the smoking-room we found Lieutenant Clayton and Szczepanik engaged in a warm talk over the telelectroscope in the German tongue. Clayton was saying:

"Well, you know *my* opinion of it, anyway!" and he brought his fist down with emphasis upon the table.

"And I do not value it," retorted the young inventor, with provoking calmness of tone and manner.

Clayton turned to Mr. K., and said:

"*I* cannot see why you are wasting money on this toy. In my opinion, the day will never come when it will do a farthing's worth of real service for any human being."

"That may be; yes, that may be; still, I have put the money in it, and am content. I think, myself, that it is only a toy; but Szczepanik claims more for it, and I know him well enough to believe that he can see farther than I can—either with his telelectroscope or without it."

The soft answer did not cool Clayton down; it seemed only to irritate him the more; and he repeated and emphasized his conviction that the invention would never do any man a farthing's worth of real service. He even made it a "brass" farthing, this time. Then he laid an English farthing on the table, and added:

"Take that, Mr. K., and put it away; and if ever the telelectroscope does any man an actual service,—mind, a *real* service,—please mail it to me as a reminder, and I will take back what I have been saying. Will you?"

"I will"; and Mr. K. put the coin in his pocket.

Mr. Clayton now turned toward Szczepanik, and began with a taunt—a taunt which did not reach a finish; Szczepanik interrupted it with a hardy retort, and followed this with a blow. There was a brisk fight for a moment or two; then the attachés separated the men.

The scene now changes to Chicago. Time, the autumn of 1901. As soon as the Paris contract released the telelectroscope, it was delivered to public use, and was soon connected with the telephonic systems of the whole world. The improved "limitless-distance" telephone was presently introduced, and the daily doings of the globe made visible to everybody, and audibly discussable, too, by witnesses separated by any number of leagues.

By and by Szczepanik arrived in Chicago. Clayton (now captain) was serving in that military department at the time. The two men resumed the Viennese quarrel of 1898. On three different occasions they quarreled, and were separated by witnesses. Then came an interval of two months, during which time Szczepanik was not seen by any of his friends, and it was at first supposed that he had gone off on a sight-seeing tour and would soon be heard from. But no; no word came from him. Then it was supposed that he had returned to Europe. Still, time drifted on, and he was not heard from. Nobody was troubled, for he was like most inventors and other kinds of poets, and went and came in a capricious way, and often without notice.

Now comes the tragedy. On the 29th of December, in a dark and unused compartment of the cellar under Captain Clayton's house, a corpse was discovered by one of Clayton's maid-servants. It was easily identified as Szczepanik's. The man had died by violence. Clayton was arrested, indicted, and brought to trial, charged with this murder. The evidence against him was perfect in every detail, and absolutely unassailable. Clayton admitted this himself. He said that a reasonable man could not examine this testimony with a dispassionate mind and not be convinced by it; yet the man would be in error, nevertheless. Clayton swore that he did not commit the murder, and that he had had nothing to do with it.

As your readers will remember, he was condemned to death. He had numerous and powerful friends, and they worked hard to save him, for none of them doubted the truth of his assertion. I did what little I could to help, for I had long since become a close friend of his, and thought I knew that it was not in his character to inveigle an enemy into a corner and assassinate him. During 1902 and 1903 he was several times reprieved by the governor; he was reprieved once more in the beginning of the present year, and the execution-day postponed to March 31.

The governor's situation has been embarrassing, from the day of the condemnation, because of the fact that Clayton's wife is the governor's niece. The marriage took place in 1899, when Clayton was thirty-four and the girl twenty-three, and has been a happy one. There is one child, a little girl three years old. Pity for the poor mother and child kept the mouths of grumblers closed at first; but this could not last forever,—for in America politics has a hand in everything,—and by and by the governor's political opponents began to call attention to his delay in allowing the law to take its course. These hints have grown more and more frequent of late, and more and more pronounced. As a natural result, his own party grew nervous. Its leaders began to visit Springfield and hold long private conferences with him. He was now between two fires. On the one hand, his niece was imploring him to pardon her husband; on the other were the leaders, insisting that he stand to his plain duty as chief magistrate of the State, and place no further bar to Clayton's execution. Duty won in the struggle, and the governor gave his word that he would not again respite the condemned man. This was two weeks ago. Mrs. Clayton now said:

"Now that you have given your word, my last hope is gone, for I know you will never go back from it. But you have done the best you could for John, and I have no reproaches for you. You love him, and you love me, and we both know that if you could honorably save him, you would do it. I will go to him now, and be what help I can to him, and get what comfort I may out of the few days that are left to us before the night comes which will have no end for me in life. You will be with me that day? You will not let me bear it alone?"

"I will take you to him myself, poor child, and I will be near you to the last."

By the governor's command, Clayton was now allowed every indulgence he might ask for which could interest his mind and soften the hardships of his imprisonment. His wife and child spent the days with him; I was his companion by night. He was removed from the narrow cell which he had occupied during such a dreary stretch of time, and given the chief warden's roomy and comfortable quarters. His mind was always busy with the catastrophe of his life, and with the slaughtered inventor, and he now took the fancy that he would like to have the telelectroscope and divert his mind with it. He had his wish. The connection was made with the international telephone-station, and day by day, and night by night, he called up one corner of the globe after another, and looked upon its life, and studied its strange sights, and spoke with its people, and realized that by grace of this marvelous instrument he was almost as free as the birds of the air, although a prisoner under locks and bars. He seldom spoke, and I never interrupted him when he was absorbed in this amusement. I sat in his parlor and read and smoked, and the nights were very quiet and reposefully sociable, and I found them pleasant. Now and then I would hear him say, "Give me Yedo"; next, "Give me Hong-Kong"; next, "Give me Melbourne." And I smoked on, and read in comfort, while he wandered about the remote under-world, where the sun was shining in the sky, and the people were at their daily work. Sometimes the talk that came from those far regions through the microphone attachment interested me, and I listened.

Yesterday—I keep calling it yesterday, which is quite natural, for certain reasons—the instrument remained unused, and that, also, was natural, for it was the eve of the execution-day. It was spent in tears and lamentations and farewells. The governor and the wife and child remained until a quarter past eleven at night, and the scenes I witnessed were pitiful to see. The execution was to take place at four in the morning. A little after eleven a sound of hammering broke out upon the still night, and there was a glare of light, and the child cried out, "What is that, papa?" and ran to the window before she could be stopped, and clapped her small hands, and said: "Oh, come and see, mama—such a pretty thing they are making!" The mother knew—and fainted. It was the gallows!

She was carried away to her lodging, poor woman, and Clayton and I were alone—alone, and thinking, brooding, dreaming. We might have been statues, we sat so motionless and still. It was a wild night, for winter was come again for a moment, after the habit of this region in the early spring. The sky was starless and black, and a strong wind was blowing from the lake. The silence in the room was so deep that all outside sounds seemed exaggerated by contrast with it. These sounds were fitting ones; they harmonized with the situation and the conditions: the boom and thunder of sudden storm-gusts among the roofs and chimneys, then the dying down into moanings and wailings about the eaves and angles; now and then a gnashing and lashing rush of sleet along the window-panes; and always the muffled and uncanny hammering of the gallows-builders in the courtyard. After an age of this, another sound—far off, and coming smothered and faint through the riot of the tempest—a bell tolling twelve! Another age, and it tolled again. By and by, again. A dreary, long interval after this, then the spectral sound floated to us once more—one, two, three; and this time we caught our breath: sixty minutes of life left!

Clayton rose, and stood by the window, and looked up into the black sky, and listened to the thrashing sleet and the piping wind; then he said: "That a dying man's last of earth should be—this!" After a little he said: "I must see the sun again—the sun!" and the next moment he was feverishly calling: "China! Give me China—Peking!"

I was strangely stirred, and said to myself: "To think that it is a mere human being who does this unimaginable miracle—turns winter into summer, night into day, storm into calm, gives the freedom of the great globe to a prisoner in his cell, and the sun in his naked splendor to a man dying in Egyptian darkness!"

I was listening.

"What light! what brilliancy! what radiance! . . . This is Peking?"

"Yes."

"The time?"

"Mid-afternoon."

"What is the great crowd for, and in such gorgeous costumes? What masses and masses of rich color and barbaric magnificence! And how they flash and glow and burn in the flooding sunlight! What *is* the occasion of it all?"

"The coronation of our new emperor—the Czar."

"But I thought that that was to take place yesterday."

"This *is* yesterday—to you."

"Certainly it is. But my mind is confused, these days; there are reasons for it. . . . Is this the beginning of the procession?"

"Oh, no; It began to move an hour ago."

"Is there much more of it still to come?"

"Two hours of it. Why do you sigh?"

"Because I should like to see it all."

"And why can't you?"

"I have to go—presently."

"You have an engagement?"

After a pause, softly: "Yes." After another pause: "Who are these in the splendid pavilion?"

"The imperial family, and visiting royalties from here and there and yonder in the earth."

"And who are those in the adjoining pavilions to the right and left?"

"Ambassadors and their families and suites to the right; unofficial foreigners to the left."

"If you will be so good, I—"

Boom! That distant bell again, tolling the half-hour faintly through the tempest of wind and sleet. The door opened, and the governor and the mother and child entered—the woman in widow's weeds! She fell upon her husband's breast in a passion of sobs, and I—I could not stay; I could not bear it. I went into the bedchamber, and closed the door. I sat there waiting—waiting—waiting, and listening to the rattling sashes and the blustering of the storm. After what seemed a long, long time, I heard a rustle and movement in the parlor, and knew that the clergyman and the sheriff and the guard were come. There was some low-voiced talking; then a hush; then a prayer, with a sound of sobbing; presently, footfalls—the departure for the gallows; then the child's happy voice: "Don't cry *now,* mama, when we've got papa again, and taking him home."

The door closed; they were gone. I was ashamed: I was the only friend of the dying man that had no spirit, no courage. I stepped into the room, and said I would be a man and would follow. But we are made as we are made, and we cannot help it. I did not go.

I fidgeted about the room nervously, and presently went to the window, and softly raised it,—drawn by that dread fascination which the terrible and the awful exert,—and looked down upon the courtyard. By the garish light of the electric lamps I saw the little group of privileged witnesses, the wife crying on her uncle's breast, the condemned man standing on the scaffold with the halter around his neck, his arms strapped to his body, the black cap on his head, the sheriff at his side with his hand on the drop, the clergyman in front of him with bare head and his book in his hand.

"I am the resurrection and the life—"

I turned away. I could not listen; I could not look. I did not know whither to go or what to do. Mechanically, and without knowing it, I put my eye to that strange instrument, and there was Peking and the Czar's procession! The next moment I was leaning out of the window, gasping, suffocating, trying to speak, but dumb from the very imminence of the necessity of speaking. The preacher could speak, but I, who had such need of words—

"And may God have mercy upon your soul. Amen."

The sheriff drew down the black cap, and laid his hand upon the lever. I got my voice.

"Stop, for God's sake! The man is innocent. Come here and see Szczepanik face to face!"

Hardly three minutes later the governor had my place at the window, and was saying:

"Strike off his bonds and set him free!"

Three minutes later all were in the parlor again. The reader will imagine the scene; I have no need to describe it. It was a sort of mad orgy of joy.

A messenger carried word to Szczepanik in the pavilion, and one could see the distressed amazement dawn in his face as he listened to the tale. Then he came to his end of the line, and talked with Clayton and the governor and the others; and the wife poured out her gratitude upon him for saving her husband's life, and in her deep thankfulness she kissed him at twelve thousand miles' range.

The telelectrophonoscopes of the globe were put to service now, and for many hours the kings and queens of many realms (with here and there a reporter) talked with Szczepanik, and praised him; and the few scientific societies which had not already made him an honorary member conferred that grace upon him.

How had he come to disappear from among us? It was easily explained. He had not grown used to being a world-famous person, and had been forced to break away from the lionizing that was robbing him of all privacy and repose. So he grew a beard, put on colored glasses, disguised himself a little in other ways, then took a fictitious name, and went off to wander about the earth in peace.

Such is the tale of the drama which began with an inconsequential quarrel in Vienna in the spring of 1898, and came near ending as a tragedy in the spring of 1904.

II

Correspondence of the "London Times"

Chicago, April 5, 1904

To-day, by a clipper of the Electric Line, and the latter's Electric Railway connections, arrived an envelop from Vienna, for Captain Clayton, containing an English farthing. The receiver of it was a good deal moved. He called up Vienna, and stood face to face with Mr. K., and said:

"I do not need to say anything; you can see it all in my face. My wife has the farthing. Do not be afraid—she will not throw it away."

III

Correspondence of the "London Times"

CHICAGO, APRIL 23, 1904

Now that the after developments of the Clayton case have run their course and reached a finish, I will sum them up. Clayton's romantic escape from a shameful death steeped all this region in an enchantment of wonder and joy—during the proverbial nine days. Then the sobering process followed, and men began to take thought, and to say: "But *a man was killed,* and Clayton killed him." Others replied: "That is true: we have been overlooking that important detail; we have been led away by excitement."

The feeling soon became general that Clayton ought to be tried again. Measures were taken accordingly, and the proper representations conveyed to Washington; for in America, under the new paragraph added to the Constitution in 1899, second trials are not State affairs, but national, and must be tried by the most august body in the land—the Supreme Court of the United States. The justices were therefore summoned to sit in Chicago. The session was held day before yesterday, and was opened with the usual impressive formalities, the nine judges appearing in their black robes, and the new chief justice (Lemaitre) presiding. In opening the case, the chief justice said:

"It is my opinion that this matter is quite simple. The prisoner at the bar was charged with murdering the man Szczepanik; he was fairly tried, and justly condemned and sentenced to death for murdering the man Szczepanik. It turns out that the man Szczepanik was not murdered at all. By the decision of the French courts in the Dreyfus matter, it is established beyond cavil or question that the decisions of courts are permanent and cannot be revised. We are obliged to respect and adopt the precedent. It is upon precedents that the enduring edifice of jurisprudence is reared. The prisoner at the bar has been fairly and righteously condemned to death for the murder of the man Szczepanik, and, in my opinion, there is but one course to pursue in the matter: he must be hanged."

Mr. Justice Crawford said:

"But, your Excellency, he was pardoned on the scaffold for that."

"The pardon is not valid, and cannot stand, because he was pardoned for killing a man whom he had not killed. A man cannot be pardoned for a crime which he has not committed; it would be an absurdity."

"But, your Excellency, he did kill a man."

"That is an extraneous detail; we have nothing to do with it. The court cannot take up this crime until the prisoner has expiated the other one."

Mr. Justice Halleck said:

"If we order his execution, your Excellency, we shall bring about a miscarriage of justice; for the governor will pardon him again."

"He will not have the power. He cannot pardon a man for a crime which he has not committed. As I observed before, it would be an absurdity."

After a consultation, Mr. Justice Wadsworth said:

"Several of us have arrived at the conclusion, your Excellency, that it would be an error to hang the prisoner for killing Szczepanik, but only for killing the other man, since it is proven that he did not kill Szczepanik."

"On the contrary, it is proven that he *did* kill Szczepanik. By the French precedent, it is plain that we must abide by the finding of the court."

"But Szczepanik is still alive."

"So is Dreyfus."

In the end it was found impossible to ignore or get around the French precedent. There could be but one result: Clayton was delivered over to the executioner. It made an immense excitement; the State rose as one man and clamored for Clayton's pardon and retrial. The governor issued the pardon, but the Supreme Court was in duty bound to annul it, and did so, and poor Clayton was hanged yesterday. The city is draped in black, and, indeed, the like may be said of the State. All America is vocal with scorn of "French justice," and of the malignant little soldiers who invented it and inflicted it upon the other Christian lands.

THE LOVES OF
ALONZO FITZ CLARENCE AND
ROSANNAH ETHELTON

I

IT WAS WELL along in the forenoon of a bitter winter's day. The town of Eastport, in the State of Maine, lay buried under a deep snow that was newly fallen. The customary bustle in the streets was wanting. One could look long distances down them and see nothing but a dead-white emptiness, with silence to match. Of course I do not mean that you could *see* the silence,—no, you could only hear it. The sidewalks were merely long, deep ditches, with steep snow walls on either side. Here and there you might hear the faint, far scrape of a wooden shovel, and if you were quick enough you might catch a glimpse of a distant black figure stooping and disappearing in one of those ditches, and reappearing the next moment with a motion which you would know meant the heaving out of a shovelful of snow. But you needed to be quick, for that black figure would not linger, but would soon drop that shovel and scud for the house, thrashing itself with its arms to warm them. Yes, it was too venomously cold for snow shovelers or anybody else to stay out long.

Presently the sky darkened; then the wind rose and began to blow in fitful, vigorous gusts, which sent clouds of powdery snow aloft, and straight ahead, and everywhere. Under the impulse of one of these gusts, great white drifts banked themselves like graves across the streets; a moment later, another gust shifted them around the other way, driving a fine spray of snow from their sharp crests, as the gale drives the spume flakes from wave-crests at sea; a third gust swept that place as clean as your hand, if it saw fit. This was fooling, this was play; but each and all of the gusts dumped some snow into the sidewalk ditches, for that was business.

Alonzo Fitz Clarence was sitting in his snug and elegant little parlor, in a lovely blue silk dressing-gown, with cuffs and facings of crimson satin, elaborately quilted. The remains of his breakfast were before him, and the dainty and costly little table service added a harmonious charm to the grace, beauty, and richness of the fixed appointments of the room. A cheery fire was blazing on the hearth.

A furious gust of wind shook the windows, and a great wave of snow washed against them with a drenching sound, so to speak. The handsome young bachelor murmured,—

"That means, no going out to-day. Well, I am content. But what to do for company? Mother is well enough, aunt Susan is well enough; but these, like the poor, I have with me always. On so grim a day as this, one needs a new interest, a fresh element, to whet the dull edge of captivity. That was very neatly said, but it does n't mean anything. One does n't *want* the edge of captivity sharpened up, you know, but just the reverse."

He glanced at his pretty French mantel clock.

"That clock's wrong again. That clock hardly ever knows what time it is; and when it does know, it lies about it—which amounts to the same thing. Alfred!"

There was no answer.

"Alfred! . . . Good servant, but as uncertain as the clock."

Alonzo touched an electrical bell-button in the wall. He waited a moment, then touched it again; waited a few moments more, and said,—

"Battery out of order, no doubt. But now that I have started, I *will* find out what time it is." He stepped to a speaking-tube in the wall, blew its whistle, and called, "Mother!" and repeated it twice.

"Well, *that's* no use. Mother's battery is out of order, too. Can't raise anybody down-stairs,—that is plain."

He sat down at a rose-wood desk, leaned his chin on the left-hand edge of it, and spoke, as if to the floor: "Aunt Susan!"

A low, pleasant voice answered, "Is that you, Alonzo?"

"Yes. I'm too lazy and comfortable to go down-stairs; I am in extremity, and I can't seem to scare up any help."

"Dear me, what is the matter?"

"Matter enough, I can tell you!"

"Oh, don't keep me in suspense, dear! What *is* it?"

"I want to know what time it is."

"You abominable boy, what a turn you did give me! Is that all?"

"All,—on my honor. Calm yourself. Tell me the time, and receive my blessing."

"Just five minutes after nine. No charge,—keep your blessing."

"Thanks. It would n't have impoverished me, aunty, nor so enriched you that you could live without other means." He got up, murmuring, "Just five minutes after nine," and faced his clock. "Ah," said he, "you are doing better than usual. You are only thirty-four minutes wrong. Let me see . . . let me see. . . . Thirty-three and twenty-one are fifty-four; four times fifty-four are two hundred and thirty-six. One off, leaves two hundred and thirty-five. That's right."

He turned the hands of his clock forward till they marked twenty-five minutes to one, and said, "Now see if you can't keep right for a while . . . else I'll raffle you!"

He sat down at the desk again, and said, "Aunt Susan!"

"Yes, dear."

"Had breakfast?"

"Yes indeed, an hour ago."

"Busy?"

"No,—except sewing. Why?"

"Got any company?"

"No, but I expect some at half past nine."

"I wish *I* did. I'm lonesome. I want to talk to somebody."

"Very well, talk to me."

"But this is very private."

"Don't be afraid,—talk right along; there's nobody here but me."

"I hardly know whether to venture or not, but"——

"But what? Oh, don't stop there! You *know* you can trust me, Alonzo,—you know you can."

"I feel it, aunt, but this is very serious. It affects me deeply,—me, and all the family,—even the whole community."

"Oh, Alonzo, tell me! I will never breathe a word of it. What is it?"

"Aunt, if I might dare"——

"Oh, please go on! I love you, and can feel for you. Tell me all. Confide in me. What *is* it?"

"The weather!"

"Plague take the weather! I don't see how you can have the heart to serve me so, Lon."

"There, there, aunty dear, I'm sorry; I am, on my honor. I won't do it again. Do you forgive me?"

"Yes, since you seem so sincere about it, though I know I ought n't to. You will fool me again as soon as I have forgotten this time."

"No, I won't, honor bright. But such weather, oh, such weather! You've *got* to keep your spirits up artificially. It is snowy, and blowy, and gusty, and bitter cold! How is the weather with you?"

"Warm and rainy and melancholy. The mourners go about the streets with their umbrellas running streams from the end of every whalebone. There's an elevated double pavement of umbrellas stretching down the sides of the streets as far as I can see. I've got a fire for cheerfulness, and the windows open to keep cool. But it is vain, it is useless: nothing comes in but the balmy breath of December, with its burden of mocking odors from the flowers that possess the realm outside, and rejoice in their lawless profusion whilst the spirit of man is low, and flaunt their gaudy splendors in his face whilst his soul is clothed in sackcloth and ashes and his heart breaketh."

Alonzo opened his lips to say, "You ought to print that, and get it framed," but checked himself, for he heard his aunt speaking to some one else. He went and stood at the window and looked out upon the wintry prospect. The storm was driving the snow before it more furiously than ever; window shutters were slamming and banging; a forlorn dog, with bowed head and tail withdrawn from service, was pressing his quaking body against a windward wall for shelter and protection; a young girl was plowing knee-deep through the drifts, with her face turned from the blast, and the cape of her water-proof blowing straight rearward over her head. Alonzo shuddered, and said with a sigh, "Better the slop, and the sultry rain, and even the insolent flowers, than this!"

He turned from the window, moved a step, and stopped in a listening attitude. The faint, sweet notes of a familiar song caught his ear. He remained there, with his head unconsciously bent forward, drinking in the melody, stirring neither hand nor foot, hardly breathing. There was a blemish in the execution of the song, but to Alonzo it seemed an added charm instead of a defect. This blemish consisted of a marked flatting of the third, fourth, fifth, sixth, and seventh notes of the refrain or chorus of the piece. When the music ended, Alonzo drew a deep breath, and said, "Ah, I never have heard In the Sweet By and By sung like that before!"

He stepped quickly to the desk, listened a moment, and said in a guarded, confidential voice, "Aunty, who is this divine singer?"

"She is the company I was expecting. Stays with me a month or two. I will introduce you. Miss"—

"For goodness' sake, wait a moment, aunt Susan! You never stop to think what you are about!"

He flew to his bed-chamber, and returned in a moment perceptibly changed in his outward appearance, and remarking, snappishly,—

"Hang it, she would have introduced me to this angel in that sky-blue dressing-gown with red-hot lappels! Women never think, when they get agoing."

He hastened and stood by the desk, and said eagerly, "Now, aunty, I am ready," and fell to smiling and bowing with all the persuasiveness and elegance that were in him.

"Very well. Miss Rosannah Ethelton, let me introduce to you my favorite nephew, Mr. Alonzo Fitz Clarence. There! You are both good people, and I like you; so I am going to trust you together while I attend to a few household affairs. Sit down, Rosannah; sit down, Alonzo. Good-by; I shan't be gone long."

Alonzo had been bowing and smiling all the while, and motioning imaginary young ladies to sit down in imaginary chairs, but now he took a seat himself, mentally saying, "Oh, this is luck! Let the winds blow now, and the snow drive, and the heavens frown! Little I care!"

While these young people chat themselves into an acquaintanceship, let us take the liberty of inspecting the sweeter and fairer of the two. She sat alone, at her graceful ease, in a richly furnished apartment which was manifestly the private parlor of a refined and sensible lady, if signs and symbols may go for anything. For instance, by a low, comfortable chair stood a dainty, top-heavy work-stand, whose summit was a fancifully embroidered shallow basket, with vari-colored crewels, and other strings and odds and ends, protruding from under the gaping lid and hanging down in negligent profusion. On the floor lay bright shreds of Turkey red, Prussian blue, and kindred fabrics, bits of ribbon, a spool or two, a pair of scissors, and a roll or so of tinted silken stuffs. On a luxurious sofa, upholstered with some sort of soft Indian goods wrought in black and gold threads interwebbed with other threads not so pronounced in color, lay a great square of coarse white stuff, upon whose surface a rich bouquet of flowers was growing, under the deft cultivation of the crochet needle. The household cat was asleep on this work of art. In a bay window stood an easel with an unfinished picture on it, and a palette and brushes on a chair beside it. There were books everywhere; Robertson's Sermons, Tennyson, Moody and Sankey, Hawthorne, Rab and his Friends, cook-books, prayerbooks, pattern-books,—and books about all kinds of odious and exasperating pottery, of course. There was a piano, with a deck-load of music, and more in a tender. There was a great plenty of pictures on the walls, on the shelves of the mantel-piece, and around generally; where coignes of vantage offered were statuettes, and quaint and pretty grimcracks, and rare and costly specimens of peculiarly devilish china. The bay window gave upon a garden that was ablaze with foreign and domestic flowers and flowering shrubs.

But the sweet young girl was the daintiest thing those premises, within or without, could offer for contemplation: delicately chiseled features, of Grecian cast; her complexion the pure snow of a japonica that is receiving a faint reflected enrichment from some scarlet neighbor of the garden; great, soft blue eyes fringed with long, curving lashes; an expression made up of the trustfulness of a child and the gentleness of a fawn; a beautiful head crowned with its own prodigal gold; a lithe and rounded figure, whose every attitude and movement were instinct with native grace.

Her dress and adornment were marked by that exquisite harmony that can come only of a fine natural taste perfected by culture. Her gown was of a simple magenta tulle, cut bias, traversed by three rows of light blue flounces, with the selvage edges turned up with ashes-of-roses chenille; overdress of dark bay tarleton, with scarlet satin lambrequins; corn-colored polonaise, *en panier,* looped with mother-of-pearl buttons and silver cord, and hauled aft and made fast by buff-velvet lashings; basque of lavender reps, picked out with valenciennes; low neck, short sleeves; maroon-velvet necktie edged with delicate pink silk; inside handkerchief of some simple three-ply ingrain fabric of a soft-saffron tint; coral bracelets and locket-chain; coiffure of forget-me-nots and lilies of the valley massed around a noble calla.

This was all; yet even in this subdued attire she was divinely beautiful. Then what must she have been when adorned for the festival or the ball?

All this time she has been busily chatting with Alonzo, unconscious of our inspection. The minutes still sped, and still she talked. But by and by she happened to look up, and saw the clock.

A crimson blush sent its rich flood through her cheeks, and she exclaimed,—

"There, good-by, Mr. Fitz Clarence; I must go now!"

She sprang from her chair with such haste that she hardly heard the young man's answering good-by. She stood radiant, graceful, beautiful, and gazed, wondering, upon the accusing clock. Presently her pouting lips parted, and she said,—

"Five minutes after eleven! Nearly two hours, and it did not seem twenty minutes! Oh, dear, what will he think of me!"

At the self-same moment Alonzo was staring at his clock. And presently he said,—

"Twenty-five minutes to three! Nearly two hours, and I didn't believe it was two minutes! Is it possible that this clock is humbugging again? Miss Ethelton! Just one moment, please. Are you there yet?"

"Yes, but be quick; I'm going right away."

"Would you be so kind as to tell me what time it is?"

The girl blushed again, murmured to herself, "It's right down cruel of him to ask me!" and then spoke up and answered with admirably counterfeited unconcern. "Five minutes after nine."

"Oh, thank you! You have to go now, have you?"

"Yes."

"I'm sorry."

No reply.

"Miss Ethelton!"

"Well?"

"You—you're there yet, *ain't* you?"

"Yes; but please hurry. What did you want to say?"

"Well, I—well, nothing in particular. It's very lonesome here. It's asking a great deal, I know, but would you mind talking with me again by and by,—that is, if it will not trouble you too much?"

"I don't know—but I'll think about it. I'll try."

"Oh, thanks! Miss Ethelton? . . . Ah me, she's gone, and here are the black clouds and the whirling snow and the raging winds come again! But she said *good-by!* She didn't say good morning, she said good-by! . . . The clock was right, after all. What a lightning-winged two hours it was!"

He sat down, and gazed dreamily into his fire for a while, then heaved a sigh and said,—

"How wonderful it is! Two little hours ago I was a free man, and now my heart's in San Francisco!"

About that time Rosannah Ethelton, propped in the window-seat of her bedchamber, book in hand, was gazing vacantly out over the rainy seas that washed the Golden Gate, and whispering to herself, "How different he is from poor Burley, with his empty head and his single little antic talent of mimicry!"

II

Four weeks later Mr. Sidney Algernon Burley was entertaining a gay luncheon company, in a sumptuous drawingroom on Telegraph Hill, with some capital imitations of the voices and gestures of certain popular actors and San Franciscan literary people and Bonanza grandees. He was elegantly upholstered, and was a handsome fellow, barring a trifling cast in his eye. He seemed very jovial, but nevertheless he kept his eye on the door with an expectant and uneasy watchfulness. By and by a nobby lackey appeared, and delivered a message to the mistress, who nodded her head understandably. That seemed to settle the thing for Mr. Burley; his vivacity decreased little by little, and a dejected look began to creep into one of his eyes and a sinister one into the other.

The rest of the company departed in due time, leaving him with the mistress, to whom he said,—

"There is no longer any question about it. She avoids me. She continually excuses herself. If I could see her, if I could speak to her only a moment,—but this suspense"—

"Perhaps her seeming avoidance is mere accident, Mr. Burley. Go to the small drawing-room up-stairs and amuse yourself a moment. I will dispatch a household order that is on my mind, and then I will go to her room. Without doubt she will be persuaded to see you."

Mr. Burley went up-stairs, intending to go to the small drawing-room, but as he was passing "aunt Susan's" private parlor, the door of which stood slightly ajar, he heard a joyous laugh which he recognized; so without knock or announcement he stepped confidently in. But before he could make his presence known he heard words that harrowed up his soul and chilled his young blood. He heard a voice say,—

"Darling, it has come!"

Then he heard Rosannah Ethelton, whose back was toward him, say,—

"So has yours, dearest!"

He saw her bowed form bend lower; he heard her kiss something,—not merely once, but again and again! His soul raged within him. The heartbreaking conversation went on:—

"Rosannah, I knew you must be beautiful, but this is dazzling, this is blinding, this is intoxicating!"

"Alonzo, it is such happiness to hear you say it. I know it is not true, but I am so grateful to have you think it is, nevertheless! I knew you must have a noble face, but the grace and majesty of the reality beggar the poor creation of my fancy."

Burley heard that rattling shower of kisses again.

"Thank you, my Rosannah! The photograph flatters me, but you must not allow yourself to think of that. Sweetheart?"

"Yes, Alonzo."

"I am so happy, Rosannah."

"Oh, Alonzo, none that have gone before me knew what love was, none that came after me will ever know what happiness is. I float in a gorgeous cloudland, a boundless firmament of enchanted and bewildering ecstasy!"

"Oh, my Rosannah!—for you are mine, are you not?"

"Wholly, oh, wholly yours, Alonzo, now and forever! All the day long, and all through my nightly dreams, one song sings itself and its sweet burden is, 'Alonzo Fitz Clarence, Alonzo Fitz Clarence, Eastport, State of Maine!'"

"Curse him, I've got his address, any way!" roared Burley, inwardly, and rushed from the place.

Just behind the unconscious Alonzo stood his mother, a picture of astonishment. She was so muffled from head to heel in furs that nothing of herself was visible but her eyes and nose. She was a good allegory of winter, for she was powdered all over with snow.

Behind the unconscious Rosannah stood "aunt Susan," another picture of astonishment. She was a good allegory of summer, for she was lightly clad, and was vigorously cooling the perspiration on her face with a fan.

Both of these women had tears of joy in their eyes.

"So ho!" exclaimed Mrs. Fitz Clarence, "this explains why nobody has been able to drag you out of your room for six weeks, Alonzo!"

"So ho!" exclaimed aunt Susan, "this explains why you have been a hermit for the past six weeks, Rosannah!"

The young couple were on their feet in an instant, abashed, and standing like detected dealers in stolen goods awaiting Judge Lynch's doom.

"Bless you, my son! I am happy in your happiness. Come to your mother's arms, Alonzo!"

"Bless you, Rosannah, for my dear nephew's sake! Come to my arms!"

Then was there a mingling of hearts and of tears of rejoicing on Telegraph Hill and in Eastport Square.

Servants were called by the elders, in both places. Unto one was given the order, "Pile this fire high with hickory wood, and bring me a roasting-hot lemonade."

Unto the other was given the order, "Put out this fire, and bring me two palm-leaf fans and a pitcher of ice-water."

Then the young people were dismissed, and the elders sat down to talk the sweet surprise over and make the wedding plans.

*

Some minutes before this Mr. Burley rushed from the mansion on Telegraph Hill without meeting or taking formal leave of anybody. He hissed through his teeth, in unconscious imitation of a popular favorite in melodrama, "Him shall she never wed! I have sworn it! Ere great Nature shall have doffed her winter's ermine to don the emerald gauds of spring, she shall be mine!"

III

Two weeks later. Every few hours, during some three or four days, a very prim and devout-looking Episcopal clergyman, with a cast in his eye, had visited Alonzo. According to his card, he was the Rev. Melton Hargrave, of Cincinnati. He said he had retired from the ministry on account of his health. If he had said on account of ill health, he would probably have erred, to judge by his wholesome looks and firm build. He was the inventor of an improvement in telephones, and hoped to make his bread by selling the privilege of using it. "At present," he continued, "a man may go and tap a telegraph wire which is conveying a song or a concert from one State to another, and he can attach his private telephone and steal a hearing of that music as it passes along. My invention will stop all that."

"Well," answered Alonzo, "if the owner of the music could not miss what was stolen, why should he care?"

"He shouldn't care," said the Reverend.

"Well?" said Alonzo, inquiringly.

"Suppose," replied the Reverend, "suppose that, instead of music that was passing along and being stolen, the burden of the wire was loving endearments of the most private and sacred nature?"

Alonzo shuddered from head to heel. "Sir, it is a priceless invention," said he; "I must have it at any cost."

But the invention was delayed somewhere on the road from Cincinnati, most unaccountably. The impatient Alonzo could hardly wait. The thought of Rosannah's sweet words being shared with him by some ribald thief was galling to him. The Reverend came frequently and lamented the delay, and told of measures he had taken to hurry things up. This was some little comfort to Alonzo.

One forenoon the Reverend ascended the stairs and knocked at Alonzo's door. There was no response. He entered, glanced eagerly around, closed the door softly, then ran to the telephone. The exquisitely soft, remote strains of the Sweet By and By came floating through the instrument. The singer was flatting, as usual, the five notes that follow the first two in the chorus, when the Reverend interrupted her with this word, in a voice which was an exact imitation of Alonzo's, with just the faintest flavor of impatience added,—

"Sweetheart?"

"Yes, Alonzo?"

"Please don't sing that any more this week,—try something modern."

The agile step that goes with a happy heart was heard on the stairs, and the Reverend, smiling diabolically, sought sudden refuge behind the heavy folds of the velvet window curtains. Alonzo entered and flew to the telephone. Said he,—

"Rosannah, dear, shall we sing something together?"

"Something *modern?*" asked she, with sarcastic bitterness.

"Yes, if you prefer."

"Sing it yourself, if you like!"

This snappishness amazed and wounded the young man. He said,—

"Rosannah, that was not like you."

"I suppose it becomes me as much as your very polite speech became you, Mr. Fitz Clarence."

"*Mister* Fitz Clarence! Rosannah, there was nothing impolite about my speech."

"Oh, indeed! Of course, then, I misunderstood you, and I most humbly beg your pardon, ha-ha-ha! No doubt you said, 'Don't sing it any more *today.*'"

"Sing *what* any more to-day?"

"The song you mentioned, of course. How very obtuse we are, all of a sudden!"

"I never mentioned any song."

"Oh, you *didn't!*"

"No, I *didn't!*"

"I am compelled to remark that you *did.*"

"And I am obliged to reiterate that I *didn't.*"

"A second rudeness! That is sufficient, sir. I will never forgive you. All is over between us."

Then came a muffled sound of crying. Alonzo hastened to say,—

"Oh, Rosannah, unsay those words! There is some dreadful mystery here, some hideous mistake. I am utterly earnest and sincere when I say I never said anything about any song. I would not hurt you for the whole world . . . Rosannah, dear? . . . Oh, speak to me, won't you?"

There was a pause; then Alonzo heard the girl's sobbings retreating, and knew she had gone from the telephone. He rose with a heavy sigh and hastened from the room, saying to himself, "I will ransack the charity missions and the haunts of the poor for my mother. She will persuade her that I never meant to wound her."

A minute later, the Reverend was crouching over the telephone like a cat that knoweth the ways of the prey. He had not very many minutes to wait. A soft, repentant voice, tremulous with tears, said,—

"Alonzo, dear, I have been wrong. You *could* not have said so cruel a thing. It must have been some one who imitated your voice in malice or in jest."

The Reverend coldly answered, in Alonzo's tones,—

"You have said all was over between us. So let it be. I spurn your proffered repentance, and despise it!"

Then he departed, radiant with fiendish triumph, to return no more with his imaginary telephonic invention forever.

Four hours afterward, Alonzo arrived with his mother from her favorite haunts of poverty and vice. They summoned the San

Francisco household; but there was no reply. They waited, and continued to wait, upon the voiceless telephone.

At length, when it was sunset in San Francisco, and three hours and a half after dark in Eastport, an answer came to the oft-repeated cry of "Rosannah!"

But, alas, it was aunt Susan's voice that spake. She said,—

"I have been out all day; just got in. I will go and find her."

The watchers waited two minutes—five minutes—ten minutes. Then came these fatal words, in a frightened tone,—

"She is gone, and her baggage with her. To visit another friend, she told the servants. But I found this note on the table in her room. Listen: 'I am gone; seek not to trace me out; my heart is broken; you will never see me more. Tell him I shall always think of him when I sing my poor Sweet By and By, but never of the unkind words he said about it.' That is her note. Alonzo, Alonzo, what does it mean? What has happened?"

But Alonzo sat white and cold as the dead. His mother threw back the velvet curtains and opened a window. The cold air refreshed the sufferer, and he told his aunt his dismal story. Meantime his mother was inspecting a card which had disclosed itself upon the floor when she cast the curtains back. It read, "Mr. Sidney Algernon Burley, San Francisco."

"The miscreant!" shouted Alonzo, and rushed forth to seek the false Reverend and destroy him; for the card explained everything, since in the course of the lovers' mutual confessions they had told each other all about all the sweethearts they had ever had, and thrown no end of mud at their failings and foibles,—for lovers always do that. It has a fascination that ranks next after billing and cooing.

IV

During the next two months, many things happened. It had early transpired that Rosannah, poor suffering orphan, had neither returned to her grandmother in Portland, Oregon, nor sent any word to her save a duplicate of the woful note she had left in the mansion on Telegraph Hill. Whosoever was sheltering her—if she was still alive—had been persuaded not to betray her whereabouts, without doubt; for all efforts to find trace of her had failed.

Did Alonzo give her up? Not he. He said to himself, "She will sing that sweet song when she is sad; I shall find her." So he took his carpet sack and a portable telephone, and shook the snow of his native city from his arctics, and went forth into the world. He wandered far and wide and in many States. Time and again, strangers were astounded to see a wasted, pale, and woe-worn man laboriously climb a telegraph pole in wintry and lonely places, perch sadly there an hour, with his ear at a little box, then come sighing down, and wander wearily away. Sometimes they shot at him, as peasants do at aeronauts, thinking him mad and dangerous. Thus his clothes were much shredded by bullets and his person grievously lacerated. But he bore it all patiently.

In the beginning of his pilgrimage he used often to say, "Ah, if I could but hear the Sweet By and By!" But toward the end of it he used to shed tears of anguish and say, "Ah, if I could but hear something else!"

Thus a month and three weeks drifted by, and at last some humane people seized him and confined him in a private mad-house in New York. He made no moan, for his strength was all gone, and with it all heart and all hope. The superintendent, in pity, gave up his own comfortable parlor and bed-chamber to him and nursed him with affectionate devotion.

At the end of a week the patient was able to leave his bed for the first time. He was lying, comfortably pillowed, on a sofa, listening to the plaintive Miserere of the bleak March winds, and the muffled sound of tramping feet in the street below,—for it was about six in the evening, and New York was going home from work. He had a bright fire and the added cheer of a couple of student lamps. So it was warm and snug within, though bleak and raw without; it was light and bright within, though outside it was as dark and dreary as if the world had been lit with Hartford gas. Alonzo smiled feebly to think how his loving vagaries had made him a maniac in the eyes of the world, and was proceeding to pursue his line of thought further, when a faint, sweet strain, the very ghost of sound, so remote and attenuated it seemed, struck upon his ear. His pulses stood still; he listened with parted lips and bated breath. The song flowed on,—he waiting, listening, rising slowly and unconsciously from his recumbent position. At last he exclaimed,—

"It is! it is she! Oh, the divine flatted notes!"

He dragged himself eagerly to the corner whence the sounds proceeded, tore aside a curtain, and discovered a telephone. He bent over, and as the last note died away he burst forth with the exclamation,—

"Oh, thank Heaven, found at last! Speak to me, Rosannah, dearest! The cruel mystery has been unraveled; it was the villain Burley who mimicked my voice and wounded you with insolent speech!"

There was a breathless pause, a waiting age to Alonzo; then a faint sound came, framing itself into language,—

"Oh, say those precious words again, Alonzo!"

"They are the truth, the veritable truth, my Rosannah, and you shall have the proof, ample and abundant proof!"

"Oh, Alonzo, stay by me! Leave me not for a moment! Let me feel that you are near me! Tell me we shall never be parted more! Oh, this happy hour, this blessed hour, this memorable hour!"

"We will make record of it, my Rosannah; every year, as this dear hour chimes from the clock, we will celebrate it with thanksgivings, all the years of our life."

"We will, we will, Alonzo!"

"Four minutes after six, in the evening, my Rosannah, shall hence-forth"—

"Twenty-three minutes after twelve, afternoon, shall"—

"Why, Rosannah, darling, where are you?"

"In Honolulu, Sandwich Islands. And where are you? Stay by me; do not leave me for a moment. I cannot bear it. Are you at home?"

"No, dear, I am in New York,—a patient in the doctor's hands."

An agonizing shriek came buzzing to Alonzo's ear, like the sharp buzzing of a hurt gnat; it lost power in traveling five thousand miles. Alonzo hastened to say,—

"Calm yourself, my child. It is nothing. Already I am getting well under the sweet healing of your presence. Rosannah?"

"Yes, Alonzo! Oh, how you terrified me! Say on."

"Name the happy day, Rosannah!"

There was a little pause. Then a diffident small voice replied, "I blush—but it is with pleasure, it is with happiness. Would—would you like to have it soon?"

"This very night, Rosannah! Oh, let us risk no more delays. Let it be now!—this very night, this very moment!"

"Oh, you impatient creature! I have nobody here but my good old uncle, a missionary for a generation, and now retired from service,—nobody but him and his wife. I would so dearly like it if your mother and your aunt Susan"—

"*Our* mother and *our* aunt Susan, my Rosannah."

"Yes, *our* mother and *our* aunt Susan,—I am content to word it so if it pleases you; I would so like to have them present."

"So would I. Suppose you telegraph aunt Susan. How long would it take her to come?"

"The steamer leaves San Francisco day after to-morrow. The passage is eight days. She would be here the 31st of March."

"Then name the 1st of April: do, Rosannah, dear."

"Mercy, it would make us April fools, Alonzo!"

"So we be the happiest ones that that day's sun looks down upon in the whole broad expanse of the globe, why need we care? Call it the 1st of April, dear."

"Then the 1st of April it shall be, with all my heart!"

"Oh, happiness! Name the hour, too, Rosannah."

"I like the morning, it is so blithe. Will eight in the morning do, Alonzo!"

"The lovliest hour in the day,—since it will make you mine."

There was a feeble but frantic sound for some little time, as if wool-lipped, disembodied spirits were exchanging kisses; then Rosannah said, "Excuse me just a moment, dear; I have an appointment, and am called to meet it."

The young girl sought a large parlor and took her place at a window which looked out upon a beautiful scene. To the left one could view the charming Nuuana Valley, fringed with its ruddy flush of tropical flowers and its plumed and graceful cocoa palms; its rising foothills clothed in the shining green of lemon, citron, and orange groves; its storied precipice beyond, where the first Kamehameha drove his defeated foes over to their destruction,—a spot that had forgotten its grim history, no doubt, for now it was smiling, as almost always at noonday, under the glowing arches of a succession of rainbows. In front of the window one could see the quaint town, and here and there a picturesque group of dusky natives, enjoying the blistering weather; and far to the right lay the restless ocean, tossing its white mane in the sunshine.

Rosannah stood there, in her filmy white raiment, fanning her flushed and heated face, waiting. A Kanaka boy, clothed in a damaged blue neck-tie and part of a silk hat, thrust his head in at the door, and announced, "'Frisco *haole!*"

"Show him in," said the girl, straightening herself up and assuming a meaning dignity. Mr. Sidney Algernon Burley entered, clad from head to heel in dazzling snow,—that is to say, in the lightest and whitest of Irish linen. He moved eagerly forward, but the girl made a gesture and gave him a look which checked him suddenly. She said, coldly, "I am here, as I promised. I believed your assertions, I yielded to your importunities, and said I would name the day. I name the 1st of April,—eight in the morning. Now go!"

"Oh, my dearest, if the gratitude of a life time"—

"Not a word. Spare me all sight of you, all communication with you, until that hour. No,—no supplications; I will have it so."

When he was gone, she sank exhausted in a chair, for the long siege of troubles she had undergone had wasted her strength. Presently she said, "What a narrow escape! If the hour appointed had been an hour earlier—Oh, horror, what an escape I have made! And to think I had come to imagine I was loving this beguiling, this truthless, this treacherous monster! Oh, he shall repent his villainy!"

*

Let us now draw this history to a close, for little more needs to be told. On the 2d of the ensuing April, the Honolulu Advertiser contained this notice:—

MARRIED.—In this city, by telephone, yesterday morning, at eight o'clock, by Rev. Nathan Hays, assisted by Rev. Nathaniel Davis, of New York, Mr. Alonzo Fitz Clarence, of Eastport, Maine, U.S., and Miss Rosannah Ethelton, of Portland, Oregon, U.S. Mrs. Susan Howland, of San Francisco, a friend of the bride, was present, she being the guest of the Rev. Mr. Hays and wife, uncle and aunt of the bride. Mr. Sidney Algernon Burley, of San Francisco, was also present, but did not remain till the conclusion of the marriage service. Captain Hawthorne's beautiful yacht, tastefully decorated, was in waiting, and the happy bride and her friends immediately departed on a bridal trip to Lahaina and Haleakala.

The New York papers of the same date contained this notice—

MARRIED.—In this city, yesterday, by telephone, at half past two in the morning, by Rev. Nathaniel Davis, assisted by Rev. Nathan Hays, of Honolulu, Mr. Alonzo Fitz Clarence, of Eastport, Maine, and Miss Rosannah Ethelton, of Portland, Oregon. The parents and several friends of the bridegroom were present, and enjoyed a sumptuous breakfast and much festivity until nearly sunrise, and then departed on a bridal trip to the Aquarium, the bridegroom's state of health not admitting of a more extended journey.

Toward the close of that memorable day, Mr. and Mrs. Alonzo Fitz Clarence were buried in sweet converse concerning the pleasures of their several bridal tours, when suddenly the young wife exclaimed: "O, Lonny, I forgot! I did what I said I would."

"Did you, dear?"

"Indeed I did. I made *him* the April fool! And I told him so, too! Ah, it was a charming surprise! There he stood, sweltering in a black dress suit, with the mercury leaking out of the top of the thermometer, waiting to be married. You should have seen the look he gave when I whispered it in his ear! Ah, his wickedness cost me many a heartache and many a tear, but the score was all squared up, then. So the vengeful feeling went right out of my heart, and I begged him to stay, and said I forgave him everything. But he wouldn't. He said he would live to be avenged; said he would make our lives a curse to us. But he can't, *can* he, dear?"

"Never in this world, my Rosannah!"

*

Aunt Susan, the Oregonian grandmother, and the young couple and their Eastport parents are all happy at this writing, and likely to remain so. Aunt Susan brought the bride from the Islands, accompanied her across our continent, and had the happiness of witnessing the rapturous meeting between an adoring husband and wife who had never seen each other until that moment.

A word about the wretched Burley, whose wicked machinations came so near wrecking the hearts and lives of our poor young friends, will be sufficient. In a murderous attempt to seize a crippled and helpless artisan who he fancied had done him some small offense, he fell into a caldron of boiling oil and expired before he could be extinguished.

MENTAL TELEGRAPHY

MAY, '78.—Another of those apparently trifling things has happened to me which puzzle and perplex all men every now and then, keep them thinking an hour or two, and leave their minds barren of explanation or solution at last. Here it is—and it looks inconsequential enough, I am obliged to say. A few days ago I said: "It must be that Frank Millet doesn't know we are in Germany, or he would have written long before this. I have been on the point of dropping him a line at least a dozen times during the past six weeks, but I always decided to wait a day or two longer, and see if we shouldn't hear from him. But now I *will* write." And so I did. I directed the letter to Paris, and thought, "*Now* we shall hear from him before this letter is fifty miles from Heidelberg—it always happens so."

True enough; but *why* should it? That is the puzzling part of it. We are always talking about letters "crossing" each other, for that is one of the very commonest accidents of this life. We call it "accident," but perhaps we misname it. We have the instinct a dozen times a year that the letter we are writing is going to "cross" the other person's letter; and if the reader will rack his memory a little he will recall the fact that this presentiment had strength enough to it to make him cut his letter down to a decided briefness, because it would be a waste of time to write a letter which was going to "cross," and hence be a useless letter. I think that in my experience this instinct has generally come to me in cases where I had put off my letter a good while in the hope that the other person would write.

Yes, as I was saying, I had waited five or six weeks; then I wrote but three lines, because I felt and seemed to know that a letter from Millet would cross mine. And so it did. He wrote the same day that I wrote. The letters crossed each other. His letter went to Berlin, care of the American minister, who sent it to me. In this letter

Millet said he had been trying for six weeks to stumble upon somebody who knew my German address, and at last the idea had occurred to him that a letter sent to the care of the embassy at Berlin might possibly find me.

Maybe it was an "accident" that he finally determined to write me at the same moment that I finally determined to write him, but I think not.

With me the most irritating thing has been to wait a tedious time in a purely business matter, hoping that the other party will do the writing, and then sit down and do it myself, perfectly satisfied that that other man is sitting down at the same moment to write a letter which will "cross" mine. And yet one must go on writing, just the same; because if you get up from your table and postpone, that other man will do the same thing, exactly as if you two were harnessed together like the Siamese twins, and must duplicate each other's movements.

Several months before I left home a New York firm did some work about the house for me, and did not make a success of it, as it seemed to me. When the bill came, I wrote and said I wanted the work perfected before I paid. They replied that they were very busy, but that as soon as they could spare the proper man the thing should be done. I waited more than two months, enduring as patiently as possible the companionship of bells which would fire away of their own accord sometimes when nobody was touching them, and at other times wouldn't ring though you struck the button with a sledgehammer. Many a time I got ready to write and then postponed it; but at last I sat down one evening and poured out my grief to the extent of a page or so, and then cut my letter suddenly short, because a strong instinct told me that the firm had begun to move in the matter. When I came down to breakfast next morning the postman had not yet taken my letter away, but the electrical man had been there, done his work, and was gone again! He had received his orders the previous evening from his employers, and had come up by the night train.

If that was an "accident," it took about three months to get it up in good shape.

One evening last summer I arrived in Washington, registered at the Arlington Hotel, and went to my room. I read and smoked until ten o'clock; then, finding I was not yet sleepy, I thought I would take a breath of fresh air. So I went forth in the rain, and tramped through one street after another in an aimless and enjoyable way. I knew that Mr. O—, a friend of mine, was in town, and I wished I might run across him; but I did not propose to hunt for him at midnight, especially as I did not know where he was stopping. Toward twelve o'clock the streets had become so deserted that I felt lonesome; so I stepped into a cigar shop far up the Avenue, and remained there fifteen minutes, listening to some bummers discussing national politics. Suddenly the spirit of prophecy came upon me, and I said to myself, "Now I will go out at this door, turn to the left, walk ten steps, and meet Mr. O— face to face." I did it, too! I could not see his face, because he had an umbrella before it, and it was pretty dark anyhow, but he interrupted the man he was walking and talking with, and I recognized his voice and stopped him.

That I should step out there and stumble upon Mr. O— was nothing, but that I should know beforehand that I was going to do it was a good deal. It is a very curious thing when you come to look at it. I stood far within the cigar shop when I delivered my prophecy: I walked about five steps to the door, opened it, closed it after me, walked down a flight of three steps to the sidewalk, then turned to the left and walked four or five more, and found my man. I repeat that in itself the thing was nothing; but to know it would happen so *beforehand,* wasn't that really curious?

I have criticised absent people so often, and then discovered, to my humiliation, that I was talking with their relatives, that I have grown superstitious about that sort of thing and dropped it. How like an idiot one feels after a blunder like that!

We are always mentioning people, and in that very instant they appear before us. We laugh, and say, "Speak of the devil," and so forth, and there we drop it, considering it an "accident." It is a cheap and convenient way of disposing of a grave and very puzzling mystery. The fact is it does seem to happen too often to be an accident.

Now I come to the oddest thing that ever happened to me. Two or three years ago I was lying in bed, idly musing, one morning—it was the 2d of March—when suddenly a red-hot new idea came whistling down into my camp, and exploded with such comprehensive effectiveness as to sweep the vicinity clean of rubbishy reflections, and fill the air with their dust and flying fragments. This idea, stated in simple phrase, was that the time was ripe and the market ready for a certain book; a book which ought to be written at once; a book which must command attention and be of peculiar interest—to wit, a book about the Nevada silver mines. The "Great Bonanza" was a new wonder then, and everybody was talking about it. It seemed to me that the person best qualified to write this book was Mr. William H. Wright, a journalist of Virginia, Nevada, by whose side I had scribbled many months when I was a reporter there ten or twelve years before. He might be alive still; he might be dead; I could not tell; but I would write him, anyway. I began by merely and modestly suggesting that he make such a book; but my interest grew as I went on, and I ventured to map out what I thought ought to be the plan of the work, he being an old friend, and not given to taking good intentions for ill. I even dealt with details, and suggested the order and sequence which they should follow. I was about to put the manuscript in an envelope, when the thought occurred to me that if this book should be written at my suggestion, and then no publisher happened to want it, I should feel uncomfortable; so I concluded to keep my letter back until I should have secured a publisher. I pigeon-holed my document, and dropped a note to my own publisher, asking him to name a day for a business consultation. He was out of town on a far journey. My note remained unanswered, and at the end of three or four days the whole matter had passed out of my mind. On the 9th of March the postman brought three or four letters, and among them a thick one whose superscription was in a hand which seemed dimly familiar to me. I could not "place" it at first, but presently I succeeded. Then I said to a visiting relative who was present:

"Now I will do a miracle. I will tell you everything this letter contains—date, signature, and all—without breaking the seal. It is from a Mr. Wright, of Virginia, Nevada, and is dated the 2d of March—seven days ago. Mr. Wright proposes to make a book about the silver mines and the Great Bonanza, and asks what I, as a friend, think of the idea. He says his subjects are to be so and so, their order and sequence so and so, and he will close with a history of the chief feature of the book, the Great Bonanza."

I opened the letter, and showed that I had stated the date and the contents correctly. Mr. Wright's letter simply contained what my own letter, written on the same date, contained, and mine still lay in its pigeon-hole, where it had been lying during the seven days since it was written.

There was no clairvoyance about this, if I rightly comprehend what clairvoyance is. I think the clairvoyant professes to actually *see* concealed writing, and read it off word for word. This was not my case. I only seemed to know, and to know absolutely, the contents of the letter in detail and due order, but I had to *word* them myself. I translated them, so to speak, out of Wrights's language into my own.

Wright's letter and the one which I had written to him but never sent were in substance the same.

Necessarily this could not come by accident; such elaborate accidents cannot happen. Chance might have duplicated one or two of the details, but she would have broken down on the rest. I could not doubt—there was no tenable reason for doubting—that Mr. Wright's mind and mine had been in close and crystal-clear communication with each other across three thousand miles of mountain and desert on the morning of the 2d of March. I did not consider that both minds *originated* that succession of ideas, but that one mind originated them, and simply telegraphed them to the other. I was curious to know which brain was the telegrapher and which the receiver, so I wrote and asked for particulars. Mr. Wright's reply showed that his mind had done the originating and telegraphing and mine the receiving. Mark that significant thing, now; consider for a moment how many a splendid "original" idea has been unconsciously stolen from a man three thousand miles away! If one should question that this is so, let him look into the cyclopaedia and con once more that curious thing in the history of inventions which has puzzled every one so much—that is, the frequency with which the same machine or other contrivance has been invented at the same time by several persons in different quarters of the globe. The world was without an electric telegraph for several thousand years; then Professor Henry, the American, Wheatstone in England, Morse on the sea, and a German in Munich, all invented it at the same time. The discovery of certain ways of applying steam was made in two or three countries in the same year. Is it not possible that inventors are constantly and unwittingly stealing each other's ideas whilst they stand thousands of miles asunder?

Last spring a literary friend of mine, who lived a hundred miles away, paid me a visit, and in the course of our talk he said he had made a discovery—conceived an entirely new idea—one which certainly had never been used in literature. He told me what it was. I handed him a manuscript, and said he would find substantially the same idea in that—a manuscript which I had written a week before. The idea had been in my mind since the previous November; it had only entered his while I was putting it on paper, a week gone by. He had not yet written his; so he left it unwritten, and gracefully made over all his right and title in the idea to me.

The following statement, which I have clipped from a newspaper, is true. I had the facts from Mr. Howells's lips when the episode was new:

> "A remarkable story of a literary coincidence is told of Mr. Howells's *Atlantic Monthly* serial 'Dr. Breen's Practice.' A lady of Rochester, New York, contributed to the magazine, after 'Dr. Breen's Practice' was in type, a short story which so much resembled Mr. Howells's that he felt it necessary to call upon her and explain the situation of affairs in order that no charge of plagiarism might be preferred against him. He showed her the proof—sheets of his story, and satisfied her that the similarity between her work and his was one of those strange coincidences which have from time to time occurred in the literary world."

I had read portions of Mr. Howells's story, both in MS. and in proof, before the lady offered her contribution to the magazine. Here is another case. I clip it from a newspaper:

> "The republication of Miss Alcott's novel *Moods* recalls to a writer in the Boston *Post* a singular coincidence which was brought to light before the book was first published: 'Miss Anna M. Crane, of Baltimore, published *Emily Chester,* a novel which was pronounced a very striking and strong story. A comparison of this book with *Moods* showed that the two writers, though entire strangers to each other, and living hundreds of miles apart, had both chosen the same subject for their novels, had followed almost the same line of treatment up to a certain point, where the parallel ceased, and the dénouements were entirely opposite. And even more curious, the leading

characters in both books had identically the same names,
so that the names in Miss Alcott's novel had to be changed.
Then the book was published by Loring.'"

Four or five times within my recollection there has been a lively newspaper war in this country over poems whose authorship was claimed by two or three different people at the same time. There was a war of this kind over "Nothing to Wear," "Beautiful Snow," "Rock Me to Sleep, Mother," and also over one of Mr. Will Carleton's early ballads, I think. These were all blameless cases of unintentional and unwitting mental telegraphy, I judge.

A word more as to Mr. Wright. He had had his book in his mind some time; consequently he, and not I, had originated the idea of it. The subject was entirely foreign to my thoughts; I was wholly absorbed in other things. Yet this friend, whom I had not seen and had hardly thought of for eleven years, was able to shoot his thoughts at me across three thousand miles of country, and fill my head with them, to the exclusion of every other interest, in a single moment. He had begun his letter after finishing his work on the morning paper—a little after three o'clock, he said. When it was three in the morning in Nevada it was about six in Hartford, where I lay awake thinking about nothing in particular; and just about that time his ideas came pouring into my head from across the continent, and I got up and put them on paper, under the impression that they were my own original thoughts.

I have never seen any mesmeric or clairvoyant performances or spiritual manifestations which were in the least degree convincing—a fact which is not of consequence, since my opportunities have been meagre; but I am forced to believe that one human mind (still inhabiting the flesh) can communicate with another, over any sort of a distance, and without any *artificial* preparation of "sympathetic conditions" to act as a transmitting agent. I suppose that when the sympathetic conditions happen to exist the two minds communicate with each other, and that otherwise they don't; and I suppose that if the sympathetic conditions could be kept up right along, the two minds would continue to correspond without limit as to time.

Now there is that curious thing which happens to everybody: suddenly a succession of thoughts or sensations flocks in upon you, which startles you with the weird idea that you have ages ago experienced just this succession of thoughts or sensations in a previous existence. The previous existence is possible, no doubt, but I am persuaded that the solution of this hoary mystery lies not there, but in the fact that some far-off stranger has been telegraphing his thoughts and sensations into your consciousness, and that he stopped because some countercurrent or other obstruction intruded and broke the line of communication. Perhaps, they seem repetitions to you because they *are* repetitions, got at second hand from the other man. Possibly Mr. Brown, the "mind-reader," reads other people's minds, possibly he does not; but I know of a surety that I have read another man's mind, and therefore I do not see why Mr. Brown shouldn't do the like also.

*

I wrote the foregoing about three years ago, in Heidelberg, and laid the manuscript aside, purposing to add to it instances of mind-telegraphing from time to time as they should fall under my experience. Meantime the "crossing" of letters has been so frequent as to become monotonous. However, I have managed to get something useful out of this hint; for now, when I get tired of waiting upon a man whom I very much wish to hear from, I sit down and *compel* him to write, whether he wants to or not; that is to say, I sit down and write him, and then tear my letter up, satisfied that my act has forced him to write me at the same moment. I do not need to mail my letter—the writing it is the only essential thing.

Of course I have grown superstitious about this letter-crossing business—this was natural. We staid awhile in Venice after leaving Heidelberg. One day I was going down the Grand Canal in a gondola, when I heard a shout behind me, and looked around to see what the matter was; a gondola was rapidly following, and the goldolier was making signs to me to stop. I did so, and the pursuing boat ranged up alongside. There was an American lady in it—a resident of Venice. She was in a good deal of distress. She said:

"There's a New York gentleman and his wife at the Hotel Britannia who arrived a week ago, expecting to find news of their son, whom they have heard nothing about during eight months. There was no news. The lady is down sick with despair; the gentleman can't sleep or eat. Their son arrived at San Francisco eight months ago, and announced the fact in a letter to his parents the same day. That is the last trace of him. The parents have been in Europe ever since; but their trip has been spoiled, for they have occupied their time simply in drifting restlessly from place to place, and writing letters everywhere and to everybody, begging for news of their son; but the mystery remains as dense as ever. Now the gentleman wants to stop writing and go to cabling. He wants to cable San Francisco. He has never done it before, because he is afraid of—of he doesn't know what—death of the son, no doubt. But he wants somebody to *advise* him to cable; wants me to do it. Now I simply can't; for if no news came, that mother yonder would die. So I have chased you up in order to get you to support me in urging him to be patient, and put the thing off a week or two longer, it may be the saving of this lady. Come along; let's not lose any time."

So I went along, but I had a programme of my own. When I was introduced to the gentleman I said: "I have some superstitions, but they are worthy of respect. If you will cable San Francisco immediately, you will hear news of your son inside of twenty-four hours. I don't know that you will get the news from San Francisco, but you will get it from somewhere. The only necessary thing is to *cable*—that is all. The news will come within twenty-four hours. Cable Peking, if you prefer; there is no choice in this matter. This delay is all occasioned by your not cabling long ago, when you were first moved to do it."

It seemed absurd that this gentleman should have been cheered up by this nonsense, but he was; he brightened up at once, and sent his cablegram; and next day, at noon, when a long letter arrived from his lost son, the man was as grateful to me as if I had really had something to do with the hurrying up of that letter. The son had shipped from San Francisco in a sailing vessel, and his letter was written from the first port he touched at, months afterward.

This incident argues nothing, and is valueless. I insert it only to show how strong is the superstition which "letter-crossing" had bred in me. I was so sure that a cablegram sent to any place, no matter where, would defeat itself by "crossing" the incoming news, that my confidence was able to raise up a hopeless man, and make him cheery and hopeful.

But here are two or three incidents which come strictly under the head of mind-telegraphing. One Monday morning, about a year ago, the mail came in, and I picked up one of the letters and said to a friend: "Without opening this letter I will tell you what it says. It is from Mrs. ——, and she says she was in New York last Saturday, and was purposing to run up here in the afternoon train and surprise us, but at the last moment changed her mind and returned westward to her home."

I was right; my details were exactly correct. Yet we had had no suspicion that Mrs. —— was coming to New York, or that she had even a remote intention of visiting us.

I smoke a good deal—that is to say, all the time—so, during seven years, I have tried to keep a box of matches handy, behind a picture on the mantel-piece; but I have had to take it out in trying, because George (colored), who makes the fires and lights the gas, always uses my matches, and never replaces them. Commands and persuasions have gone for nothing with him all these seven years. One day last summer, when our family had been away from home several months, I said to a member of the household:

"Now, with all this long holiday, and nothing in the way to interrupt—"

"I can finish the sentence for you," said the member of the household.

"Do it, then," said I.

"George ought to be able, by practising, to learn to let those matches alone."

It was correctly done. That was what I was going to say. Yet until that moment George and the matches had not been in my mind for three months, and it is plain that the part of the sentence which I uttered offers not the least cue or suggestion of what I was purposing to follow it with.

My mother is descended from the younger of two English brothers named Lambton, who settled in this country a few generations ago. The tradition goes that the elder of the two eventually fell heir to a certain estate in England (now an earldom), and died right away. This has always been the way with our family. They always die when they could make anything by not doing it. The two Lambtons left plenty of Lambtons behind them; and when at last, about fifty years ago, the English baronetcy was exalted to an earldom, the great tribe of American Lambtons began to bestir themselves—that is, those descended from the elder branch. Ever since that day one or another of these has been fretting his life uselessly away with schemes to get at his "rights." The present "rightful earl"—I mean the American one— used to write me occasionally, and try to interest me in his projected raids upon the title and estates by offering me a share in the latter portion of the spoil; but I have always managed to resist his temptations.

Well, one day last summer I was lying under a tree, thinking about nothing in particular, when an absurd idea flashed into my head, and I said to a member of the household, "Suppose I should live to be ninety-two, and dumb and blind and toothless, and just as I was gasping out what was left of me on my death-bed—"

"Wait, I will finish the sentence," said the member of the household.

"Go on," said I.

"Somebody should rush in with a document, and say, 'All the other heirs are dead, and you are the Earl of Durham!'"

That is truly what I was going to say. Yet until that moment the subject had not entered my mind or been referred to in my hearing for months before. A few years ago this thing would have astounded me, but the like could not much surprise me now, though it happened every week; for I think I *know* now that mind can communicate accurately with mind without the aid of the slow and clumsy vehicle of speech.

This age does seem to have exhausted invention nearly; still, it has one important contract on its hands yet—the invention of the *phrenophone*; that is to say, a method whereby the communicating of mind with mind may be brought under command and reduced to certainty and system. The telegraph and the telephone are going to become too slow and wordy for our needs. We must have the *thought* itself shot into our minds from a distance; then, if we need to put it into words, we can do that tedious work at our leisure. Doubtless the something which conveys our thoughts through the air from brain to brain is a finer and subtler form of electricity, and all we need do is to find out how to capture it and how to force it to do its work, as we have had to do in the case of the electric currents. Before the day of telegraphs neither one of these marvels would have seemed any easier to achieve than the other.

While I am writing this, doubtless somebody on the other side of the globe is writing it too. The question is, am I inspiring him or is he inspiring me? I cannot answer that; but that these thoughts have been passing through somebody else's mind all the time I have been setting them down I have no sort of doubt.

I will close this paper with a remark which I found some time ago in Boswell's *Johnson*:

"Voltaire's *Candide* is wonderfully similar in its plan and conduct to Johnson's *Rasselas*; insomuch that I have heard Johnson say that if they had not been published so closely one after the other that there was not time for imitation, *it would have been in vain to deny that the scheme of that which came latest was taken from the other.*"

The two men were widely separated from each other at the time, and the sea lay between.

POSTSCRIPT

In the *Atlantic* for June, 1882, Mr. John Fiske refers to the often-quoted Darwin-and-Wallace "coincidence":

"I alluded, just now, to the 'unforeseen circumstance' which led Mr. Darwin in 1859 to break his long silence, and to write and publish the *Origin of Species*. This circumstance served, no less than the extraordinary success of his book, to show how ripe the minds of men had become for entertaining such views as those which Mr. Darwin propounded. In 1858 Mr. Wallace, who was then engaged in studying the natural history of the Malay Archipelago, sent to Mr. Darwin (as to the man most likely to understand him) a paper, in which he sketched the outlines of a theory identical with that upon which Mr. Darwin had so long been at work. The same sequence of observed facts and inferences that had led Mr. Darwin to the discovery of natural selection and its consequences had led Mr. Wallace to the very threshold of the same discovery; but in Mr. Wallace's mind the theory had by no means been wrought out to the same degree of completeness to which it had been wrought in the mind of Mr. Darwin. In the preface to his charming book on Natural Selection, Mr. Wallace, with rare modesty and candor, acknowledges that whatever value his speculations may have had, they have been utterly surpassed in richness and cogency of proof by those of Mr. Darwin. This is no doubt true, and Mr. Wallace had done such good work in further illustration of the theory that he can well afford to rest content with the second place in the first announcement of it.

"The coincidence, however, between Mr. Wallace's conclusions and those of Mr. Darwin was very remarkable. But, after all, coincidences of this sort have not been uncommon in the history of scientific inquiry. Nor is it at all surprising that they should occur now and then, when we remember that a great and pregnant discovery must always be

concerned with some question which many of the foremost
minds in the world are busy in thinking about. It was so with
the discovery of the differential calculus, and again with the
discovery of the planet Neptune. It was so with the
interpretation of the Egyptian hieroglyphics, and with the
establishment of the undulatory theory of light. It was so, to
a considerable extent, with the introduction of the new
chemistry, with the discovery of the mechanical equivalent
of heat, and the whole doctrine of the correlation of forces.
It was so with the invention of the electric telegraph and with
the discovery of spectrum [*sic*] analysis. And it is not at all
strange that it should have been so with the doctrine of the
origin of species through natural selection."

He thinks these "coincidences" were apt to happen because the
matters from which they sprang were matters which many of the
foremost minds in the world were busy thinking about. But
perhaps *one* man in each case did the telegraphing to the others.
The aberrations which gave Leverrier the idea that there must be a
planet of such and such mass and such and such an orbit hidden
from sight out yonder in the remote abysses of space were not new;
they had been noticed by astronomers for generations. Then why
should it happen to occur to three people, widely separated—
Leverrier, Mrs. Somerville, and Adams—to suddenly go to
worrying about those aberrations all at the same time, and set
themselves to work to find out what caused them, and to measure
and weigh an invisible planet, and calculate its orbit, and hunt it
down and catch it?—a strange project which nobody but they had
ever thought of before. If one astronomer had invented that odd
and happy project fifty years before, don't you think he would have
telegraphed it to several others without knowing it?

But now I come to a puzzler. How is it that *inanimate* objects are
able to affect the mind? They seem to do that. However, I wish to
throw in a parenthesis first—just a reference to a thing everybody is
familiar with—the experience of receiving a clear and particular *answer*
to your telegram before your telegram has reached the sender of the
answer. That is a case where your telegram has gone straight from
your brain to the man it was meant for, far outstripping the wire's slow
electricity, and it is an exercise of mental telegraphy which is as
common as dining. To return to the influence of inanimate things. In

the cases of non-professional clairvoyance examined by the Psychical Society the clairvoyant has usually been blindfolded, then some object which has been touched or worn by a person is placed in his hand; the clairvoyant immediately describes that person, and goes on and gives a history of some event with which the test object has been connected. If the inanimate object is also to affect and inform the clairvoyant's mind, maybe it can do the same when it is working in the interest of mental telegraphy. Once a lady in the West wrote me that her son was coming to New York to remain three weeks, and would pay me a visit if invited, and she gave me his address. I mislaid the letter, and forgot all about the matter till the three weeks were about up. Then a sudden and fiery irruption of remorse burst up in my brain that illuminated all the region round about, and I sat down at once and wrote to the lady and asked for that lost address. But, upon reflection, I judged that the stirring up of my recollection had not been an accident, so I added a postscript to say, never mind, I should get a letter from her son before night. And I did get it; for the letter was already in the town, although not delivered yet. It had influenced me somehow. I have had so many experiences of this sort—a dozen of them at least—that I am nearly persuaded that inanimate objects do not confine their activities to helping the clairvoyant, but do every now and then give the mental telegraphist a lift.

The case of mental telegraphy which I am coming to now comes under I don't exactly know what head. I clipped it from one of our local papers six or eight years ago. I know the details to be right and true, for the story was told to me in the same form by one of the two persons concerned (a clergyman of Hartford) at the time that the curious thing happened:

"A REMARKABLE COINCIDENCE.—Strange coincidences make the most interesting of stories and most curious of studies. Nobody can quite say how they come about, but everybody appreciates the fact when they do come, and it is seldom that any more complete and curious coincidence is recorded of minor importance than the following, which is absolutely true, and occurred in this city:

"At the time of the building of one of the finest residences of Hartford, which is still a very new house, a local firm supplied the wallpaper for certain rooms, contracting both to furnish and to put on the paper. It happened that they did not calculate the size of one room exactly right, and the paper of the design selected for it fell short just half a roll. They asked for delay enough to send on to the manufacturers for what was needed, and were told that there was no especial hurry. It happened that the manufacturers had none on hand, and had destroyed the blocks from which it was printed. They wrote that they had a full list of the dealers to whom they had sold that paper, and that they would write to each of these, and get from some of them a roll. It might involve a delay of a couple of weeks, but they would surely get it.

"In the course of time came a letter saying that, to their great surprise, they could not find a single roll. Such a thing was very unusual, but in this case it had so happened. Accordingly the local firm asked for further time, saying they would write to their own customers who had bought of that pattern, and would get this piece from them. But, to their surprise, this effort also failed. A long time had now elapsed, and there was no use of delaying any longer. They had contracted to paper the room, and their only course was to take off that which was insufficient and put on some other of which there was enough to go around. Accordingly at length a man was sent out to remove the paper. He got his apparatus ready and was about to begin work, under the direction of the owner of the building, when the latter was for the moment called away. The house was large and very interesting, and so many people had rambled about it that finally admission had been refused by a sign at the door. On the occasion, however, when a gentleman had knocked and asked for leave to look about, the owner, being on the premises, had been sent for to reply to the request in person. That was the call that for the moment delayed the final preparations. The gentleman went to the door and admitted the stranger, saying he would show him about the house, but first must return for a moment to that room to finish his directions there, and he told the curious story about the paper as they went on. They entered the room together, and the first thing the stranger, who lived fifty miles away, said on looking about was, 'Why, I have that very paper on a room in my house, and I have an extra roll of it laid away, which is at your service.' In a few days the wall was papered according to the original contract. Had not the owner been at the house, the stranger would not have been admitted; had he called a day later, it would have been too late; had not the facts been almost accidentally told to him, he would probably have said nothing of the paper, and so on. The exact fitting of all the circumstances is something very remarkable, and makes one of those stories that seem hardly accidental in their nature."

Something had happened the other day brought my hoary MS. to mind, and that is how I came to dig it out from its dusty pigeon-hole grave for publication. The thing that happened was a question. A lady asked it: "Have you ever had a vision—when awake?" I was about to answer promptly, when the last two words of the question began to grow and spread and swell, and presently they attained to vast dimensions. She did not know that they were important; and I did not at first, but I soon saw that they were putting me on the track of the solution of a mystery which had perplexed me a good deal. You will see what I mean when I get down to it. Ever since the English Society for Psychical Research began its searching investigations of ghost stories, haunted houses, and apparitions of the living and the dead, I have read their pamphlets with avidity as fast as they arrived. Now one of their commonest inquiries of a dreamer or a vision-seer is, "Are you sure you were awake at the time?" If the man can't say he is sure he was awake, a doubt falls upon his tale right there. But if he is positive he was awake, and offers reasonable evidence to substantiate it, the fact counts largely for the credibility of his story. It does with the society, and it did with me until that lady asked me the above question the other day.

The question set me to considering, and brought me to the conclusion that you can be asleep—at least wholly unconscious—for a time, and not suspect that it has happened, and not have any way to prove that it *has* happened. A memorable case was in my mind. About a year ago I was standing on the porch one day, when I saw a man coming up the walk. He was a stranger, and I hoped he would ring and carry his business into the house without stopping to argue with me; he would have to pass the front door to get to me, and I hoped he wouldn't take the trouble; to help, I tried to look like a stranger myself—it often works. I was looking straight at that man; he had got to within ten feet of the door and within twenty-five feet of me—and suddenly he disappeared. It was as astounding as if a church should vanish from before your face and leave nothing behind it but a vacant lot. I was unspeakably delighted. I had seen an apparition at last, with my own eyes, in broad daylight. I made up my mind to write an account of it to the society. I ran to where the spectre had been, to make sure he was playing fair, then I ran to the other end of the porch, scanning the open grounds as I went. No, everything was perfect; he couldn't have escaped without my seeing him; he was an apparition, without the slightest doubt, and I would write him up before he was cold. I ran, hot with excitement, and let myself in with a latch-key. When I stepped into the hall my lungs collapsed and my heart stood still. For there sat that same apparition in a chair, all alone, and as quiet and reposeful as if he had come to stay a year! The shock kept me dumb for a moment or two, then I said, "Did you come in at that door?"

"Yes."

"Did *you* open it, or did you ring?"

"I rang, and the colored man opened it."

I said to myself: "This is astonishing. It takes George all of two minutes to answer the door-bell when he is in a hurry and I have never seen him in a hurry. How *did* this man stand two minutes at that door, within five steps of me, and I did not see him?"

I should have gone to my grave puzzling over that riddle but for that lady's chance question last week: "Have you ever had a vision— when awake?" It stands explained now. During at least sixty seconds that day I was asleep or at least totally unconscious, without suspecting it. In that interval the man came to my immediate vicinity, rang, stood there and waited, then entered and closed the door, and I did not see him and did not hear the door slam.

If he had slipped around the house in that interval and gone into the cellar—he had time enough—I should have written him up for the society, and magnified him, and gloated over him, and hurrahed about him, and thirty yoke of oxen could not have pulled the belief out of me that I was of the favored ones of the earth, and had seen a vision—while wide awake.

Now how are you to tell when you are awake? What are you to go by? People bite their fingers to find out. Why, you can do that in a dream.

MENTAL TELEGRAPHY AGAIN

I HAVE THREE or four curious incidents to tell about. They seem to come under the head of what I named "Mental Telegraphy" in a paper written seventeen years ago, and published long afterward.

Several years ago I made a campaign on the platform with Mr. George W. Cable. In Montreal we were honored with a reception. It began at two in the afternoon in a long drawing-room in the Windsor Hotel. Mr. Cable and I stood at one end of this room, and the ladies and gentlemen entered it at the other end, crossed it at that end, then came up the long left-hand side, shook hands with us, said a word or two, and passed on, in the usual way. My sight is of the telescopic sort, and I presently recognized a familiar face among the throng of strangers drifting in at the distant door, and I said to myself, with surprise and high gratification, "That is Mrs. R.; I had forgotten that she was a Canadian." She had been a great friend of mine in Carson City, Nevada, in the early days. I had not seen her or heard of her for twenty years; I had not been thinking about her; there was nothing to suggest her to me, nothing to bring her to my mind; in fact, to me she had long ago ceased to exist, and had disappeared from my consciousness. But I knew her instantly; and I saw her so clearly that I was able to note some of the particulars of her dress, and did note them, and they remained in my mind. I was impatient for her to come. In the midst of the hand-shakings I snatched glimpses of her and noted her progress with the slow-moving file across the end of the room, then I saw her start up the side, and this gave me a full front view of her face. I saw her last when she was within twenty-five feet of me. For an hour I kept thinking she must still be in the room somewhere and would come at last, but I was disappointed.

When I arrived in the lecture-hall that evening some one said: "Come into the waiting-room; there's a friend of yours there who wants to see you. You'll not be introduced—you are to do the recognizing without help if you can."

I said to myself, "It is Mrs. R.; I sha'n't have any trouble."

There were perhaps ten ladies present, all seated. In the midst of them was Mrs. R., as I had expected. She was dressed exactly as she was when I had seen her in the afternoon. I went forward and shook hands with her and called her by name, and said,

"I knew you the moment you appeared at the reception this afternoon."

She looked surprised, and said: "But I was not at the reception. I have just arrived from Quebec, and have not been in town an hour."

It was my turn to be surprised now. I said: "I can't help it. I give you my word of honor that it's as I say. I saw you at the reception, and you were dressed precisely as you are now. When they told me a moment ago that I should find a friend in this room, your image rose before me, dress and all, just as I had seen you at the reception."

Those are the facts. She was not at the reception at all, or anywhere near it: but I saw her there nevertheless, and most clearly and unmistakably. To that I could make oath. How is one to explain this? I was not thinking of her at the time; had not thought of her for years. But she had been thinking of me, no doubt; did her thought flit through leagues of air to me, and bring with it that clear and pleasant vision of herself? I think so. That was and remains my sole experience in the matter of apparitions—I mean apparitions that come when one is (ostensibly) awake. I could have been asleep for a moment: the apparition could have been the creature of a dream. Still, that is nothing to the point; the feature of interest is the happening of the thing just at that time, instead of at an earlier or later time, which is argument that its origin lay in thought-transference.

My next incident will be set aside by most persons as being merely a "coincidence," I suppose. Years ago I used to think sometimes of making a lecturing trip through the antipodes and the borders of the Orient, but always gave up the idea, partly because of the great length of the journey and partly because my wife could not well manage to go with me. Toward the end of last January that idea, after an interval of years, came suddenly into my head again—forcefully, too, and without any apparent reason. Whence came it? What suggested it? I will touch upon that presently.

I was at that time where I am now—in Paris. I wrote at once to Henry M. Stanley (London), and asked him some questions about his Australian lecture tour, and inquired who had conducted him and what were the terms. After a day or two his answer came. It began:

"The lecture agent for Australia and New Zealand is *par excellence* Mr. R. S. Smythe, of Melbourne."

He added his itinerary, terms, sea expenses, and some other matters, and advised me to write Mr. Smythe, which I did—February 3d. I began my letter by saying in substance that while he did not know me personally we had a mutual friend in Stanley, and that would answer for an introduction. Then I proposed my trip, and asked if he would give me the same terms which he had given Stanley.

I mailed my letter to Mr. Smythe February 6th, and three days later I got a letter from the selfsame Smythe, dated Melbourne, December 17th. I would as soon have expected to get a letter from the late George Washington. The letter began somewhat as mine to him had begun—with a self-introduction:

"DEAR MR. CLEMENS,—It is so long since Archibald Forbes and I spent that pleasant afternoon in your comfortable house at Hartford that you have probably quite forgotten the occasion."

In the course of his letter this occurs:

"I am willing to give you" [here he named the terms which he had given Stanley "for an antipodean tour to last, say, three months."

Here was the single essential detail of my letter answered three days after I had mailed my inquiry. I might have saved myself the trouble and the postage—and a few years ago I would have done that very thing, for I would have argued that my sudden and strong impulse to write and ask some questions of a stranger on the under side of the globe meant that the impulse came from that stranger, and that he would answer my questions of his own motion if I would let him alone.

Mr. Smythe's letter probably passed under my nose on its way to lose three weeks travelling to America and back, and gave me a whiff of its contents as it went along. Letters often act like that. Instead of the *thought* coming to you in an instant from Australia, the (apparently) unsentient letter imparts it to you as it glides invisibly past your elbow in the mail-bag.

Next incident. In the following month—March—I was in America. I spent a Sunday at Irvington-on-the-Hudson with Mr. John Brisben Walker, of the *Cosmopolitan* magazine. We came into New York next morning, and went to the Century Club for luncheon. He said some praiseful things about the character of the club and the orderly serenity and pleasantness of its quarters, and asked if I had never tried to acquire membership in it. I said I had not, and that New York clubs were a continuous expense to the country members without being of frequent use or benefit to them.

"And now I've got an idea!" said I. "There's the Lotos—the first New York club I was ever a member of—my very earliest love in that line. I have been a member of it for considerably more than twenty years, yet have seldom had a chance to look in and see the boys. They turn gray and grow old while I am not watching. And *my dues go on*. I am going to Hartford this afternoon for a day or two, but as soon as I get back I will go to John Elderkin very privately and say: 'Remember the veteran and confer distinction upon him, for the sake of old times. Make me an honorary member and abolish the tax. If you haven't any such thing as honorary membership, all the better—create it for my honor and glory.' That would be a great thing; I will go to John Elderkin as soon as I get back from Hartford."

I took the last express that afternoon, first telegraphing Mr. F. G. Whitmore to come and see me next day. When he came he asked,

"Did you get a letter from Mr. John Elderkin, secretary of the Lotos Club, before you left New York?"

"No."

"Then it just missed you. If I had known you were coming I would have kept it. It is beautiful, and will make you proud. The Board of Directors, by unanimous vote, have made you a life member, and *squelched those dues;* and you are to be on hand and receive your distinction on the night of the 30th, which is the twenty-fifth anniversary of the founding of the club, and it will not surprise me if they have some great times there."

What put the honorary membership in my head that day in the Century Club? for I had never thought of it before. I don't know what brought the thought to me at *that* particular time instead of earlier, but I am well satisfied that it originated with the Board of Directors, and had been on its way to my brain through the air ever since the moment that saw their vote recorded.

Another incident. I was in Hartford two or three days as a guest of the Rev. Joseph H. Twichell. I have held the rank of Honorary Uncle to his children for a quarter of a century, and I went out with him in the trolley-car to visit one of my nieces, who is at

Miss Porter's famous school in Farmington. The distance is eight or nine miles. On the way, talking, I illustrated something with an anecdote. This is the anecdote:

Two years and a half ago I and the family arrived at Milan on our way to Rome, and stopped at the Continental. After dinner I went below and took a seat in the stone-paved court, where the customary lemon-trees stand in the customary tubs, and said to myself, "Now *this* is comfort, comfort and repose, and nobody to disturb it; I do not know anybody in Milan."

Then a young gentleman stepped up and shook hands, which damaged my theory. He said, in substance:

"You won't remember me, Mr. Clemens, but I remember you very well. I was a cadet at West Point when you and Rev. Joseph H. Twichell came there some years ago and talked to us on a Hundredth Night. I am a lieutenant in the regular army now, and my name is H. I am in Europe, all alone, for a modest little tour; my regiment is in Arizona."

We became friendly and sociable, and in the course of the talk he told me of an adventure which had befallen him—about to this effect:

"I was at Bellagio, stopping at the big hotel there, and ten days ago I lost my letter of credit. I did not know what in the world to do. I was a stranger; I knew no one in Europe; I hadn't a penny in my pocket; I couldn't even send a telegram to London to get my lost letter replaced; my hotel bill was a week old, and the presentation of it imminent—so imminent that it could happen at any moment now. I was so frightened that my wits all seemed to leave me. I tramped and tramped, back and forth, like a crazy person. If anybody approached me I hurried away, for no matter what a person looked like, I took him for the head waiter with the bill.

"I was at last in such a desperate state that I was ready to do any wild thing that promised even the shadow of help, and so this is the insane thing that I did. I saw a family lunching at a small table on the veranda, and recognized their nationality—Americans—father, mother, and several young daughters—young, tastefully dressed, and pretty—the rule with our people. I went straight there in my civilian costume, named my name, said I was a lieutenant in the army, and told my story and asked for help.

"What do you suppose the gentleman did? But you would not guess in twenty years. He took out a handful of gold coin and told me to help myself—freely. That is what he did."

The next morning the lieutenant told me his new letter of credit had arrived in the night, so we strolled to Cook's to draw money to pay back the benefactor with. We got it, and then went strolling through the great arcade. Presently he said, "Yonder they are; come and be introduced." I was introduced to the parents and the young ladies, then we separated, and I never saw him or them any m—"

"Here we are at Farmington," said Twichell, interrupting.

We left the trolley-car and tramped through the mud a hundred yards or so to the school, talking about the time we and Warner walked out there years ago, and the pleasant time we had.

We had a visit with my niece in the parlor; then started for the trolley again. Outside the house we encountered a double rank of twenty or thirty of Miss Porter's young ladies arriving from a walk, and we stood aside, ostensibly to let them have room to file past, but really to look at them. Presently one of them stepped out of the rank and said,

"You don't know me, Mr. Twichell, but I know your daughter, and that gives me the privilege of shaking hands with you."

Then she put out her hand to me, and said:

"And I wish to shake hands with you too, Mr. Clemens. You don't remember me, but you were introduced to me in the arcade in Milan two years and a half ago by Lieutenant H."

What had put that story into my head after all that stretch of time? Was it just the proximity of that young girl, or was it merely an odd accident?

EXTRACTS FROM ADAM'S DIARY

MONDAY—This new creature with the long hair is a good deal in the way. It is always hanging around and following me about. I don't like this; I am not used to company. I wish it would stay with the other animals. . . . Cloudy today, wind in the east; think we shall have rain. . . . *We?* Where did I get that word—the new creature uses it.

Tuesday—Been examining the great waterfall. It is the finest thing on the estate, I think. The new creature calls it Niagara Falls—why, I am sure I do not know. Says it *looks* like Niagara Falls. That is not a reason, it is mere waywardness and imbecility. I get no chance to name anything myself. The new creature names everything that comes along, before I can get in a protest. There is a dodo, for instance. Says the moment one looks at it one sees at a glance that it "looks like a dodo." It will have to keep that name, no doubt. It wearies me to fret about it, and it does no good, anyway. Dodo! It looks no more like a dodo than I do.

Wednesday—Built me a shelter against the rain, but could not have it to myself in peace. The new creature intruded. When I tried to put it out it shed water out of the holes it looks with, and wiped it away with the back of its paws, and made a noise such as some of the other animals make when they are in distress. I wish it would not talk; it is always talking. That sounds like a cheap fling at the poor creature, a slur; but I do not mean it so. I have never heard the human voice before, and any new and strange sound intruding itself here upon the solemn hush of these dreaming solitudes offends my ear and seems a false note. And this new sound is so close to me; it is right at my shoulder, tight at my ear, first on one side and then on the other, and I am used only to sounds that are more or less distant from me.

Friday—The naming goes recklessly on, in spite of anything I can do. I had a very good name for the estate, and it was musical and pretty—*garden of Eden*. Privately, I continue to call it that, but not any longer publicly. The new creature says it is all woods and rocks and scenery, and therefore has no resemblance to a garden. Says it *looks* like a park, and does not look like anything *but* a park. Consequently, without consulting me, it has been new-named *Niagara falls park*. This is sufficiently high-handed, it seems to me. And already there is a sign up:

> KEEP OFF
> THE GRASS

My life is not as happy as it was.

Saturday—The new creature eats too much fruit. We are going to run short, most likely. "We" again—that is *its* word; mine, too, now, from hearing it so much. Good deal of fog this morning. I do not go out in the fog myself. This new creature does. It goes out in all weathers, and stumps right in with its muddy feet. And talks. It used to be so pleasant and quiet here.

Sunday—Pulled through. This day is getting to be more and more trying. It was selected and set apart last November as a day of rest. I had already six of them per week before. This morning found the new creature trying to clod apples out of that forbidden tree.

Monday—The new creature says its name is Eve. That is all right, I have no objections. Says it is to call it by, when I want it to come. I said it was superfluous, then. The word evidently raised me in its respect; and indeed it is a large, good word and will bear repetition. It says it is not an It, it is a She. This is probably doubtful; yet it is all one to me; what she is were nothing to me if she would but go by herself and not talk.

Tuesday—She has littered the whole estate with execrable names and offensive signs:

→ **This way to the Whirlpool**

→ **This way to Goat Island**

→ **Cave of the Winds this way**

She says this park would make a tidy summer resort if there was any custom for it. Summer resort—another invention of hers—just words, without any meaning. What is a summer resort? But it is best not to ask her, she has such a rage for explaining.

Friday—She has taken to beseeching me to stop going over the Falls. What harm does it do? Says it makes her shudder. I wonder why; I have always done it—always liked the plunge, and coolness. I supposed it was what the Falls were for. They have no other use that I can see, and they must have been made for something. She says they were only made for scenery—like the rhinoceros and the mastodon.

I went over the Falls in a barrel—not satisfactory to her. Went over in a tub—still not satisfactory. Swam the Whirlpool and the Rapids in a fig-leaf suit. It got much damaged. Hence, tedious complaints about my extravagance. I am too much hampered here. What I need is a change of scene.

Saturday—I escaped last Tuesday night, and traveled two days, and built me another shelter in a secluded place, and obliterated my tracks as well as I could, but she hunted me out by means of a beast which she has tamed and calls a wolf, and came making that pitiful noise again, and shedding that water out of the places she looks with. I was obliged to return with her, but will presently emigrate again when occasion offers. She engages herself in many foolish things; among others; to study out why the animals called lions and tigers live on grass and flowers, when, as she says, the sort of teeth they wear would indicate that they were intended to eat each other. This is foolish, because to do that would be to kill each other, and that would introduce what, as I understand, is called "death"; and death, as I have been told, has not yet entered the Park. Which is a pity, on some accounts.

Sunday—Pulled through.

Monday—I believe I see what the week is for: it is to give time to rest up from the weariness of Sunday. It seems a good idea. . . . She has been climbing that tree again. Clodded her out of it. She said nobody was looking. Seems to consider that a sufficient justification for chancing any dangerous thing. Told her that. The word justification moved her admiration—and envy, too, I thought. It is a good word.

Tuesday—She told me she was made out of a rib taken from my body. This is at least doubtful, if not more than that. I have not missed any rib. . . . She is in much trouble about the buzzard; says grass does not agree with it; is afraid she can't raise it; thinks it was intended to live on decayed flesh. The buzzard must get along the best it can with what is provided. We cannot overturn the whole scheme to accommodate the buzzard.

Saturday—She fell in the pond yesterday when she was looking at herself in it, which she is always doing. She nearly strangled, and said it was most uncomfortable. This made her sorry for the creatures which live in there, which she calls fish, for she continues to fasten names on to things that don't need them and don't come when they are called by them, which is a matter of no consequence to her, she is such a numbskull, anyway; so she got a lot of them out and brought them in last night and put them in my bed to keep warm, but I have noticed them now and then all day and I don't see that they are any happier there then they were before, only quieter. When night comes I shall throw them outdoors. I will not sleep with them again, for I find them clammy and unpleasant to lie among when a person hasn't anything on.

Sunday—Pulled through.

Tuesday—She has taken up with a snake now. The other animals are glad, for she was always experimenting with them and bothering them; and I am glad because the snake talks, and this enables me to get a rest.

Friday—She says the snake advises her to try the fruit of the tree, and says the result will be a great and fine and noble education. I told her there would be another result, too—it would introduce death into the world. That was a mistake—it had been better to keep the remark to myself; it only gave her an idea she could save the sick buzzard, and furnish fresh meat to the despondent lions and tigers. I advised her to keep away from the tree. She said she wouldn't. I foresee trouble. Will emigrate.

Wednesday—I have had a variegated time. I escaped last night, and rode a horse all night as fast as he could go, hoping to get clear of the Park and hide in some other country before the trouble should begin; but it was not to be. About an hour after sun-up, as I was riding through a flowery plain where thousands of animals were grazing, slumbering, or playing with each other, according to their wont, all of a sudden they broke into a tempest of frightful noises, and in one moment the plain was a frantic commotion and every beast was destroying its neighbor. I knew what it meant— Eve had eaten that fruit, and death was come into the world. . . . The tigers ate my house, paying no attention when I ordered them to desist, and they would have eaten me if I had stayed—which I didn't, but went away in much haste. . . . I found this place, outside the Park, and was fairly comfortable for a few days, but she has found me out. Found me out, and has named the place Tonawanda—says it *looks* like that. In fact I was not sorry she came, for there are but meager pickings here, and she brought some of those apples. I was obliged to eat them, I was so hungry. It was against my principles, but I find that principles have no real force except when one is well fed. . . . She came curtained in boughs and bunches of leaves, and when I asked her what she meant by such nonsense, and snatched them away and threw them down, she tittered and blushed. I had never seen a person titter and blush before, and to me it seemed unbecoming and idiotic. She said I would soon know how it was myself. This was correct. Hungry as I was, I laid down the apple half-eaten—certainly the best one I ever saw, considering the lateness of the season—and arrayed myself in the discarded boughs and branches, and then spoke to her with some severity and ordered her to go and get some more and not make a spectacle of herself. She did it, and after this we crept down to where the wild-beast battle had been, and collected some skins, and I made her patch together a couple of suits proper for public occasions. They are uncomfortable, it is true, but stylish, and that is the main point about clothes. . . . I find she is a good deal of a companion. I see I should be lonesome and depressed without her, now that I have lost my property. Another thing, she says it is ordered that we work for our living hereafter. She will be useful. I will superintend.

Ten days later—She accuses *me* of being the cause of our disaster! She says, with apparent sincerity and truth, that the Serpent assured her that the forbidden fruit was not apples, it was chestnuts. I said I was innocent, then, for I had not eaten any chestnuts. She said the Serpent informed her that "chestnut" was a figurative term meaning an aged and moldy joke. I turned pale at that, for I have made many jokes to pass the weary time, and some of them could have been of that sort, though I had honestly supposed that they were new when I made them. She asked me if I had made one just at the time of the catastrophe. I was obliged to admit that I had made one to myself, though not aloud. It was this. I was thinking about the Falls, and I said to myself, "How wonderful it is to see that vast body of water tumble down there!" Then in an instant a bright thought flashed into my head, and I let it fly, saying, "It would be a deal more wonderful to see it tumble *up* there!"—and I was just about to kill myself with laughing at it when all nature broke loose in war and death and I had to flee for my life. "There," she said, with triumph, "that is just it; the Serpent mentioned that very jest, and called it the First Chestnut, and said it was coeval with the creation." Alas, I am indeed to blame. Would that I were not witty; oh, that I had never had that radiant thought!

Next year—We have named it Cain. She caught it while I was up country trapping on the North Shore of the Erie; caught it in the timber a couple of miles from our dug-out—or it might have been four, she isn't certain which. It resembles us in some ways, and may be a relation. That is what she thinks, but this is an error, in my judgment. The difference in size warrants the conclusion that it is a different and new kind of animal—a fish, perhaps, though when I put it in the water to see, it sank, and she plunged in and snatched it out before there was opportunity for the experiment to determine the matter. I still think it is a fish, but she is indifferent about what it is, and will not let me have it to try. I do not understand this. The coming of the creature seems to have changed her whole nature and made her unreasonable about experiments. She thinks more of it than she does of any of the other animals, but is not able to explain why. Her mind is disordered—everything shows it. Sometimes she carries the fish in her arms half the night when it complains and wants to get to the water. At such times the water comes out of the places in her face that she looks out of, and she pats the fish on the back and makes soft sounds with her mouth to soothe it, and betrays sorrow and solicitude in a hundred ways. I have never seen her do like this with any other fish, and it troubles me greatly. She used to carry the young tigers around so, and play with them, before we lost our property, but it was only play; she never took on about them like this when their dinner disagreed with them.

Sunday—She doesn't work, Sundays, but lies around all tired out, and likes to have the fish wallow over her; and she makes fool noises to amuse it, and pretends to chew its paws, and that makes it laugh. I have not seen a fish before that could laugh. This makes me doubt. . . . I have come to like Sunday myself. Superintending all the week tires a body so. There ought to be more Sundays. In the old days they were tough, but now they come handy.

Wednesday—It isn't a fish. I cannot quite make out what it is. It makes curious devilish noises when not satisfied, and says "goo-goo" when it is. It is not one of us, for it doesn't walk; it is not a bird, for it doesn't fly; it is not a frog, for it doesn't hop; it is not a snake, for it doesn't crawl; I feel sure it is not a fish, though I cannot get a chance to find out whether it can swim or not. It merely lies around, and mostly on its back, with its feet up. I have not seen any other animal do that before. I said I believed it was an enigma; but she only admired the word without understanding it. In my judgment it is either an enigma or some kind of a bug. If it dies, I will take it apart and see what its arrangements are. I never had a thing perplex me so.

Three months later—The perplexity augments instead of diminishing. I sleep but little. It has ceased from lying around, and goes about on its four legs now. Yet it differs from the other four-legged animals, in that its front legs are unusually short, consequently this causes the main part of its person to stick up uncomfortably high in the air, and this is not attractive. It is built much as we are, but its method of traveling shows that it is not of our breed. The short front legs and long hind ones indicate that it is of the kangaroo family, but it is a marked variation of that species, since the true kangaroo hops, whereas this one never does. Still it is a curious and interesting variety, and has not been catalogued before. As I discovered it, I have felt justified in securing the credit of the discovery by attaching my name to it, and hence have called it KANGAROORUM ADAMIENSIS. . . . It must have been a young one when it came, for it has grown exceedingly since. It must be five times as big, now, as it was then, and when discontented it is able to make from twenty-two to thirty-eight times the noise it made at first. Coercion does not modify this, but has the contrary effect. For this reason I discontinued the system. She reconciles it by persuasion, and by giving it things which she had previously told me she wouldn't give it. As already observed, I was not at home when it first came, and she told me she found it in the woods. It seems odd that it should be the only one, yet it must be so, for I have worn myself out these many weeks trying to find another one to add to my collection, and for this to play with; for surely then it would be quieter and we could tame it more easily. But I find none, nor any vestige of any; and strangest of all, no tracks. It has to live on the ground, it cannot help itself; therefore, how does it get about without leaving a track? I have set a dozen traps, but they do no good. I catch all small animals except that one; animals that merely go into the trap out of curiosity, I think, to see what the milk is there for. They never drink it.

Three months later—The Kangaroo still continues to grow, which is very strange and perplexing. I never knew one to be so long getting its growth. It has fur on its head now; not like kangaroo fur, but exactly like our hair except that it is much finer and softer, and instead of being black is red. I am like to lose my mind over the capricious and harassing developments of this unclassifiable zoological freak. If I could catch another one—but that is hopeless; it is a new variety, and the only sample; this is plain. But I caught a true kangaroo and brought it in, thinking that this one, being lonesome, would rather have that for company than have no kin at all, or any animal it could feel a nearness to or get sympathy from in its forlorn condition here among strangers who do not know its ways or habits, or what to do to make it feel that it is among friends; but it was a mistake—it went into such fits at the sight of the kangaroo that I was convinced it had never seen one before. I pity the poor noisy little animal, but there is nothing I can do to make it happy. If I could tame it—but that is out of the question; the more I try the worse I seem to make it. It grieves me to the heart to see it in its little storms of sorrow and passion. I wanted to let it go, but she wouldn't hear of it. That seemed cruel and not like her; and yet she may be right. It might be lonelier than ever; for since I cannot find another one, how could *it*?

Five months later—It is not a kangaroo. No, for it supports itself by holding to her finger, and thus goes a few steps on its hind legs, and then falls down. It is probably some kind of a bear; and yet it has no tail—as yet—and no fur, except upon its head. It still keeps on growing—that is a curious circumstance, for bears get their growth earlier than this. Bears are dangerous—since our catastrophe—and I shall not be satisfied to have this one prowling about the place much longer without a muzzle on. I have offered to get her a kangaroo if she would let this one go, but it did no good—she is determined to run us into all sorts of foolish risks, I think. She was not like this before she lost her mind.

A fortnight later—I examined its mouth. There is no danger yet: it has only one tooth. It has no tail yet. It makes more noise now than it ever did before—and mainly at night. I have moved out. But I shall go over, mornings, to breakfast, and see if it has more teeth. If it gets a mouthful of teeth it will be time for it to go, tail or no tail, for a bear does not need a tail in order to be dangerous.

Four months later—I have been off hunting and fishing a month, up in the region that she calls Buffalo; I don't know why, unless it is because there are not any buffaloes there. Meantime the bear has learned to paddle around all by itself on its hind legs, and says "poppa" and "momma." It is certainly a new species. This resemblance to words may be purely accidental, of course, and may have no purpose or meaning; but even in that case it is still extraordinary, and is a thing which no other bear can do. This imitation of speech, taken together with general absence of fur and entire absence of tail, sufficiently indicates that this is a new kind of bear. The further study of it will be exceedingly interesting. Meantime I will go off on a far expedition among the forests of the north and make an exhaustive search. There must certainly be another one somewhere, and this one will be less dangerous when it has company of its own species. I will go straightway; but I will muzzle this one first.

Three months later—It has been a weary, weary hunt, yet I have had no success. In the mean time, without stirring from the home estate, she has caught another one! I never saw such luck. I might have hunted these woods a hundred years, I never would have run across that thing.

Next day—I have been comparing the new one with the old one, and it is perfectly plain that they are of the same breed. I was going to stuff one of them for my collection, but she is prejudiced against it for some reason or other; so I have relinquished the idea, though I think it is a mistake. It would be an irreparable loss to science if they should get away. The old one is tamer than it was and can laugh and talk like a parrot, having learned this, no doubt, from being with the parrot so much, and having the imitative faculty in a high developed degree. I shall be astonished if it turns out to be a new kind of parrot; and yet I ought not to be astonished, for it has already been everything else it could think of since those first days when it was a fish. The new one is as ugly as the old one was at first; has the same sulphur-and-raw-meat complexion and the same singular head without any fur on it. She calls it Abel.

Ten years later—They are *boys*; we found it out long ago. It was their coming in that small immature shape that puzzled us; we were not used to it. There are some girls now. Abel is a good boy, but if Cain had stayed a bear it would have improved him. After all these years, I see that I was mistaken about Eve in the beginning; it is better to live outside the Garden with her than inside it without her. At first I thought she talked too much; but now I should be sorry to have that voice fall silent and pass out of my life. Blessed be the chestnut that brought us near together and taught me to know the goodness of her heart and the sweetness of her spirit!

EVE'S DIARY
Translated from the Original

SATURDAY—I am almost a whole day old, now. I arrived yesterday. That is as it seems to me. And it must be so, for if there was a day-before-yesterday I was not there when it happened, or I should remember it. It could be, of course, that it did happen, and that I was not noticing. Very well; I will be very watchful now, and if any day-before-yesterdays happen I will make a note of it. It will be best to start right and not let the record get confused, for some instinct tells me that these details are going to be important to the historian some day. For I feel like an experiment, I feel exactly like an experiment; it would be impossible for a person to feel more like an experiment than I do, and so I am coming to feel convinced that that is what I *am*—an experiment; just an experiment, and nothing more.

Then if I am an experiment, am I the whole of it? No, I think not; I think the rest of it is part of it. I am the main part of it, but I think the rest of it has its share in the matter. Is my position assured, or do I have to watch it and take care of it? The latter, perhaps. Some instinct tells me that eternal vigilance is the price of supremacy. [That is a good phrase, I think, for one so young.]

Everything looks better today than it did yesterday. In the rush of finishing up yesterday, the mountains were left in a ragged condition, and some of the plains were so cluttered with rubbish and remnants that the aspects were quite distressing. Noble and beautiful works of art should not be subjected to haste; and this majestic new world is indeed a most noble and beautiful work. And certainly marvelously near to being perfect, notwithstanding the shortness of the time. There are too many stars in some places and not enough in others, but that can be remedied presently, no doubt. The moon got loose last night, and slid down and fell out of the

65

scheme—a very great loss; it breaks my heart to think of it. There isn't another thing among the ornaments and decorations that is comparable to it for beauty and finish. It should have been fastened better. If we can only get it back again—But of course there is no telling where it went to. And besides, whoever gets it will hide it; I know it because I would do it myself. I believe I can be honest in all other matters, but I already begin to realize that the core and center of my nature is love of the beautiful, a passion for the beautiful, and that it would not be safe to trust me with a moon that belonged to another person and that person didn't know I had it. I could give up a moon that I found in the daytime, because I should be afraid some one was looking; but if I found it in the dark, I am sure I should find some kind of an excuse for not saying anything about it. For I do love moons, they are so pretty and so romantic. I wish we had five or six; I would never go to bed; I should never get tired lying on the moss-bank and looking up at them.

Stars are good, too. I wish I could get some to put in my hair. But I suppose I never can. You would be surprised to find how far off they are, for they do not look it. When they first showed, last night, I tried to knock some down with a pole, but it didn't reach, which astonished me; then I tried clods till I was all tired out, but I never got one. It was because I am left-handed and cannot throw good. Even when I aimed at the one I wasn't after I couldn't hit the other one, though I did make some close shots, for I saw the black blot of the clod sail light into the midst of the golden clusters forty or fifty times, just barely missing them, and if I could have held out a little longer maybe I could have got one.

So I cried a little, which was natural, I suppose, for one of my age, and after I was rested I got a basket and started for a place on the extreme rim of the circle, where the stars were close to the ground and I could get them with my hands, which would be better, anyway, because I could gather them tenderly then, and not break them. But it was farther than I thought, and at last I had to give it up; I was so tired I couldn't drag my feet another step; and besides, they were sore and hurt me very much.

I couldn't get back home; it was too far and turning cold; but I found some tigers and nestled in among them and was most adorably comfortable, and their breath was sweet and pleasant, because they live on strawberries. I had never seen a tiger before, but I knew them in a minute by the stripes. If I could have one of those skins, it would make a lovely gown.

Today I am getting better ideas about distances. I was so eager to get hold of every pretty thing that I giddily grabbed for it, sometimes when it was too far off, and sometimes when it was but six inches away but seemed a foot—alas, with thorns between! I learned a lesson; also I made an axiom, all out of my own head— my very first one; *the scratched experiment shuns the thorn*. I think it is a very good one for one so young.

I followed the other Experiment around, yesterday afternoon, at a distance, to see what it might be for, if I could. But I was not able to make out. I think it is a man. I had never seen a man, but it looked like one, and I feel sure that that is what it is. I realize that I feel more curiosity about it than about any of the other reptiles. If it is a reptile, and I suppose it is; for it has frowzy hair and blue eyes, and looks like a reptile. It has no hips; it tapers like a carrot; when it stands, it spreads itself apart like a derrick; so I think it is a reptile, though it may be architecture.

I was afraid of it at first, and started to run every time it turned around, for I thought it was going to chase me; but by and by I found it was only trying to get away, so after that I was not timid any more, but tracked it along, several hours, about twenty yards behind, which made it nervous and unhappy. At last it was a good deal worried, and climbed a tree. I waited a good while, then gave it up and went home.

Today the same thing over. I've got it up the tree again.

Sunday—It is up there yet. Resting, apparently. But that is a subterfuge: Sunday isn't the day of rest; Saturday is appointed for that. It looks to me like a creature that is more interested in resting than in anything else. It would tire me to rest so much. It tires me just to sit around and watch the tree. I do wonder what it is for; I never see it do anything.

They returned the moon last night, and I was *so* happy! I think it is very honest of them. It slid down and fell off again, but I was not distressed; there is no need to worry when one has that kind of neighbors; they will fetch it back. I wish I could do something to show my appreciation. I would like to send them some stars, for we have more than we can use. I mean I, not we, for I can see that the reptile cares nothing for such things.

It has low tastes, and is not kind. When I went there yesterday evening in the gloaming it had crept down and was trying to catch the little speckled fishes that play in the pool, and I had to clod it to make it go up the tree again and let them alone. I wonder if *that* is what it is for? Hasn't it any heart? Hasn't it any compassion for those little creatures? Can it be that it was designed and manufactured for such ungentle work? It has the look of it. One of the clods took it back of the ear, and it used language. It gave me a thrill, for it was the first time I had ever heard speech, except my own. I did not understand the words, but they seemed expressive.

When I found it could talk I felt a new interest in it, for I love to talk; I talk, all day, and in my sleep, too, and I am very interesting, but if I had another to talk to I could be twice as interesting, and would never stop, if desired.

If this reptile is a man, it isn't an *it,* is it? That wouldn't be grammatical, would it? I think it would be *he.* I think so. In that case one would parse it thus: nominative, *he*; dative, *him*; possessive, HIS'N. Well, I will consider it a man and call it he until it turns out to be something else. This will be handier than having so many uncertainties.

Next week Sunday—All the week I tagged around after him and tried to get acquainted. I had to do the talking, because he was shy, but I didn't mind it. He seemed pleased to have me around, and I used the sociable "we" a good deal, because it seemed to flatter him to be included.

Wednesday—We are getting along very well indeed, now, and getting better and better acquainted. He does not try to avoid me any more, which is a good sign, and shows that he likes to have me with him. That pleases me, and I study to be useful to him in every way I can, so as to increase his regard. During the last day or two I have taken all the work of naming things off his hands, and this has been a great relief to him, for he has no gift in that line, and is evidently very grateful. He can't think of a rational name to save him, but I do not let him see that I am aware of his defect. Whenever a new creature comes along I name it before he has time to expose himself by an awkward silence. In this way I have saved him many embarrassments. I have no defect like this. The minute

I set eyes on an animal I know what it is. I don't have to reflect a moment; the right name comes out instantly, just as if it were an inspiration, as no doubt it is, for I am sure it wasn't in me half a minute before. I seem to know just by the shape of the creature and the way it acts what animal it is.

When the dodo came along he thought it was a wildcat—I saw it in his eye. But I saved him. And I was careful not to do it in a way that could hurt his pride. I just spoke up in a quite natural way of pleasing surprise, and not as if I was dreaming of conveying information, and said, "Well, I do declare, if there isn't the dodo!" I explained—without seeming to be explaining—how I knew it for a dodo, and although I thought maybe he was a little piqued that I knew the creature when he didn't, it was quite evident that he admired me. That was very agreeable, and I thought of it more than once with gratification before I slept. How little a thing can make us happy when we feel that we have earned it!

Thursday—My first sorrow. Yesterday he avoided me and seemed to wish I would not talk to him. I could not believe it, and thought there was some mistake, for I loved to be with him, and loved to hear him talk, and so how could it be that he could feel unkind toward me when I had not done anything? But at last it seemed true, so I went away and sat lonely in the place where I first saw him the morning that we were made and I did not know what he was and was indifferent about him; but now it was a mournful place, and every little thing spoke of him, and my heart was very sore. I did not know why very clearly, for it was a new feeling; I had not experienced it before, and it was all a mystery, and I could not make it out.

But when night came I could not bear the lonesomeness, and went to the new shelter which he has built, to ask him what I had done that was wrong and how I could mend it and get back his kindness again; but he put me out in the rain, and it was my first sorrow.

Sunday—It is pleasant again, now, and I am happy; but those were heavy days; I do not think of them when I can help it.

I tried to get him some of those apples, but I cannot learn to throw straight. I failed, but I think the good intention pleased him.

They are forbidden, and he says I shall come to harm; but so I come to harm through pleasing him, why shall I care for that harm?

Monday—This morning I told him my name, hoping it would interest him. But he did not care for it. It is strange. If he should tell me his name, I would care. I think it would be pleasanter in my ears than any other sound.

He talks very little. Perhaps it is because he is not bright, and is sensitive about it and wishes to conceal it. It is such a pity that he should feel so, for brightness is nothing; it is in the heart that the values lie. I wish I could make him understand that a loving good heart is riches, and riches enough, and that without it intellect is poverty.

Although he talks so little, he has quite a considerable vocabulary. This morning he used a surprisingly good word. He evidently recognized, himself, that it was a good one, for he worked it in twice afterward, casually. It was good casual art, still it showed that he possesses a certain quality of perception. Without a doubt that seed can be made to grow, if cultivated.

Where did he get that word? I do not think I have ever used it.

No, he took no interest in my name. I tried to hide my disappointment, but I suppose I did not succeed. I went away and sat on the moss-bank with my feet in the water. It is where I go when I hunger for companionship, some one to look at, some one to talk to. It is not enough—that lovely white body painted there in the pool—but it is something, and something is better than utter loneliness. It talks when I talk; it is sad when I am sad; it comforts me with its sympathy; it says, "Do not be down-hearted, you poor friendless girl; I will be your friend." It is a good friend to me, and my only one; it is my sister.

That first time that she forsook me! ah, I shall never forget that—never, never. My heart was lead in my body! I said, "She was all I had, and now she is gone!" In my despair I said, "Break, my heart; I cannot bear my life any more!" and hid my face in my hands, and there was no solace for me. And when I took them away, after a little, there she was again, white and shining and beautiful, and I sprang into her arms!

That was perfect happiness; I had known happiness before, but it was not like this, which was ecstasy. I never doubted her afterward. Sometimes she stayed away—maybe an hour, maybe almost the whole day, but I waited and did not doubt; I said, "She is busy, or she is gone on a journey, but she will come." And it was so: she always did. At night she would not come if it was dark, for she was a timid little thing; but if there was a moon she would come. I am not afraid of the dark, but she is younger than I am; she was born after I was. Many and many are the visits I have paid her; she is my comfort and my refuge when my life is hard—and it is mainly that.

Tuesday—All the morning I was at work improving the estate; and I purposely kept away from him in the hope that he would get lonely and come. But he did not.

At noon I stopped for the day and took my recreation by flitting all about with the bees and the butterflies and reveling in the flowers, those beautiful creatures that catch the smile of God out of the sky and preserve it! I gathered them, and made them into wreaths and garlands and clothed myself in them while I ate my luncheon—apples, of course; then I sat in the shade and wished and waited. But he did not come.

But no matter. Nothing would have come of it, for he does not care for flowers. He called them rubbish, and cannot tell one from another, and thinks it is superior to feel like that. He does not care for me, he does not care for flowers, he does not care for the painted sky at eventide—is there anything he does care for, except building shacks to coop himself up in from the good clean rain, and thumping the melons, and sampling the grapes, and fingering the fruit on the trees, to see how those properties are coming along?

I laid a dry stick on the ground and tried to bore a hole in it with another one, in order to carry out a scheme that I had, and soon I got an awful fright. A thin, transparent bluish film rose out of the hole, and I dropped everything and ran! I thought it was a spirit, and I *was* so frightened! But I looked back, and it was not coming; so I leaned against a rock and rested and panted, and let my limbs go on trembling until they got steady again; then I crept warily back, alert, watching, and ready to fly if there was occasion; and when I was come near, I parted the branches of a rose-bush and peeped through—wishing the man was about, I was looking so cunning and pretty—but the sprite was gone. I went there, and there was a pinch of delicate pink dust in the hole. I put my finger in, to feel it, and said *Ouch!* and took it out again. It was a cruel pain. I put my finger in my mouth; and by standing first on one foot and then the other, and grunting, I presently eased my misery; then I was full of interest, and began to examine.

I was curious to know what the pink dust was. Suddenly the name of it occurred to me, though I had never heard of it before. It was *fire*! I was as certain of it as a person could be of anything in the world. So without hesitation I named it that—fire.

I had created something that didn't exist before; I had added a new thing to the world's uncountable properties; I realized this, and was proud of my achievement, and was going to run and find him and tell him about it, thinking to raise myself in his esteem—but I reflected, and did not do it. No—he would not care for it. He would ask what it was good for, and what could I answer? for if it was not *good* for something, but only beautiful, merely beautiful— So I sighed, and did not go. For it wasn't good for anything; it could not build a shack, it could not improve melons, it could not hurry a fruit crop; it was useless, it was a foolishness and a vanity; he would despise it and say cutting words. But to me it was not despicable; I said, "Oh, you fire, I love you, you dainty pink creature, for you are *beautiful*—and that is enough!" and was going to gather it to my breast. But refrained. Then I made another maxim out of my head, though it was so nearly like the first one that I was afraid it was only a plagiarism: *"the burnt experiment shuns the fire."*

I wrought again; and when I had made a good deal of fire-dust I emptied it into a handful of dry brown grass, intending to carry it home and keep it always and play with it; but the wind struck it and it sprayed up and spat out at me fiercely, and I dropped it and ran. When I looked back the blue spirit was towering up and stretching and rolling away like a cloud, and instantly I thought of the name of it—*smoke!*—though, upon my word, I had never heard of smoke before.

Soon brilliant yellow and red flares shot up through the smoke, and I named them in an instant—*flames*—and I was right, too, though these were the very first flames that had ever been in the world. They climbed the trees, then flashed splendidly in and out of the vast and increasing volume of tumbling smoke, and I had to clap my hands and laugh and dance in my rapture, it was so new and strange and so wonderful and so beautiful!

He came running, and stopped and gazed, and said not a word for many minutes. Then he asked what it was. Ah, it was too bad that he should ask such a direct question. I had to answer it, of course, and I did. I said it was fire. If it annoyed him that I should know and he must ask; that was not my fault; I had no desire to annoy him. After a pause he asked:

"How did it come?"

Another direct question, and it also had to have a direct answer. "I made it."

The fire was traveling farther and farther off. He went to the edge of the burned place and stood looking down, and said:

"What are these?"

"Fire-coals."

He picked up one to examine it, but changed his mind and put it down again. Then he went away. *Nothing* interests him.

But I was interested. There were ashes, gray and soft and delicate and pretty—I knew what they were at once. And the embers; I knew the embers, too. I found my apples, and raked them out, and was glad; for I am very young and my appetite is active. But I was disappointed; they were all burst open and spoiled. Spoiled apparently; but it was not so; they were better than raw ones. Fire is beautiful; some day it will be useful, I think.

Friday—I saw him again, for a moment, last Monday at nightfall, but only for a moment. I was hoping he would praise me for trying to improve the estate, for I had meant well and had worked hard. But he was not pleased, and turned away and left me. He was also displeased on another account: I tried once more to persuade him to stop going over the Falls. That was because the fire had revealed to me a new passion—quite new, and distinctly different from love, grief, and those others which I had already discovered—*fear*. And it is horrible!—I wish I had never discovered it; it gives me dark moments, it spoils my happiness, it makes me shiver and tremble and shudder. But I could not persuade him, for he has not discovered fear yet, and so he could not understand me.

Extract from Adam's Diary

Perhaps I ought to remember that she is very young, a mere girl, and make allowances. She is all interest, eagerness, vivacity, the world is to her a charm, a wonder, a mystery, a joy; she can't speak for delight when she finds a new flower, she must pet it and caress it and smell it and talk to it, and pour out endearing names upon it. And she is color-mad: brown rocks, yellow sand, gray moss, green foliage, blue sky; the pearl of the dawn, the purple shadows on the mountains, the golden islands floating in crimson seas at sunset, the pallid moon sailing through the shredded cloud-rack, the star-jewels glittering in the wastes of space—none of them is of any practical value, so far as I can see, but because they have color and majesty, that is enough for her, and she loses her mind over them. If she could quiet down and keep still a couple minutes at a time, it would be a reposeful spectacle. In that case I think I could enjoy looking at her; indeed I am sure I could, for I am coming to realize that she is a quite remarkably comely creature—lithe, slender, trim, rounded, shapely, nimble, graceful; and once when she was standing marble-white and sun-drenched on a boulder, with her young head tilted back and her hand shading her eyes, watching the flight of a bird in the sky, I recognized that she was beautiful.

Monday noon—If there is anything on the planet that she is not interested in it is not in my list. There are animals that I am indifferent to, but it is not so with her. She has no discrimination, she takes to all of them, she thinks they are all treasures, every new one is welcome.

When the mighty brontosaurus came striding into camp, she regarded it as an acquisition, I considered it a calamity; that is a good sample of the lack of harmony that prevails in our views of things. She wanted to domesticate it, I wanted to make it a present of the homestead and move out. She believed it could be tamed by kind treatment and would be a good pet; I said a pet twenty-one feet high and eighty-four feet long would be no proper thing to have about the place, because, even with the best intentions and without meaning any harm, it could sit down on the house and mash it, for any one could see by the look of its eye that it was absent-minded.

Still, her heart was set upon having that monster, and she couldn't give it up. She thought we could start a dairy with it, and wanted me to help milk it; but I wouldn't; it was too risky. The sex wasn't right, and we hadn't any ladder anyway. Then she wanted to ride it, and look at the scenery. Thirty or forty feet of its tail was lying on the ground, like a fallen tree, and she thought she could climb it, but she was mistaken; when she got to the steep place it was too slick and down she came, and would have hurt herself but for me.

Was she satisfied now? No. Nothing ever satisfies her but demonstration; untested theories are not in her line, and she won't have them. It is the right spirit, I concede it; it attracts me; I feel the influence of it; if I were with her more I think I should take it up myself. Well, she had one theory remaining about this colossus: she thought that if we could tame it and make him friendly we could stand in the river and use him for a bridge. It turned out that he was already plenty tame enough—at least as far as she was concerned—so she tried her theory, but it failed: every time she got him properly placed in the river and went ashore to cross over him, he came out and followed her around like a pet mountain. Like the other animals. They all do that.

Eve's Diary

Friday—Tuesday—Wednesday—Thursday—and today: all without seeing him. It is a long time to be alone; still, it is better to be alone than unwelcome.

I *had* to have company—I was made for it, I think—so I made friends with the animals. They are just charming, and they have the kindest disposition and the politest ways; they never look sour, they never let you feel that you are intruding, they smile at you and wag their tail, if they've got one, and they are always ready for a romp or an excursion or anything you want to propose. I think they are perfect gentlemen. All these days we have had such good times, and it hasn't been lonesome for me, ever. Lonesome! No, I should say not. Why, there's always a swarm of them around—sometimes as much as four or five acres—you can't count them; and when you stand on a rock in the midst and look out over the furry expanse it is so mottled and splashed and gay with color and frisking sheen and sun-flash, and so rippled with stripes, that you might think it was a lake, only you know it isn't; and there's storms of sociable birds, and hurricanes of whirring wings; and when the sun strikes all that feathery commotion, you have a blazing up of all the colors you can think of: enough to put your eyes out.

We have made long excursions, and I have seen a great deal of the world; almost all of it, I think; and so I am the first traveler, and the only one. When we are on the march, it is an imposing sight—there's nothing like it anywhere. For comfort I ride a tiger or a leopard, because it is soft and has a round back that fits me, and because they are such pretty animals; but for long distance or for scenery I ride the elephant. He hoists me up with his trunk, but I can get off myself; when we are ready to camp, he sits and I slide down the back way.

The birds and animals are all friendly to each other, and there are no disputes about anything. They all talk, and they all talk to me, but it must be a foreign language, for I cannot make out a word they say; yet they often understand me when I talk back, particularly the dog and the elephant. It makes me ashamed. It shows that they are brighter than I am, for I want to be the principal Experiment myself—and I intend to be, too.

I have learned a number of things, and am educated, now, but I wasn't at first. I was ignorant at first. At first it used to vex me because, with all my watching, I was never smart enough to be around when the water was running uphill; but now I do not mind it. I have experimented and experimented until now I know it never does run uphill, except in the dark. I know it does in the dark, because the pool never goes dry, which it would, of course, if the water didn't come back in the night. It is best to prove things by actual experiment; then you *know;* whereas if you depend on guessing and supposing and conjecturing, you never get educated.

Some things you *can't* find out; but you will never know you can't by guessing and supposing: no, you have to be patient and go on experimenting until you find out that you can't find out. And it is delightful to have it that way, it makes the world so interesting. If there wasn't anything to find out, it would be dull. Even trying to find out and not finding out is just as interesting as trying to find out and finding out, and I don't know but more so. The secret of the water was a treasure until I *got* it; then the excitement all went away, and I recognized a sense of loss.

By experiment I know that wood swims, and dry leaves, and feathers, and plenty of other things; therefore by all that cumulative evidence you know that a rock will swim; but you have to put up with simply knowing it, for there isn't any way to prove it—up to now. But I shall find a way—then *that* excitement will go. Such things make me sad; because by and by when I have found out everything there won't be any more excitements, and I do love excitements so! The other night I couldn't sleep for thinking about it.

At first I couldn't make out what I was made for, but now I think it was to search out the secrets of this wonderful world and be happy and thank the Giver of it all for devising it. I think there are many things to learn yet—I hope so; and by economizing and not hurrying too fast I think they will last weeks and weeks. I hope so. When you cast up a feather it sails away on the air and goes out of sight; then you throw up a clod and it doesn't. It comes down, every time. I have tried it and tried it, and it is always so. I wonder why it is? Of course it *doesn't* come down, but why should it *seem* to? I suppose it is an optical illusion. I mean, one of them is. I don't know which one. It may be the feather, it may be the clod; I can't prove which it is, I can only demonstrate that one or the other is a fake, and let a person take his choice.

By watching, I know that the stars are not going to last. I have seen some of the best ones melt and run down the sky. Since one can melt, they can all melt; since they can all melt, they can all melt the same night. That sorrow will come—I know it. I mean to sit up every night and look at them as long as I can keep awake; and I will impress those sparkling fields on my memory, so that by and by when they are taken away I can by my fancy restore those lovely myriads to the black sky and make them sparkle again, and double them by the blur of my tears.

After the Fall

When I look back, the Garden is a dream to me. It was beautiful, surpassingly beautiful, enchantingly beautiful; and now it is lost, and I shall not see it any more.

The Garden is lost, but I have found *him*, and am content. He loves me as well as he can; I love him with all the strength of my passionate nature, and this, I think, is proper to my youth and sex. If I ask myself why I love him, I find I do not know, and do not really much care to know; so I suppose that this kind of love is not a product of reasoning and statistics, like one's love for other reptiles and animals. I think that this must be so. I love certain birds because of their song; but I do not love Adam on account of his singing—no, it is not that; the more he sings the more I do not get reconciled to it. Yet I ask him to sing, because I wish to learn to like everything he is interested in. I am sure I can learn, because at first I could not stand it, but now I can. It sours the milk, but it doesn't matter; I can get used to that kind of milk.

It is not on account of his brightness that I love him—no, it is not that. He is not to blame for his brightness, such as it is, for he did not make it himself; he is as God made him, and that is sufficient. There was a wise purpose in it, *that* I know. In time it will develop, though I think it will not be sudden; and besides, there is no hurry; he is well enough just as he is.

It is not on account of his gracious and considerate ways and his delicacy that I love him. No, he has lacks in this regard, but he is well enough just so, and is improving.

It is not on account of his industry that I love him—no, it is not that. I think he has it in him, and I do not know why he conceals it from me. It is my only pain. Otherwise he is frank and open with me, now. I am sure he keeps nothing from me but this. It grieves me that he should have a secret from me, and sometimes it spoils my sleep, thinking of it, but I will put it out of my mind; it shall not trouble my happiness, which is otherwise full to overflowing.

It is not on account of his education that I love him—no, it is not that. He is self-educated, and does really know a multitude of things, but they are not so.

It is not on account of his chivalry that I love him—no, it is not that. He told on me, but I do not blame him; it is a peculiarity of sex, I think, and he did not make his sex. Of course I would not have told on him, I would have perished first; but that is a peculiarity of sex, too, and I do not take credit for it, for I did not make my sex.

Then why is it that I love him? *Merely because he is masculine,* I think.

At bottom he is good, and I love him for that, but I could love him without it. If he should beat me and abuse me, I should go on loving him. I know it. It is a matter of sex, I think.

He is strong and handsome, and I love him for that, and I admire him and am proud of him, but I could love him without those qualities. If he were plain, I should love him; if he were a wreck, I should love him; and I would work for him, and slave over him, and pray for him, and watch by his bedside until I died.

Yes, I think I love him merely because he is *mine* and is *masculine*. There is no other reason, I suppose. And so I think it is as I first said: that this kind of love is not a product of reasonings and statistics. It just *comes*—none knows whence—and cannot explain itself. And doesn't need to.

It is what I think. But I am only a girl, the first that has examined this matter, and it may turn out that in my ignorance and inexperience I have not got it right.

Forty Years Later

It is my prayer, it is my longing, that we may pass from this life together—a longing which shall never perish from the earth, but shall have place in the heart of every wife that loves, until the end of time; and it shall be called by my name.

But if one of us must go first, it is my prayer that it shall be I; for he is strong, I am weak, I am not so necessary to him as he is to me—life without him would not be life; how could I endure it? This prayer is also immortal, and will not cease from being offered up while my race continues. I am the first wife; and in the last wife I shall be repeated.

At Eve's Grave

Adam: Wheresoever she was, *there* was Eden.

THE GREAT DARK

Before It Happened

STATEMENT BY MRS. EDWARDS

WE WERE IN no way prepared for this dreadful thing. We were a happy family, we had been happy from the beginning; we did not know what trouble was, we were not thinking of it nor expecting it.

My husband was thirty-five years old, and seemed ten years younger, for he was one of those fortunate people who by nature are overcharged with breezy spirits and vigorous health, and from whom cares and troubles slide off without making any impression. He was my ideal, and indeed my idol. In my eyes he was everything that a man ought to be, and in spirit and body beautiful. We were married when I was a girl of 16, and we now had two children, comely and dear little creatures: Jessie, 8 years old, and Bessie, 6.

The house had been in a pleasant turmoil all day, this 19th of March, for it was Jessie's birthday. Henry (my husband) had romped with the children till I was afraid he would tire them out and unfit them for their party in the evening, which was to be a children's fancy dress dance; and so I was glad when at last in the edge of the evening he took them to our bedroom to show them the grandest of all the presents, the microscope. I allowed them fifteen minutes for this show. I would put the children into their costumes, then, and have them ready to receive their great flock of little friends and the accompanying parents. Henry would then be free to jot down in short-hand (he was a past-master in that art) an essay which he was to read at the social club the next night. I would show the children to him in their smart costumes when the party should be over and the good-night kisses due.

I left the three in a state of great excitement over the microscope, and at the end of the fifteen minutes I returned for the children. They and their papa were examining the wonders of a drop of water through a powerful lens. I delivered the children to a maid and they went away. Henry said—

"I will take forty winks and then go to work. But I will make a new experiment with the drop of water first. Won't you please strengthen the drop with the merest touch of Scotch whisky and stir up the animals?"

Then he threw himself on the sofa and before I could speak he uttered a snore. That came of romping the whole day. In reaching for the whisky decanter I knocked off the one that contained brandy and it broke. The noise stopped the snore. I stooped and gathered up the broken glass hurriedly in a towel, and when I rose to put it out of the way he was gone. I dipped a broomstraw in the Scotch whisky and let a wee drop fall upon the glass slide where the water-drop was, then I crossed to the glass door to tell him it was ready. But he had lit the gas and was at his table writing. It was the rule of the house not to disturb him when he was at work; so I went about my affairs in the picture gallery, which was our house's ballroom.

STATEMENT BY MR. EDWARDS

We were experimenting with the microscope. And pretty ignorantly. Among the little glass slides in the box we found one labeled "section of a fly's eye." In its centre was faintly visible a dot. We put it under a low-power lens and it showed up like a fragment of honey-comb. We put it under a stronger lens and it became a window-sash. We put in under the most powerful lens of all, then there was room in the field for only one pane of the several hundred. We were childishly delighted and astonished at the magnifying capacities of that lens, and said, "Now we can find out if there really are living animals in a drop of water, as the books say."

We brought some stale water from a puddle in the carriage-house where some rotten hay lay soaking, sucked up a dropperful and allowed a tear of it to fall on a glass slide. Then we worked the screws and brought the lens down until it almost touched the water; then shut an eye and peered eagerly down through the barrel. A disappointment—nothing showed. Then we worked the screws again and made the lens *touch* the water. Another disappointment—nothing visible. Once more we worked the screws and projected the lens hard *against* the glass slide itself. *Then* we saw the animals! Not frequently, but now and then. For a time there would be a great empty blank; then a monster would enter one horizon of this great white sea made so splendidly luminous by the reflector and go plowing across and disappear beyond the opposite horizon. Others would come and go at intervals and disappear. The lens was pressing *against* the glass slide; therefore how could those bulky creatures crowd through between and not get stuck? Yet they swam with perfect freedom; it was plain that they had all the room and all the water that they needed. Then how unimaginably little they must be! Moreover, that wide circular sea which they were traversing was only a small part of our drop of stale water; it was not as big as the head of a pin; whereas the entire drop, flattened out on the glass, was as big around as a child's finger-ring. If we could have gotten the whole drop under the lens we could have seen those gruesome fishes swim leagues and leagues before they dwindled out of sight at the further shore!

*

I threw myself on the sofa profoundly impressed by what I had seen, and oppressed with thinkings. An ocean in a drop of water—and unknown, uncharted, unexplored by man! By man, who gives all his time to the Africas and the poles, with this unsearched marvelous world right at his elbow. Then the Superintendent of Dreams appeared at my side, and we talked it over. He was willing to provide a ship and crew, but said—

"It will be like any other voyage of the sort—not altogether a holiday excursion."

"That is all right; it is not an objection."

"You and your crew will be much diminished, as to size, but you need not trouble about that, as you will not be aware of it. Your ship itself, stuck upon the point of a needle, would not be discoverable except through a microscope of very high power."

"I do not mind these things. Get a crew of whalers. It will be well to have men who will know what to do in case we have trouble with those creatures."

"Better still if you avoid them."

"I shall avoid them if I can, for they have done me no harm, and I would not wantonly hurt any creature, but I shan't run from them. They have an ugly look, but I thank God I am not afraid of the ugliest that ever plowed a drop of water."

"You think so *now,* with your five feet eight, but it will be a different matter when the mote that floats in a sunbeam is Mont Blanc compared to you."

"It is no matter; you have seen me face dangers before—"

"Finish with your orders—the night is slipping away."

"Very well, then. Provide me a naturalist to tell me the names of the creatures we see; and let the ship be a comfortable one and perfectly appointed and provisioned, for I take my family with me."

*

Half a minute later (as it seemed to me), a hoarse voice broke on my ear—

"Topsails all—let go the lee brace—sheet home the stuns'l boom—hearty, now, and all together!"

I turned out, washed the sleep out of my eyes with a dash of cold water, and stepped out of my cabin, leaving Alice quietly sleeping in her berth. It was a blustering night and dark, and the air was thick with a driving mist out of which the tall masts and bellying clouds of sail towered spectrally, faintly flecked here and there aloft by the smothered signal lanterns. The ship was heaving and wallowing in the heavy seas, and it was hard to keep one's footing on the moist deck. Everything was dimmed to obliteration, almost; the only thing sharply defined was the foamy mane of white water, sprinkled with phosphorescent sparks, which broke away from the lee bow. Men were within twenty steps of me, but I could not make out their figures; I only knew they were there by their voices. I heard the quartermaster report to the second mate—

"Eight bells, sir."

"Very well—make it so."

Then I heard the muffled sound of the distant bell, followed by a far-off cry—

"Eight bells and a cloudy morning—anchor watch turn out!"

I saw the glow of a match photograph a pipe and part of a face against a solid bank of darkness, and groped my way thither and found the second mate.

"What of the weather, mate?"

"I don't see that it's any better, sir, than it was the first day out, ten days ago; if anything it's worse—thicker and blacker, I mean. You remember the spitting snow-flurries we had that night?"

"Yes."

"Well, we've had them again to-night. And hail and sleet besides, b'George! And here it comes again."

We stepped into the sheltering lee of the galley, and stood there listening to the lashing of the hail along the deck and the singing of the wind in the cordage. The mate said—

"I've been at sea thirty years, man and boy, but for a level ten-day stretch of unholy weather this bangs anything I ever struck, north of the Horn—if we *are* north of it. For I'm blest if I know *where* we are—do you?"

It was an embarrassing question. I had been asked it very confidentially by my captain, long ago, and had been able to state that I didn't know; and had been discreet enough not to go into any particulars; but this was the first time that any officer of the ship had approached me with the matter. I said—

"Well, no, I'm not a sailor, but I am surprised to hear *you* say you don't know where we are."

He was caught. It was his turn to be embarrassed. First he began to hedge, and vaguely let on that perhaps he did know, after all; but he made a lame fist of it, and presently gave it up and concluded to be frank and take me into his confidence.

"I'm going to be honest with you, sir—and don't give me away." He put his mouth close to my ear and sheltered it against the howling wind with his hand to keep from having to shout, and said impressively, "Not only I don't know where we are, sir, but by God the captain himself don't know!"

I had met the captain's confession by pretending to be frightened and distressed at having engaged a man who was ignorant of his business; and then he had changed his note and told me he had only meant that he had lost his bearings in the thick weather—a thing which would rectify itself as soon as he could get a glimpse of the sun. But I was willing to let the mate tell me all he would, so long as I was not to "give it away."

"No, sir, he don't know where he is; lets on to, but he don't. I mean, he lets on to the crew, and his daughters, and young Phillips the purser, and of course to you and your family, but here lately he don't let on any more to the chief mate and me. And worried? I tell you he's worried plumb to his vitals."

"I must say I don't much like the look of this, Mr. Turner."

"Well, don't let on, sir; keep it to yourself—maybe it'll come out all right; hope it will. But you look at the facts—just look at the facts. We sail north—see? North-and-by-east-half-east, to be exact. Noon the fourth day out, heading for Sable island—ought to see it, weather rather thin for *this* voyage. *Don't* see it. Think the dead reckoning ain't right, maybe. We bang straight along, all the afternoon. No Sable island. *Damned if we didn't run straight over it!* It warn't there. What do you think of that?"

"Dear me, it is awful—awful—if true."

"*If* true. Well, it *is* true. True as anything that ever was, I take my oath on it. And then Greenland. We three banked our hopes on Greenland. Night before last we couldn't sleep for uneasiness; just anxiety, you know, to see if Greenland was going to be there. By the dead reckoning she was due to be in sight along anywhere from five to seven in the morning, if clear enough. But we staid on deck all night. Of course two of us had no business there, and had to scuttle out of the way whenever a man came along, or they would have been suspicious. But five o'clock came, seven o'clock, eight o'clock, ten o'clock, and at last twelve—and then the captain groaned and gave in! He knew well enough that if there had been any Greenland left we'd have knocked a corner off of it long before that."

"This is appalling!"

"You may hunt out a bigger word than that and it won't cover it, sir. And Lord, to see the captain, gray as ashes, sweating and worrying over his chart all day yesterday and all day to-day, and spreading his compasses here and spreading them there, and getting suspicious of his chronometer, and damning the dead-reckoning— just suffering death and taxes, you know, and me and the chief mate helping and suffering, and that purser and the captain's oldest girl spooning and cackling around, just in heaven! I'm a poor man, sir, but I could buy out half of each of 'em's ignorance and put it together and make it a whole, blamed if I wouldn't put up my last nickel to do it, you hear *me*. Now—"

A wild gust of wind drowned the rest of his remark and smothered us in a fierce flurry of snow and sleet. He darted away and disappeared in the gloom, but first I heard his voice hoarsely shouting—

"Turn out, all hands, shorten sail!"

There was a rush of feet along the deck, and then the gale brought the dimmed sound of far-off commands—

"Mizzen foretop halyards there—all clue-garnets heave and away—now then, with a will—sheet home!"

And then the plaintive notes had told that the men were handling the kites—

> "If you get there, before I do—
>   Hi-ho-o-o, roll a man down;
> If you get there before I do,
>   O, give a man time to roll a man down!"

By and by all was still again. Meantime I had shifted to the other side of the galley to get out of the storm, and there Mr. Turner presently found me.

"That's a specimen," said he. "I've never struck any such weather anywhere. You are bowling along on a wind that's as steady as a sermon, and just as likely to last, and before you can say Jack Robinson the wind whips around from weather to lee, and if you don't jump for it you'll have your canvas blown out of the cat-heads and sailing for heaven in rags and tatters. I've never seen anything to begin with it. But then I've never been in the middle of Greenland before—in a *ship*—middle of where it *used* to be, I mean. Would it worry you if I was to tell you something, sir?"

"Why, no, I think not. What is it?"

"Let me take a turn up and down, first, to see if anybody's in earshot." When he came back he said, "What should you think if you was to see a whale with hairy spider-legs to it as long as the foretogallant backstay and as big around as the mainmast?"

I recognized the creature; I had seen it in the microscope. But I didn't say so. I said—

"I should think I had a little touch of the jimjams."

"The very thing *I* thought, so help me! It was the third day out, at a quarter to five in the morning. I was out astraddle of the bowsprit in the drizzle, bending on a scuttle-butt, for I don't trust that kind of a job to a common sailor, when all of a sudden that creature plunged up out of the sea the way a porpoise does, not a hundred yards away—I saw two hundred and fifty feet of him and his fringes—and then he turned in the air like a triumphal arch, shedding Niagaras of water, and plunged head first under the sea with an awful swash of sound, and by that time we were close aboard him and in another ten yards we'd have hit him. It was my belief that he tried to hit *us*, but by the mercy of God he was out of practice. The lookout on the foc'sle was the only man around, and thankful I was, or there could have been a mutiny. He was asleep on the binnacle—they always sleep on the binnacle, it's the best place to see from—and it woke him up and he said, "Good land, what's that, sir?" and I said, "It's nothing, but it *might* have been, for any good a stump like you is for a lookout." I was pretty far gone, and said I was sick, and made him help me onto the foc'sle; and then I went straight off and took the pledge; for I had been going it pretty high for a week before we sailed, and I made up my mind that I'd rather go dry the rest of my life than see the like of that thing again."

"Well, I'm glad it was only the jimjams."

"Wait a minute, I ain't done. Of course I didn't enter it on the log—"

"Of course not—"

"For a man in his right mind don't put nightmares in the log. He only puts the word 'pledge' in, and takes credit for it if anybody inquires; and knows it will please the captain, and hopes it'll get to the owners. Well, two days later the chief mate took the pledge!"

"You don't mean it!"

"Sure as I'm standing here. I saw the word on the hook. I didn't say anything, but I felt encouraged. Now then, listen to this: day before yesterday I'm dumm'd if the *captain* didn't take the pledge!"

"Oh, come!"

"It's a true bill—I take my oath. There was the word. Then we begun to put this and that together, and next we began to look at each other kind of significant and willing, you know; and of course giving the captain the pre*ce*edence, for it wouldn't become *us* to begin, and we nothing but mates. And so yesterday, sure enough, out comes the captain—and we called his hand. Said he was out astern in a snow-flurry about dawn, and saw a creature shaped like a wood-louse and as big as a turreted monitor, go racing by and tearing up the foam, in chase of a fat animal the size of an elephant and creased like a caterpillar—and saw it dive after it and disappear; and he begun to prepare *his* soul for the pledge and break it to his entrails."

"It's terrible!"

"The pledge?—you bet your bottom dollar. If I—"

"No, I don't mean the pledge; I mean it is terrible to be lost at sea among such strange, uncanny brutes."

"Yes, there's something in that, too, I don't deny it. Well, the thing that the mate saw was like one of these big long lubberly canal boats, and it was ripping along like the Empire Express; and the look of it gave him the cold shivers, and so he begun to arrange *his* earthly affairs and go for pledge."

"Turner, it is dreadful—dreadful. Still, good has been done; for these pledges—"

"Oh, they're off!"

"Off?"

"Cert'nly. Can't be jimjams; couldn't all three of us have them at once, it ain't likely. What do you want with a pledge when there ain't any occasion for it? *There* he goes!"

He was gone like a shot, and the night swallowed him up. Now all of a sudden, with the wind still blowing hard, the seas went down and the deck became as level as a billiard table! Were *all* the laws of Nature suspended? It made my flesh creep; it was like being in a haunted ship. Pretty soon the mate came back panting, and sank down on a cable-tier, and said—

"Oh, this is an awful life; I don't think we can stand it long. There's too many horribles in it. Let me pant a little, I'm in a kind of a collapse."

"What's the trouble?"

"Drop down by me, sir—I mustn't shout. There—now you're all right." Then he said sorrowfully, "I reckon we've got to take it again."

"Take what?"

"The pledge."

"Why?"

"Did you see that thing go by?"

"What thing?"

"A *man.*"

"No. What of it?"

"This is four times that *I've* seen it; and the mate has seen it, and so has the captain. Haven't you ever seen it?"

"I suppose not. Is there anything extraordinary about it?"

"Extra-*or*dinary? Well, I should *say!*"

"How is it extraordinary?"

He said in an awed voice that was almost like a groan—

"Like this, for instance: you put your hand on him and he *ain't there.*"

"What do you mean, Turner?"

"It's as true as I'm sitting here; I wish I may never stir. The captain's getting morbid and religious over it, and says he wouldn't give a damn for ship and crew if that thing stays aboard."

"You curdle my blood. What is the man like? Isn't it just one of the crew, that you glimpse and lose in the dark?"

"You take note of *this:* it wears a broad slouch hat and a long cloak. Is that a whaler outfit, I'll ask you? A minute ago I was as close to him as I am to you; and I made a grab for him, and what did I get? A handful of air, that's all. There warn't a sign of him left."

"I do hope the pledge will dispose of it. It must be a work of the imagination, or the crew would have seen it."

"We're afraid they have. There was a deal of whispering going on last night in the middle watch. The captain dealt out grog, and got their minds on something else; but he is mighty uneasy, because of course he don't want you or your family to hear about that man, and would take my scalp if he knew what I'm doing now; and besides, if such a thing got a start with the crew, there'd be a mutiny, sure."

"I'll keep quiet, of course; still, I think it must be an output of imaginations overstrung by the strange fishes you think you saw; and I am hoping that the pledge—"

"I want to take it now. And I will."

"I'm witness to it. Now come to my parlor and I'll give you a cup of hot coffee and—"

"Oh, my goodness, there it is again! . . . It's gone. . . . Lord, it takes a body's breath . . . It's the jimjams I've got—I know it for sure. I want the coffee; it'll do me good. If you could help me a little, sir—I feel as weak as Sabbath grog."

We groped along the sleety deck to my door and entered, and there in the bright glare of the lamps sat (as I was half expecting) the man of the long cloak and the slouch hat, on the sofa,—my friend the Superintendent of Dreams. I was annoyed, for a moment, for of course I expected Turner to make a jump at him, get nothing, and be at once in a more miserable state than he already was. I reached for my cabin door and closed it, so that Alice might not hear the scuffle and get a fright. But there wasn't any. Turner went on talking, and took no notice of the Superintendent. I gave the Superintendent a grateful look; and it was an honest one, for this thing of making himself visible and scaring people could do harm.

"Lord, it's good to be in the light, sir," said Turner, rustling comfortably in his yellow oilskins, "it lifts a person's spirits right up. I've noticed that these cussed jimjam blatherskites ain't as apt to show up in the light as they are in the dark, except when you've got the trouble in your attic pretty bad." Meantime we were dusting the snow off each other with towels. "You're mighty well fixed here, sir—chairs and carpets and rugs and tables and lamps and books and everything lovely, and so warm and comfortable and homy; and the roomiest parlor I ever struck in a ship, too. Land, hear the wind, don't she sing! And not a sign of motion!—rip goes the sleet again!—ugly, you bet!—and here? why here it's only just the more cosier on account of it. Dern that jimjam, if I had him in here once I bet you I'd sweat him. Because I don't mind saying that I don't grab at him as earnest as I want to, outside there, and ain't as disappointed as I ought to be when I don't get him; but here in the light I ain't afraid of *no* jimjam."

It made the Superintendent of Dreams smile a smile that was full of pious satisfaction to hear him. I poured a steaming cup of coffee and handed it to Turner and told him to sit where he pleased and make himself comfortable and at home; and before I could interfere he had sat down in the Superintendent of Dreams' lap!—no, sat down *through* him. It cost me a gasp, but only that, nothing more. [The] Superintendent of Dreams' head was larger than Turner's, and *surrounded* it, and was a transparent spirit-head fronted with a transparent spirit-face; and this latter smiled at me as much as to say give myself no uneasiness, it is all right. Turner was smiling comfort and contentment at me at the same time, and the double result was very curious, but I could tell the smiles apart without trouble. The Superintendent of Dreams' body enclosed Turner's, but I could see Turner through it, just as one sees objects through thin smoke. It was interesting and pretty. Turner tasted his coffee and set the cup down in front of him with a hearty—

"Now I call that prime! 'George, it makes me feel the way old Cap'n Jimmy Starkweather did, I reckon, the first time he tasted grog after he'd been off his allowance three years. The way of it was this. It was there in Fairhaven by New Bedford, away back in the old early whaling days before I was born; but I heard about it the first day I *was* born, and it was a ripe old tale then, because they keep only the one fleet of yarns in commission down New Bedford-way, and don't ever re-stock and don't ever repair. And I came near hearing it in old Cap'n Jimmy's own presence once, when I was ten years old and he was ninety-two; but I didn't, because the man that asked Cap'n Jimmy to tell about it got crippled and the thing didn't materialize. It was Cap'n Jimmy that crippled him. Land, I thought I sh'd die! The very recollection of it—"

The very recollection of it so powerfully affected him that it shut off his speech and he put his head back and spread his jaws and laughed himself purple in the face. And while he was doing it the Superintendent of Dreams emptied the coffee into the slop bowl and set the cup back where it was before. When the explosion had spent itself Turner swabbed his face with his handkerchief and said—

"There—that laugh has scoured me out and done me good; I hain't had such another one—well, not since I struck *this* ship, now that's sure. I'll whet up and start over."

He took up his cup, glanced into it, and it was curious to observe the two faces that were framed in the front of his head. Turner's was long and distressed; the Superintendent of Dreams' was wide, and broken out of all shape with a convulsion of silent laughter. After a little, Turner said in a troubled way—

"I'm dumm'd if *I* recollect drinking that."

I didn't say anything, though I knew he must be expecting me to say something. He continued to gaze into the cup a while, then looked up wistfully and said—

"Of course I must have drunk it, but I'm blest if I can recollect whether I did or not. Lemme see. First you poured it out, then I set down and put it before me here; next I took a sup and said it was good, and set it down and begun about old Cap'n Jimmy—and then—and then—" He was silent a moment, then said, "It's as far as I can get. It beats me. I reckon that after that I was so kind of full of my story that I didn't notice whether I—." He stopped again, and there was something almost pathetic about the appealing way in which he added, "But I *did* drink it, *didn't* I? You *see* me do it—*didn't* you?"

I hadn't the heart to say no.

"Why, yes, I think I did. I wasn't noticing particularly, but it seems to me that I saw you drink it—in fact, I am about certain of it."

I was glad I told the lie, it did him so much good, and so lightened his spirits, poor old fellow.

"Of course I done it! I'm such a fool. As a general thing I wouldn't care, and I wouldn't bother anything about it; but when there's jimjams around the least little thing makes a person suspicious, you know. If you don't mind, sir—thanks, ever so much." He took a large sup of the new supply, praised it, set the cup down—leaning forward and fencing it around with his arms, with a labored pretense of not noticing that he was doing that— then said—

"Lemme see—where was I? Yes. Well, it happened like this. The Washingtonian Movement started up in those old times, you know, and it was Father Matthew here and Father Matthew there and Father Matthew yonder—nothing but Father Matthew and temperance all over everywheres. And temperance societies? There was millions of them, and everybody joined and took the pledge. We had one in New Bedford. Every last whaler joined—captain, crew and all. All, down to old Cap'n Jimmy. He was an old bach, his grog was his darling, he owned his ship and sailed her himself, he was independent, and he wouldn't give in. So at last they gave it up and quit pestering him. Time rolled along, and he got awful lonesome. There wasn't anybody to drink with, you see, and it got unbearable. So finally the day he sailed for Bering Strait he caved, and sent in his name to the society. Just as he was starting, his mate broke his leg and stopped ashore and he shipped a stranger in his place from down New York way. This fellow didn't belong to any society, and he went aboard fixed for the voyage. Cap'n Jimmy was out three solid years; and all the whole time he had the spectacle of that mate whetting up every day and leading a life that was worth the trouble; and it nearly killed him for envy to see it. Made his mouth water, you know, in a way that was pitiful. Well, he used to get out on the peak of the bowsprit where it was private, and set there and cuss. It was his only relief from his sufferings. Mainly he cussed himself; but when he had used up all his words and couldn't think of any new rotten things to call himself, he would turn his vocabulary over and start fresh and lay into Father Matthew and give *him* down the banks; and then the society; and so put in his watch as satisfactory as he could. Then he would count the days he was out, and try to reckon up about when he could hope to get home and resign from the society and start in on an all-compensating drunk that would make up for lost time. Well, when he was out three thousand years—which was *his* estimate, you know, though really it was only three years—he came rolling down the home-stretch with every rag stretched on his poles. Middle of winter, it was, and terrible cold and stormy. He made the landfall just at sundown and had to stand watch on deck all night of course, and the rigging was caked with ice three inches thick, and the yards was bearded with icicles five foot long, and the snow laid nine inches deep on the deck and hurricanes more of it being shoveled down onto him out of the skies. And so he plowed up and down all night, cussing himself and Father Matthew and the society, and doing it better than he ever done before; and his mouth was watering so, on account of the mate whetting up right in his sight all the time, that every cuss-word come out damp, and froze solid as it fell, and in his insufferable indignation he would hit it a whack with his cane and knock it a hundred yards, and one of them took the mate in the mouth and fetched away a rank of teeth and lowered *his* spirits considerable. He made the dock just at early breakfast time and never waited to tie up, but jumped ashore with his jug in his hand and rushed for the society's quarters like a deer. He met the seckatary coming out and yelled at him—

" 'I've resigned my membership!—I give you just two minutes to scrape my name off your log, d'ye hear?'

"And then the seckatary told him he'd been black-balled three years before—*hadn't ever been a member!* Land, I can't hold in, it's coming again!"

He flung up his arms, threw his head back, spread his jaws, and made the ship quake with the thunder of his laughter, while the Superintendent of Dreams emptied the cup again and set it back in its place. When Turner came out of his fit at last he was limp and exhausted, and sat mopping his tears away and breaking at times into little feebler and feebler barks and catches of expiring laughter. Finally he fetched a deep sigh of comfort and satisfaction, and said—

"Well, it *does* do a person good, no mistake—on a voyage like *this*. I reckon—"

His eye fell on the cup. His face turned a ghastly white—

"By God she's empty again!"

He jumped up and made a sprawling break for the door. I was frightened; I didn't know what he might do—jump overboard, maybe. I sprang in front of him and barred the way, saying, "Come, Turner, be a man, be a man! don't let your imagination run away with you like this"; and over his shoulder I threw a pleading look at the Superintendent of Dreams, who answered my prayer and refilled the cup from the coffee urn.

"Imagination you call it, sir! Can't I *see*?—with my own eyes? Let me go—don't stop me—I can't stand it, I can't stand it!"

"Turner, be reasonable—you know perfectly well your cup isn't empty, and *hasn't* been."

That hit him. A dim light of hope and gratitude shone in his eye, and he said in a quivery voice—

"Say it again—and say it's true. *Is* it true? Honor bright—you wouldn't deceive a poor devil that's—"

"Honor bright, man, I'm not deceiving you—look for yourself."

Gradually he turned a timid and wary glance toward the table; then the terror went out of his face, and he said humbly—

"Well, you see I reckon I hadn't quite got over thinking it happened the first time, and so maybe without me knowing it, that made me kind of suspicious that it would happen again, because the jimjams make you untrustful that way; and so, sure enough, I didn't half look at the cup, and just jumped to the conclusion it *had* happened." And talking so, he moved toward the sofa, hesitated a moment, and then sat down in that figure's body again. "But I'm all right, now, and I'll just shake these feelings off and be a man, as you say."

The Superintendent of Dreams separated himself and moved along the sofa a foot or two away from Turner. I was glad of that; it looked like a truce. Turner swallowed his cup of coffee; I poured another; he began to sip it, the pleasant influence worked a change, and soon he was a rational man again, and comfortable. Now a sea came aboard, hit our deck-house a stunning thump, and went hissing and seething aft.

"Oh, that's the ticket," said Turner, "the dummdest weather that ever I went pleasure-excursioning in. And how did it get aboard?— You answer me that: there ain't any motion to the ship. These mysteriousnesses—well, they just give me the cold shudders. And that reminds me. Do you mind my calling your attention to another peculiar thing or two?—on conditions as before—solid secrecy, you know."

"I'll keep it to myself. Go on."

"The Gulf Stream's gone to the devil!"

"What do you mean?"

"It's the fact, I wish I may never die. From the day we sailed till now, the water's been the same temperature right along, I'll take my oath. The Gulf Stream don't exist any more; she's gone to the devil."

"It's incredible, Turner! You make me gasp."

"Gasp away, if you want to; if things go on so, you ain't going to forget how for want of practice. It's the wooliest voyage, take it by and large—why, look here! You are a landsman, and there's no telling what a landsman can't overlook if he tries. For instance, have you noticed that the nights and days are exactly alike, and you can't tell one from 'tother except by keeping tally?"

"Why, yes, I have noticed it in a sort of indifferent general way, but—"

"Have you kept a tally, sir?"

"No, it didn't occur to me to do it."

"I thought so. Now you know, you couldn't keep it in your head, because you and your family are free to sleep as much as you like, and as it's always dark, you sleep a good deal, and you are pretty irregular, naturally. You've all been a little seasick from the start—tea and toast in your own parlor here—no regular time—order it as each of you pleases. You see? You don't go down to meals—*they* would keep tally for you. So you've lost your reckoning. I noticed it an hour ago."

"How?"

"Well, you spoke of *to-night*. It ain't to-night at all; it's just noon, now."

"The fact is, I don't believe I have often thought of its being day, since we left. I've got into the habit of considering it night all the time; it's the same with my wife and the children."

"There it is, you see. Mr. Edwards, it's perfectly awful; now ain't it, when you come to look at it? Always night—and such dismal nights, too. It's like being up at the pole in the winter time. And I'll ask you to notice another thing: this sky is as empty as my sou-wester there."

"Empty?"

"Yes, sir. I know it. You can't get up a day, in a Christian country, that's so solid black the sun can't make a blurry glow of *some* kind in the sky at high noon—now can you?"

"No, you can't."

"Have you ever seen a suspicion of any such a glow in this sky?"

"Now that you mention it, I haven't."

He dropped his voice and said impressively—

"Because there ain't any *sun*. She's gone where the Gulf Stream twineth."

"Turner! Don't talk like that."

"It's confidential, or I wouldn't. And the moon. She's at the full—by the almanac she is. Why don't *she* make a blur? Because there *ain't* any moon. And moreover—you might rake this on-completed sky a hundred year with a drag-net and you'd never scoop a star! Why? Because there *ain't* any. Now then, what is your opinion about all this?"

"Turner, it's so gruesome and creepy that I don't like to think about it—and I haven't any. What is yours?"

He said, dismally—

"That the world has come to an end. Look at it yourself. Just look at the facts. Put them together and add them up, and what have you got? No Sable island; no Greenland; no Gulf Stream; no day, no proper night; weather that don't jibe with any sample known to the Bureau; animals that would start a panic in any menagerie, chart no more use than a horse-blanket, and the heavenly bodies gone to hell! And on top of it all, that jimjam that I've put my hand on more than once and he warn't there—I'll swear it. The ship's bewitched. You don't believe in the jim, and I've sort of lost faith myself, here in the bright light; but if this cup of coffee was to—"

The cup began to glide slowly away, along the table. The hand that moved it was not visible to him. He rose slowly to his feet and stood trembling as if with an ague, his teeth knocking together and his glassy eyes staring at the cup. It slid on and on, noiseless; then it rose in the air, gradually reversed itself, poured its contents down the Superintendent's throat—I saw the dark stream trickling its way down through his hazy breast—then it returned to the table, and without sound of contact, rested there. The mate continued to stare at it for as much as a minute; then he drew a deep breath, took up his sou-wester, and without looking to the right or the left, walked slowly out of the room like one in a trance, muttering—

"I've *got* them—I've had the proof."

I said, reproachfully—

"Superintendent, why do you do that?"

"Do what?"

"Play these tricks."

"What harm is it?"

"Harm? It could make that poor devil jump overboard."

"No, he's not as far gone as that."

"For a while he was. He is a good fellow, and it was a pity to scare him so. However there are other matters that I am more concerned about just now.

"Can I help?"

"Why yes, you can; and I don't know any one else that can."

"Very well, go on."

"By the dead-reckoning we have come twenty-three hundred miles."

"The actual distance is twenty-three-fifty."

"Straight as a dart in the one direction—mainly."

"Apparently."

"Why do you say apparently? Haven't we come straight?"

"Go on with the rest. What were you going to say?"

"This. Doesn't it strike you that this is a pretty large drop of water?"

"No. It is about the usual size—six thousand miles across."

"Six thousand miles!"

"Yes."

"Twice as far as from New York to Liverpool?"

"Yes."

"I must say it is more of a voyage than I counted on. And we are not a great deal more than halfway across, yet. When shall we get in?"

"It will be some time yet."

"That is not very definite. Two weeks?"

"More than that."

I was getting a little uneasy.

"But how *much* more? A week?"

"All of that. More, perhaps."

"Why don't you tell me? A month more, do you think?"

"I am afraid so. Possibly two—possibly longer, even."

I was getting seriously disturbed by now.

"Why, we are sure to run out of provisions and water."

"No you'll not. I've looked out for that. It is what you are loaded with."

"Is that so? How does that come?"

"Because the ship is chartered for a voyage of discovery. Ostensibly she goes to England, takes aboard some scientists, then sails for the South pole."

"I see. You are deep."

"I understand my business."

I turned the matter over in my mind a moment, then said—

"It is more of a voyage than I was expecting, but I am not of a worrying disposition, so I do not care, so long as we are not going to suffer hunger and thirst."

"Make yourself easy, as to that. Let the trip last as long as it may, you will not run short of food and water, I go bail for that."

"All right, then. Now explain this riddle to me. Why is it always night?"

"That is easy. All of the drop of water is outside the luminous circle of the microscope except one thin and delicate rim of it. We are in the shadow; consequently in the dark."

"In the shadow of what?"

"Of the brazen end of the lens-holder."

"How can it cover such a spread with its shadow?"

"Because it is several thousand miles in diameter. For dimensions, that is nothing. The glass slide which it is pressing against, and which forms the bottom of the ocean we are sailing upon, is thirty thousand miles long, and the length of the microscope barrel is a hundred and twenty thousand. Now then, if—"

"You make me dizzy. I—"

"If you should thrust that glass slide through what you call the 'great' globe, eleven thousand miles of it would stand out on each side—it would be like impaling an orange on a table-knife. And so—"

"It gives me the head-ache. Are these the fictitious proportions which we and our surroundings and belongings have acquired by being reduced to microscopic objects?"

"They are the proportions, yes—but they are not fictitious. You do not notice that you yourself are in any way diminished in size, do you?"

"No, I am my usual size, so far as I can see."

"The same with the men, the ship and everything?"

"Yes—all natural."

"Very good; nothing but the laws and conditions have undergone a change. You came from a small and very insignificant world. The one you are in now is proportioned according to microscopic standards—that is to say, it is inconceivably stupendous and imposing."

It was food for thought. There was something overpowering in the situation, something sublime. It took me a while to shake off the spell and drag myself back to speech. Presently I said—

"I am content; I do not regret the voyage—far from it. I would not change places with any man in that cramped little world. But tell me—is it always going to be dark?"

"Not if you ever come into the luminous circle under the lens. Indeed you will not find *that* dark!"

"If we ever. What do you mean by that? We are making steady good time; we are cutting across this sea on a straight course."

"Apparently."

"There is no apparently about it."

"You might be going around in a small and not rapidly widening circle."

"Nothing of the kind. Look at the tell-tale compass over your head."

"I see it."

"We changed to this easterly course to satisfy—well, to satisfy everybody but me. It is a pretense of aiming for England—in a drop of water! Have you noticed that needle before?"

"Yes, a number of times."

"To-day, for instance?"

"Yes—often."

"Has it varied a jot?"

"Not a jot."

"Hasn't it always kept the place appointed for it—from the start?"

"Yes, always."

"Very well. First we sailed a northerly course; then tilted easterly; and now it is more so. How is *that* going around in a circle?"

He was silent. I put it at him again. He answered with lazy indifference—

"I merely threw out the suggestion."

"All right, then; cornered; let it stand at that. Whenever you happen to think of an argument in support of it, I shall be glad to hear about it."

He did not like that very well, and muttered something about my being a trifle airy. I retorted a little sharply, and followed it up by finding fault with him again for playing tricks on Turner. He said Turner called him a blatherskite. I said—

"No matter; you let him alone, from this out. And moreover, stop appearing to people—stop it entirely."

His face darkened. He said—

"I would advise you to moderate your manner. I am not used to it, and I am not pleased with it."

The rest of my temper went, then. I said, angrily—

"You may like it or not, just as you choose. And moreover, if my style doesn't suit you, you can end the dream as soon as you please—right now, if you like."

He looked me steadily in the eye for a moment, then said, with deliberation—

"The dream? *Are you quite sure it is a dream?*"

It took my breath away.

"What do you mean? *Isn't* it a dream?"

He looked at me in that same way again; and it made my blood chilly, this time. Then he said—

"You have spent your whole life in this ship. And this is *real* life. Your other life was the dream!"

It was as if he had hit me, it stunned me so. Still looking at me, his lip curled itself into a mocking smile, and he wasted away like a mist and disappeared.

I sat a long time thinking uncomfortable thoughts.

We are strangely made. We think we are wonderful creatures. Part of the time we think that, at any rate. And during that interval we consider with pride our mental equipment, with its penetration, its power of analysis, its ability to reason out clear conclusions from confused facts, and all the lordly rest of it; and then comes a rational interval and disenchants us. Disenchants us and lays us bare to ourselves, and we see that intellectually we are really no great things; that we seldom really know the thing we think we know; that our best-built certainties are but sand-houses and subject to damage from any wind of doubt that blows.

So little a time before, I *knew* that this voyage was a dream, and nothing more; a wee little puff or two of doubt had blown against that certainty, unhelped by fact or argument, and already it was dissolving away. It seemed an incredible thing, and it hurt my pride of intellect, but it had to be confessed.

When I came to consider it, these ten days had been such intense realities!—so intense that by comparison the life I had lived before them seemed distant, indistinct, slipping away and fading out in a far perspective—exactly as a dream does when you sit at breakfast trying to call back its details. I grew steadily more and more nervous and uncomfortable—and a little frightened, though I would not quite acknowledge this to myself.

Then came this disturbing thought: if this transformation goes on, how am I going to conceal it from my wife? Suppose she should say to me, "Henry, there is something the matter with you, you are acting strangely; something is on your mind that you are concealing from me; tell me about it, let me help you"—what answer could I make?

I was *bound* to act strangely if this went on—bound to bury myself in deeps of troubled thought; I should not be able to help it. She had a swift eye to notice, where her heart was concerned, and a sharp intuition, and I was an impotent poor thing in her hands when I had things to hide and she had struck the trail.

I have no large amount of fortitude, staying power. When there is a fate before me I cannot rest easy until I know what it is. I am not able to wait. I want to know, right away. So, I would call Alice, now, and take the consequences. If she drove me into a corner and I found I could not escape, I would act according to my custom—come out and tell her the truth. She had a better head than mine, and a surer instinct in grouping facts and getting their meaning out of them. If I was drifting into dangerous waters, now, she would be sure to detect it and as sure to set me right and save me. I would call her, and keep out of the corner if I could; if I couldn't, why—I couldn't, that is all.

She came, refreshed with sleep, and looking her best self: that is to say, looking like a girl of nineteen, not a matron of twenty-five; she wore a becoming wrapper, or tea gown, or whatever it is called, and it was trimmed with ribbons and limp stuff—lace, I suppose; and she had her hair balled up and nailed to its place with a four-pronged tortoise-shell comb. She brought a basket of pink and gray crewels with her, for she was crocheting a jacket—for the cat, probably, judging by the size of it. She sat down on the sofa and set the basket on the table, expecting to have a chance to get to work by and by; not right away, because a kitten was curled up in it asleep, fitting its circle snugly, and the repose of the children's kittens was a sacred thing and not to be disturbed. She said—

"I noticed that there was no motion—it was what waked me, I think—and I got up to enjoy it, it is such a rare thing."

"Yes, rare enough, dear; we do have the most unaccountably strange weather."

"Do you think so, Henry? Does it seem strange weather to you?"

She looked so earnest and innocent that I was rather startled, and a little in doubt as to what to say. Any sane person could see that it was perfectly devilish weather and crazy beyond imagination, and so how could she feel uncertain about it?

"Well, Alice, I may be putting it too strong, but I don't think so; I think a person may call our weather by any hard name he pleases and be justified."

"Perhaps you are right, Henry. I have heard the sailors talk the same way about it, but I did not think that that meant much, they speak so extravagantly about everything. You are not always extravagant in your speech—often you are, but not always—and so it surprised me a little to hear you." Then she added tranquilly and musingly, "I don't remember any different weather."

It was not quite definite.

"You mean on *this* voyage, Alice."

"Yes, of course. Naturally. I haven't made any other."

She was softly stroking the kitten—and apparently in her right mind. I said cautiously, and with seeming indifference—

"You mean you haven't made any other this year. But the time we went to Europe—well, that was very different weather."

"The time we went to Europe, Henry?"

"Certainly, certainly—when Jessie was a year old."

She stopped stroking the kitty, and looked at me inquiringly.

"I don't understand you, Henry."

She was not a joker, and she was always truthful. Her remark blew another wind of doubt upon my wasting sand-edifice of certainty. Had I only *dreamed* that we went to Europe? It seemed a good idea to put this thought into words.

"Come, Alice, the first thing you know you will be imagining that we went to Europe in a dream."

She smiled, and said—

"Don't let me spoil it, Henry, if it is pleasant to you to think we went. I will consider that we did go, and that I have forgotten it."

"But Alice dear we *did* go!"

"But Henry dear we *didn't* go!"

She had a good head and a good memory, and she was always truthful. My head had been injured by a fall when I was a boy, and the physicians had said at the time that there could be ill effects from it some day. A cold wave struck me, now; perhaps the effects had come. I was losing confidence in the European trip. However, I thought I would make another try.

"Alice, I will give you a detail or two; then maybe you will remember."

"A detail or two from the dream?"

"I am not at all sure that it was a dream; and five minutes ago I was sure that it wasn't. It was seven years ago. We went over in the *Batavia*. Do you remember the *Batavia*?"

"I don't, Henry."

"Captain Moreland. Don't you remember him?"

"To me he is a myth, Henry."

"Well, it beats anything. We lived two or three months in London, then six weeks in a private hotel in George Street, Edinburgh—Veitch's. Come!"

"It sounds pleasant, but I have never heard of these things before, Henry."

"And Doctor John Brown, of *Rab and His Friends*—you were ill, and he came every day; and when you were well again he still came every day and took us all around while he paid his visits, and we waited in his carriage while he prescribed for his patients. And he was so dear and lovely. You *must* remember all that, Alice."

"None of it, dear; it is only a dream."

"Why, Alice, have you ever had a dream that remained as distinct as that, and which you could remember so long?"

"So long? It is more than likely that you dreamed it last night."

"No indeed! It has been in my memory seven years."

"Seven years in a dream, yes—it is the way of dreams. They put seven years into two minutes, without any trouble—isn't it so?"

I had to acknowledge that it was.

"It seems almost as if it couldn't have been a dream, Alice; it seems as if you ought to remember it."

"Wait! It begins to come back to me." She sat thinking a while, nodding her head with satisfaction from time to time. At last she said, joyfully, "I remember almost the whole of it, now."

"Good!"

"I am glad I got it back. Ordinarily I remember my dreams very well; but for some reason this one—"

"*This* one, Alice? Do you really consider it a dream, yet?"

"I don't consider anything about it, Henry, I know it; I know it positively."

The conviction stole through me that she must be right, since she felt so sure. Indeed I almost knew she was. I was privately becoming ashamed of myself now, for mistaking a clever illusion for a fact. So I gave it up, then, and said I would let it stand as a dream. Then I added—

"It puzzles me; even now it seems almost as distinct as the microscope."

"Which microscope?"

"Well, Alice, there's only the one."

"Very well, which one is *that*?"

"Bother it all, the one we examined this ocean in, the other day."

"Where?"

"Why, at home—Of course."

"What home?"

"Alice it's provoking—why, *our* home. In Springport."

"Dreaming again. I've never heard of it."

That was stupefying. There was no need of further beating about the bush; I threw caution aside, and came out frankly.

"Alice, what do you call the life we are leading in this ship? Isn't it a dream?"

She looked at me in a puzzled way and said—

"A dream, Henry? Why should I think that?"

"Oh, dear me, I don't know! I thought I did, but I don't. Alice, haven't we ever had a home? Don't you remember one?"

"Why, yes—three. That is, dream-homes, not real ones. I have never regarded them as realities."

"Describe them."

She did it, and in detail, also our life in them. Pleasant enough homes, and easily recognizable by me. I could also recognize an average of 2 out of 7 of the episodes and incidents which she threw in. Then I described the home and the life which (as it appeared to me) we had so recently left. She recognized it—but only as a dream-home. She remembered nothing about the microscope and the children's party. I was in a corner; but it was not the one which I had arranged for.

"Alice, if those were dream-homes, how long have you been in this ship?—you say this is the only voyage you have ever made."

"I don't know. I don't remember. It *is* the only voyage we have made—unless breaking it to pick up this crew of strangers in place of the friendly dear men and officers we had sailed with so many years makes two voyages of it. How I do miss them—Captain Hall, and Williams the sail-maker, and Storrs the chief mate, and—"

She choked up, and the tears began to trickle down her cheeks. Soon she had her handkerchief out and was sobbing.

I realized that I remembered those people perfectly well. Damnation! I said to myself, are we real creatures in a real world, all of a sudden, and have we been feeding on dreams in an imaginary one since nobody knows when—or how *is* it? My head was swimming.

"Alice! Answer me this. Do you know the Superintendent of Dreams?"

"Certainly."

"Have you seen him often?"

"Not often, but several times."

"When did you see him first?"

"The time that Robert the captain's boy was eaten."

"*Eaten?*"

"Yes. Surely you haven't forgotten that?"

"But I have, though. I never heard of it before." (I spoke the truth. For the moment I could not recall the incident.)

Her face was full of reproach.

"I am sorry, if that is so. He was always good to you. If you are jesting, I do not think it is in good taste."

"Now don't treat me like that, Alice, I don't deserve it. I am not jesting, I am in earnest. I mean the boy's memory no offence, but although I remember him I do not remember the circumstance— I swear it. Who ate him?"

"Do not be irreverent, Henry, it is out of place. It was not a *who*, at all."

"What then—a *which*?"

"Yes."

"What kind of a which?"

"A spider-squid. *Now* you remember it I hope."

"Indeed and deed and double-deed I don't, Alice, and it is the real truth. Tell me about it, please."

"I suppose you see, now, Henry, what your memory is worth. You can remember dream-trips to Europe well enough, but things in real life—even the most memorable and horrible things—pass out of your memory in twelve years. There is something the matter with your mind."

It was very curious. How *could* I have forgotten that tragedy? It must have happened; she was never mistaken in her facts, and she never spoke with positiveness of a thing which she was in any degree uncertain about. And this tragedy—*twelve years* ago—

"Alice, how long *have* we been in this ship?"

"Now how can I know, Henry? It goes too far back. Always, for all I know. The earliest thing I can call to mind was papa's death by the sun-heat and mamma's suicide the same day. I was four years old, then. Surely you must remember that, Henry."

"Yes. . . . Yes. But it is so dim. Tell me about it—refresh my memory."

"Why, you must remember that we were in the edge of a great white glare once for a little while—a day, or maybe two days,—only a little while, I think, but I remember it, because it was the only time I was ever out of the dark, and there was a great deal of talk of it for long afterwards—why, Henry, you *must* remember a wonderful thing like that."

"Wait. Let me think." Gradually, detail by detail the whole thing came back to me; and with it the boy's adventure with the spider-squid; and then I recalled a dozen other incidents, which Alice verified as incidents of our ship-life, and said I had set them forth correctly.

It was a puzzling thing—my freaks of memory; Alice's, too. By testing, it was presently manifest that the vacancies in my ship-life memories were only apparent, not real; a few words by way of reminder enabled me to fill them up, in almost all cases, and give them clarity and vividness. What had caused these temporary lapses? Didn't these very lapses indicate that the ship-life was a dream, and not real?

It made Alice laugh.

I did not see anything foolish in it, or anything to laugh at, and I told her so. And I reminded her that her own memory was as bad as mine, since many and many a conspicuous episode of our land-life was gone from her, even so striking an incident as the water-drop exploration with the microscope—

It made her shout.

I was wounded; and said that if I could not be treated with respect I would spare her the burden of my presence and conversation. She stopped laughing, at once, and threw her arms about my neck. She said she would not have hurt me for the world, but she supposed I was joking; it was quite natural to think I was not in earnest in talking gravely about this and that and the other dream-phantom as if it were a reality.

"But Alice I *was* in earnest, and I *am* in earnest. Look at it—examine it. If the land-life was a dream-life, how is it that you remember so much of it exactly as *I* remember it?"

She was amused again, inside—I could feel the quiver; but there was no exterior expression of it, for she did not want to hurt me again.

"Dear heart, throw the whole matter aside! Stop puzzling over it; it isn't worth it. It is perfectly simple. It is true that I remember a little of that dream-life just as you remember it—but that is an accident; the rest of it—and by far the largest part—does not correspond with your recollections. And how *could* it? People can't be expected to remember each other's dreams, but only their own. You have put me into your land-dreams a thousand times, but I didn't always know I was there; so how could I remember it? Also I have put you into my land-dreams a thousand times when you didn't know it—and the natural result is that when I name the circumstances you don't always recall them. But how different it is with this real life, this genuine life in the ship! Our recollections of it are just alike. You have been forgetting episodes of it to-day—I don't know why; it has surprised me and puzzled me—but the lapse was only temporary; your memory soon rallied again. Now it hasn't rallied in the case of land-dreams of mine—in most cases it hasn't. And it's not going to, Henry. You can be sure of that."

She stopped, and tilted her head up in a thinking attitude and began to unconsciously tap her teeth with the ivory knob of a crochet needle. Presently she said, "I think I know what is the matter. I have been neglecting you for ten days while I have been grieving for our old shipmates and pretending to be seasick so that I might indulge myself with solitude; and here is the result—you haven't been taking exercise enough."

I was glad to have a reason—any reason that would excuse my memory—and I accepted this one, and made confession. There was no truth in the confession, but I was already getting handy with these evasions. I was a little sorry for this, for she had always trusted my word, and I had honored this trust by telling her the truth many a time when it was a sharp sacrifice to me to do it. She looked me over with gentle reproach in her eye, and said—

"Henry, how can you be so naughty? I watch you so faithfully and make you take such good care of your health that you owe me the grace to do my office for me when for any fair reason I am for a while not on guard. When have you boxed with George last?"

What an idea it was! It was a good place to make a mistake, and I came near to doing it. It was on my tongue's end to say that I had never boxed with anyone; and as for boxing with a colored man-servant—and so on; but I kept back my remark, and in place of it tried to look like a person who didn't know what to say. It was easy to do, and I probably did it very well.

"You do not say anything, Henry. I think it is because you have a good reason. When have you fenced with him? Henry, you are avoiding my eye. Look up. Tell me the truth: have you fenced with him a single time in the last ten days?"

So far as I was aware I knew nothing about foils, and had never handled them; so I was able to answer—

"I will be frank with you, Alice—I haven't."

"I suspected it. Now, Henry, what can you say?"

I was getting some of my wits back, now, and was not altogether unprepared, this time.

"Well, Alice, there hasn't been much fencing weather, and when there was any, I—well, I was lazy, and that is the shameful truth."

"There's a chance now, anyway, and you mustn't waste it. Take off your coat and things."

She rang for George, then she got up and raised the sofa-seat and began to fish out boxing-gloves, and foils and masks from the locker under it, softly scolding me all the while. George put his head in, noted the preparations, then entered and put himself in boxing trim. It was his turn to take the witness stand, now.

"George, didn't I tell you to keep up Mr. Henry's exercises just the same as if I were about?"

"Yes, madam, you did."

"Why haven't you done it?"

George chuckled, and showed his white teeth and said—

"Bless yo' soul, honey, I dasn't."

"Why?"

"Because the first time I went to him—it was that Tuesday, you know, when it was ca'm—he wouldn't hear to it, and said he didn't want no exercise and warn't going to take any, and tole me to go 'long. Well, I didn't stop there, of course, but went to him agin, every now and then, trying to persuade him, tell at last he let into me" (he stopped and comforted himself with an unhurried laugh over the recollection of it,) "and give me a most solid good cussing, and tole me if I come agin he'd take and thow me overboard— there, ain't that so, Mr. Henry?"

My wife was looking at me pretty severely.

"Henry, what have you to say to that?"

It was my belief that it hadn't happened, but I was steadily losing confidence in my memory; and moreover my new policy of recollecting whatever anybody required me to recollect seemed the safest course to pursue in my strange and trying circumstances; so I said—

"Nothing, Alice—I did refuse."

"Oh, I'm not talking about that; of course you refused—George had already said so."

"Oh, I see."

"Well, why do you stop?"

"Why do I stop?"

"Yes. Why don't you answer my question?"

"Why, Alice, I've answered it. You asked me—you asked me— What *is* it I haven't answered?"

"Henry, you know very well. You broke a promise; and you are trying to talk around it and get me away from it; but I am not going to let you. You know quite well you promised me you wouldn't swear any more in calm weather. And it is such a little thing to do. It is hardly ever calm, and—"

"Alice, dear, I beg ever so many pardons! I had clear forgotten it; but I won't offend again, I give you my word. Be good to me, and forgive."

She was always ready to forgive, and glad to do it, whatever my crime might be; so things were pleasant again, now, and smooth and happy. George was gloved and skipping about in an imaginary fight, by this time, and Alice told me to get to work with him. She took pencil and paper and got ready to keep game. I stepped forward to position—then a curious thing happened: I seemed to remember a thousand boxing-bouts with George, the whole boxing art came flooding in upon me, and I knew just what to do! I was a prey to no indecisions, I had no trouble. We fought six rounds, I held my own all through, and I finally knocked George out. I was not astonished; it seemed a familiar experience. Alice showed no surprise, George showed none; apparently it was an old story to them.

The same thing happened with the fencing. I suddenly knew that I was an experienced old fencer; I expected to get the victory, and when I got it, it seemed but a repetition of something which had happened numberless times before.

We decided to go down to the main saloon and take a regular meal in the regular way—the evening meal. Alice went away to dress. Just as I had finished dressing, the children came romping in, warmly and prettily clad, and nestled up to me, one on each side, on the sofa, and began to chatter. Not about a former home; no, not a word of that, but only about this ship-home and its concerns and its people. After a little I threw out some questions—feelers. They did not understand. Finally I asked them if they had known no home but this one. Jessie said, with some little enthusiasm—

"Oh, yes, dream-homes. They were pretty—some of them." Then, with a shrug of her shoulders, "But they *are* so queer!"

"How, Jessie?"

"Well, you know, they have such curious things in them; and they fade, and don't stay. Bessie doesn't like them at all."

"Why don't you, Bessie?"

"Because they scare me so."

"What is it that scares you?"

"Oh, everything, papa. Sometimes it is so light. That hurts my eyes. And it's too many lamps—little sparkles all over, up high, and large ones that are dreadful. They could fall on me, you know."

"But I am not much afraid," said Jessie, "because mamma says they are not real, and if they did fall they wouldn't hurt."

"What else do you see there besides the lights, Bessie?"

"Ugly things that go on four legs like our cat, but bigger."

"Horses?"

"I forget names."

"Describe them, dear."

"I can't, papa. They are not alike; they are different kinds; and when I wake up I can't just remember the shape of them, they are so dim."

"And I wouldn't wish to remember them," said Jessie, "they make me feel creepy. Don't let's talk about them, papa, let's talk about something else."

"That's what I say, too," said Bessie.

So then we talked about our ship. That interested them. They cared for no other home, real or unreal, and wanted no better one. They were innocent witnesses and free from prejudice.

When we went below we found the roomy saloon well lighted and brightly and prettily furnished, and a very comfortable and inviting place altogether. Everything seemed substantial and genuine, there was nothing to suggest that it might be a work of the imagination.

At table the captain (Davis) sat at the head, my wife at his right with the children, I at his left, a stranger at my left. The rest of the company consisted of Rush Phillips, purser, aged 27; his sweetheart the Captain's daughter Lucy, aged 22; her sister Connie (short for Connecticut), aged 10; Arnold Blake, surgeon, 25; Harvey Pratt, naturalist, 36; at the foot sat Sturgis the chief mate, aged 35, and completed the snug assemblage. Stewards waited upon the general company, and George and our nurse Germania had charge of our family. Germania was not the nurse's name, but that was our name for her because it was shorter than her own. She was 28 years old, and had always been with us; and so had George. George was 30, and had once been a slave, according to my record, but I was losing my grip upon that, now, and was indeed getting shadowy and uncertain about all my traditions.

The talk and the feeding went along in a natural way, I could find nothing unusual about it anywhere. The captain was pale, and had a jaded and harassed look, and was subject to little fits of absence of mind; and these things could be said of the mate, also, but this was all natural enough considering the grisly time they had been having, and certainly there was nothing about it to suggest that they were dream-creatures or that their troubles were unreal.

The stranger at my side was about 45 years old, and he had the half-subdued, half-resigned look of a man who had been under a burden of trouble a long time. He was tall and thin; he had a bushy black head, and black eyes which burned when he was interested, but were dull and expressionless when his thoughts were far away—and that happened every time he dropped out of the conversation. He forgot to eat, then, his hands became idle, his dull eye fixed itself upon his plate or upon vacancy, and now and then he would draw a heavy sigh out of the depths of his breast.

These three were exceptions; the others were chatty and cheerful, and they were like a pleasant little family party together. Phillips and Lucy were full of life, and quite happy, as became engaged people; and their furtive love-passages had everybody's sympathy and approval. Lucy was a pretty creature, and simple in her ways and kindly, and Phillips was a blithesome and attractive young fellow. I seemed to be familiarly acquainted with everybody, I didn't quite know why. That is, with everybody except the stranger at my side; and as he seemed to know me well, I had to let on to know him, lest I cause remark by exposing the fact that I didn't know him. I was already tired of being caught up for ignorance at every turn.

The captain and the mate managed to seem confortable enough until Phillips raised the subject of the day's run, the position of the ship, distance out, and so on; then they became irritable, and sharp of speech, and were unkinder to the young fellow than the case seemed to call for. His sweetheart was distressed to see him so treated before all the company, and she spoke up bravely in his defence and reproached her father for making an offence out of so harmless a thing. This only brought her into trouble, and procured for her so rude a retort that she was consumed with shame, and left the table crying.

The pleasure was all gone, now; everybody felt personally affronted and wantonly abused. Conversation ceased and an uncomfortable silence fell upon the company; through it one could hear the wailing of the wind and the dull tramp of the sailors and the muffled words of command overhead, and this made the silence all the more dismal. The dinner was a failure. While it was still unfinished the company began to break up and slip out, one after another; and presently none was left but me.

I sat long, sipping black coffee and smoking. And thinking; groping about in my dimming land-past. An incident of my American life would rise upon me, vague at first, then grow more distinct and articulate, then sharp and clear; then in a moment it was gone, and in its place was a dull and distant image of some long-past episode whose theatre was this ship—and then *it* would develop, and clarify, and become strong and real. It was fascinating, enchanting, this spying among the elusive mysteries of my bewitched memory, and I went up to my parlor and continued it, with the help of punch and pipe, hour after hour, as long as I could keep awake. With this curious result: that the main incidents of both my lives were now recovered, but only those of one of them persistently gathered strength and vividness—our life in the ship! Those of our land-life were good enough, plain enough, but in minuteness of detail they fell perceptibly short of those others; and in matters of feeling—joy, grief, physical pain, physical pleasure—immeasurably short!

Some mellow notes floated to my ear, muffled by the moaning wind—six bells in the morning watch. So late! I went to bed.

When I woke in the middle of the so-called day the first thing I thought of was my night's experience. Already my land-life had faded a little—but not the other.

BOOK II

Chapter I

I have long ago lost Book I, but it is no matter. It served its purpose—writing it was an entertainment to me. We found out that our little boy set it adrift on the wind, sheet by sheet, to see if it would fly. It did. And so two of us got entertainment out of it. I have often been minded to begin Book II, but natural indolence and the pleasant life of the ship interfered.

There have been little happenings, from time to time. The principal one, for us of the family, was the birth of our Harry, which stands recorded in the log under the date of June 8, and happened about three months after we shipped the present crew, poor devils! They still think we are bound for the South Pole, and that we are a long time on the way. It is pathetic, after a fashion. They regard their former life in the World as their real life and this present one as—well, they hardly know what; but sometimes they get pretty tired of it, even at this late day. We hear of it now and then through the officers—mainly Turner, who is a puzzled man.

During the first four years we had several mutinies, but things have been reasonably quiet during the past two. One of them had really a serious look. It occurred when Harry was a month old, and at an anxious time, both he and his mother were weak and ill. The master spirit of it was Stephen Bradshaw the carpenter, of course—a hard lot I know, and a born mutineer I think.

In those days I was greatly troubled, for a time, because my wife's memories still refused to correspond with mine. It had been an ideal life, and naturally it was a distress not to be able to live it over again in its entirety with her in our talks. At first she did not feel about it as I did, and said she could not understand my interest in those dreams, but when she found how much I took the matter to heart, and that to me the dreams had come to have a seeming of reality and were freighted with tender and affectionate impressions besides, she began to change her mind and wish she could go back in spirit with me to that mysterious land. And so she tried to get back that forgotten life. By my help, and by patient probing and searching of her memory she succeeded. Gradually it all came back, and her reward was sufficient. We now had the recollections of two lives to draw upon, and the result was a double measure of happiness for us. We even got the children's former lives back for them—with a good deal of difficulty—next the servants'. It made a new world for us all, and an entertaining one to explore. In the beginning George the colored man was an unwilling subject, because by heredity he was superstitious, and believed that no good could come of meddling with dreams; but when he presently found that no harm came of it his disfavor dissolved away.

Talking over our double-past—particularly our dream-past— became our most pleasant and satisfying amusement, and the search for missing details of it our most profitable labor. One day when the baby was about a month old, we were at this pastime in our parlor. Alice was lying on the sofa, propped with pillows—she was by no means well. It was a still and solemn black day, and cold; but the lamps made the place cheerful, and as for comfort, Turner had taken care of that; for he had found a kerosene stove with an isinglass front among the freight, and had brought it up and lashed it fast and fired it up, and the warmth it gave and the red glow it made took away all chill and cheerlessness from the parlor and made it homelike. The little girls were out somewhere with George and Delia (the maid).

Alice and I were talking about the time, twelve years before, when Captain Hall's boy had his tragic adventure with the spider-squid, and I was reminding her that she had misstated the case when she mentioned it to me, once. She had said the squid *ate* the boy. Out of my memory I could call back all the details, now, and I remembered that the boy was only badly hurt, not eaten.

For a month or two the ship's company had been glimpsing vast animals at intervals of a few days, and at first the general terror was so great that the men openly threatened, on two occasions, to seize the ship unless the captain turned back; but by a resolute bearing he tided over the difficulty; and by pointing out to the men that the animals had shown no disposition to attack the ship and might therefore be considered harmless, he quieted them down and restored order. It was good grit in the captain, for privately he was very much afraid of the animals himself and had but a shady opinion of their innocence. He kept his gatlings in order, and had gun-watches, which he changed with the other watches.

I had just finished correcting Alice's history of the boy's adventure with the squid when the ship, plowing through a perfectly smooth sea, went heeling away down to starboard and stayed there! The floor slanted like a roof, and every loose thing in the room slid to the floor and glided down against the bulkhead. We were greatly alarmed, of course. Next we heard a rush of feet along the deck and an uproar of cries and shoutings, then the rush of feet coming back, with a wilder riot of cries. Alice exclaimed—

"Go find the children—quick!"

I sprang out and started to run aft through the gloom, and then I saw the fearful sight which I had seen twelve years before when that boy had his shocking misadventure. For the moment I turned the corner of the deck-house and had an unobstructed view astern, there it was—apparently two full moons rising close over the stern of the ship and lighting the decks and rigging with a sickly yellow glow—the eyes of the colossal squid. His vast beak and head were plain to be seen, swelling up like a hill above our stern; he had flung one tentacle forward and gripped it around the peak of the main-mast and was pulling the ship over; he had gripped the mizzen-mast with another, and a couple more were writhing about dimly away above our heads searching for something to take hold of. The stench of his breath was suffocating everybody.

I was like the most of the crew, helpless with fright; but the captain and the officers kept their wits and courage. The gatlings on the starboard side could not be used, but the four on the port side were brought to bear, and inside of a minute they had poured more than two thousand bullets into those moons. That blinded the creature, and he let go; and by squirting a violent Niagara of water out of his mouth which tore the sea into a tempest of foam he shot himself backward three hundred yards and the ship forward as far, drowning the deck with a racing flood which swept many of the men off their feet and crippled some, and washed all loose deck-plunder overboard. For five minutes we could hear him thrashing about, there in the dark, and lashing the sea with his giant tentacles in his pain; and now and then his moons showed, then vanished again; and all the while we were rocking and plunging in the booming seas he made. Then he quieted down. We took a thankful full breath, believing him dead.

Now I thought of the children, and ran all about inquiring for them, but no one had seen them. I thought they must have been washed overboard, and for a moment my heart stopped beating. Then the hope came that they had taken refuge with their mother; so I ran there; and almost swooned when I entered the place, for it was vacant. I ran out shouting the alarm, and after a dozen steps almost ran over her. She was lying against the bulwarks drenched and insensible. The surgeon and young Phillips helped me carry her in; then the surgeon and I began to work over her and Phillips rushed away to start the hunt for the children. It was all of half an hour before she showed any sign of life; then her eyes opened with a dazed and wondering look in them, then they recognized me and into them shot a ghastly terror.

"The children! the children!" she gasped; and I, with the heart all gone out of me, answered with such air of truth as I could assume—

"They are safe."

I could never deceive her. I was transparent to her.

"It is not true! The truth speaks out all over you—they are lost, oh they are lost, they are lost!"

We were strong, but we could not hold her. She tore loose from us and was gone in a moment, flying along the dark decks and shrieking the children's names with a despairing pathos that broke one's heart to hear it. We fled after her, and urged that the flitting lanterns meant that all were searching, and begged her for the children's sake and mine if not for her own to go to bed and save her life. But it went for nothing, she would not listen. For she was a mother, and her children were lost. That says it all. She would hunt for them as long as she had strength to move. And that is what she did, hour after hour, wailing and mourning, and touching the hardest hearts with grief, until she was exhausted and fell in a swoon. Then the stewardess and I put her to bed, and as soon as she came to and was going to creep out of her bed and take up her search again the doctor encouraged her in it and gave her a draught to restore her strength; and it put her into a deep sleep, which was what he expected.

We left the stewardess on watch and went away to join the searchers. Not a lantern was twinkling anywhere, and every figure that emerged from the gloom moved upon tip-toe. I collared one of them and said angrily

"What does this mean? Is the search stopped?"

Turner's voice answered—very low: "—'sh! Captain's orders. The beast ain't dead—it's hunting for us."

It made me sick with fear.

"Do you mean it, Turner? How do you know?"

"Listen."

There was a muffled swashing sound out there somewhere, and then the two moons appeared for a moment, then turned slowly away and were invisible again.

"He's been within a hundred yards of us, feeling around for us with his arms. He could reach us, but he couldn't locate us because he's blind. Once he mighty near had us; one of his arms that was squirming around up there in the dark just missed the foremast, and he hauled in the slack of it without suspecting anything. It made my lungs come up into my throat. He has edged away, you see, but he ain't done laying for us." Pause. Then in a whisper, "He's wallowing around closer to us again, by gracious. Look—look at that. See it? Away up in the air—writhing around like a crooked mainmast. Dim, but—there, *now* don't you see it?"

We stood dead still, hardly breathing. Here and there at little distances the men were gathering silently together and watching and pointing. The deep hush lay like a weight upon one's spirit. Even the faintest quiver of air that went idling by gave out a ghost of sound. A couple of mellow notes floated lingering and fading down from forward:

Booooom——booooom. (Two bells in the middle watch.)

A hoarse low voice—the captain's:

"Silence that damned bell!"

Instantly there was a thrashing commotion out there, with a thundering rush of discharged water, and the monster came charging for us. I caught my breath, and had to seize Turner or I should have fallen, so suddenly my strength collapsed. Then vaguely we saw the creature, waving its arms aloft, tear past the ship stern first, pushing a vast swell ahead and trailing a tumultuous wake behind, and the next moment it was far away and we were plunging and tossing in the sea it made.

"Thank God, *he's* out of practice!" said Turner, with emotion.

The majestic blind devil stopped out there with its moons toward us, and we were miserable again. We had so hoped it would go home.

I resumed my search. Below I found Phillips and Lucy Davis and a number of others searching, but with no hope. They said they had been everywhere, and were merely going over the ground again and again because they could not bear to have it reported to the mother that the search had ceased. She must be told that they were her friends and that she could depend upon them.

Four hours later I gave it up, wearied to exhaustion, and went and sat down by Alice's bed, to be at hand and support her when she should wake and have to hear my desolate story. After a while she stirred, then opened her eyes and smiled brightly and said—

"Oh, what bliss it is! I dreamed that the children—" She flung her arms about me in a transport of grief. "I remember—oh, my God it is true!"

And so, with sobs and lamentations and frantic self-reproaches she poured out her bitter sorrow, and I clasped her close to me, and could not find one comforting word to say.

"Oh, Henry, Henry, your silence means—oh, we cannot live, we cannot bear it!"

There was a flurry of feet along the deck, the door was burst in, and Turner's voice shouted—

"They're found, by God they're found!"

A joy like that brings the shock of a thunderbolt, and for a little while we thought Alice was gone; but then she rallied, and by that time the children were come, and were clasped to her breast, and she was steeped in a happiness for which there were no words. And she said she never dreamed that profanity could sound so dear and sweet, and she asked the mate to say it again; and he did, but left out the profanity and spoiled it.

The children and George and Delia had seen the squid come and lift its moons above our stern and reach its vast tentacles aloft; and they had not waited, but had fled below, and had not stopped till they were deep down in the hold and hidden in a tunnel among the freight. When found, they had had several hours' sleep and were much refreshed.

Between seeing the squid, and getting washed off her feet, and losing the children, the day was a costly one for Alice. It marks the date of her first gray hairs. They were few, but they were to have company.

We lay in a dead calm, and helpless. We could not get away from the squid's neighborhood. But I was obliged to have some sleep, and I took it. I took all I could get, which was six hours. Then young Phillips came and turned me out and said there were signs that the spirit of mutiny was abroad again and that the captain was going to call the men aft and talk to them. Phillips thought I would not want to miss it.

He was right. We had private theatricals, we had concerts, and the other usual time-passers customary on long voyages; but a speech from the captain was the best entertainment the ship's talent could furnish. There was character back of his oratory. He was all sailor. He was sixty years old, and had known no life but sea life. He had no gray hairs, his beard was full and black and shiny; he wore no mustache, therefore his lips were exposed to view; they fitted together like box and lid, and expressed the pluck and resolution that were in him. He had bright black eyes in his old bronze face and they eloquently interpreted all his moods, and his moods were many: for at times he was the youngest man in the ship, and the most cheerful and vivacious and skittish; at times he was the best-natured man in the ship, and he was always the most lovable; sometimes he was sarcastic, sometimes he was serious even to solemnity, sometimes he was stern, sometimes he was as sentimental as a school-girl; sometimes he was silent, quiet, withdrawn within himself, sometimes he was talkative and argumentative; he was remarkably and sincerely and persistently pious, and marvelously and scientifically profane; he was much the strongest man in the ship, and he was also the largest, excepting that plotting, malicious and fearless devil, Stephen Bradshaw the carpenter; he could smile as sweetly as a girl, and it was a pleasure to see him do it. He was entirely self-educated, and had made a vast and picturesque job of it. He was an affectionate creature, and in his family relations he was beautiful; in the eyes of his daughters 'he was omniscient, omnipotent, a mixed sun-god and storm-god, and they feared him and adored him accordingly. He was fond of oratory, and thought he had the gift of it; and so he practiced it now and then, upon occasion, and did it with easy confidence. He was a charming man and a manly man, with a right heart and a fine and daring spirit.

Phillips and I slipped out and moved aft. Things had an unusual and startling aspect. There were flushes of light here and there and yonder; the captain stood in one of them, the officers stood a little way back of him.

"How do matters stand, Phillips?"

"You notice that the battle-lanterns are lit, all the way forward?"

"Yes. The gun-watches are at their posts; I see that. The captain means business, I reckon."

"The gun-watches are mutineers!"

I steadied my voice as well as I could, but there was still a quaver in it when I said—

"Then they've sprung a trap on us, and we are at their mercy, of course."

"It has the look of it. They've caught the old man napping, and we are in a close place this time."

We joined the officers, and just then we heard the measured tramp of the men in the distance. They were coming down from forward. Soon they came into view and moved toward us until they were within three or four paces of the captain.

"Halt!"

They had a leader this time, and it was he that gave the command—Stephen Bradshaw, the carpenter. He had a revolver in his hand. There was a pause, then the captain drew himself up, put on his dignity, and prepared to transact business in a properly impressive and theatrical way. He cleared his voice and said, in a fatherly tone—

"Men, this is your spokesman, duly appointed by you?"

Several responded timidly—

"Yes, sir."

"You have a grievance, and you desire to have it redressed?"

"Yes, sir."

"He is not here to represent himself, lads, but only you?"

"Yes, sir."

"Very well. Your complaint shall be heard, and treated with justice." (Murmur of approbation from the men.) Then the captain's soft manner hardened a little, and he said to the carpenter, "Go on."

Bradshaw was eager to begin, and he flung out his words with aggressive confidence—

"Captain Davis, in the first place this crew wants to know where they *are*. Next, they want this ship put about and pointed for home—straight off, and no fooling. They are tired of this blind voyage, and they ain't going to have any more of it—and that's the word with the bark on it." He paused a moment, for his temper was rising and obstructing his breath; then he continued in a raised and insolent voice and with a showy flourish of his revolver. "Before, they've had no leader, and you talked them down and cowed them; but that ain't going to happen this time. And they hadn't any plans, and warn't fixed for business; but it's different, now." He grew exultant. "Do you see this?"—his revolver. "And do you see that?" He pointed to the gatlings. "We've got the guns; we are boss of the ship. Put her about! That's the order, and it's going to be obeyed."

There was an admiring murmur from the men. After a pause the captain said, with dignity—

"Apparently you are through. Stand aside."

"Stand aside, is it? Not till I have heard what answer you—"

The captain's face darkened and an evil light began to flicker in his eyes, and his hands to twitch. The carpenter glanced at him, then stepped a pace aside, shaking his head and grumbling. "Say your say, then, and cut it short, for I've got something more to say when you're done, if it ain't satisfactory."

The captain's manner at once grew sweet, and even tender, and he turned toward the men with his most genial and winning smile on his face, and proceeded to take them into his confidence.

"You want to know where you are, boys. It is reasonable; it is natural. If we don't know where we are—if we are lost—who is worst off, you or me? You have no children in this ship—I have. If we are in danger have I put us there intentionally? Would I have done it purposely—with my children aboard? Come, what do you think?"

There was a stir among the men, and an approving nodding of heads which conceded that the point was well taken.

"Don't I know my trade, or am I only an apprentice to it? Have I sailed the seas for sixty years and commanded ships for thirty to be taught what to do in a difficulty by—by a damned carpenter?"

He was talking in such a pleading way, such an earnest, and moving and appealing way that the men were not prepared for the close of his remark, and it caught them out and made some of them laugh. He had scored one—and he knew it. The carpenter's back was turned—he was playing indifference. He whirled around and covered the captain with his revolver. Everybody shrank together and caught his breath, except the captain, who said gently—

"Don't be afraid—pull the trigger; it isn't loaded."

The carpenter pulled—twice, thrice, and threw the pistol away. Then he shouted—

"Fall back, men—out of the way!" They surged apart, and he fell back himself. The captain and the officers stood alone in the circle of light. "Gun 4, fire!" The officers threw themselves on their faces on the deck, but the captain remained in his place. The gunner spun the windlass around—there was no result. "Gun 3, fire!" The same thing happened again. The captain said—

"Come back to your places, men." They obeyed, looking puzzled, surprised, and a good deal demoralized. The officers got up, looking astonished and rather ashamed. "Carpenter, come back to your place." He did it, but reluctantly, and swearing to himself. It was easy to see that the captain was contented with his dramatic effects. He resumed his speech, in his pleasantest manner—

"You have mutinied two or three times, boys. It is all right—up to now. I would have done it myself in my common-seaman days, I reckon, if my ship was bewitched and I didn't know where I was. Now then, can you be trusted with the facts? Are we rational men, manly men, men who can stand up and face hard luck and a big difficulty that has been brought about by nobody's fault, and say live or die, survive or perish, we are in for it, for good or bad, and we'll stand by the ship if she goes to hell!" (The men let go a tol[erably] hearty cheer.) "Are we men—grown men—salt-sea men—men nursed upon dangers and cradled in storms—men made in the image of God and ready to do when He commands and die when He calls—or are we just sneaks and curs and carpenters!" (This brought both cheers and laughter, and the captain was happy.) "There—that's the kind. And so I'll tell you how the thing stands. *I* don't know where this ship is, but she's in the hands of God, and that's enough for me, it's enough for you, and it's enough for anybody but a carpenter. If it is God's will that we pull through, we pull through—otherwise not. We haven't had an observation for four months, but we are going ahead, and do our best to fetch up somewhere."

CAPTAIN STORMFIELD'S
VISIT TO HEAVEN

CHAPTER I

I WAS DYING, and knew it. I was making gasps, with long spaces between, and they were standing around the bed, quiet and still, waiting for me to go. Now and then they spoke; and what they said got dimmer and dimmer, and further and further away. I heard it all, though. The mate said—

"He's going out with the tide."

Chips the carpenter said—

"How do you know? No tide out here in the middle of the ocean."

"Yes there is. And anyway, they always do."

It was still again, a while—only the heaving and creaking, and the dull lanterns swinging this way and that, and the wind wheezing and piping, far off. Then I heard a voice, away off—

"Eight bells, sir."

"Make it so," said the mate.

"Ay-ay, sir."

Another voice—

"Freshening up, sir—coming on to blow."

"Sheet home," says the mate. "Reef tops'ls and sky-scrapers, and stand by."

"Ay-ay, sir."

By and by the mate says—

"How's it now?"

"He's cold, up to his ribs," says the doctor. "Give him ten minutes."

"Everything ready, Chips?"

"Canvas, cannon balls and all, sir."

"Bible and burial service?"

"All handy, sir."

Quiet again, for a while—wind so vague it sounded like dream-wind. Then the doctor's voice—

"Is he prepared for the change, do you think?"

"To hell? Oh, I guess so."

"I reckon there ain't any doubt."

It was Chips said it; kind of mournful, too.

"Doubt?" said the mate. "Hadn't any himself, if that's any sign."

"No," says Chips, "he always said he judged he was booked for there."

Long, long stillness. Then the doctor's voice, so far off and dim it sounded like it was down a deep well—

"There—it's over! Just at 12:14!"

Dark? Oh, pitch dark—all in a second! I was dead, and knew it.

I felt myself make a plunge, and recognized that I was flashing through the air like a bird. I had a quick, dim glimpse of the sea and the ship, then everything was black darkness, and nothing visible, and I went whizzing through it. I said to myself, "I'm all here, clothes and all, nothing missing; they'll sink a counterfeit in the sea; it's not me, I'm all here."

Next, it began to get light, and straight off I plunged into a whole universe of blinding fire, and straight through it. It was 12:22 by my watch.

Do you know where I was? In the sun. That was my guess, and it turned out afterwards that I was right. Eight minutes out from port. It gave me my gait—exactly the speed of light, 186,000 miles a second. Ninety-three million miles in eight minutes by the watch. There wasn't ever a prouder ghost. I was as pleased as a child, and wished I had something to race with.

Before I was done thinking these things I was out on the other side and the sun shriveling up to a luminous wad behind me. It was less than a million miles in diameter, and I was through before I had time to get warm. I was in the dark again, now. In the dark; but I myself wasn't dark. My body gave out a soft and ghostly glow and I felt like a lightning bug. I couldn't make out the why of this, but I could read my watch by it, and that was more to the point.

Presently I noticed a glow like my own a little way off, and was glad, and made a trumpet of my hands and hailed it—

"Shipmate ahoy!"

"Same to you!"

"Where from?"

"Chatham Street."

"Whither bound?"

"I vish I knew—aind it?"

"I reckon you're going my way. Name?"

"Solomon Goldstein. Yours?"

"Captain Ben Stormfield, late of Fairhaven and 'Frisco. Come alongside, friend."

He did it. It was a great improvement, having company. I was born sociable, and never could stand solitude. I was trained to a prejudice against Jews—Christians always are, you know—but such of it as I had was in my head, there wasn't any in my heart. But if I had been full of it it would have disappeared then, I was so lonesome and so anxious for company. Dear me, when you are going to—to—where I was going—you are humble-mindeder than you used to be, and thankful for whatever you can get, never mind the quality of it.

We spun along together, and talked, and got acquainted and had a good time. I thought it would be a kindness to Solomon to dissipate his doubts, so that he would have a quiet mind. I could never be comfortable in a state of doubt myself. So I reasoned the thing out, and showed him that his being pointed the same as me was proof of where he was bound for. It cost him a good deal of distress, but in the end he was reconciled and said it was probably best the way it was, he wouldn't be suitable company for angels and they would turn him down if he tried to work in; he had been treated like that in New York, and he judged that the ways of high society were about the same everywhere. He wanted me not to desert him when we got to where we were going, but stay by him, for he would be a stranger and friendless. Poor fellow, I was touched; and promised—"to all eternity."

Then we were quiet a long time, and I let him alone, and let him think. It would do him good. Now and then he sighed, and by and by I found he was crying. You know, I was mad with him in a minute; and says to myself, "Just like a Jew! He has promised some hayseed or other a coat for four dollars, and now he has made up his mind that if he was back he could work off a worse one on him for five. They haven't any heart—that race—nor any principles."

He sobbed along to himself, and I got colder and colder and harder and harder towards him. At last I broke out and said—

"Cheese it! Damn the coat! Drop it out of your mind."

"Goat?"

"Yes. Find something else to cry about."

"Why, I wasn't crying apoud a goat."

"What then?"

"Oh, captain. I lost my little taughter, and now I never, never see her again any more. It break my heart!"

By God, it went through me like a knife! I wouldn't feel so mean again, and so grieved, not for a fleet of ships. And I spoke out and said what I felt; and went on damning myself for a hound till he was so distressed I had to stop; but I wasn't half through. He begged me not to talk so, and said I oughtn't to make so much of what I had done; he said it was only a mistake, and a mistake wasn't a crime.

There now—wasn't it magnanimous? I ask you—wasn't it? I think so. To my mind there was the stuff in him for a Christian; and I came out flat-footed and told him so. And if it hadn't been too late I would have reformed him and made him one, or died in the act.

We were good friends again, and he didn't need to keep his sorrows to himself any more, he could pour them right into my heart, which was wide open and ready; and he did; till it seemed to me I couldn't bear it. Lord, the misery of it! She was his pet, his playfellow, the apple of his eye; she was ten years old, and dead six months, and he was glad to die, himself, so he could have her in his arms again and be with her always—and now that dream was over. Why, she was gone—*forever*. The word had a new meaning. It took my breath, it made me gasp. All our lives we believe we are going to see our lost friends again—we are not disturbed with doubts, we think we *know* it. It is what keeps us alive. And here, in this father's heart that hope was dead. I had never seen that before. This was the first time, and I—why it was I that had killed it. If I had only thought! If I had only kept still, and left him to find it out for himself. He let his tears run, and now and then his trouble wrung a groan out of him, and his lips quivered and he said—

"Poor little Minnie—and poor me."

And to myself I said the same—

"Poor little Minnie—and poor me."

That feeling stayed by me, and never left me. And many's the time, when I was thinking of that poor Jew's disaster, I have said in my thoughts, "I wish I was bound for heaven, and could trade places with him, so he could see his child, damned if I wouldn't do it." If ever you are situated like that, you will understand the feeling.

CHAPTER II

We talked late, and fell asleep pretty tired, about two in the morning;
had a sound sleep, and woke refreshed and fine towards noon. Pitch
dark, still. We were not hungry, but I could have smoked with a
relish, if I had had the things. Also, I could have enjoyed a drink.

We had to stop and think a minute, when we woke, before we
came fully to ourselves and realized our situation, for we thought
we had been dreaming. In fact it was hard to get rid of the idea that
it was all a dream. But we had to get rid of it, and we did. Then a
ghastly cold shock went through us—we remembered where we
were pointed for. Next, we were astonished. Astonished because
we hadn't arrived. Astonished and glad. Glad we hadn't arrived.
Hopeful that we might not arrive for some little time yet.

"How far is it that ve haf come, Captain Sthormfilt?"

"Eleven or twelve hundred million miles."

"Ach Gott, it is a speed!"

"Right you are. There isn't anything that can pass us but thought.
It would take the lightning express twenty-four or twenty-five days
to fly around the globe; we could do it four times in a second—yes,
sir, and do it easy. Solomon, I wish we had something to race with."

Along in the afternoon we saw a soft blur of light a little way off,
north-east-half-east, about two points off the weather bow, and
hailed it. It closed up on us, and turned out to be a corpse by the
name of Bailey, from Oshkosh, that had died at 7:10 the night
before. A good creature, but moody and reflective. Republican in
politics, and had the idea that nothing could save civilization but
that party. He was melancholy, and we got him to talk, so as to
cheer him up; and along by spells, as he got to feeling better, his
private matters got to leaking out—among others, the fact that he
had committed suicide. You know, we had suspected it; he had a
hole through his forehead that you couldn't have plugged with a
marlinespike.

By and by his spirits sagged again. Then the cause came out. He
was delicate and sensitive in his morals, and he had been doing
something in politics, the last thing, which he was wondering if it
was exactly straight. There was an election to fill a vacancy in his
town government, and it was such a close fit that one vote would
decide it. He wasn't going to be there to vote—he was going to be
up here, with us. But if he could keep a democrat from voting, that

would answer just as well, and the republican candidate would pull through. So, when he was ready for suicide he went to a rigidly honorable friend, who was a democrat, and got him to pair off with him. The republican ticket was safe, then, and he killed himself. So he was a little troubled about it, and uncertain; afraid that maybe he hadn't played quite fair, for a Presbyterian.

But Solomon admired him, and thought it was an amazingly smart idea, and just gloated over him with envy, and grinned that Jew grin of intense satisfaction, you know, and slapped his thigh and said—

"Py Chorge, Pailey, almost thou persuadest me to pe a Ghristian."

It was about his girl that he killed himself—Candace Miller. He couldn't ever quite get her to say she loved him, though she seemed to, and had good hopes. But the thing that decided him was a note from her, in which she told him she loved him as a friend, and hoped they would always be friends, but she found her heart belonged to another. Poor Bailey, he broke down there and cried.

Curious! Just then we sighted a blue light a little astern, and hailed it, and when it ranged up alongside Bailey shouted—

"Why Tom Wilson! what a happy surprise; what ever brought you here, comrade?"

Wilson gave him an appealing look that was sort of heartbreaking to see, and said—

"Don't welcome me like that, George, I'm not worthy. I'm a low-down dog, and not fit for any clean man's company."

"Don't!" said Bailey. "Don't talk like that. What is it?"

"George, I did a treacherous thing. To think I could do it to an old playfellow like you, that I was born and raised with! But it was only a silly practical joke, and I never dreamed that any harm could come of it. I wrote that letter. She loved you, George."

"My God!"

"Yes, she did. She was the first one to the house; and when she saw you lying dead in your blood and the letter by you, signed with her name, she read it and knew! She flung herself on your corpse, and kissed your face and your eyes, and poured out her love and her grief and despair, and I saw it. I had murdered you, I had broken her heart, I couldn't bear it—and I am here."

Another suicide, you see. Bailey—well, he couldn't go back, you know, and it was pitiful to see him, he was so frantic over what he had lost by killing himself before ever stopping to find out whether she wrote the letter or not. He kept on regretting and lamenting and wishing he had waited and been more rational, and arranging over and over again in different ways, how he ought to have acted, and how he would act now, if he could only have the chance over again. All no good, of course, and made us miserable to hear it, for he couldn't ever have his chance again forever—we realized that, and the whole ghastliness of the situation. Some people think you are at rest when you die. Let them wait, they'll see.

Solomon took Bailey aside to comfort him—a good idea; people that carry griefs in their hearts know how to comfort others' griefs.

We whizzed along about a week before we picked up another straggler. This time it was a nigger. He was about thirty-eight or forty, and had been a slave nearly half of his life. Named Sam. A cheerful, good-natured cuss, and likeable. As I learned later, a pick-up is a depressing influence upon the company for some time, because he is full of thinkings about his people at home and their grief over losing him; and so his talk is all about that, and he wants sympathy, and cries a good deal, and tells you how dear and good his wife was, or his poor old mother, or his sisters and brothers, and of course in common kindness you have to listen, and it keeps the company feeling desolate and wretched for days together, and starts up their own sorrows over their own loss of family and friends; but when the pick-up is a young person that has lost a sweetheart, that is the worst. There isn't any end to their talk, and their sorrow and their tears. And dear, dear, that one tiresome everlasting question that they keep on asking till you are worn to the bone with it: *don't* we think he (or she) will die soon, and come? What can you say? There's only one thing: *yes,* we hope he will. And when you have said it a couple of thousand times, you lose patience and wish you hadn't died. But dead people are people, just the same, and they bring their habits with them, which is natural. On the earth, when you arrive in a city—any city on the globe—the people peck at you with the same old regular questions—

"First time you have visited our city?"

"How does it impress you?"

"When did you arrive?"

"How long are you going to stay?"

Sometimes you have to leave next day, to get a rest. We arranged differently with the lovers, by and by: we bunched them together to themselves and made them burn their own smoke. And it was no harm; they like it best that way. There was plenty of sympathy and sentiment, and that was what they wanted.

Sam had pipe, tobacco and matches; I cannot tell you how glad I was. But only for a little moment; then there was a sharp disappointment: the matches wouldn't light. Bailey explained it: there was no atmosphere there in space, and the match couldn't burn without oxygen. I said we would keep the things—we might strike through the atmosphere of a planet or a sun, sometime or other, and if it was a big one we might have time for one whiff, anyway. But he said no, it wasn't on the cards.

"Ours are spiritualized bodies and spiritualized clothes and things," he said, "otherwise they would have been consumed in a flash when we first darted through the earth's atmosphere. This is spiritualized tobacco, and fire-proof."

It was very annoying. But I said we would keep it, just the same— "It will burn in hell, anyway."

When the nigger found that that was where I was going, it filled him with distress, and he hoped I was mistaken, and did his best to persuade me I was; but I hadn't any doubts, and so he had to give in. He was as grieved about it as my best friend could be, and tried his best to believe it wouldn't be as hot there as people said, and hoped and believed I would get used to it after a while, and not mind it. His kindly talk won me completely; and when he gave me the pipe and tobacco, and begged me to think of him sometimes when I was smoking, I was a good deal moved. He was a good chap, and like his race: I have seen but few niggers that hadn't their hearts in the right place.

As week after week slipped along by we picked up a straggler at intervals, and at the end of the first year our herd numbered 36. It looked like a flock of glow-worms, and was a quite pretty sight. We could have had a regiment if we had kept all we came across, but the speeds were various and that was an interference. The slowest ship makes the pace for the fleet, of course. I raised our gait a little, as an accommodation, and established it at 200,000 miles a second. Some wanted to get on faster, on account of wanting to join lost friends, so we let them go. I was not in a particular hurry, myself—my business would keep. Some that had been consumptives and such like, were rickety and slow, and they dropped behind and disappeared. Some that were troublesome and disagreeable, and always raising Cain over any little thing that didn't suit them, I ordered off the course, with a competent cursing and a warning to stand clear. We had all sorts left, young and old, and on the whole they were satisfactory enough, though a few of them were not up to standard, I will admit.

CHAPTER III

Well, when I had been dead about thirty years, I begun to get a little anxious. Mind you, I had been whizzing through space all that time, like a comet. *Like* a comet! Why, Peters, I laid over the lot of them! Of course there warn't any of them going my way, as a steady thing, you know, because they travel in a long circle like the loop of a lasso, whereas I was pointed as straight as a dart for Hereafter; but I happened on one every now and then that was going my way for an hour or so, and then we had a bit of a brush together. But it was generally pretty one-sided, because I sailed by them the same as if they were standing still. An ordinary comet don't make more than about 200,000 miles a minute. Of course when I came across one of that sort—like Encke's and Halley's comets, for instance—it warn't anything but just a flash and a vanish, you see. You couldn't rightly call it a race. It was as if the comet was a gravel-train and I was a telegraph despatch. But after I got outside of our astronomical system, I used to flush a comet occasionally that was something *like*. We haven't got any such comets—ours don't begin. One night I was swinging along at a good round gait, everything taut and trim, and the wind in my favor—I judged I was going about a million miles a minute—it might have been more, it couldn't have been less—when I flushed a most uncommonly big one about three points off my starboard bow. By his stern lights I judged he was bearing about northeast-and-by-north-half-east. Well, it was so near my course that I wouldn't throw away the chance; so I fell off a point, steadied my helm, and went for him. You should have heard me whiz, and seen the electric fur fly! In about a minute and a half I was fringed out with an electrical nimbus that flamed around for miles and miles and lit up all space like broad day. The comet was burning blue in the distance, like a sickly torch, when I first sighted him, but he begun to grow bigger and bigger as I crept up on him. I slipped up on him so fast that when I had gone about 150,000,000 miles I was close enough to be swallowed up in the phosphorescent glory of his wake, and I couldn't see anything for the glare. Thinks I, it won't do to run into him, so I shunted to one side and tore along. By and by I closed up abreast of his tail. Do you know what it was like? It was like a gnat closing up on the continent of America. I forged along. By and by I had sailed along his coast for a little upwards of a hundred and fifty million miles and then I could see by the shape of him that I hadn't even got up to his waistband yet. Why, Peters, we don't know anything about comets, down here. If you want to see comets that are comets, you've got to go outside of our solar system—where there's room for them, you understand. My friend, I've seen comets out there that couldn't even lay down inside the *orbits* of our noblest comets without their tails hanging over.

Well, I boomed along another hundred and fifty million miles, and got up abreast his shoulder, as you may say. I was feeling pretty fine, I tell you; but just then I noticed the officer of the deck come to the side and hoist his glass in my direction. Straight off I heard him sing out—

"Below there, ahoy! Shake her up, shake her up! Heave on a hundred million billion tons of brimstone!"

"Ay—ay, sir!"

"Pipe the stabboard watch! All hands on deck!"

"Ay—ay, sir!"

"Send two hundred thousand million men aloft to shake out royals and sky-scrapers!"

"Ay—ay, sir!"

"Hand the stuns'ls! Hang out every rag you've got! Clothe her from stem to rudder-post!"

"Ay—ay, sir!"

In about a second I begun to see I'd woke up a pretty ugly customer, Peters. In less than ten seconds that comet was just a blazing cloud of red-hot canvas. It was piled up into the heavens clean out of sight—the old thing seemed to swell out and occupy all space; the sulphur smoke from the furnaces—oh, well, nobody can describe the way it rolled and tumbled up into the skies, and nobody can half describe the way it smelt. Neither can anybody begin to describe the way the monstrous craft begun to crash along. And such another powwow—thousands of bo's'n's whistles screaming at once, and a crew like the populations of a hundred thousand worlds like ours all swearing at once. Well, I never heard the like of it before.

We roared and thundered along side by side, both doing our level best, because I'd never struck a comet before that could lay over me, and so I was bound to beat this one or break something. I judged I had some reputation in space, and I calculated to keep it. I noticed I wasn't gaining as fast, now, as I was before, but still I was gaining. There was a power of excitement on board the comet. Upwards of a hundred billion passengers swarmed up from below and rushed to the side and begun to bet on the race. Of course this careened her and damaged her speed. My, but wasn't the mate mad! He jumped at the crowd, with his trumpet in his hand, and sung out—

"Amidships! amidships, you—! or I'll brain the last idiot of you!"

Well, sir, I gained and gained, little by little, till at last I went skimming sweetly by the magnificent old conflagration's nose. By this time the captain of the comet had been rousted out, and he stood there in the red glare for'ard, by the mate, in his shirt-sleeves and slippers, his hair all rats' nests and one suspender hanging, and how sick those two men did look! I just simply couldn't help putting my thumb to my nose as I glided away and singing out:

"Ta-ta! ta-ta! Any word to send to your family?"

Peters, it was a mistake. Yes, sir, I've often regretted that—it was a mistake. You see, the captain had given up the race, but that remark was too tedious for him—he couldn't stand it. He turned to the mate, and says he—

"Have we got brimstone enough of our own to make the trip?"

"Yes, sir."

"Sure?"

"Yes, sir, more than enough."

"How much have we got in cargo for Satan?"

"Eighteen hundred thousand billion quintillions of kazarks."

"Very well, then, let his boarders freeze till the next comet comes. Lighten ship! Lively, now, lively, men! Heave the whole cargo overboard!"

Peters, look me in the eye, and be calm. I found out, over there, that a kazark is exactly the bulk of a *hundred and sixty-nine worlds like ours*! They hove all that load overboard. When it fell it wiped out a considerable raft of stars just as clean as if they'd been candles and somebody blowed them out. As for the race, that was at an end. The minute she was lightened the comet swung along by me the same as if I was anchored. The captain stood on the stern, by the afterdavits, and put his thumb to his nose and sung out—

"Ta-ta! ta-ta! Maybe *you've* got some message to send your friends in the Everlasting Tropics!"

Then he hove up on his other suspender and started for'ard, and inside of three-quarters of an hour his craft was only a pale torch again in the distance. Yes, it was a mistake, Peters—that remark of mine. I don't reckon I'll ever get over being sorry about it. I'd 'a' beat the bully of the firmament if I'd kept my mouth shut.

*

But I've wandered a little off the track of my tale; I'll get back on my course again. Now you see what kind of speed I was making. So, as I said, when I had been tearing along this way about thirty years I begun to get uneasy. Oh, it was pleasant enough, with a good deal to find out, but then it was kind of lonesome, you know. Besides, I wanted to get somewhere. I hadn't shipped with the idea of cruising forever. First off, I liked the delay, because I judged I was going with its fire and its glare—light enough then, of course, but towards the last I begun to feel that I'd rather go to— well, most any place, so as to finish up the uncertainty.

Well, one night—it was always night, except when I was rushing by some star that was occupying the whole universe with its fire and its glare—light enough then, of course, but I necessarily left it behind in a minute or two and plunged into a solid week of darkness again. The stars ain't so close together as they look to be. Where was I? Oh yes; one night I was sailing along, when I discovered a tremendous long row of blinking lights away on the horizon ahead. As I approached, they begun to tower and swell and look like mighty furnaces. Says I to myself—

"By George, I've arrived at last—and at the wrong place, just as I expected!"

Then I fainted. I don't know how long I was insensible, but it must have been a good while, for, when I came to, the darkness was all gone and there was the loveliest sunshine and the balmiest, fragrantest air in its place. And there was such a marvellous world spread out before me—such a glowing, beautiful, bewitching country. The things I took for furnaces were gates, miles high, made all of flashing jewels, and they pierced a wall of solid gold that you couldn't see the top of, nor yet the end of, in either direction. I was pointed straight for one of these gates, and a-coming like a house afire. Now I noticed that the skies were black with millions of people, pointed for those gates. What a roar they made, rushing through the air! The ground was as thick as ants with people, too— billions of them, I judge.

I lit. I drifted up to a gate with a swarm of people, and when it was my turn the head clerk says, in a businesslike way—

"Well, quick! Where are you from?"

"San Francisco," says I.

"San Fran—*what?*" says he.

"San Francisco."

He scratched his head and looked puzzled, then he says—

"Is it a planet?"

By George, Peters, think of it! "*Planet?*" says I; "it's a city. And moreover, it's one of the biggest and finest and—"

"There, there!" says he, "no time here for conversation. We don't deal in cities here. Where are you from in a *general* way?"

"Oh," I says, "I beg your pardon. Put me down for California."

I had him *again*, Peters! He puzzled a second, then he says, sharp and irritable—

"I don't know any such planet—is it a constellation?"

"Oh, my goodness!" says I. "Constellation, says you? No—it's a State."

"Man, we don't deal in States here. *Will* you tell me where you are from *in general—at large,* don't you understand?"

"Oh, now I get your idea," I says. "I'm from America—the United States of America."

Peters, do you know I had him *again?* If I hadn't I'm a clam! His face was as blank as a target after a militia shooting-match. He turned to an under clerk and says—

"Where is America? *What* is America?"

The under clerk answered up prompt and says—

"There ain't any such orb."

"*Orb?*" says I. "Why, what are you talking about, young man? It ain't an orb; it's a country; it's a continent. Columbus discovered it; I reckon likely you've heard of *him*, anyway. America—why, sir, America—"

"Silence!" says the head clerk. "Once for all, where—are—you—*from?*"

"Well," says I, "I don't know anything more to say—unless I lump things, and just say I'm from the world."

"Ah," says he, brightening up, "now that's something like! *What* world?"

Peters, he had *me,* that time. I looked at him, puzzled, he looked at me, worried. Then he burst out—

"Come, come, what world?"

Says I, "Why, *the* world, of course."

"*The* world!" he says. "H'm! there's billions of them! . . . Next!"

That meant for me to stand aside. I done so, and a skyblue man with seven heads and only one leg hopped into my place. I took a walk. It just occurred to me, then, that all the myriads I had seen swarming to that gate, up to this time, were just like that creature. I tried to run across somebody I was acquainted with, but they were out of acquaintances of mine just then. So I thought the thing all over and finally sidled back there pretty meek and feeling rather stumped, as you may say.

"Well?" said the head clerk.

"Well, sir," I says, pretty humble, "I don't seem to make out which world it is I'm from. But you may know it from this—it's the one the Saviour saved."

He bent his head at the Name. Then he says, gently—

"The worlds He has saved are like to the gates of heaven in number—none can count them. What astronomical system is your world in?—perhaps that may assist."

"It's the one that has the sun in it—and the moon—and Mars"— he shook his head at each name—hadn't ever heard of them, you see—"and Neptune—and Uranus—and Jupiter—"

"Hold on!" says he—"hold on a minute! Jupiter . . . Jupiter . . . Seems to me we had a man from there eight or nine hundred years ago—but people from that system very seldom enter by this gate." All of a sudden he begun to look me so straight in the eye that I thought he was going to bore through me. Then he says, very deliberate, "Did you come *straight here* from your system?"

"Yes, sir" I says—but I blushed the least little bit in the world when I said it.

He looked at me very stern, and says—

"That is not true, and this is not the place for prevarication. You wandered from your course. How did that happen?"

Says I, blushing again—

"I'm sorry, and I take back what I said, and confess. I raced a little with a comet one day—only just the least little bit—only the tiniest lit—"

"So—so," says he—and without any sugar in his voice to speak of.

I went on, and says—

"But I only fell off just a bare point, and I went right back on my course again the minute the race was over."

"No matter—that divergence has made all this trouble. It has brought you to a gate that is billions of leagues from the right one. If you had gone to your own gate they would have known all about your world at once and there would have been no delay. But we will try to accommodate you." He turned to an under clerk and says—

"What system is Jupiter in?"

"I don't remember, sir, but I think there is such a planet in one of the little new systems away out in one of the thinly worlded corners of the universe. I will see."

He got a balloon and sailed up and up and up, in front of a map that was as big as Rhode Island. He went on till he was out of sight, and by and by he came down and got something to eat and went up again. To cut a long story short, he kept on doing this for a day or two, and finally he came down and said he thought he had found that solar system, but it might be fly-specks. So he got a microscope and went back. It turned out better than he feared. He had rousted out our system, sure enough. He got me to describe our planet and its distance from the sun, and then he says to his chief—

"Oh, I know the one he means now, sir. It is on the map. It is called the Wart."

Says I to myself, "Young man, it wouldn't be wholesome for you to go down *there* and call it the Wart."

Well, they let me in, then, and told me I was safe forever and wouldn't have any more trouble.

Then they turned from me and went on with their work, the same as if they considered my case all complete and shipshape. I was a good deal surprised at this, but I was diffident about speaking up and reminding them. I did so hate to do it, you know; it seemed a pity to bother them, they had so much on their hands. Twice I thought I would give up and let the thing go; so twice I started to leave, but immediately I thought what a figure I should cut stepping out amongst the redeemed in such a rig, and that made me hang back and come to anchor again. People got to eying me—clerks, you know—wondering why I didn't get under way. I couldn't stand this long—it was too uncomfortable. So at last I plucked up courage and tipped the head clerk a signal. He says—

"What! you here yet? What's wanting?"

Says I, in a low voice and very confidential, making a trumpet with my hand at his ear—

"I beg pardon, and you mustn't mind my reminding you, and seeming to meddle, but hain't you forgot something?"

He studied a second, and says—

"Forgot something? . . . No, not that I know of."

"Think," says I.

He thought. Then he says—

"No, I can't seem to have forgot anything. What is it?"

"Look at me," says I, "look me all over."

He done it.

"Well?" says he.

"Well," says I, "you don't notice anything? If I branched out amongst the elect looking like this, wouldn't I attract considerable attention?—wouldn't I be a little conspicuous?"

"Well," he says, "I don't see anything the matter. What do you lack?"

"Lack! Why, I lack my harp, and my wreath, and my halo, and my hymn-book, and my palm branch—I lack everything that a body naturally requires up here, my friend."

Puzzled? Peters, he was the worst puzzled man you ever saw. Finally he says—

"Well, you seem to be a curiosity every way a body takes you. I never heard of these things before."

I looked at the man awhile in solid astonishment; then I says—

"Now, I hope you don't take it as an offence, for I don't mean any, but really, for a man that has been in the Kingdom as long as I reckon you have, you do seem to know powerful little about its customs."

"Its customs!" says he. "Heaven is a large place, good friend. Large empires have many and diverse customs. Even small dominions have, as you know by what you have seen of the matter on a small scale in the Wart. How can you imagine I could ever learn the varied customs of the countless kingdoms of heaven? It makes my head ache to think of it. I know the customs that prevail in those portions inhabited by peoples that are appointed to enter by my own gate—and hark ye, that is quite enough knowledge for one individual to try to pack into his head in the thirty-seven millions of years I have devoted night and day to that study. But the idea of learning the customs of the whole appalling expanse of heaven—O man, how insanely you talk! Now I don't doubt that this odd costume you talk about is the fashion in that district of heaven you belong to, but you won't be conspicuous in this section without it."

I felt all right, if that was the case, so I bade him good-day and left. All day I walked towards the far end of a prodigious hall of the office, hoping to come out into heaven any moment, but it was a mistake. That hall was built on the general heavenly plan—it naturally couldn't be small. At last I got so tired I couldn't go any farther; so I sat down to rest, and begun to tackle the queerest sort of strangers and ask for information; but I didn't get any; they couldn't understand my language, and I could not understand theirs. I got dreadfully lonesome. I was so downhearted and home-sick I wished a hundred times I never had died. I turned back, of course. About noon next day, I got back at last and was on hand at the booking-office once more. Says I to the head clerk—

"I begin to see that a man's got to be in his own heaven to be happy."

"Perfectly correct," says he. "Did you imagine the same heaven would suit all sorts of men?"

"Well, I had that idea—but I see the foolishness of it. Which way am I to go to get to my district?"

He called the under clerk that had examined the map, and he gave me general directions. I thanked him and started; but he says—

"Wait a minute; it is millions of leagues from here. Go outside and stand on that red wishing-carpet; shut your eyes, hold your breath, and wish yourself there."

"I'm much obliged," says I; "why didn't you dart me through when I first arrived?"

"We have a good deal to think of here; it was your place to think of it and ask for it. Good-by; we probably shan't see you in this region for a thousand centuries or so."

"In that case, *o revoor*," says I.

I hopped onto the carpet and held my breath and shut my eyes and wished I was in the booking-office of my own section. The very next instant a voice I knew sung out in a business kind of way—

"A harp and a hymn-book, pair of wings and a halo, size 13, for Cap'n Eli Stormfield, of San Francisco!—make him out a clean bill of health, and let him in."

I opened my eyes. Sure enough, it was a Pi Ute Injun I used to know in Tulare County; mighty good fellow—I remember being at his funeral, which consisted of him being burnt and the other Injuns gauming their faces with his ashes and howling like wildcats. He was powerful glad to see me, and you may make up your mind I was just as glad to see him, and feel that I was in the right kind of a heaven at last.

Just as far as your eye could reach, there was swarms of clerks, running and bustling around, tricking out thousands of Yanks and Mexicans and English and A-rabs, and all sorts of people in their new outfits; and when they gave me my kit and I put on my halo and took a look in the glass, I could have jumped over a house for joy, I was so happy.

"Now *this* is something like!" says I.

"Now," says I, "I'm all right—show me a cloud."

Inside of fifteen minutes I was a mile on my way towards the cloud-banks and about a million people along with me. Most of us tried to fly, but some got crippled and nobody made a success of it. So we concluded to walk, for the present, till we had had some wing practice.

We begun to meet swarms of folks who were coming back. Some had harps and nothing else; some had hymn-books and nothing else; some had nothing at all; all of them looked meek and uncomfortable; one young fellow hadn't anything left but his halo, and he was carrying that in his hand; all of a sudden he offered it to me and says—

"Will you hold it for me a minute?"

Then he disappeared in the crowd. I went on. A woman asked me to hold her palm branch, and then *she* disappeared. A girl got me to hold her harp for her, and by George, *she* disappeared; and so on and so on, till I was about loaded down to the guards. Then comes a smiling old gentleman and asked me to hold *his* things. I swabbed off the perspiration and says, pretty tart—

"I'll have to get you to excuse me, my friend,—*I* ain't no hat-rack."

About this time I begun to run across piles of those traps, lying in the road. I just quietly dumped my extra cargo along with them. I looked around, and, Peters, that whole nation that was following me were loaded down the same as I'd been. The return crowd had got them to hold their things a minute, you see. They all dumped their loads, too, and we went on.

When I found myself perched on a cloud, with a million other people, I never felt so good in my life. Says I, "Now this is according to the promises; I've been having my doubts, but now I *am* in heaven, sure enough." I gave my palm branch a wave or two, for luck, and then I tautened up my harp-strings and struck in. Well, Peters, you can't imagine anything like the row we made. It was grand to listen to, and made a body thrill all over, but there was considerable many tunes going on at once, and that was a drawback to the harmony, you understand; and then there was a lot of Injun tribes, and they kept up such another war-whooping that they kind of took the tuck out of the music. By and by I quit performing, and judged I'd take a rest. There was quite a nice mild old gentleman sitting next me, and I noticed he didn't take a hand; I encouraged him, but he said he was naturally bashful, and was afraid to try before so many people. By and by the old gentleman said he never could seem to enjoy music somehow. The fact was I was beginning to feel the same way; but I didn't say anything. Him and I had a considerable long silence, then, but of course it warn't noticeable in that place. After about sixteen or seventeen hours, during which I played and sung a little, now and then—always the same tune, because I didn't know any other—I laid down my harp and begun to fan myself with my palm branch. Then we both got to sighing pretty regular. Finally says he—

"Don't you know any tune but the one you've been pegging at all day?"

"Not another blessed one," says I.

"Don't you reckon you could learn another one?" says he.

"Never," says I; "I've tried to, but I couldn't manage it."

"It's a long time to hang to the one—eternity, you know."

"Don't break my heart," says I; "I'm getting low-spirited enough already."

After another long silence, says he—

"Are you glad to be here?"

Says I, "Old man, I'll be frank with you. This *ain't* just as near my idea of bliss as I thought it was going to be, when I used to go to church."

Says he, "What do you say to knocking off and calling it half a day?"

'That's me," says I. "I never wanted to get off watch so bad in my life."

So we started. Millions were coming to the cloud-bank all the time, happy and hosannahing; millions were leaving it all the time, looking mighty quiet, I tell you. We laid for the new-comers, and pretty soon I'd got them to hold my things a minute, and then I was a free man again and most outrageously happy. Just then I ran across old Sam Bartlett, who had been dead a long time, and stopped to have a talk with him. Says I—

"Now tell me—is this to go on forever? Ain't there anything else for a change?"

Says he—

"I'll set you right on that point very quick. People take the figurative language of the Bible and the allegories for literal, and the first thing they ask for when they get here is a halo and a harp, and so on. Nothing that's harmless and reasonable is refused a body here, if he asks it in the right spirit. So they are outfitted with these things without a word. They go and sing and play just about one day, and that's the last you'll ever see them in the choir. They don't need anybody to tell them that that sort of thing wouldn't make a heaven—at least not a heaven that a sane man could stand a week and remain sane. That cloud-bank is placed where the noise can't disturb the old inhabitants, and so there ain't any harm in letting everybody get up there and cure himself as soon as he comes.

"Now you just remember this—heaven is as blissful and lovely as it can be; but it's just the busiest place you ever heard of. There ain't any idle people here after the first day. Singing hymns and waving palm branches through all eternity is pretty when you hear about it in the pulpit, but it's as poor a way to put in valuable time as a body could contrive. It would just make a heaven of warbling ignoramuses, don't you see? Eternal Rest sounds comforting in the pulpit, too. Well, you try it once, and see how heavy time will hang on your hands. Why, Stormfield, a man like you, that had been active and stirring all his life, would go mad in six months in a heaven where he hadn't anything to do. Heaven is the very last place to come to *rest* in,—and don't you be afraid to bet on that!"

Says I—

"Sam, I'm as glad to hear it as I thought I'd be sorry. I'm glad I come, now."

Says he——

"Cap'n, ain't you pretty physically tired?"

Says I—

"Sam, it ain't any name for it! I'm dog-tired."

"Just so—just so. You've earned a good sleep, and you'll get it. You've earned a good appetite, and you'll enjoy your dinner. It's the same here as it is on earth—you've got to earn a thing, square and honest, before you enjoy it. You can't enjoy first and earn afterwards. But there's this difference, here: you can choose your own occupation, and all the powers of heaven will be put forth to help you make a success of it, if you do your level best. The shoemaker on earth that had the soul of a poet in him won't have to make shoes here."

"Now that's all reasonable and right," says I. "Plenty of work, and the kind you hanker after; no more pain, no more suffering—"

"Oh, hold on; there's plenty of pain here—but it don't kill. There's plenty of suffering here, but it don't last. You see, happiness ain't a *thing in itself*—it's only a *contrast* with something that ain't pleasant. That's all it is. There ain't a thing you can mention that is happiness in its own self—it's only so by contrast with the other thing. And so, as soon as the novelty is over and the force of the contrast dulled, it ain't happiness any longer, and you have to get something fresh. Well, there's plenty of pain and suffering in heaven—consequently there's plenty of contrasts and just no end of happiness."

Says I, "It's the sensiblest heaven I've heard of yet, Sam, though it's about as different from the one I was brought up on as a live princess is different from her own wax figger."

Along in the first months I knocked around about the Kingdom, making friends and finally settled down in a pretty likely region, to have a rest before taking another start. I went on making acquaintances and gathering up information. I had a good deal of talk with an old bald-headed angel by the name of Sandy McWilliams. He was from somewhere in New Jersey. I went about with him, considerable. We used to lay around, warm afternoons, in the shade of a rock, on some meadow-ground that was pretty high and out of the marshy slush of his cranberry-farm, and there we used to talk about all kinds of things and smoke pipes. One day, says I—

"About how old might you be, Sandy?"

"Seventy-two."

"I judged so. How long you been in heaven?"

"Twenty-seven years, come Christmas."

"How old was you when you come up?"

"Why, seventy-two, of course."

"You can't mean it!"

"Why can't I mean it!"

"Because, if you was seventy-two then, you are naturally ninety-nine now."

"No, but I ain't. I stay the same age I was when I come."

"Well," says I, "come to think, there's something just here that I want to ask about. Down below, I always had an idea that in heaven we would all be young, and bright, and spry."

"Well, you *can* be young if you want to. You've only got to wish."

"Well, then why didn't you wish?"

"I did. They all did. You'll try it, some day, like enough; but you'll get tired of the change pretty soon."

"Why?"

"Well, I'll tell you. Now you've always been a sailor; did you ever try some other business?"

"Yes, I tried keeping grocery, once, up in the mines; but I couldn't stand it; it was too dull—no stir, no storm, no life about it; it was like being part dead and part alive, both at the same time. I wanted to be one thing or t'other. I shut up shop pretty quick and went to sea."

"That's it. Grocery people like it, but you couldn't. You see you wasn't used to it. Well, I wasn't used to being young, and I couldn't seem to take any interest in it. I was strong, and handsome, and had curly hair,—yes, and wings, too!—gay wings like a butterfly. I went to picnics and dances and parties with the fellows, and tried to carry on and talk nonsense with the girls, but it wasn't any use; I couldn't take to it—fact is, it was an awful bore. What I wanted was early to bed and early to rise, and something to *do;* and when my work was done, I wanted to sit quiet, and smoke and think—not tear around with a parcel of giddy young kids. You can't think what I suffered whilst I was young."

"How long was you young?"

"Only two weeks. That was plenty for me. Laws, I was so lonesome! You see, I was full of the knowledge and experience of seventy-two years; the deepest subject those young folks could strike was only *a-b-c-* to me. And to hear them argue—oh, my! it would have been funny, if it hadn't been so pitiful. Well, I was so hungry for the ways and the sober talk I was used to, that I tried to ring in with the old people, but they wouldn't have it. They considered me a conceited young upstart, and gave me the cold shoulder. Two weeks was a-plenty for me. I was glad to get back my bald head again, and my pipe, and my old drowsy reflections in the shade of a rock or a tree."

"Well," says I, "do you mean to say you're going to stand still at seventy-two, forever?"

"I don't know, and I ain't particular. But I ain't going to drop back to twenty-five any more—I know that, mighty well. I know a sight more than I did twenty-seven years ago, and I enjoy learning, all the time, but I don't seem to get any older. That is, bodily—my mind gets older, and stronger, and better seasoned, and more satisfactory."

Says I, "If a man comes here at ninety, don't he ever set himself back?"

"Of course he does. He sets himself back to fourteen; tries it a couple of hours, and feels like a fool; sets himself forward to twenty; it ain't much improvement; tries thirty, fifty, eighty, and finally ninety—finds he is more at home and comfortable at the same old figure he is used to than any other way. Or, if his mind begun to fail him on earth at eighty, that's where he finally sticks up here. He sticks at the place where his mind was last at its best, for there's where his enjoyment is best, and his ways most set and established."

"Does a chap of twenty-five stay always twenty-five, and look it?"

"If he is a fool, yes. But if he is bright, and ambitious and industrious, the knowledge he gains and the experiences he has, change his ways and thoughts and likings, and make him find his best pleasure in the company of people above that age; so he allows his body to take on that look of as many added years as he needs to make him comfortable and proper in that sort of society; he lets his body go on taking the look of age, according as he progresses, and by and by he will be bald and wrinkled outside, and wise and deep within."

"Babies the same?"

"Babies the same. Laws, what asses we used to be, on earth, about these things! We said we'd be always young in heaven. We didn't say *how* young—we didn't think of that, perhaps—that is, we didn't all think alike, anyway. When I was a boy of seven, I suppose I thought we'd all be twelve, in heaven; when I was twelve, I suppose I thought we'd all be eighteen or twenty in heaven; when I was forty, I begun to go back; I remember I hoped we'd all be about *thirty* years old in heaven. Neither a man nor a boy ever thinks the age he *has* is exactly the best one—he puts the *right* age a few years older or a few years younger than he is. Then he makes that ideal age the general age of the heavenly people. And he expects everybody to

stick at that age—stand stock-still—and expects them to enjoy it!—
Now just think of the idea of standing still in heaven! Think of a
heaven made up entirely of hoop-rolling, marble-playing cubs of
seven years!—or of awkward, diffident, sentimental immaturities of
nineteen—or of vigorous people of thirty, healthy-minded,
brimming with ambition, but chained hand and foot to that one
age and its limitations like so many galley-slaves! Think of the dull
sameness of a society made up of people all of one age and one set
of looks, habits, tastes and feelings. Think how superior to it earth
would be, with its variety of types and faces and ages, and the
enlivening attrition of the myriad interests that come into pleasant
collision in such a variegated society."

"Look here," says I, "do you know what you're doing?"

"Well, what am I doing?"

"You are making heaven pretty comfortable in one way, but you
are playing the mischief with it in another."

"How'd you mean?"

"Well," I says, "take a young mother that's lost her child, and—"

" 'Sh!" he says. "Look!"

It was a woman. Middle-aged, and had grizzled hair. She was
walking slow, and her head was bent down, and her wings hanging
limp and droopy; and she looked ever so tired, and was crying,
poor thing! She passed along by, with her head down, that way,
and the tears running down her face, and didn't see us. Then Sandy
said, low and gentle, and full of pity:

"*She's* hunting for her child! No, *found* it, I reckon. Lord, how she's
changed! But I recognized her in a minute, though it's twenty-seven
years since I saw her. A young mother she was, about twenty-two
or four, or along there; and blooming and lovely and sweet! oh, just
a flower! And all her heart and all her soul was wrapped up in her
child, her little girl, two years old. And it died, and she went wild
with grief, just wild! Well, the only comfort she had was that she'd
see her child again, in heaven—'never more to part,' she said, and
kept on saying it over and over, 'never more to part.' And the
words made her happy; yes, they did; they made her joyful; and
when I was dying, twenty-seven years ago, she told me to find her
child the first thing, and say she was coming—'soon, soon, *very*
soon, she hoped and believed!' "

"Why, it's pitiful, Sandy."

He didn't say anything for a while, but sat looking at the ground,
thinking. Then he says, kind of mournful:

"And now she's come!"

"Well? Go on."

"Stormfield, maybe she hasn't found the child, but I think she has. Looks so to me. I've seen cases before. You see, she's kept that child in her head just the same as it was when she jounced it in her arms a little chubby thing. But here it didn't elect to *stay* a child. No, it elected to grow up, which it did. And in these twenty-seven years it has learned all the deep scientific learning there is to learn, and is studying and studying and learning and learning more and more, all the time, and don't give a damn for anything *but* learning; just learning, and discussing gigantic problems with people like herself."

"Well?"

"Stormfield, don't you see? Her mother knows *cranberries,* and how to tend them, and pick them, and put them up, and market them; and not another blamed thing! Her and her daughter can't be any more company for each other *now* than mud turtle and bird o' paradise. Poor thing, she was looking for a baby to jounce; I think she's struck a disapp'intment."

"Sandy, what will they do—stay unhappy forever in heaven?"

"No, they'll come together and get adjusted by and by. But not this year, and not next. By and by."

CHAPTER IV

I had been having considerable trouble with my wings. The day after I helped the choir I made a dash or two with them, but was not lucky. First off, I flew thirty yards, and then fouled an Irishman and brought him down—brought us both down, in fact. Next, I had a collision with a Bishop—and bowled him down, of course. We had some sharp words, and I felt pretty cheap, to come banging into a grave old person like that, with a million strangers looking on and smiling to themselves.

I saw I hadn't got the hang of the steering, and so couldn't rightly tell where I was going to bring up when I started. I went afoot the rest of the day, and let my wings hang. Early next morning I went to a private place to have some practice. I got up on a pretty high rock, and got a good start, and went swooping down, aiming for a bush a little over three hundred yards off; but I couldn't seem to calculate for the wind, which was about two points abaft my beam.

I could see I was going considerable to looard of the bush, so I worked my starboard wing slow and went ahead strong on the port one, but it wouldn't answer; I could see I was going to broach to, so I slowed down on both, and lit. I went back to the rock and took another chance at it. I aimed two or three points to starboard of the bush—yes, more than that—enough so as to make it nearly a head-wind. I done well enough, but made pretty poor time. I could see, plain enough, that on a head-wind, wings was a mistake. I could see that a body could sail pretty close to the wind, but he couldn't go in the wind's eye. I could see that if I wanted to go a-visiting any distance from home, and the wind was ahead, I might have to wait days, maybe, for a change; and I could see, too, that these things could not be any use at all in a gale; if you tried to run before the wind, you would make a mess of it, for there isn't any way to shorten sail—like reefing, you know—you have to take it *all* in—shut your feathers down flat to your sides. That would *land* you, of course. You could lay to, with your head to the wind—that is the best you could do, and right hard work you'd find it, too. If you tried any other game, you would founder, sure.

I judge it was about a couple of weeks or so after this that I dropped old Sandy McWilliams a note one day—it was a Tuesday—and asked him to come over and take his manna and quails with me next day; and the first thing he did when he stepped in was to twinkle his eye in a sly way, and say—

"Well, Cap, what you done with your wings?"

I saw in a minute that there was some sarcasm done up in that rag somewheres, but I never let on. I only says—

"Gone to the wash."

"Yes," he says, in a dry sort of way, "they mostly go to the wash—about this time—I've often noticed it. Fresh angels are powerful neat. When do you look for 'em back?"

"Day after to-morrow," says I.

He winked at me, and smiled.

Says I—

"Sandy, out with it. Come—no secrets among friends. I notice you don't ever wear wings—and plenty others don't. I've been making an ass of myself—is that it?"

"That is about the size of it. But it is no harm. We all do it at first. It's perfectly natural. You see, on earth we jump to such foolish conclusions as to things up here. In the pictures we always saw the angels with wings on—and that was all right; but we jumped to the conclusion that that was their way of getting around—and that was all wrong. The wings ain't anything but a uniform, that's all. When they are in the field—so to speak,—they always wear them; you never see an angel going with a message anywhere without his wings, any more than you would see a military officer presiding at a court-martial without his uniform, or a postman delivering letters, or a policeman walking his beat, in plain clothes. But they ain't to *fly* with! The wings are for show, not for use. Old experienced angels are like officers of the regular army—they dress plain, when they are off duty. New angels are like the militia—never shed the uniform—always fluttering and floundering around in their wings, butting people down, flapping here, and there, and everywhere, always imagining they are attracting the admiring eye—well, they just think they are the very most important people in heaven. And when you see one of them come sailing around with one wing tipped up and t'other down, you make up your mind he is saying to himself: 'I wish Mary Ann in Arkansaw could see me now. I reckon she'd wish she hadn't shook me.' No, they're just for show, that's all—only just for show."

"I judge you've got it about right, Sandy," says I.

"Why, look at it yourself," says he. "*You* ain't built for wings—no man is. You know what a grist of years it took you to come here from the earth—and yet you were booming along faster than any cannon-ball could go. Suppose you had to fly that distance with your wings—wouldn't eternity have been over before you got here? Certainly. Well, angels have to go to the earth every day—millions of them—to appear in visions to dying children and good people, you know—it's the heft of their business. They appear with their wings, of course, because they are on official service, and because the dying persons wouldn't know they were angels if they hadn't wings—but do you reckon they fly with them? It stands to reason they don't. The wings would wear out before they got half-way; even the pin-feathers would be gone; the wing frames would be as bare as kite sticks before the paper is pasted on. The distances in heaven are billions of times greater, angels have to go all over heaven every day; could they do it with their wings alone? No, indeed; they wear the wings for style, but they travel any distance in an instant by *wishing*. The wishing-carpet of the Arabian Nights was a sensible idea—but our earthly idea of angels flying these awful distances with their clumsy wings was foolish.

"Our young saints, of both sexes, wear wings all the time—blazing red ones, and blue and green, and gold, and variegated, and rainbowed, and ring-streaked-and-striped ones—and nobody finds fault. It is suitable to their time of life. The things are beautiful, and they set the young people off. They are the most striking and lovely part of their outfit—a halo don't *begin*."

"Well," says I, "I've tucked mine away in the cupboard, and I allow to let them lay there till there's mud."

"Yes—or a reception."

"What's that?"

"Well, you can see one to-night if you want to. There's a bar-keeper from Jersey City going to be received."

"Go on—tell me about it."

"This barkeeper got converted at a Moody and Sankey meeting, in New York, and started home on the ferry-boat, and there was a collision and he got drowned. He is of a class that think all heaven goes wild with joy when a particularly hard lot like him is saved; they think all heaven turns out hosannahing to welcome them; they think there isn't anything talked about in the realms of the blest but their case, for that day. This barkeeper thinks there hasn't been such another stir here in years, as his coming is going to raise.—And I've always noticed this peculiarity about a dead barkeeper—he not only expects all hands to turn out when he arrives, but he expects to be received with a torchlight procession."

"I reckon he is disappointed, then."

"No, he isn't. No man is allowed to be disappointed here. Whatever he wants, when he comes—that is, any reasonable and unsacrilegious thing—he can have. There's always a few millions or billions of young folks around who don't want any better entertainment than to fill up their lungs and swarm out with their torches and have a high time over a barkeeper. It tickles the barkeeper till he can't rest, it makes a charming lark for the young folks, it don't do anybody any harm, it don't cost a rap, and it keeps up the place's reputation for making all comers happy and content."

"Very good. I'll be on hand and see them land the barkeeper."

"It is manners to go in full dress. You want to wear your wings, you know, and your other things."

"Which ones?"

"Halo, and harp, and palm branch, and all that."

"Well," says I, "I reckon I ought to be ashamed of myself, but the fact is I left them laying around that day I resigned from the choir. I haven't got a rag to wear but this robe and the wings."

"That's all right. You'll find they've been raked up and saved for you. Send for them."

"I'll do it, Sandy. But what was it you was saying about unsacrilegious things, which people expect to get, and will be disappointed about?"

"Oh, there are a lot of such things that people expect and don't get. For instance, there's a Brooklyn preacher by the name of Talmage, who is laying up a considerable disappointment for himself. He says, every now and then in his sermons, that the first thing he does when he gets to heaven, will be to fling his arms around Abraham, Isaac and Jacob, and kiss them and weep on them. There's millions of people down there on earth that are promising themselves the same thing. As many as sixty thousand people arrive here every single day, that want to run straight to Abraham, Isaac and Jacob, and hug them and weep on them. Now mind you, sixty thousand a day is a pretty heavy contract for those old people. If they were a mind to allow it, they wouldn't ever have anything to do, year in and year out, but stand up and be hugged and wept on thirty-two hours in the twenty-four. They would be tired and as wet as muskrats all the time. What would heaven be, to *them?* It would be a mighty good place to get out of— you know that, yourself. Those are kind and gentle old Jews, but they ain't any fonder of kissing the emotional highlights of Brooklyn than you be. You mark my words, Mr. T's endearments are going to be declined, with thanks. There are limits to the privileges of the elect, even in heaven. Why, if Adam was to show himself to every new comer that wants to call and gaze at him and strike him for his autograph, he would never have time to do anything else but just that. Talmage has said he is going to give Adam some of his attentions, as well as A., I. and J. But he will have to change his mind about that."

"Do you think Talmage will really come here?"

"Why, certainly, he will; but don't you be alarmed; he will run with his own kind, and there's plenty of them. That is the main charm of heaven—there's all kinds here—which wouldn't be the case if you let the preachers tell it. Anybody can find the sort he prefers, here, and he just lets the others alone, and they let him alone. When the Deity builds a heaven, it is built right, and on a liberal plan."

Sandy sent home for his things, and I sent for mine, and about nine in the evening we begun to dress. Sandy says—

"This is going to be a grand time for you, Stormy. Like as not some of the patriarchs will turn out."

"No, but will they?"

"Like as not. Of course they are pretty exclusive. They hardly ever show themselves to the common public. I believe they never turn out except for an eleventh-hour convert. They wouldn't do it then, only earthly tradition makes a grand show pretty necessary on that kind of an occasion."

"Do they all turn out, Sandy?"

"Who?—all the patriarchs? Oh, no—hardly ever more than a couple. You will be here fifty thousand years—maybe more—before you get a glimpse of all the patriarchs and prophets. Since I have been here, Job has been to the front once, and once Ham and Jeremiah both at the same time. But the finest thing that has happened in my day was a year or so ago; that was Charles Peace's reception—him they called 'the Bannercross Murderer'—an Englishman. There were four patriarchs and two prophets on the Grand Stand that time— there hasn't been anything like it since Captain Kidd came; Abel was there—the first time in twelve hundred years. A report got around that Adam was coming; well, of course, Abel was enough to bring a crowd, all by himself, but there is nobody that can draw like Adam. It was a false report, but it got around, anyway, as I say, and it will be a long day before I see the like of it again. The reception was in the English department, of course, which is eight hundred and eleven million miles from the New Jersey line. I went, along with a good many of my neighbors, and it was a sight to see, I can tell you. Flocks came from all the departments. I saw Esquimaux there, and Tartars, negroes, Chinamen—people from everywhere. You see a mixture like that in the Grand Choir, the first day you land here, but you hardly ever see it again. There were billions of people; when they were singing or hosannahing, the noise was wonderful; and even when their tongues were still the drumming of the wings was nearly enough to burst your head, for all the sky was as thick as if it was snowing angels. Although Adam was not there, it was a great time anyway, because we had three archangels on the Grand Stand—it is a seldom thing that even one comes out."

"What did they look like, Sandy?"

"Well, they had shining faces, and shining robes, and wonderful rainbow wings, and they stood eighteen feet high, and wore swords, and held their heads up in a noble way, and looked like soldiers."

"Did they have halos?"

"No—anyway, not the hoop kind. The archangels and the upper-class patriarchs wear a finer thing than that. It is a round, solid, splendid glory of gold, that is blinding to look at. You have often seen a patriarch in a picture, on earth, with that thing on— you remember it?—he looks as if he had his head in a brass platter. That don't give you the right idea of it at all—it is much more shining and beautiful."

"Did you talk with those archangels and patriarchs, Sandy?"

"Who—*I*? Why, what can you be thinking about, Stormy? I ain't worthy to speak to such as they."

"Is Talmage?"

"Of course not. You have got the same mixed-up idea about these things that everybody has down there. I had it once, but I got over it. Down there they talk of the heavenly King—and that is right—but then they go right on speaking as if this was a republic and everybody was on a dead level with everybody else, and privileged to fling his arms around anybody he comes across, and be hail-fellow-well-met with all the elect, from the highest down. How tangled up and absurd that is! How are you going to have a republic under a king? How are you going to have a republic at all, where the head of the government is absolute, holds his place forever, and has no parliament, no council to meddle or make in his affairs, nobody voted for, nobody elected, nobody in the whole universe with a voice in the government, nobody asked to take a hand in its matters, and nobody *allowed* to do it? Fine republic, ain't it?"

"Well, yes—it *is* a little different from the idea I had—but I thought I might go around and get acquainted with the grandees, anyway—not exactly splice the main-brace with them, you know, but shake hands and pass the time of day."

"Could Tom, Dick and Harry call on the Cabinet of Russia and do that?—on Prince Gortschakoff, for instance?"

"I reckon not, Sandy."

"Well, this is Russia—only more so. There's not the shadow of a republic about it anywhere. There are ranks, here. There are viceroys, princes, governors, sub-governors, sub-sub-governors, and a hundred

orders of nobility, grading along down from grand-ducal archangels, stage by stage, till the general level is struck, where there ain't any titles. Do you know what a prince of the blood is, on earth?"

"No."

"Well, a prince of the blood don't belong to the royal family exactly, and he don't belong to the mere nobility of the kingdom; he is lower than the one, and higher than t'other. That's about the position of the patriarchs and prophets here. There's some mighty high nobility here—people that you and I ain't worthy to polish sandals for—and *they* ain't worthy to polish sandals for the patriarchs and prophets. That gives you a kind of an idea of their rank, don't it? You begin to see how high up they are, don't you? Just to get a two-minute glimpse of one of them is a thing for a body to remember and tell about for a thousand years. Why, Captain, just think of this: if Abraham was to set foot down here by this door, there would be a railing set up around that foot-track right away, and a shelter put over it, and people would flock here from all over heaven, for hundreds and hundreds of years, to look at it. Abraham is one of the parties that Mr. Talmage, of Brooklyn, is going to embrace, and kiss, and weep on, when he comes. He wants to lay in a good stock of tears, you know, or five to one he will go dry before he gets a chance to do it."

"Sandy," says I, "I had an idea that *I* was going to be equals with everybody here, too, but I will let that drop. It don't matter, and I am plenty happy enough anyway."

"Captain, you are happier than you would be, the other way. These old patriarchs and prophets have got ages the start of you; they know more in two minutes than you know in a year. Did you ever try to have a sociable improving-time discussing winds, and currents and variations of compass with an undertaker?"

"I get your idea, Sandy. He couldn't interest me. He would be an ignoramus in such things—he would bore me, and I would bore him."

"You have got it. You would bore the patriarchs when you talked, and when they talked they would shoot over your head. By and by you would say, 'Good morning, your Eminence, I will call again'—but you wouldn't. Did you ever ask the slush-boy to come up in the cabin and take dinner with you?"

"I get your drift again, Sandy. I wouldn't be used to such grand people as the patriarchs and prophets, and I would be sheepish and tongue-tied in their company, and mighty glad to get out of it. Sandy, which is the highest rank, patriarch or prophet?"

"Oh, the prophets hold over the patriarchs. The newest prophet, even, is of a sight more consequence than the oldest patriarch. Yes, sir, Adam himself has to walk behind Shakespeare."

"Was Shakespeare a prophet?"

"Of course he was; and so was Homer, and heaps more. But Shakespeare and the rest have to walk behind a common tailor from Tennessee, by the name of Billings; and behind a horse-doctor named Sakka, from Afghanistan. Jeremiah, and Billings and Buddha walk together, side by side, right behind a crowd from planets not in our astronomy; next come a dozen or two from Jupiter and other worlds; next come Daniel, and Sakka and Confucius; next a lot from systems outside of ours; next come Ezekiel, and Mahomet, Zoroaster, and a knife-grinder from ancient Egypt; then there is a long string, and after them, away down toward the bottom, come Shakespeare and Homer, and a shoe-maker named Marais, from the back settlements of France."

"Have they really rung in Mahomet and all those other heathens?"

"Yes—they all had their message, and they all get their reward. The man who don't get his reward on earth, needn't bother—he will get it here, sure."

"But why did they throw off on Shakespeare, that way, and put him away down there below those shoemakers and horse-doctors and knife-grinders—a lot of people nobody ever heard of?"

"That is the heavenly justice of it—they warn't rewarded according to their deserts, on earth, but here they get their rightful rank. That tailor Billings, from Tennessee, wrote poetry that Homer and Shakespeare couldn't begin to come up to; but nobody would print it, nobody read it but his neighbors, an ignorant lot, and they laughed at it. Whenever the village had a drunken frolic and a dance, they would drag him in and crown him with cabbage leaves, and pretend to bow down to him; and one night when he was sick and nearly starved to death, they had him out and crowned him, and then they rode him on a rail about the village, and everybody followed along, beating tin pans and yelling. Well, he died before morning. He wasn't ever expecting to go to heaven, much less that there was going to be any fuss made over him, so I reckon he was a good deal surprised when the reception broke on him."

"Was you there, Sandy?"

"Bless you, no!"

"Why? Didn't you know it was going to come off?"

"Well, I judge I did. It was the talk of these realms—not for a day, like this barkeeper business, but for twenty years before the man died."

"Why the mischief didn't you go, then?"

"Now how you talk! The like of me go meddling around at the reception of a prophet? A mudsill like me trying to push in and help receive an awful grandee like Edward J. Billings? Why, I should have been laughed at for a billion miles around. I shouldn't ever heard the last of it."

"Well, who did go, then?"

"Mighty few people that you and I will ever get a chance to see, Captain. Not a solitary commoner ever has the luck to see a reception of a prophet, I can tell you. All the nobility, and all the patriarchs and prophets—every last one of them—and all the archangels, and all the princes and governors and viceroys, were there,—and *no* small fry—not a single one. And mind you, I'm not talking about only the grandees from *our* world, but the princes and patriarchs and so on from *all* the worlds that shine in our sky, and from billions more that belong in systems upon systems away outside of the one our sun is in. There were some prophets and patriarchs there that ours ain't a circumstance to, for rank and illustriousness and all that. Some were from Jupiter and other worlds in our own system, but the most celebrated were three poets, Saa, Bo and Soof, from great planets in three different and very remote systems. These three names are common and familiar in every nook and corner of heaven, clear from one end of it to the other—fully as well known as the eighty Supreme Archangels, in fact—whereas our Moses, and Adam, and the rest, have not been heard of outside of our world's little corner of heaven, except by a few very learned men scattered here and there—and they always spell their names wrong, and get the performances of one mixed up with the doings of another, and they almost always locate them simply *in our solar system,* and think that is enough without going into little details such as naming the particular world they are from. It is like a learned Hindoo showing off how much he knows by saying Longfellow lives in the United States—as if he lived all over the United States, and as if the country was so small you couldn't throw a brick there without hitting him. Between you and me, it does gravel me, the cool way people from those monster worlds outside our system snub our little world, and even our system. Of course we think a good deal of Jupiter, because our world is only a potato to it, for size; but then there are worlds in other systems that Jupiter isn't even a mustard-seed to—like the planet Goobra, for instance, which you couldn't squeeze inside the orbit of Halley's comet without straining the rivets. Tourists from Goobra (I mean parties that lived and died there—natives) come here, now and then, and inquire about our world, and when they find out it is so little that a streak of lightning can flash clear around it in the eighth of a second, they have to lean up against something to laugh. Then they screw a glass into their eye and go to examining *us,* as if we were a curious kind of foreign bug, or something of that sort. One of them asked me how long our day was; and when I told him it was twelve hours long, as a general thing, he asked me if people where I was from considered it worth while to get up and wash for such a day as that. That is the way with those Goobra people—they can't seem to let a chance go by to throw it in your face that their day is three hundred and twenty-two of our years long. This young snob was just of age— he was six or seven thousand of his days old—say two million of our years—and he had all the puppy airs that belong to that time of life— that turning-point when a person has got over being a boy and yet ain't quite a man exactly. If it had been anywhere else but in heaven, I would have given him a piece of my mind. Well, anyway, Billings had the grandest reception that has been seen in thousands of centuries, and I think it will have a good effect. His name will be carried pretty far, and it will make our system talked about, and maybe our world, too, and raise us in the respect of the general public of heaven. Why, look here—Shakespeare walked backwards before that tailor from Tennessee, and scattered flowers for him to walk on, and Homer stood behind his chair and waited on him at the banquet. Of course that didn't go for much *there,* amongst all those big foreigners from other systems, as they hadn't heard of Shakespeare or Homer either, but it would amount to considerable down there on our little earth if they could know about it. I wish there was something *in* that miserable spiritualism, so we could send them word. That Tennessee village would set up a monument to Billings, then, and his autograph would outsell Satan's. Well, they had grand times at that reception—a small-fry noble from Hoboken told me all about it—Sir Richard Duffer, Baronet."

"What, Sandy, a nobleman from Hoboken? How is that?"

"Easy enough. Duffer kept a sausage-shop and never saved a cent in his life because he used to give all his spare meat to the poor, in a quiet way. Not tramps—no, the other sort—the sort that will starve before they will beg—honest square people out of work. Dick used to watch hungry-looking men and women and children, and track them home, and find out all about them from the neighbors, and then feed them and find them work. As nobody ever *saw* him give anything to anybody, he had the reputation of being mean; he died with it, too, and everybody said it was a good riddance; but the minute he landed here, they made him a baronet, and the very first words Dick the sausage-maker of Hoboken heard when he stepped upon the heavenly shore were, 'Welcome, Sir Richard Duffer!' It surprised him some, because he thought he had reasons to believe he was pointed for a warmer climate than this one."

All of a sudden the whole region fairly rocked under the crash of eleven hundred and one thunder blasts, all let off at once, and Sandy says—

"There, that's for the barkeep."

I jumped up and says—

"Then let's be moving along, Sandy; we don't want to miss any of this thing, you know."

"Keep your seat," he says; "he is only just telegraphed, that is all."

"How?"

"That blast only means that he has been sighted from the signal-station. He is off Sandy Hook. The committees will go down to meet him, now, and escort him in. There will be ceremonies and delays; they won't be coming up the Bay for a considerable time, yet. It is several billion miles away, anyway."

"*I* could have been a barkeeper and a hard lot just as well as not," says I, remembering the lonesome way I arrived, and how there wasn't any committee nor anything.

"I notice some regret in your voice," says Sandy, "and it is natural enough; but let bygones be bygones; you went according to your lights, and it is too late now to mend the thing."

"No, let it slide, Sandy, I don't mind. But you've got a Sandy Hook *here,* too, have you?"

"We've got everthing here, just as it is below. All the States and Territories of the Union, and all the kingdoms of the earth and the islands of the sea are laid out here just as they are on the globe—all the same shape they are down there, and all graded to the relative size, only each State and realm and island is a good many billion times bigger here than it is below. There goes another blast."

"What is that one for?"

"That is only another fort answering the first one. They each fire eleven hundred and one thunder blasts at a single dash—it is the usual salute for an eleventh-hour guest; a hundred for each hour and an extra one for the guest's sex; if it was a woman we would know it by their leaving off the extra gun."

"How do we know there's eleven hundred and one, Sandy, when they all go off at once?—and yet we certainly do know."

"Our intellects are a good deal sharpened up, here, in some ways, and that is one of them. Numbers and sizes and distances are so great, here, that we have to be made so we can *feel* them—our old ways of counting and measuring and ciphering wouldn't ever give us an idea of them, but would only confuse us and oppress us and make our heads ache."

After some more talk about this, I says: "Sandy, I notice that I hardly ever see a white angel; where I run across one white angel, I strike as many as a hundred million copper-colored ones—people that can't speak English. How is that?"

"Well, you will find it the same in any State or Territory of the American corner of heaven you choose to go to. I have shot along, a whole week on a stretch, and gone millions and millions of miles, through perfect swarms of angels, without ever seeing a single white one, or hearing a word I could understand. You see, America was occupied a billion years and more, by Injuns and Aztecs, and that sort of folks, before a white man ever set his foot in it. During the first three hundred years after Columbus's discovery, there wasn't ever more than one good lecture audience of white people, all put together, in America—I mean the whole thing, British Possessions and all; in the beginning of our century there were only 6,000,000 or 7,000,000—say seven; 12,000,000 or 14,000,000 in 1825; say 23,000,000 in 1850; 40,000,000 in 1875. Our death-rate has always been 20 in 1000 per annum. Well, 140,000 died the first year of the century; 280,000 the twenty-fifth year; 500,000 the fiftieth year; about a million the seventy-fifth year. Now I am going to be liberal about this thing, and consider that fifty million whites have died in America from the beginning up to today—make it sixty, if you want to; make it a hundred million—it's no difference about a few millions one way or t'other. Well, now, you can see, yourself, that when you come to spread a little dab of people like that over these hundreds of billions of miles of American territory here in heaven, it is like scattering a ten-cent box of homeopathic pills over the Great Sahara and expecting to find them again. You can't expect us to amount to anything in heaven, and we *don't*—now that is the simple fact, and we have got to do the best we can with it. The learned men from other planets and other systems come here and hang around a while, when they are touring around the Kingdom, and then go back to their own section of heaven and write a book of travels, and they give America about five lines in it. And what do they say about us? They say this wilderness is populated with a scattering few hundred thousand billions of red angels, with now and then a curiously completed *diseased* one. You see, they think we whites and the occasional nigger are Injuns that have been bleached out or blackened by some leprous disease or other—for some peculiarly rascally *sin*, mind you. It is a mighty sour pill for us all, my friend—even the modestest of us, let alone the other kind, that think they are going to be received like a long-lost government bond, and hug Abraham into the bargain. I haven't asked you any of the particulars, Captain, but I judge it goes without saying—if my experience is worth anything—that there wasn't much of a hooraw made over you when you arrived—now was there?"

"Don't mention it, Sandy," says I, coloring up a little; "I wouldn't have had the family see it for any amount you are a mind to name. Change the subject, Sandy, change the subject."

"Well, do you think of settling in the California department of bliss?"

"I don't know. I wasn't calculating on doing anything really definite in that direction till the family come. I thought I would just look around, meantime, in a quiet way, and make up my mind. Besides, I know a good many dead people, and I was calculating to hunt them up and swap a little gossip with them about friends, and old times, and one thing or another, and ask them how they like it here, as far as they have got. I reckon my wife will want to camp in the California range, though, because most all her departed will be there, and she likes to be with folks she knows."

"Don't you let her. You see what the Jersey district of heaven is, for whites; well, the Californian district is a thousand times worse. It swarms with a mean kind of leather-headed mud-colored angels—and your nearest white neighbor is likely to be a million miles away.

What a man mostly misses, in heaven, is company—company of his own sort and color and language. I have come near settling in the European part of heaven once or twice on that account."

"Well, why didn't you, Sandy?"

"Oh, various reasons. For one thing, although you *see* plenty of whites there, you can't understand any of them, hardly, and so you go about as hungry for talk as you do here. I like to look at a Russian or a German or an Italian—I even like to look at a Frenchman if I ever have the luck to catch him engaged in anything that ain't indelicate—but *looking* don't cure the hunger—what you want is talk."

"Well, there's England, Sandy—the English district of heaven."

"Yes, but it is not so very much better than this end of the heavenly domain. As long as you run across Englishmen born this side of three hundred years ago, you are all right; but the minute you get back of Elizabeth's time the language begins to fog up, and the further back you go the foggier it gets. I had some talk with one Langland and a man by the name of Chaucer—old-time poets—but it was no use, I couldn't quite understand them, and they couldn't quite understand me. I have had letters from them since, but it is such broken English I can't make it out. Back of those men's time the English are just simply foreigners, nothing more, nothing less; they talk Danish, German, Norman French, and sometimes a mixture of all three; back of *them,* they talk Latin, and ancient British, Irish, and Gaelic; and then back of these come billions and billions of pure savages that talk a gibberish that Satan himself couldn't understand. The fact is, where you strike one man in the English settlements that you can understand, you wade through awful swarms that talk something you can't make head nor tail of. You see, every country on earth has been overlaid so often, in the course of a billion years, with different kinds of people and different sorts of languages, that this sort of mongrel business was bound to be the result in heaven."

"Sandy," says I, "did you see a good many of the great people history tells about?"

"Yes—plenty. I saw kings and all sorts of distinguished people."

"Do the kings rank just as they did below?"

"No; a body can't bring his rank up here with him. Divine right is a good-enough earthly romance, but it don't go, here. Kings drop down to the general level as soon as they reach the realms of grace. I knew Charles the Second very well—one of the most popular comedians in the English section—draws first rate. There are better, of course—people that were never heard of on earth—but Charles is making a very good reputation indeed, and is considered a rising man. Richard the Lion-hearted is in the prize-ring, and coming into considerable favor. Henry the Eighth is a tragedian, and the scenes where he kills people are done to the very life. Henry the Sixth keeps a religious book stand."

"Did you ever see Napoleon, Sandy?"

"Often—sometimes in the Corsican range, sometimes in the French. He always hunts up a conspicuous place, and goes frowning around with his arms folded and his field-glass under his arm, looking as grand, gloomy and peculiar as his reputation calls for, and very much bothered because he don't stand as high, here, for a soldier, as he expected to."

"Why, who stand higher?"

"Oh, a *lot* of people we never heard of before—the shoemaker and horse-doctor and knife-grinder kind, you know—clodhoppers from goodness knows where, that never handled a sword or fired a shot in their lives—but the soldier-ship was in them, though they never had a chance to show it. But here they take their right place, and Caesar and Napoleon and Alexander have to take a back seat. The greatest military genius our world ever produced was a bricklayer from somewhere back of Boston—died during the Revolution—by the name of Absalom Jones. Wherever he goes, crowds flock to see him. You see, everybody knows that if he had had a chance he would have shown the world some generalship that would have made all generalship before look like child's play and 'prentice work. But he never got a chance; he tried heaps of times to enlist as a private, but he had lost both thumbs and a couple of front teeth, and the recruiting sergeant wouldn't pass him. However, as I say, everybody knows, now, what he *would* have been, and so they flock by the million to get a glimpse of him whenever they hear he is going to be anywhere. Caesar, and Hannibal, and Alexander, and Napoleon are all on his staff, and ever so many more great generals; but the public hardly care to look at *them* when *he* is around. Boom! There goes another salute. The barkeeper's off quarantine now."

*

Sandy and I put on our things. Then we made a wish, and in a second we were at the reception-place. We stood on the edge of the ocean of space, and looked out over the dimness, but couldn't make out anything. Close by us was the Grand Stand—tier on tier of dim thrones rising up toward the zenith. From each side of it spread away the tiers of seats for the general public. They spread away for leagues and leagues—you couldn't see the ends. They were empty and still, and hadn't a cheerful look, but looked dreary, like a theatre before anybody comes—gas turned down. Sandy says—

"We'll sit down here and wait. We'll see the head of the procession come in sight away off yonder pretty soon, now."

Says I—

"It's pretty lonesome, Sandy; I reckon there's a hitch somewheres. Nobody but just you and me—it ain't much of a display for the barkeeper."

"Don't you fret, it's all right. There'll be one more gunfire—then you'll see."

In a little while we noticed a sort of a lightish flush, away off on the horizon.

"Head of the torchlight procession," says Sandy.

It spread, and got lighter and brighter: soon it had a strong glare like a locomotive headlight; it kept on getting brighter and brighter till it was like the sun peeping above the horizon-line at sea—the big red rays shot high up into the sky.

"Keep your eyes on the Grand Stand and the miles of seats—sharp!" says Sandy, "and listen for the gunfire."

Just then it burst out, "Boom-boom-boom!" like a million thunderstorms in one, and made the whole heavens rock. Then there was a sudden and awful glare of light all about us, and in that very instant every one of the millions of seats was occupied, and as far as you could see, in both directions, was just a solid pack of people, and the place was all splendidly lit up! It was enough to take a body's breath away. Sandy says—

"That is the way we do it here. No time fooled away; nobody straggling in after the curtain's up. Wishing is quicker work than traveling. A quarter of a second ago these folks were millions of miles from here. When they heard the last signal, all they had to do was to wish, and here they are."

The prodigious choir struck up—

> We long to hear thy voice,
> To see thee face to face.

It was noble music, but the uneducated chipped in and spoilt it, just as the congregation used to do on earth.

The head of the procession began to pass, now, and it was a wonderful sight. It swept along, thick and solid, five hundred thousand angels abreast, and every angel carrying a torch and singing—the whirring thunder of the wings made a body's head ache. You could follow the line of the procession back, and slanting upward into the sky, far away in a glittering snaky rope, till it was only a faint streak in the distance. The rush went on and on, for a long time, and at last, sure enough, along comes the barkeeper, and then everybody rose, and a cheer went up that made the heavens shake, I tell you! He was all smiles, and had his halo tilted over one ear in a cocky way, and was the most satisfied-looking saint I ever saw. While he marched up the steps of the Grand Stand, the choir struck up—

> The whole wide heaven groans,
> And waits to hear that voice

There were four gorgeous tents standing side by side in the place of honor, on a broad railed platform in the centre of the Grand Stand, with a shining guard of honor round about them. The tents had been shut up all this time. As the barkeeper climbed along up, bowing and smiling to everybody, and at last got to the platform, these tents were jerked up aloft all of a sudden, and we saw four noble thrones of gold, all caked with jewels, and in the two middle ones sat old white-whiskered men, and in the two others a couple of the most glorious and gaudy giants, with platter halos and beautiful armor. All the millions went down on their knees, and stared, and looked glad, and burst out into a joyful kind of murmurs. They said—

"Two archangels!—that is splendid. Who can the others be?"

The archangels gave the barkeeper a stiff little military bow; the two old men rose; one of them said, "Moses and Esau welcome thee!" and then all the four vanished, and the thrones were empty.

The barkeeper looked a little disappointed, for he was calculating to hug those old people, I judge; but it was the gladdest and proudest multitude you ever saw—because they had seen Moses and Esau. Everybody was saying, "Did you see them?—I did— Esau's side face was to me, but I saw Moses full in the face, just as plain as I see you this minute."

The procession took up the barkeeper and moved on with him again, and the crowd broke up and scattered. As we went along home, Sandy said it was a great success, and the barkeeper would have a right to be proud of it forever. And he said *we* were in luck, too; said we might attend receptions for forty thousand years to come, and not have a chance to see a brace of such grand moguls as Moses and Esau. We found afterwards that we had come near seeing another patriarch, and likewise a genuine prophet besides, but at the last moment they sent regrets. Sandy said there would be a monument put up there, where Moses and Esau had stood, with the date and circumstances, and all about the whole business, and travelers would come for thousands of years and gawk at it, and climb over it, and scribble their names on it.

CHAPTER V

Captain Stormfield Resumes

I

When I had been in heaven some time I begun to feel restless, the same as I used to on earth when I had been ashore a month, so I sejested to Sandy that we do some excursions. He said all right, and with that we started with a whiz—not that you could *hear* us go, but it was as if you ought to.—On account of our going so fast, for you go by *thought*. If you went only as fast as light or electricity you would be forever getting to any place, heaven is so big. Even when you are traveling by thought it takes you days and days and days to cover the territory of any Christian State, and days and days to cover the uninhabited stretch between that State and the next one.

"You can't put it into miles," Sandy says.

"Becuz there ain't enough of them. If you had all the miles God ever made they wouldn't reach from the Catholic camp to the High Church Piscopalian—nor half way, for that matter; and yet they are the nearest together of any. Professor Higgins tries to work the miles on the measurements, on account of old earthly habit, and p'raps he gets a sort of grip on the distances out of the result, but you couldn't, and I can't."

"How do *you* know I couldn't, Sandy? Speak for yourself, hadn't you better? You just tell me his game, and wait till I look at my hand."

"Well, it's this. He used to be astronomical professor of astronomy at Harvard—"

"This was before he was dead?"

"Certainly. How could he be *after* he was dead?"

"Oh, well, it ain't important. But a *soldier* can be a soldier after he's dead. And he can breed, too. There's eleven million dead soldiers drawing pension at home, now—some that's been dead 125 years—and we've never had three millions on the pay-roll since the first Fourth of July. Go on, Sandy. Maybe it was before he was dead; maybe it wasn't; but it ain't important."

"Well, he was astronomical professor, and can't get rid of his habits. So he tries to figure out these heavenly distances by astronomical measurements. That is to say, he computes them in light-years."

"What is a light-year, Sandy?"

"He says light travels 186,000 miles a second, and—"

"How many?"

"186,000."

"In a *second,* Sandy—not a week?"

"No, in a second. He says the sun is 93,000,000 miles from the earth, and it takes light 8 minutes to cover the distance. Then he ciphers out how far the light would travel in a year of 365 days at that gait, and he calls that distance a light-year."

"It's considerable, ain't it, Sandy?"

"Don't you doubt it!"

"How far is it, Sandy?"

"It's 63,280 times the distance from the earth to the sun."

"Land! Say it again, Sandy, and say it slow."

"63,280 times 93,000,000 miles."

"Sandy, it beats the band. Do you think there's room for a straight stretch like that? Don't you reckon it would come to the edge and stick out over? What does a light-year foot up, Sandy, in a lump?"

"Six thousand million miles."

"Sandy, it is certainly a corker! ls there any known place as far off as a light-year?"

"Shucks, Stormy, *one* light-year is nothing. He says it's *four* light-years from our earth to the nearest star—and nothing between."

"Nothing between? Nothing but just emptiness?"

"That's it; nothing but emptiness. But he says there's not a star in the Milky Way nor anywhere else in the sky that's not *further* away from its nearest neighbor than that."

"Why, Sandy, if that is true, the sky is emptier than heaven."

"Oh, indeed, no! Far from it. In the Milky Way, the professor says, no star is more than six or seven light-years distant from its nearest neighbor, but there ain't any Christian sect in heaven that is nearer that 5,000 light-years from the camp of the next sect. Oh, no, he says the sky *is* a howling wilderness, but it can't show with heaven. No, sir, he says of all the lonesome places that ever was, give him heaven. Every now and then he gets so lonesome here that he makes an excursion amongst the stars, so's to have a sense of company."

"Why, Sandy, what have they made heaven so large for?"

"So's to have room in the future. The redeemed will still be coming for billions and billions and billions and billions of years, but there'll always be room, you see. This heaven ain't built on any 'Gates Ajar' proportions."

. . . Time drifted along. We went on excursioning amongst the colonies and over the monstrous spaces between, till at last I was so weighed down by the awful bigness of heaven that I said I'd got to see something small to back my natural focus and lift off some of the load, I couldn't stand it any longer. Sandy says,

"Well, then, suppose we try an asterisk, or asteroid, or whatever the professor calls them. They're little enough to fit the case, I reckon."

II

Journey to the Asterisk

So we went, and it was quite interesting. It was a very nice little world, twenty-five or thirty miles in circumference; almost exactly a thousand times smaller than the earth, and just a miniature of it, in every way: little wee Atlantic oceans and Pacific oceans and Indian oceans, all in the right places; the same with the rivers, the same with the lakes; the same old familiar mountain ranges, the same continents and islands, the same Sahara—all in the right proportions and as exact as a photograph. We walked around it one afternoon, and waded the oceans, and had a most uncommon good time. We spent weeks and weeks walking around over it and getting acquainted with the nations and their ways.

Nice little dollies, they were, and not bigger than Gulliver's Lilliput people. Their ways were like ours. In their America they had a republic on our own plan, and in their Europe, their Asia and their Africa they had monarchies and established churches, and a pope and a Czar, and all the rest of it. They were not afraid of us; in fact they held us in rather frank contempt, because we were giants. Giants have never been respected, in any world. These people had a quite good opinion of themselves, and many of them no bigger that a clothes pin. In church it was a common thing for the preacher to look out over his congregation and speak of them as the noblest work of God—and never a clothes pin smirked! These little animals were having wars all the time, and raising armies and building navies, and striving after the approval of God every way they could. And whenever there was a savage country that needed civilizing, they went there and took it, and divided it up among the several enlightened monarchs, and civilized it—each monarch in his own way, but generally with Bibles and bullets and taxes. And the way they did whoop-up Morals, and Patriotism, and Religion, and the Brotherhood of Man was noble to see.

I couldn't see that they differed from us, except in size. It was like looking at ourselves through the wrong end of the spyglass. But Sandy said there was one difference, and a big one. It was this: each person could look right into every other person's mind and read what was in it, but he thought his own mind was concealed from everybody but himself!

CHAPTER VI

From Captain Stormfield's Reminiscences

One day, whilst I was there in Heaven, I says to Sandy—"Sandy," I says, "you was telling me, a while back, that you knowed how the human race came to be created; and now, if you don't mind,"

I says, "I'd like you to pull off the narrative, for I reckon it's interesting."

So he done it. This is it.

Sandy's Narrative

Well, it was like this. I got it from Slattery. Slattery was there at the time, being an eye-witness, you see; and so Slattery, he—

"Who's Slattery, Sandy?"

One of the originals.

"Original *which*?"

Original inventions. He used to be an angel, in the early times, two hunderd thousand years ago; and so, as it happened—

"Two hun—do you mean to say—"

Yes, I *do*. It was two hunderd thousand years ago. Slattery was born here in heaven, and so time don't count. As I was a-telling you, he was an angel, first-off, but when Satan fell, he fell, too, becuz he was a connexion of Satan's, by marriage or blood or somehow or other, and it put him under suspicion, though they warn't able to prove anything on him. Still, they judged a little term down below in the fires would be a lesson to him and do him good, so they give him a thousand years down in them tropics, and—

"A *thousand*, Sandy?"

Certainly. It ain't anything to these people, Cap'n Stormfield. When you've been here as long as I have—but never mind about that. When he got back, he was different. The vacation done him good. You see, he had had experience, and it sharpened him up. And besides, he had traveled, and it made him important, which he warn't, before. Satan came near getting a thousand years himself, that time—

"But I thought he *did,* Sandy. I thought he went down for good and all."

No, sir, not that time.

"What saved him?"

Influence.

"M-m. So they have it here, too, do they?"

Oh, well, I sh'd *think*! Satan has fell a lot of times, but he hasn't ever been sent down permanent, yet—but only the small fry.

"Just the same it used to was, down on earth, Sandy. Ain't it interesting? Go on. Slattery he got reinstated, as I understand it?"

Yes, so he did. And he was a considerable person by now, as I was a-saying, partly on accounts of his relative, and partly on accounts of him having been abroad, and all that, and affecting to talk with a foreign accent, which he picked up down below. So he was around when the first attempts was made. They had a mould for a man, and a mould for a woman, and they mixed up the materials and poured it in. They came out very handsome to look at, and everybody said it was a success. So they made some more, and kept on making them and setting them one side to dry, till they had about ten thousand. Then they blew in the breath, and put the dispositions in, and turned them loose in a pleasant piece of territory, and told them to go it.

"Put in the dispositions?"

Yes, the *Moral Qualities*. That's what makes dispositions. They distributed 'em around perfectly fair and honorable. There was 28 of them, according to the plans and specifications, and the whole 28 went to each man and woman in equal measure, nobody getting more of a quality than anybody else, nor less. I'll give you the list, just as Slattery give it to me:

1. Magnanimity.	2. Meanness.
3. Moral courage.	4. Moral cowardice.
5. Physical courage.	6. Physical cowardice.
7. Honesty.	8. Dishonesty.
9. Truthfulness.	10. Untruthfulness.
11. Love.	12. Hate.
13. Chastity.	14. Unchastity.
15. Firmness.	16. Unfirmness.
17. Diligence.	18. Indolence.
19. Selfishness.	20. Unselfishness.
21. Prodigality.	22. Stinginess.
23. Reverence.	24. Irreverence.
25. Intellectuality.	26. Unintellectuality.
27. Self-Conceit.	28. Humility.

"And a mighty good layout, Sandy. And all fair and square, too, and no favors to anybody. I like it. Looks to me elegant, and the way it had ought to be. Blamed if it ain't interesting. Go on."

Well, the new creatures settled in the territory that was app'inted for them, and begun to hatch, and multiply and replenish, and all that, and everything went along to the queen's taste, as the saying is. But by and by Slattery noticed something, and got Satan to go out there and take a look, which he done, and says,

"Well, something the matter, you think! What is it?"

"I'll show you," Slattery says. "Warn't they to be something fresh, something new and surprising?"

"Cert'nly," Satan says. "Ain't they?"

"Oh, well," says Slattery, "if you come right down to the fine shades, I ain't able to deny that they *are* new—but *how* new? What's the idea? Moreover, what I want to know is, is what's new an *improvement*?"

"Go on," says Satan, a little impatient, "what's your point? Get at it!"

"Well, it's this. These new people don't differ from the angels. Except that they hain't got wings, and they don't get sick, and they don't die. Otherwise they're just angels—just the old usual thing. They're all the same size, they're all exactly alike—hair, eyes, noses, gait, everything—just the same as angels. Now, then, here's the point: the only solitary new thing about 'em is a new arrangement of their morals. It's the only fresh thing."

"Very well," says Satan, "ain't that enough? What are you complaining about?"

"No, it *ain't* enough, unless it's an improvement over the old regular arrangement."

"Come, get down to particulars!" says Satan, in that snappish way some people has.

"All right. Look at the old arrangement, and what do you find? Just this: the entire and complete and rounded-out sum of an angel's morals is *goodness*—plain, simple *goodness*. What's his equipment—a great long string of Moral Qualities with 28 specifications in it? No, there's only one—*love*. It's the whole outfit. They can't hate, they don't know how, becuz they can't help loving everything and everybody. Just the same, they don't know anything about envy, or jealousy, or avarice, or meanness, or lying, or selfishness, or *any* of those things. And so they're never unhappy, there not being any way for them to *get* unhappy. It makes *character*, don't it? And Al."

"Correct. Go on."

"Now then, look at these new creatures. They've got an immense layout in the way of Moral Qualities, and you'd think they'd have a stunning future in front of them—but it ain't so. For why? Because they've got Love *and* Hate, in the same proportions. The one neutralizes the other. They don't really love, and they don't really hate. They *can't,* you see. It's the same with the whole invoice: Honesty and Dishonesty, exactly the same quantity of each; selfishness and unselfishness; reverence and irreverence; courage and cowardice—and so on and so on. They are all exactly alike, inside and out, these new people—and *characterless.* They're ciphers, nothings, just wax-works. What do you say?"

"I see the point," says Satan. "The old arrangement was better."

*

Well, they got to talking around, and by and by others begun to see the point—and criticize. But not loud—only continuous. In about two hundred thousand years it got all around and come to be common talk everywheres. So at last it got to the Authorities.

"Would it take all that time, Sandy?"

"Here? Yes. It ain't long here, where a thousand years is as a day. It ain't six months, heavenly time. You've often noticed, in history, where the awful oppression of a nation has been going on eight or nine hundred years before Providence interferes, and everybody surprised at the delay. Providence *does* interfere, and mighty prompt, too, as you reconnize when you come to allow for the difference betwixt heavenly time and real time."

"By gracious I never thought of that before! I've been unfair to Providence a many and a many a time, but it was becuz I didn't think. Russia's a case in point; it looks like procrasination, but I see now, it ain't."

"Yes, you see, a thousand years earthly time being exactly a day of heavenly time, then of course a year of earthly time is only just a shade over a minute of heavenly time; and if you don't keep these facts in mind you are naturally bound to think Providence is procrasturing when it's just the other way. It's on accounts of this ignorance that many and many a person has got the idea that prayer ain't ever answered, and stuck to it to his dying day; whereas, prayer is *always* answered. Take praying for rain, f'instance. The prayer comes up; Providence reflects a minute, judges it's all right, and says to the Secretary of State, "turn it on." Down she comes, in a flood. But don't do any good of course, becuz it's a year late. Providence reflecting a minute has made all the trouble, you see. If people would only take the Bible at its word, and reconnize the difference betwixt heavenly time and earthly time, they'd pray for rain a year before they want it, and then they'd be all right. Prayer is always answered, but not inside of a year, becuz Providence has *got* to have a minute to reflect. Otherwise there'd be mistakes, on accounts of too much hurry."

"Why, Sandy, blamed if it don't make everything perfectly plain and understandable, which it never was before. Well, go on about what we was talking about."

"All right. The Authorities got wind of the talk, so they reckoned they would take a private view of them wax figures and see what was to be done. The end was, They concluded to start another Race, and do it better this time. Well, this was the Human Race."

"Wasn't the other the human race too, Sandy?"

"No. That one is neither one thing nor t'other. It ain't human, becuz it's immortal; and it ain't any account, becuz everybody is just alike and hasn't any character. The Holy Doughnuts—that is what they're called, in private."

"Can we go and see them some time, Sandy?" I says.

"Cert'nly. There's excursions every week-day. Well, the Authorities started out on the hypotheneuse that the thing to go for in the new race was *variety*. You see, that's where the Doughnuts failed. Now then, was the Human Race an easy job? Yes, sir, it was. They made rafts of moulds, this time, no two of them alike—so there's your physical differentiations, till you can't rest! Then all They had to do was to take the same old 28 Moral Qualities, and mix them up, helter-skelter, in all sorts of different proportions and ladle them into the moulds—and there's your *dispositional* differentiations, b'George! Variety? Oh, don't mention it! Slattery says to me, 'Sandy,' he says, 'this dreamy old quiet heaven of ourn had been asleep for ages, but if that Human Race didn't wake it up don't you believe *me* no more!'

"Wake it up? Oh, yes, that's what it done. Slattery says the Authorities was awful suprised when they come to examine that Human Race and see how careless They'd been in the distribution of them Qualities, and the results that was a flowing from it.

" 'Sandy,' he says, 'there wasn't any foreman to the job, nor any plan about the distributing. Anybody could help that wanted to; no instructions, only look out and provide *variety*. So these 'commodating volunteers would heave a dipperful of Hate into a mould and season it with a teaspoonful of Love, and there's your

Murderer, all ready for business. And into another mould they'd heave a teaspoonful of Chastity, and flavor it up with a dipperful of Unchastity—and so on and so on. A dipperful of Honesty and a spoonful of Dishonesty; a dipperful of Moral Courage and a spoonful of Moral Cowardice—and there's your splendid man, ready to stand up for an unpopular cause and stake his life on it; in another mould they'd dump considerable Magnanimity, and then dilute it down with Meanness till there wasn't any strength left in it—and so on and so on—the worst mixed-up mess of good and bad dispositions and half-good and half-bad ones a body could imagine—just a tagrag and bobtail Mob of nondescripts, and not worth propagating, of course; but what could the Authorities *do*? Not a thing. It was too late.'"

THE MYSTERIOUS STRANGER

1

IT WAS IN 1590—winter. Austria was far away from the world, and asleep; it was still the Middle Ages in Austria, and promised to remain so forever. Some even set it away back centuries upon centuries and said that by the mental and spiritual clock it was still the Age of Belief in Austria. But they meant it as a compliment, not a slur, and it was so taken, and we were all proud of it. I remember it well, although I was only a boy; and I remember, too, the pleasure it gave me.

Yes, Austria was far from the world, and asleep, and our village was in the middle of that sleep, being in the middle of Austria. It drowsed in peace in the deep privacy of a hilly and woodsy solitude where news from the world hardly ever came to disturb its dreams, and was infinitely content. At its front flowed the tranquil river, its surface painted with cloud-forms and the reflections of drifting arks and stone-boats; behind it rose the woody steeps to the base of the lofty precipice; from the top of the precipice frowned a vast castle, its long stretch of towers and bastions mailed in vines; beyond the river, a league to the left, was a tumbled expanse of forest-clothed hills cloven by winding gorges where the sun never penetrated; and to the right a precipice overlooked the river, and between it and the hills just spoken of lay a far-reaching plain dotted with little homesteads nested among orchards and shade trees.

The whole region for leagues around was the hereditary property of a prince, whose servants kept the castle always in perfect condition for occupancy, but neither he nor his family came there oftener than once in five years. When they came it was as if the lord of the world had arrived, and had brought all the glories of its kingdoms along; and when they went they left a calm behind which was like the deep sleep which follows an orgy.

Eseldorf was a paradise for us boys. We were not overmuch pestered with schooling. Mainly we were trained to be good Christians; to revere the Virgin, the Church, and the saints above everything. Beyond these matters we were not required to know much; and, in fact, not allowed to. Knowledge was not good for the common people, and could make them discontented with the lot which God had appointed for them, and God would not endure discontentment with His plans. We had two priests. One of them, Father Adolf, was a very zealous and strenuous priest, much considered.

There may have been better priests, in some ways, than Father Adolf, but there was never one in our commune who was held in more solemn and awful respect. This was because he had absolutely no fear of the Devil. He was the only Christian I have ever known of whom that could be truly said. People stood in deep dread of him on that account; for they thought that there must be something supernatural about him, else he could not be so bold and so confident. All men speak in bitter disapproval of the Devil, but they do it reverently, not flippantly; but Father Adolf's way was very different; he called him by every name he could lay his tongue to, and it made everyone shudder that heard him; and often he would even speak of him scornfully and scoffingly; then the people crossed themselves and went quickly out of his presence, fearing that something fearful might happen.

Father Adolf had actually met Satan face to face more than once, and defied him. This was known to be so. Father Adolf said it himself. He never made any secret of it, but spoke it right out. And that he was speaking true there was proof in at least one instance, for on that occasion he quarreled with the enemy, and intrepidly threw his bottle at him; and there, upon the wall of his study, was the ruddy splotch where it struck and broke.

But it was Father Peter, the other priest, that we all loved best and were sorriest for. Some people charged him with talking around in conversation that God was all goodness and would find a way to save all his poor human children. It was a horrible thing to say, but there was never any absolute proof that Father Peter said it; and it was out of character for him to say it, too, for he was always good and gentle and truthful. He wasn't charged with saying it in the pulpit, where all the congregation could hear and testify, but only outside, in talk; and it is easy for enemies to manufacture *that*. Father Peter had an enemy and a very powerful one, the astrologer who lived in a tumbled old tower up the valley, and put in his nights studying the stars. Every one knew he could foretell wars and famines, though that was not so hard, for there was always a war and generally a famine somewhere. But he could also read any man's life through the stars in a big book he had, and find lost property, and every one in the village except Father Peter stood in awe of him. Even Father Adolf, who had defied the Devil, had a wholesome respect for the astrologer when he came through our village wearing his tall, pointed hat and his long, flowing robe with stars on it, carrying his big book, and a staff which was known to have magic power. The bishop himself sometimes listened to the astrologer, it was said, for, besides studying the stars and prophesying, the astrologer made a great show of piety, which would impress the bishop, of course.

But Father Peter took no stock in the astrologer. He denounced him openly as a charlatan—a fraud with no valuable knowledge of any kind, or powers beyond those of an ordinary and rather inferior human being, which naturally made the astrologer hate Father Peter and wish to ruin him. It was the astrologer, as we all believed, who originated the story about Father Peter's shocking remark and carried it to the bishop. It was said that Father Peter had made the remark to his niece, Marget, though Marget denied it and implored the bishop to believe her and spare her old uncle from poverty and disgrace. But the bishop wouldn't listen. He suspended Father Peter indefinitely, though he wouldn't go so far as to excommunicate him on the evidence of only one witness; and now Father Peter had been out a couple of years, and our other priest, Father Adolf, had his flock.

Those had been hard years for the old priest and Marget. They had been favorites, but of course that changed when they came under the shadow of the bishop's frown. Many of their friends fell away entirely, and the rest became cool and distant. Marget was a lovely girl of eighteen when the trouble came, and she had the best head in the village, and the most in it. She taught the harp, and earned all her clothes and pocket money by her own industry. But her scholars fell off one by one now; she was forgotten when there were dances and parties among the youth of the village; the young fellows stopped coming to the house, all except Wilhelm Meidling—and he could have been spared; she and her uncle were sad and forlorn in their neglect and disgrace, and the sunshine was gone out of their lives. Matters went worse and worse, all through the two years. Clothes were wearing out, bread was harder and harder to get. And now, at last, the very end was come. Solomon Isaacs had lent all the money he was willing to put on the house, and gave notice that to-morrow he would foreclose.

2

Three of us boys were always together, and had been so from the cradle, being fond of one another from the beginning. and this affection deepened as the years went on—Nikolaus Bauman, son of the principal judge of the local court; Seppi Wohlmeyer, son of the keeper of the principal inn, the "Golden Stag," which had a nice garden, with shade trees reaching down to the riverside, and pleasure boats for hire; and I was the third—Theodor Fischer, son of the church organist, who was also leader of the village musicians, teacher of the violin, composer, tax-collector of the commune, sexton, and in other ways a useful citizen, and respected by all. We knew the hills and the woods as well as the birds knew them; for we were always roaming them when we had leisure—at least, when we were not swimming or boating or fishing, or playing on the ice or sliding down hill.

And we had the run of the castle park, and very few had that. It was because we were pets of the oldest servingman in the castle—Felix Brandt; and often we went there, nights, to hear him talk about old times and strange things, and to smoke with him (he taught us that) and to drink coffee; for he had served in the wars, and was at the siege of Vienna; and there, when the Turks were defeated and driven away, among the captured things were bags of coffee, and the Turkish prisoners explained the character of it and how to make a pleasant drink out of it, and now he always kept coffee by him, to drink himself and also to astonish the ignorant with. When it stormed he kept us all night; and while it thundered and lightened outside he told us about ghosts and horrors of every kind, and of battles and murders and mutilations, and such things, and made it pleasant and cozy inside; and he told these things from his own experience largely. He had seen many ghosts in his time, and witches and enchanters, and once he was lost in a fierce storm at midnight in the mountains, and by the glare of the lightning had seen the Wild Huntsman rage on the blast with his specter dogs chasing after him through the driving cloud-rack. Also he had seen an incubus once, and several times he had seen the great bat that sucks the blood from the necks of people while they are asleep, fanning them softly with its wings and so keeping them drowsy till they die.

He encouraged us not to fear supernatural things, such as ghosts, and said they did no harm, but only wandered about because they were lonely and distressed and wanted kindly notice and compassion; and in time we learned not to be afraid, and even went down with him in the night to the haunted chamber in the dungeons of the castle. The ghost appeared only once, and it went by very dim to the sight and floated noiseless through the air, and then disappeared; and we scarcely trembled, he had taught us so well. He said it came up sometimes in the night and woke him by passing its clammy hand over his face, but it did him no hurt; it only wanted sympathy and notice. But the strangest thing was that he had seen angels— actual angels out of heaven—and had talked with them. They had no wings, and wore clothes, and talked and looked and acted just like any natural person, and you would never know them for angels except for the wonderful things they did which a mortal could not do, and the way they suddenly disappeared while you were talking with them, which was also a thing which no mortal could do. And he said they were pleasant and cheerful, not gloomy and melancholy, like ghosts.

It was after that kind of a talk one May night that we got up next morning and had a good breakfast with him and then went down and crossed the bridge and went away up into the hills on the left to a woody hill-top which was a favorite place of ours, and there we stretched out on the grass in the shade to rest and smoke and talk over these strange things, for they were in our minds yet, and impressing us. But we couldn't smoke, because we had been heedless and left our flint and steel behind.

Soon there came a youth strolling toward us through the trees, and he sat down and began to talk in a friendly way, just as if he knew us. But we did not answer him, for he was a stranger and we were not used to strangers and were shy of them. He had new and good clothes on, and was handsome and had a winning face and a pleasant voice, and was easy and graceful and unembarrassed, not slouchy and awkward and diffident, like other boys. We wanted to be friendly with him, but didn't know how to begin. Then I thought of the pipe, and wondered if it would be taken as kindly meant if I offered it to him. But I remembered that we had no fire, so I was sorry and disappointed. But he looked up bright and pleased, and said:

"Fire? Oh, that is easy; I will furnish it."

I was so astonished I couldn't speak; for I had not said anything. He took the pipe and blew his breath on it, and the tobacco glowed red, and spirals of blue smoke rose up. We jumped up and were going to run, for that was natural; and we did run a few steps, although he was yearningly pleading for us to stay, and giving us his word that he would not do us any harm, but only wanted to be friends with us and have company. So we stopped and stood, and wanted to go back, being full of curiosity and wonder, but afraid to venture. He went on coaxing, in his soft, persuasive way; and when we saw that the pipe did not blow up and nothing happened, our confidence returned by little and little, and presently our curiosity got to be stronger than our fear, and we ventured back—but slowly, and ready to fly at any alarm.

He was bent on putting us at ease, and he had the right art; one could not remain doubtful and timorous where a person was so earnest and simple and gentle, and talked so alluringly as he did; no, he won us over, and it was not long before we were content and comfortable and chatty, and glad we had found this new friend. When the feeling of constraint was all gone we asked him how he had learned to do that strange thing, and he said he hadn't learned it at all; it came natural to him—like other things—other curious things.

"What ones?"

"Oh, a number; I don't know how many."

"Will you let us see you do them?"

"Do—please!" the others said.

"You won't run away again?"

"No—indeed we won't. Please do. Won't you?"

"Yes, with pleasure; but you mustn't forget your promise, you know."

We said we wouldn't, and he went to a puddle and came back with water in a cup which he had made out of a leaf, and blew upon it and threw it out, and it was a lump of ice the shape of the cup. We were astonished and charmed, but not afraid any more; we were very glad to be there, and asked him to go on and do some more things. And he did. He said he would give us any kind of fruit we liked, whether it was in season or not. We all spoke at once;

"Orange!"

"Apple!"

"Grapes!"

"They are in your pockets," he said, and it was true. And they were of the best, too, and we ate them and wished we had more, though none of us said so.

"You will find them where those came from," he said, "and everything else your appetites call for; and you need not name the thing you wish; as long as I am with you, you have only to wish and find."

And he said true. There was never anything so wonderful and so interesting. Bread, cakes, sweets, nuts—whatever one wanted, it was there. He ate nothing himself, but sat and chatted, and did one curious thing after another to amuse us. He made a tiny toy squirrel out of clay, and it ran up a tree and sat on a limb overhead and barked down at us. Then he made a dog that was not much larger than a mouse, and it treed the squirrel and danced about the tree, excited and barking, and was as alive as any dog could be. It frightened the squirrel from tree to tree and followed it up until both were out of sight in the forest. He made birds out of clay and set them free, and they flew away, singing.

At last I made bold to ask him to tell us who he was.

"An angel," he said, quite simply, and set another bird free and clapped his hands and made it fly away.

A kind of awe fell upon us when we heard him say that, and we were afraid again; but he said we need not be troubled, there was no occasion for us to be afraid of an angel, and he liked us, anyway. He went on chatting as simply and unaffectedly as ever; and while he talked he made a crowd of little men and women the size of your finger, and they went diligently to work and cleared and leveled off a space a couple of yards square in the grass and began to build a cunning little castle in it, the women mixing the mortar and carrying it up the scaffoldings in pails on their heads, just as our work-women have always done, and the men laying the courses of masonry—five hundred of these toy people swarming briskly about and working diligently and wiping the sweat off their faces as natural as life. In the absorbing interest of watching those five hundred little people make the castle grow step by step and course by course, and take shape and symmetry, that feeling and awe soon passed away and we were quite comfortable and at home again. We asked if we might make some people, and he said yes, and told Seppi to make some cannon for the walls, and told Nikolaus to make some halberdiers, with breastplates and greaves and helmets, and I was to make some cavalry, with horses, and in allotting these tasks he called us by our names, but did not say how he knew them. Then Seppi asked him what his own name was, and he said, tranquilly, "Satan," and held out a chip and caught a little woman on it who was falling from the scaffolding and put her back where she belonged, and said, "She is an idiot to step backward like that and not notice what she is about."

It caught us suddenly, that name did, and our work dropped out of our hands and broke to pieces—a cannon, a halberdier, and a horse. Satan laughed, and asked what was the matter. I said, "Nothing, only it seemed a strange name for an angel." He asked why.

"Because it's—it's—well, it's his name, you know."

"Yes—he is my uncle."

He said it placidly, but it took our breath for a moment and made our hearts beat. He did not seem to notice that, but mended our halberdiers and things with a touch, handing them to us finished, and said, "Don't you remember?—he was an angel himself, once."

"Yes—it's true," said Seppi; "I didn't think of that."

"Before the Fall he was blameless."

"Yes," said Nikolaus, "he was without sin."

"It is a good family—ours," said Satan; "there is not a better. He is the only member of it that has ever sinned."

I should not be able to make any one understand how exciting it all was. You know that kind of quiver that trembles around through you when you are seeing something so strange and enchanting and wonderful that it is just a fearful joy to be alive and look at it; and you know how you gaze, and your lips turn dry and your breath comes short, but you wouldn't be anywhere but there, not for the world. I was bursting to ask one question—I had it on my tongue's end and could hardly hold it back—but I was ashamed to ask it; it might be a rudeness. Satan set an ox down that he had been making, and smiled up at me and said:

"It wouldn't be a rudeness, and I should forgive it if it was. Have I seen him? Millions of times. From the time that I was a little child a thousand years old I was his second favorite among the nursery angels of our blood and lineage—to use a human phrase—yes, from that time until the Fall, eight thousand years, measured as you count time."

"Eight—thousand!"

"Yes." He turned to Seppi, and went on as if answering something that was in Seppi's mind: "Why, naturally I look like a boy, for that is what I am. With us what you call time is a spacious thing; it takes a long stretch of it to grow an angel to full age." There was a question in my mind, and he turned to me and answered it, "I am sixteen thousand years old—counting as you count." Then he turned to Nikolaus and said: "No, the Fall did not affect me nor the rest of the relationship. It was only he that I was named for who ate of the fruit of the tree and then beguiled the man and the woman with it. We others are still ignorant of sin; we are not able to commit it; we are without blemish, and shall abide in that estate always. We—" Two of the little workmen were quarreling, and in buzzing little bumblebee voices they were cursing and swearing at each other; now came blows and blood; then they locked themselves together in a life-and-death struggle. Satan reached out his hand and crushed the life out of them with his fingers, threw them away, wiped the red from his fingers on his handkerchief, and went on talking where he had left off: "We cannot do wrong; neither have we any disposition to do it, for we do not know what it is."

It seemed a strange speech, in the circumstances, but we barely noticed that, we were so shocked and grieved at the wanton murder he had committed—for murder it was, that was its true name, and it was without palliation or excuse, for the men had not wronged him in any way. It made us miserable, for we loved him, and had thought him so noble and so beautiful and gracious, and had honestly believed he was an angel; and to have him do this cruel thing—ah, it lowered him so, and we had had such pride in him. He went right on talking, just as if nothing had happened, telling about his travels, and the interesting things he had seen in the big worlds of our solar systems and of other solar systems far away in the remotenesses of space, and about the customs of the immortals that inhabit them, somehow fascinating us, enchanting us, charming us in spite of the pitiful scene that was now under our eyes, for the wives of the little dead men had found the crushed and shapeless bodies and were crying over them, and sobbing and lamenting, and a priest was kneeling there with his hands crossed upon his breast, praying; and crowds and crowds of pitying friends were massed about them, reverently uncovered, with their bare heads bowed, and many with the tears running down—a scene which Satan paid no attention to until the small noise of the weeping and praying began to annoy him, then he reached out and took the heavy board seat out of our swing and brought it down and mashed all those people into the earth just as if they had been flies, and went on talking just the same.

An angel, and kill a priest! An angel who did not know how to do wrong, and yet destroys in cold blood hundreds of helpless poor men and women who had never done him any harm! It made us sick to see that awful deed, and to think that none of those poor creatures was prepared except the priest, for none of them had ever heard a mass or seen a church. And we were witnesses; we had seen these murders done and it was our duty to tell, and let the law take its course.

But he went on talking right along, and worked his enchantments upon us again with that fatal music of his voice. He made us forget everything; we could only listen to him, and love him, and be his slaves, to do with us as he would. He made us drunk with the joy of being with him, and of looking into the heaven of his eyes, and of feeling the ecstasy that thrilled along our veins from the touch of his hand.

3

The stranger had seen everything, he had been everywhere, he knew everything, and he forgot nothing. What another must study, he learned at a glance; there were no difficulties for him. And he made things live before you when he told about them. He saw the world made; he saw Adam created; he saw Samson surge against the pillars and bring the temple down in ruins about him; he saw Cæsar's death; he told of the daily life in heaven; he had seen the damned writhing in the red waves of hell; and he made us see all these things, and it was as if we were on the spot and looking at them

with our own eyes. And we felt them, too, but there was no sign
that they were anything to him beyond mere entertainments.
Those visions of hell, those poor babes and women and girls and
lads and men shrieking and supplicating in anguish—why, we could
hardly bear it, but he was as bland about it as if it had been so many
imitation rats in an artificial fire.

And always when he was talking about men and women here on
the earth and their doings—even their grandest and sublimest—we
were secretly ashamed, for his manner showed that to him they and
their doings were of paltry poor consequence; often you would
think he was talking about flies, if you didn't know. Once he even
said, in so many words, that our people down here were quite
interesting to him, notwithstanding they were so dull and ignorant
and trivial and conceited, and so diseased and rickety, and such a
shabby, poor, worthless lot all around. He said it in a quite matter-
of-course way and without bitterness, just as a person might talk
about bricks or manure or any other thing that was of no consequence and hadn't feelings. I could see he meant no offense, but in
my thoughts I set it down as not very good manners.

"Manners!" he said. "Why, it is merely the truth, and truth is
good manners; manners are a fiction. The castle is done. Do you
like it?"

Any one would have been obliged to like it. It was lovely to look
at, it was so shapely and fine, and so cunningly perfect in all its
particulars, even to the little flags waving from the turrets. Satan
said we must put the artillery in place now, and station the
halberdiers and display the cavalry. Our men and horses were a
spectacle to see, they were so little like what they were intended
for; for, of course, we had no art in making such things. Satan said
they were the worst he had seen; and when he touched them and
made them alive, it was just ridiculous the way they acted, on
account of their legs not being of uniform lengths. They reeled and
sprawled around as if they were drunk, and endangered everybody's
lives around them, and finally fell over and lay helpless and kicking.
It made us all laugh, though it was a shameful thing to see. The
guns were charged with dirt, to fire a salute, but they were so
crooked and so badly made that they all burst when they went off,
and killed some of the gunners and crippled the others. Satan said
we would have a storm now, and an earthquake, if we liked, but
we must stand off a piece, out of danger. We wanted to call the

people away, too, but he said never mind them; they were of no consequence, and we could make more, some time or other, if we needed them.

A small storm-cloud began to settle down black over the castle, and the miniature lightning and thunder began to play, and the ground to quiver, and the wind to pipe and wheeze, and the rain to fall, and all the people flocked into the castle for shelter. The cloud settled down blacker and blacker, and one could see the castle only dimly through it; the lightning blazed out flash upon flash and pierced the castle and set it on fire, and the flames shone out red and fierce through the cloud, and the people came flying out, shrieking, but Satan brushed them back, paying no attention to our begging and crying and imploring; and in the midst of the howling of the wind and volleying of the thunder the magazine blew up, the earthquake rent the ground wide, and the castle's wreck and ruin tumbled into the chasm, which swallowed it from sight, and closed upon it, with all that innocent life, not one of the five hundred poor creatures escaping. Our hearts were broken; we could not keep from crying.

"Don't cry," Satan said; "they were of no value."

"But they are gone to hell!"

"Oh, it is no matter; we can make plenty more."

It was of no use to try to move him; evidently he was wholly without feeling, and could not understand. He was full of bubbling spirits, and as gay as if this were a wedding instead of a fiendish massacre. And he was bent on making us feel as he did, and of course his magic accomplished his desire. It was no trouble to him; he did whatever he pleased with us. In a little while we were dancing on that grave, and he was playing to us on a strange, sweet instrument which he took out of his pocket; and the music—but there is no music like that, unless perhaps in heaven, and that was where he brought it from, he said. It made one mad, for pleasure; and we could not take our eyes from him, and the looks that went out of our eyes came from our hearts, and their dumb speech was worship. He brought the dance from heaven, too, and the bliss of paradise was in it.

Presently he said he must go away on an errand. But we could not bear the thought of it, and clung to him, and pleaded with him to stay; and that pleased him, and he said so, and said he would not go yet, but would wait a little while and we would sit down and talk a few minutes longer; and he told us Satan was only his real name, and he was to be known by it to us alone, but he had chosen another one to be called by in the presence of others; just a common one, such as people have—Philip Traum.

It sounded so odd and mean for such a being! But it was his decision, and we said nothing; his decision was sufficient.

We had seen wonders this day; and my thoughts began to run on the pleasure it would be to tell them when I got home, but he noticed those thoughts, and said:

"No, all these matters are a secret among us four. I do not mind your trying to tell them, if you like, but I will protect your tongues, and nothing of the secret will escape from them."

It was a disappointment, but it couldn't be helped, and it cost us a sigh or two. We talked pleasantly along, and he was always reading our thoughts and responding to them, and it seemed to me that this was the most wonderful of all the things he did, but he interrupted my musings and said:

"No, it would be wonderful for you, but it is not wonderful for me. I am not limited like you. I am not subject to human conditions. I can measure and understand your human weaknesses, for I have studied them; but I have none of them. My flesh is not real, although it would seem firm to your touch; my clothes are not real; I am a spirit. Father Peter is coming." We looked around, but did not see any one. "He is not in sight yet, but you will see him presently."

"Do you know him, Satan?"

"No."

"Won't you talk with him when he comes? He is not ignorant and dull, like us, and he would so like to talk with you. Will you?"

"Another time, yes, but not now. I must go on my errand after a little. There he is now; you can see him. Sit still, and don't say anything."

We looked up and saw Father Peter approaching through the chestnuts. We three were sitting together in the grass, and Satan sat in front of us in the path. Father Peter came slowly along with his head down, thinking, and stopped within a couple of yards of us and took off his hat and got out his silk handkerchief, and stood there mopping his face and looking as if he were going to speak to us, but he didn't. Presently he muttered, "I can't think what brought me here; it seems as if I were in my study a minute ago—

but I suppose I have been dreaming along for an hour and have come all this stretch without noticing; for I am not myself in these troubled days." Then he went mumbling along to himself and walked straight through Satan, just as if nothing were there. It made us catch our breath to see it. We had the impulse to cry out, the way you nearly always do when a startling thing happens, but something mysteriously restrained us and we remained quiet, only breathing fast. Then the trees hid Father Peter after a little, and Satan said:

"It is as I told you—I am only a spirit."

"Yes, one perceives it now," said Nikolaus, "but we are not spirits. It is plain he did not see you, but were we invisible, too? He looked at us, but he didn't seem to see us. "

"No, none of us was visible to him, for I wished it so."

It seemed almost too good to he true, that we were actually seeing these romantic and wonderful things, and that it was not a dream. And there he sat, looking just like anybody—so natural and simple and charming, and chatting along again the same as ever, and—well, words cannot make you understand what we felt. It was an ecstasy; and an ecstasy is a thing that will not go into words; it feels like music, and one cannot tell about music so that another person can get the feeling of it. He was back in the old ages once more now, and making them live before us. He had seen so much, so much! It was just a wonder to look at him and try to think how it must seem to have such experience behind one.

But it made you seem sorrowfully trivial, and the creature of a day, and such a short and paltry day, too. And he didn't say anything to raise up your drooping pride—no, not a word. He always spoke of men in the same old indifferent way—just as one speaks of bricks and manure-piles and such things; you could see that they were of no consequence to him, one way or the other. He didn't mean to hurt us, you could see that; just as we don't mean to insult a brick when we disparage it; a brick's emotions are nothing to us; it never occurs to us to think whether it has any or not.

Once when he was bunching the most illustrious kings and conquerors and poets and prophets and pirates and beggars together—just a brick-pile—I was shamed into putting in a word for man, and asked him why he made so much difference between men and himself. He had to struggle with that a moment; he didn't seem to understand how I could ask such a strange question. Then he said:

"The difference between man and me? The difference between a mortal and an immortal? between a cloud and a spirit?" He picked up a wood-louse that was creeping along a piece of bark: "What is the difference between Cæsar and this?"

I said, "One cannot compare things which by their nature and by the interval between them are not comparable."

"You have answered your own question," he said. "I will expand it. Man is made of dirt—I saw him made. I am not made of dirt. Man is a museum of diseases, a home of impurities; he comes to-day and is gone to-morrow; he begins as dirt and departs as stench; I am of the aristocracy of the Imperishables. And man has the *Moral Sense*. You understand? He has the *Moral Sense*. That would seem to be difference enough between us, all by itself."

He stopped there, as if that settled the matter. I was sorry, for at that time I had but a dim idea of what the Moral Sense was. I merely knew that we were proud of having it, and when he talked like that about it, it wounded me, and I felt as a girl feels who thinks her dearest finery is being admired and then overhears strangers making fun of it. For a while we were all silent, and I, for one, was depressed. Then Satan began to chat again, and soon he was sparkling along in such a cheerful and vivacious vein that my spirits rose once more. He told some very cunning things that put us in a gale of laughter; and when he was telling about the time that Samson tied the torches to the foxes' tails and set them loose in the Philistines' corn, and Samson sitting on the fence slapping his thighs and laughing, with the tears running down his cheeks, and lost his balance and fell off the fence, the memory of that picture got him to laughing, too, and we did have a most lovely and jolly time. By and by he said:

"I am going on my errand now."

"Don't!" we all said. "Don't go; stay with us; You won't come back."

"Yes, I will; I give you my word."

"When? To-night? Say when."

"It won't be long. You will see."

"We like you."

"And I you. And as a proof of it I will show you something fine to see. Usually when I go I merely vanish; but now I will dissolve myself and let you see me do it."

He stood up, and it was quickly finished. He thinned away and thinned away until he was a soap-bubble, except that he kept his shape. You could see the bushes through him as clearly as you see things through a soap-bubble, and all over him played and flashed the delicate iridescent colors of the bubble, and along with them was that thing shaped like a window-sash which you always see on the globe of the bubble. You have seen a bubble strike the carpet and lightly bound along two or three times before it bursts. He did that. He sprang—touched the grass—bounded—floated along—touched again—and so on, and presently exploded—puff! and in his place was vacancy.

It was a strange and beautiful thing to see. We did not say anything, but sat wondering and dreaming and blinking; and finally Seppi roused up and said, mournfully sighing:

"I suppose none of it has happened."

Nikolaus sighed and said about the same.

I was miserable to hear them say it, for it was the same cold fear that was in my own mind. Then we saw poor old Father Peter wandering along back, with his head bent down, searching the ground. When he was pretty close to us he looked up and saw us, and said, "How long have you been here, boys?"

"A little while, Father."

"Then it is since I came by, and maybe you can help me. Did you come up by the path?"

"Yes, Father."

"That is good. I came the same way. I have lost my wallet. There wasn't much in it, but a very little is much to me, for it was all I had. I suppose you haven't seen anything of it?"

"No, Father, but we will help you hunt."

"It is what I was going to ask you. Why, here it is!"

We hadn't noticed it; yet there it lay, right where Satan stood when he began to melt—if he did melt and it wasn't a delusion. Father Peter picked it up and looked very much surprised.

"It is mine," he said, "but not the contents. This is fat; mine was flat; mine was light; this is heavy." He opened it; it was stuffed as full as it could hold with gold coins. He let us gaze our fill; and of course we did gaze, for we had never seen so much money at one time before. All our mouths came open to say "Satan did it!" but nothing came out. There it was, you see—we couldn't tell what Satan didn't want told; he had said so himself.

"Boys, did you do this?"

It made us laugh. And it made him laugh, too, as soon as he thought what a foolish question it was.

"Who has been here?"

Our mouths came open to answer, but stood so for a moment, because we couldn't say "Nobody," for it wouldn't be true, and the right word didn't seem to come; then I thought of the right one, and said it:

"Not a human being."

"That is so," said the others, and let their mouths go shut.

"It is not so," said Father Peter, and looked at us very severely. "I came by here a while ago, and there was no one here, but that is nothing; some one has been here since. I don't mean to say that the person didn't pass here before you came, and I don't mean to say you saw him, but some one did pass, that I know. On your honor—you saw no one?"

"Not a human being."

"That is sufficient; I know you are telling me the truth."

He began to count the money on the path, we on our knees eagerly helping to stack it in little piles.

"It's eleven hundred ducats odd!" he said. "Oh dear! if it were only mine—and I need it so!" and his voice broke and his lips quivered.

"It is yours, sir!" we all cried out at once, "every heller!"

"No—it isn't mine. Only four ducats are mine; the rest . . . !" He fell to dreaming, poor old soul, and caressing some of the coins in his hands, and forgot where he was, sitting there on his heels with his old gray head bare; it was pitiful to see. "No," he said, waking up, "it isn't mine. I can't account for it. I think some enemy . . . it must be a trap."

Nikolaus said: "Father Peter, with the exception of the astrologer you haven't a real enemy in the village—nor Marget, either. And not even a half-enemy that's rich enough to chance eleven hundred ducats to do you a mean turn. I'll ask you if that's so or not?"

He couldn't get around that argument, and it cheered him up. "But it isn't mine, you see—it isn't mine, in any case."

He said it in a wistful way, like a person that wouldn't be sorry, but glad, if anybody would contradict him.

"It is yours, Father Peter, and we are witness to it. Aren't we, boys?"

"Yes, we are—and we'll stand by it, too."

"Bless your hearts, you do almost persuade me; you do, indeed. If I had only a hundred-odd ducats of it! The house is mortgaged for it, and we've no home for our heads if we don't pay to-morrow. And that four ducats is all we've got in the—"

"It's yours, every bit of it, and you've got to take it—we are bail that it's all right. Aren't we, Theodor? Aren't we, Seppi?"

We two said yes, and Nikolaus stuffed the money back into the shabby old wallet and made the owner take it. So he said he would use two hundred of it, for his house was good enough security for that, and would put the rest at interest till the rightful owner came for it; and on our side we must sign a paper showing how he got the money—a paper to show to the villagers as proof that he had not got out of his troubles dishonestly.

4

It made immense talk next day, when Father Peter paid Solomon Isaacs in gold and left the rest of the money with him at interest. Also, there was a pleasant change; many people called at the house to congratulate him, and a number of cool old friends became kind and friendly again; and, to top all, Marget was invited to a party.

And there was no mystery; Father Peter told the whole circumstance just as it happened, and said he could not account for it, only it was the plain hand of Providence, so far as he could see.

One or two shook their heads and said privately it looked more like the hand of Satan; and really that seemed a surprisingly good guess for ignorant people like that. Some came slyly buzzing around and tried to coax us boys to come out and "tell the truth"; and promised they wouldn't ever tell, but only wanted to know for their own satisfaction, because the whole thing was so curious. They even wanted to buy the secret, and pay money for it; and if we could have invented something that would answer—but we couldn't; we hadn't the ingenuity, so we had to let the chance go by, and it was a pity.

We carried that secret around without any trouble, but the other one, the big one, the splendid one, burned the very vitals of us, it was so hot to get out and we so hot to let it out and astonish people with it. But we had to keep it in; in fact, it kept itself in. Satan said it would, and it did. We went off every day and got to ourselves in the woods so that we could talk about Satan, and really that was the only subject we thought of or cared anything about; and day and night we watched for him and hoped he would come, and we got more and more impatient all the time. We hadn't any interest in the other boys any more, and wouldn't take part in their games and enterprises. They seemed so tame, after Satan; and their doings so trifling and commonplace after his adventures in antiquity and the constellations, and his miracles and meltings and explosions, and all that.

During the first day we were in a state of anxiety on account of one thing, and we kept going to Father Peter's house on one pretext or another to keep track of it. That was the gold coin; we were afraid it would crumble and turn to dust, like fairy money. If it did— But it didn't. At the end of the day no complaint had been made about it, so after that we were satisfied that it was real gold, and dropped the anxiety out of our minds.

There was a question which we wanted to ask Father Peter, and finally we went there the second evening, a little diffidently, after drawing straws, and I asked it as casually as I could, though it did not sound as casual as I wanted, because I didn't know how:

"What is the Moral Sense, sir?"

He looked down, surprised, over his great spectacles, and said, "Why, it is the faculty which enables us to distinguish good from evil."

It threw some light, but not a glare, and I was a little disappointed, also to some degree embarrassed. He was waiting for me to go on, so, in default of anything else to say, I asked, "Is it valuable?"

"Valuable? Heavens! lad, it is the one thing that lifts man above the beasts that perish and makes him heir to immortality!"

This did not remind me of anything further to say, so I got out, with the other boys, and we went away with that indefinite sense you have often had of being filled but not fatted. They wanted me to explain, but I was tired.

We passed out through the parlor, and there was Marget at the spinnet teaching Marie Lueger. So one of the deserting pupils was back; and an influential one, too; the others would follow. Marget jumped up and ran and thanked us again, with tears in her eyes— this was the third time—for saving her and her uncle from being turned into the street, and we told her again we hadn't done it; but that was her way, she never could be grateful enough for anything a person did for her; so we let her have her say. And as we passed through the garden, there was Wilhelm Merdling sitting there waiting, for it was getting toward the edge of the evening, and he would be asking Marget to take a walk along the river with him when she was done with the lesson. He was a young lawyer, and succeeding fairly well and working his way along, little by little. He was very fond of Marget, and she of him. He had not deserted along with the others, but had stood his ground all through. His faithfulness was not lost on Marget and her uncle. He hadn't so very much talent, but he was handsome and good, and these are a kind of talents themselves and help along. He asked us how the lesson was getting along, and we told him it was about done. And maybe it was so; we didn't know anything about it, but we judged it would please him, and it did, and didn't cost us anything.

5

On the fourth day comes the astrologer from his crumbling old tower up the valley, where he had heard the news, I reckon. He had a private talk with us, and we told him what we could, for we were mightily in dread of him. He sat there studying and studying awhile to himself; then he asked:

"How many ducats did you say?"

"Eleven hundred and seven, sir."

Then he said, as if he were talking to himself: "It is ver-y singular. Yes . . . very strange. A curious coincidence." Then he began to ask questions, and went over the whole ground from the beginning, we answering. By and by he said: "Eleven hundred and six ducats. It is a large sum."

"Seven," said Seppi, correcting him.

"Oh, seven, was it? Of course a ducat more or less isn't of consequence, but you said eleven hundred and six before."

It would not have been safe for us to say he was mistaken, but we knew he was. Nikolaus said, "We ask pardon for the mistake, but we meant to say seven."

"Oh, it is no matter, lad; it was merely that I noticed the discrepancy. It is several days, and you cannot be expected to remember precisely. One is apt to be inexact when there is no particular circumstance to impress the count upon the memory."

"But there was one, sir," said Seppi, eagerly.

"What was it, my son?" asked the astrologer, indifferently.

"First, we all counted the piles of coin, each in turn, and all made it the same—eleven hundred and six. But I had slipped one out, for fun, when the count began, and now I slipped it back and said, 'I think there is a mistake—there are eleven hundred and seven; let us count again.' We did, and of course I was right. They were astonished; then I told how it came about."

The astrologer asked us if this was so, and we said it was.

"That settles it," he said. "I know the thief now. Lads, the money was stolen."

Then he went away, leaving us very much troubled, and wondering what he could mean. In about an hour we found out; for by that time it was all over the village that Father Peter had been arrested for stealing a great sum of money from the astrologer. Everybody's tongue was loose and going. Many said it was not in Father Peter's character and must be a mistake; but the others shook their heads and said misery and want could drive a suffering man to almost anything. About one detail there were no differences; all agreed that Father Peter's account of how the money came into his hands was just about unbelievable—it had such an impossible look. They said it might have come into the astrologer's hands in some such way, but into Father Peter's, never! Our characters began to suffer now. We were Father Peter's only witnesses; how much did he probably pay us to back up his fantastic tale? People talked that kind of talk to us pretty freely and frankly, and were full of scoffings when we begged them to believe really we had told only the truth. Our parents were harder on us than any one else. Our fathers said we were disgracing our families, and they commanded us to purge ourselves of our lie, and there was no limit to their anger when we continued to say we had spoken true. Our mothers cried over us and begged us to give back our bribe and get back our honest names and save our families from shame, and come out and honorably confess. And at last we were so worried and harassed that we tried to tell the whole thing, Satan and all—but no, it wouldn't come out. We were hoping and longing all the time that Satan would come and help us out of our trouble, but there was no sign of him.

Within an hour after the astrologer's talk with us, Father Peter was in prison and the money sealed up and in the hands of the officers of the law. The money was in a bag, and Solomon Isaacs said he had not touched it since he had counted it; his oath was taken that it was the same money, and that the amount was eleven hundred and seven ducats. Father Peter claimed trial by the ecclesiastical court, but our other priest, Father Adolf, said an ecclesiastical court hadn't jurisdiction over a suspended priest. The bishop upheld him. That settled it; the case would go to trial in the civil court. The court would not sit for some time to come. Wilhelm Meidling would be Father Peter's lawyer and do the best he could, of course, but he told us privately that a weak case on his side and all the power and prejudice on the other made the outlook bad.

So Marget's new happiness died a quick death. No friends came to condole with her, and none were expected; an unsigned note withdrew her invitation to the party. There would be no scholars to take lessons. How could she support herself? She could remain in the house, for the mortgage was paid off, though the government and not poor Solomon Isaacs had the mortgage-money in its grip for the present. Old Ursula, who was cook, chambermaid, housekeeper, laundress, and everything else for Father Peter, and had been Marget's nurse in earlier years, said God would provide. But she said that from habit, for she was a good Christian. She meant to help in the providing, to make sure, if she could find a way.

We boys wanted to go and see Marget and show friendliness for her, but our parents were afraid of offending the community and wouldn't let us. The astrologer was going around inflaming everybody against Father Peter, and saying he was an abandoned thief and had stolen eleven hundred and seven gold ducats from him. He said he knew he was a thief from that fact, for it was exactly the sum he had lost and which Father Peter pretended he had "found."

In the afternoon of the fourth day after the catastrophe old Ursula appeared at our house and asked for some washing to do, and begged my mother to keep this secret, to save Marget's pride, who would stop this project if she found it out, yet Marget had not enough to eat and was growing weak. Ursula was growing weak herself, and showed it; and she ate of the food that was offered her like a starving person, but could not be persuaded to carry any home, for Marget would not eat charity food. She took some clothes down to the stream to wash them, but we saw from the window that handling the bat was too much for her strength; so she was called back and a trifle of money offered her, which she was afraid to take lest Marget should suspect; then she took it, saying she would explain that she found it in the road. To keep it from being a lie and damning her soul, she got me to drop it while she watched; then she went along by there and found it, and exclaimed with surprise and joy, and picked it up and went her way. Like the rest of the village, she could tell every-day lies fast enough and without taking any precautions against fire and brimstone on their account; but this was a new kind of lie, and it had a dangerous look because she hadn't had any practice in it. After a week's practice it wouldn't have given her any trouble. It is the way we are made.

I was in trouble, for how would Marget live? Ursula could not find a coin in the road every day—perhaps not even a second one. And I was ashamed, too, for not having been near Marget, and she so in need of friends; but that was my parents' fault, not mine, and I couldn't help it.

I was walking along the path, feeling very downhearted, when a most cheery and tingling freshening-up sensation went rippling through me, and I was too glad for any words, for I knew by that sign that Satan was by. I had noticed it before. Next moment he was alongside of me and I was telling him all my trouble and what had been happening to Marget and her uncle. While we were talking we turned a curve and saw old Ursula resting in the shade of a tree, and she had a lean stray kitten in her lap and was petting it. I asked her where she got it, and she said it came out of the woods and followed her; and she said it probably hadn't any mother or any friends and she was going to take it home and take care of it. Satan said:

"I understand you are very poor. Why do you want to add another mouth to feed? Why don't you give it to some rich person?"

Ursula bridled at this and said: "Perhaps you would like to have it. You must be rich, with your fine clothes and quality airs." Then she sniffed and said: "Give it to the rich—the idea! The rich don't care for anybody but themselves; it's only the poor that have feeling for the poor, and help them. The poor and God. God will provide for this kitten."

"What makes you think so?"

Ursula's eyes snapped with anger. "Because I know it!" she said. "Not a sparrow falls to the ground without His seeing it."

"But it falls, just the same. What good is seeing it fall?"

Old Ursula's jaws worked, but she could not get any word out for the moment, she was so horrified. When she got her tongue she stormed out, "Go about your business, you puppy, or I will take a stick to you!"

I could not speak, I was so scared. I knew that with his notions about the human race Satan would consider it a matter of no consequence to strike her dead, there being "plenty more"; but my tongue stood still, I could give her no warning. But nothing happened; Satan remained tranquil—tranquil and indifferent. I suppose he could not be insulted by Ursula any more than the king could be insulted by a tumble-bug. The old woman jumped to her feet when she made her remark, and did it as briskly as a young girl. It had been many years since she had done the like of that. That was Satan's influence; he was a fresh breeze to the weak and the sick, wherever he came. His presence affected even the lean kitten, and it skipped to the ground and began to chase a leaf. This surprised Ursula, and she stood looking at the creature and nodding her head wonderingly, her anger quite forgotten.

"What's come over it?" she said. "Awhile ago it could hardly walk."

"You have not seen a kitten of that breed before," said Satan.

Ursula was not proposing to be friendly with the mocking stranger, and she gave him an ungentle look and retorted: "Who asked you to come here and pester me, I'd like to know? And what do you know about what I've seen and what I haven't seen?"

"You haven't seen a kitten with the hair-spines on its tongue pointing to the front, have you?"

"No—nor you, either."

"Well, examine this one and see."

Ursula was become pretty spry, but the kitten was spryer, and she could not catch it, and had to give it up. Then Satan said:

"Give it a name, and maybe it will come."

Ursula tried several names, but the kitten was not interested. "Call it Agnes. Try that."

The creature answered to the name and came. Ursula examined its tongue. "Upon my word, it's true!" she said. "I have not seen this kind of a cat before. Is it yours?"

"No."

"Then how did you know its name so pat?"

"Because all cats of that breed are named Agnes; they will not answer to any other."

Ursula was impressed. "It is the most wonderful thing!" Then a shadow of trouble came into her face, for her superstitions were aroused, and she reluctantly put the creature down, saying: "I suppose I must let it go; I am not afraid—no, not exactly that, though the priest—well, I've heard people—indeed, many people

. . . And, besides, it is quite well now and can take care of itself." She sighed, and turned to go, murmuring: "It is such a pretty one, too, and would be such company—and the house is so sad and lonesome these troubled days . . . Miss Marget so mournful and just a shadow, and the old master shut up in jail."

"It seems a pity not to keep it," said Satan.

Ursula turned quickly—just as if she were hoping some one would encourage her.

"Why?" she asked, wistfully.

"Because this breed brings luck."

"Does it? Is it true? Young man, do you know it to be true? How does it bring luck?"

"Well, it brings money, anyway."

Ursula looked disappointed. "Money? A cat bring money? The idea! You could never sell it here; people do not buy cats here: one can't even give them away." She turned to go.

"I don't mean sell it. I mean have an income from it. This kind is called the Lucky Cat. Its owner finds four silver groschen in his pocket every morning."

I saw the indignation rising in the old woman's face. She was insulted. This boy was making fun of her. That was her thought. She thrust her hands into her pockets and straightened up to give him a piece of her mind. Her temper was all up, and hot. Her mouth came open and let out three words of a bitter sentence, . . . then it fell silent, and the anger in her face turned to surprise or wonder or fear, or something, and she slowly brought out her hands from her pockets and opened them and held them so. In one was my piece of money, in the other lay four silver groschen. She gazed a little while, perhaps to see if the groschen would vanish away; then she said, fervently:

"It's true—it's true—and I'm ashamed and beg forgiveness, O dear master and benefactor!" And she ran to Satan and kissed his hand, over and over again, according to the Austrian custom.

In her heart she probably believed it was a witch-cat and an agent of the Devil; but no matter, it was all the more certain to be able to keep its contract and furnish a daily good living for the family, for in matters of finance even the piousest of our peasants would have more confidence in an arrangement with the Devil than with an archangel. Ursula started homeward, with Agnes in her arms, and I said I wished I had her privilege of seeing Marget.

Then I caught my breath, for we were there. There in the parlor, and Marget standing looking at us, astonished. She was feeble and pale, but I knew that those conditions would not last in Satan's atmosphere, and it turned out so. I introduced Satan—that is, Philip Traum—and we sat down and talked. There was no constraint. We were simple folk, in our village, and when a stranger was a pleasant person we were soon friends. Marget wondered how we got in without her hearing us. Traum said the door was open, and we walked in and waited until she should turn around and greet us. This was not true; no door was open; we entered through the walls or the roof or down the chimney, or somehow; but no matter, what Satan wished a person to believe, the person was sure to believe, and so Marget was quite satisfied with that explanation. And then the main part of her mind was on Traum, anyway; she couldn't keep her eyes off him, he was so beautiful. That gratified me, and made me proud. I hoped he would show off some, but he didn't. He seemed only interested in being friendly and telling lies. He said he was an orphan. That made Marget pity him. The water came into her eyes. He said he had never known his mamma; she passed away while he was a young thing; and said his papa was in shattered health, and had no property to speak of—in fact, none of any earthly value—but he had an uncle in business down in the tropics, and he was very well off and had a monopoly, and it was from this uncle that he drew his support. The very mention of a kind uncle was enough to remind Marget of her own, and her eyes filled again. She said she hoped their two uncles would meet, some day. It made me shudder. Philip said he hoped so, too; and that made me shudder again.

"Maybe they will," said Marget. "Does your uncle travel much?"

"Oh yes, he goes all about; he has business everywhere."

And so they went on chatting, and poor Marget forgot her sorrow for one little while, anyway. It was probably the only really bright and cheery hour she had known lately. I saw she liked Philip, and I knew she would. And when he told her he was studying for the ministry I could see that she liked him better than ever. And then, when he promised to get her admitted to the jail so that she could see her uncle, that was the capstone. He said he would give the guards a little present, and she must always go in the evening after dark, and say nothing, "but just show this paper and pass in, and show it again when you come out"—and he scribbled some queer marks on the paper and gave it to her, and she was ever so thankful, and right away was in a fever for the sun to go down; for in that old, cruel time prisoners were not allowed to see their friends, and sometimes they spent years in the jails without ever seeing a friendly face. I judged that the marks on the paper were an enchantment, and that the guards would not know what they were doing, nor have any memory of it afterward; and that was indeed the way of it. Ursula put her head in at the door now and said:

"Supper's ready, miss." Then she saw us and looked frightened, and motioned me to come to her, which I did, and she asked if we had told about the cat. I said no, and she was relieved, and said please don't; for if Miss Marget knew, she would think it was an unholy cat and would send for a priest and have its gifts all purified out of it, and then there wouldn't be any more dividends. So I said we wouldn't tell, and she was satisfied. Then I was beginning to say good-by to Marget, but Satan interrupted and said, ever so politely—well, I don't remember just the words, but anyway he as good as invited himself to supper, and me, too. Of course Marget was miserably embarrassed, for she had no reason to suppose there would be half enough for a sick bird. Ursula heard him, and she came straight into the room, not a bit pleased. At first she was astonished to see Marget looking so fresh and rosy, and said so; then she spoke up in her native tongue, which was Bohemian, and said—as I learned afterward— "Send him away, Miss Marget; there's not victuals enough."

Before Marget could speak, Satan had the word, and was talking back to Ursula in her own language—which was a surprise to her, and for her mistress, too. He said, "Didn't I see you down the road awhile ago?"

"Yes, sir."

"Ah, that pleases me; I see you remember me." He stepped to her and whispered: "I told you it is a Lucky Cat. Don't be troubled; it will provide."

That sponged the slate of Ursula's feelings clean of its anxieties, and a deep, financial joy shone in her eyes. The cat's value was augmenting. It was getting full time for Marget to take some sort of notice of Satan's invitation, and she did it in the best way, the honest way that was natural to her. She said she had little to offer, but that we were welcome if we would share it with her.

We had supper in the kitchen, and Ursula waited at table. A small fish was in the frying-pan, crisp and brown and tempting, and one could see that Marget was not expecting such respectable food as this. Ursula brought it, and Marget divided it between Satan and me, declining to take any of it herself; and was beginning to say she did not care for fish to-day, but she did not finish the remark. It was because she noticed that another fish had appeared in the pan. She looked surprised, but did not say anything. She probably meant to inquire of Ursula about this later. There were other surprises: flesh and game and wines and fruits—things which had been strangers in that house lately; but Marget made no exclamations, and now even looked unsurprised, which was Satan's influence, of course. Satan talked right along, and was entertaining, and made the time pass pleasantly and cheerfully; and although he told a good many lies, it was no harm in him, for he was only an angel and did not know any better. They do not know right from wrong; I knew this, because I remembered what he had said about it. He got on the good side of Ursula. He praised her to Marget, confidentially, but speaking just loud enough for Ursula to hear. He said she was a fine woman, and he hoped some day to bring her and his uncle together. Very soon Ursula was mincing and simpering around in a ridiculous girly way, and smoothing out her gown and prinking at herself like a foolish old hen, and all the time pretending she was not hearing what Satan was saying. I was ashamed, for it showed us to be what Satan considered us, a silly race and trivial. Satan said his uncle entertained a great deal, and to have a clever woman presiding over the festivities would double the attractions of the place.

"But your uncle is a gentleman, isn't he?" asked Marget.

"Yes," said Satan indifferently; "some even call him a Prince, out of compliment, but he is not bigoted; to him personal merit is everything, rank nothing."

My hand was hanging down by my chair; Agnes came along and licked it; by this act a secret was revealed. I started to say, "It is all a mistake; this is just a common, ordinary cat; the hair-needles on her tongue point inward, not outward." But the words did not come, because they couldn't. Satan smiled upon me, and I understood.

When it was dark Marget took food and wine and fruit, in a basket, and hurried away to the jail, and Satan and I walked toward my home. I was thinking to myself that I should like to see what the inside of the jail was like; Satan overheard the thought, and the next moment we were in the jail. We were in the torture-chamber, Satan said. The rack was there, and the other instruments, and there was a smoky lantern or two hanging on the walls and helping to make the place look dim and dreadful. There were people there—and executioners—but as they took no notice of us, it meant that we were invisible. A young man lay bound, and Satan said he was suspected of being a heretic, and the executioners were about to inquire into it. They asked the man to confess to the charge, and he said he could not, for it was not true. Then they drove splinter after splinter under his nails, and he shrieked with the pain. Satan was not disturbed, but I could not endure it, and had to be whisked out of there. I was faint and sick, but the fresh air revived me, and we walked toward my home. I said it was a brutal thing.

"No, it was a human thing. You should not insult the brutes by such a misuse of that word; they have not deserved it," and he went on talking like that. "It is like your paltry race—always lying, always claiming virtues which it hasn't got, always denying them to the higher animals, which alone possess them. No brute ever does a cruel thing—that is the monopoly of those with the Moral Sense. When a brute inflicts pain he does it innocently; it is not wrong; for him there is no such thing as wrong. And he does not inflict pain for the pleasure of inflicting it—only man does that. Inspired by that mongrel Moral Sense of his! A sense whose function is to distinguish between right and wrong, with liberty to choose which of them he will do. Now what advantage can he get out of that? He is always choosing, and in nine cases out of ten he prefers the wrong. There shouldn't be any wrong; and without the Moral Sense there couldn't be any. And yet he is such an unreasoning creature that he is not able to perceive that the Moral Sense degrades him to the bottom layer of animated beings and is a shameful possession. Are you feeling better? Let me show you something."

6

In a moment we were in a French village. We walked through a great factory of some sort, where men and women and little children were toiling in heat and dirt and a fog of dust; and they were clothed in rags, and drooped at their work, for they were worn and half starved, and weak and drowsy. Satan said:

"It is some more Moral Sense. The proprietors are rich, and very holy; but the wage they pay to these poor brothers and sisters of theirs is only enough to keep them from dropping dead with hunger. The work-hours are fourteen per day, winter and summer—from six in the morning till eight at night—little children and all. And they walk to and from the pigsties which they inhabit—four miles each way, through mud and slush, rain, snow, sleet, and storm, daily, year in and year out. They get four hours of sleep. They kennel together, three families in a room, in unimaginable filth and stench; and disease comes, and they die off like flies. Have they committed a crime, these mangy things? No. What have they done, that they are punished so? Nothing at all, except getting themselves born into your foolish race. You have seen how they treat a misdoer there in the jail; now you see how they treat the innocent and the worthy. Is your race logical? Are these ill-smelling innocents better off than that heretic? Indeed, no; his punishment is trivial compared with theirs. They broke him on the wheel and smashed him to rags and pulp after we left, and he is dead now, and free of your precious race; but these poor slaves here—why, they have been dying for years, and some of them will not escape from life for years to come. It is the Moral Sense which teaches the factory proprietors the difference between right and wrong—you perceive the result. They think themselves better than dogs. Ah, you are such an illogical, unreasoning race! And paltry—oh, unspeakably!"

Then he dropped all seriousness and just overstrained himself making fun of us, and deriding our pride in our warlike deeds, our great heroes, our imperishable fames, our mighty kings, our ancient aristocracies, our venerable history—and laughed and laughed till it was enough to make a person sick to hear him; and finally he sobered a little and said, "But, after all, it is not all ridiculous; there is a sort of pathos about it when one remembers how few are your days, how childish your pomps, and what shadows you are!"

Presently all things vanished suddenly from my sight, and I knew what it meant. The next moment we were walking along in our village; and down toward the river I saw the twinkling lights of the Golden Stag. Then in the dark I heard a joyful cry:

"He's come again!"

It was Seppi Wohlmeyer. He had felt his blood leap and his spirits rise in a way that could mean only one thing, and he knew Satan was near, although it was too dark to see him. He came to us, and we walked along together, and Seppi poured out his gladness like water. It was as if he were a lover and had found his sweetheart who had been lost. Seppi was a smart and animated boy, and had enthusiasm and expression, and was a contrast to Nikolaus and me. He was full of the last new mystery, now—the disappearance of Hans Oppert, the village loafer. People were beginning to be curious about it, he said. He did not say anxious—curious was the right word, and strong enough. No one had seen Hans for a couple of days.

"Not since he did that brutal thing, you know," he said.

"What brutal thing?" It was Satan that asked.

"Well, he is always clubbing his dog, which is a good dog, and his only friend, and is faithful, and loves him, and does no one any harm; and two days ago he was at it again, just for nothing—just for pleasure—and the dog was howling and begging, and Theodor and I begged, too, but he threatened us, and struck the dog again with all his might and knocked one of his eyes out, and he said to us, 'There, I hope you are satisfied now; that's what you have got for him by your damned meddling'—and he laughed, the heartless brute." Seppi's voice trembled with pity and anger. I guessed what Satan would say, and he said it.

"There is that misused word again—that shabby slander. Brutes do not act like that, but only men."

"Well, it was inhuman, anyway."

"No, it wasn't, Seppi; it was human—quite distinctly human. It is not pleasant to hear you libel the higher animals by attributing to them dispositions which they are free from, and which are found nowhere but in the human heart. None of the higher animals is tainted with the disease called the Moral Sense. Purify your language, Seppi; drop those lying phrases out of it."

He spoke pretty sternly—for him—and I was sorry I hadn't warned Seppi to be more particular about the word he used. I knew how he was feeling. He would not want to offend Satan; he would rather offend all his kin. There was an uncomfortable silence, but relief soon came, for that poor dog came along now, with his eye hanging down, and went straight to Satan, and began to moan and mutter brokenly, and Satan began to answer in the same way, and it was plain that they were talking together in the dog language. We all sat down in the grass, in the moonlight, for the clouds were breaking away now, and Satan took the dog's head in his lap and put the eye back in its place, and the dog was comfortable, and he wagged his tail and licked Satan's hand, and looked thankful and said the same; I knew he was saying it, though I did not understand the words. Then the two talked together a bit, and Satan said:

"He says his master was drunk."

"Yes, he was," said we.

"And an hour later he fell over the precipice there beyond the Cliff Pasture."

"We know the place; it is three miles from here."

"And the dog has been often to the village, begging people to go there, but he was only driven away and not listened to."

We remembered it, but hadn't understood what he wanted.

"He only wanted help for the man who had misused him, and he thought only of that, and has had no food nor sought any. He has watched by his master two nights. What do you think of your race? Is heaven reserved for it, and this dog ruled out, as your teachers tell you? Can your race add anything to this dog's stock of morals and magnanimities?" He spoke to the creature, who jumped up, eager and happy, and apparently ready for orders and impatient to execute them. "Get some men; go with the dog—he will show you that carrion; and take a priest along to arrange about insurance, for death is near."

With the last word he vanished, to our sorrow and disappointment. We got the men and Father Adolf, and we saw the man die. Nobody cared but the dog; he mourned and grieved, and licked the dead face, and could not be comforted. We buried him where he was, and without a coffin, for he had no money, and no friend but the dog. If we had been an hour earlier the priest would have been in time to send that poor creature to heaven, but now he was gone down into the awful fires, to burn forever. It seemed such a pity that in a world where so many people have difficulty to put in their time, one little hour could not have been spared for this poor creature who needed it so much, and to whom it would have made the difference between eternal joy and eternal pain. It gave an appalling idea of the value of an hour, and I thought I could never waste one again without remorse and terror. Seppi was depressed and grieved, and said it must be so much better to be a dog and not run such awful risks. We took this one home with us and kept him for our own. Seppi had a very good thought as we were walking along, and it cheered us up and made us feel much better. He said the dog had forgiven the man that had wronged him so, and maybe God would accept that absolution.

There was a very dull week, now, for Satan did not come, nothing much was going on, and we boys could not venture to go and see Marget, because the nights were moonlit and our parents might find us out if we tried. But we came across Ursula a couple of times taking a walk in the meadows beyond the river to air the cat, and we learned from her that things were going well. She had natty new clothes on and bore a prosperous look. The four groschen a day were arriving without a break, but were not being spent for food and wine and such things—the cat attended to all that.

Marget was enduring her forsakenness and isolation fairly well, all things considered, and was cheerful, by help of Wilhelm Meidling. She spent an hour or two every night in the jail with her uncle, and had fattened him up with the cat's contributions. But she was curious to know more about Philip Traum, and hoped I would bring him again. Ursula was curious about him herself, and asked a good many questions about his uncle. It made the boys laugh, for I had told them the nonsense Satan had been stuffing her with. She got no satisfaction out of us, our tongues being tied.

Ursula gave us a small item of information: money being plenty now, she had taken on a servant to help about the house and run errands. She tried to tell it in a commonplace, matter-of-course way, but she was so set up by it and so vain of it that her pride in it leaked out pretty plainly. It was beautiful to see her veiled delight in this grandeur, poor old thing, but when we heard the name of the servant we wondered if she had been altogether wise; for although we were young, and often thoughtless, we had fairly good perception on some matters. This boy was Gottfried Narr, a dull, good creature, with no harm in him and nothing against him personally; still, he was under a cloud, and properly so, for it had not been six months since a social blight had mildewed the family—his grandmother had been burned as a witch. When that kind of a malady is in the blood it does not always come out with just one burning. Just now was not a good time for Ursula and Marget to be having dealings with a member of such a family, for the witch-terror had risen higher during the past year than it had ever reached in the memory of the oldest villagers. The mere mention of a witch was almost enough to frighten us out of our wits. This was natural enough, because of late years there were more kinds of witches than there used to be; in old times it had been only old women, but of late years they were of all ages—even children of eight and nine; it was getting so that anybody might turn out to be a familiar of the Devil—age and sex hadn't anything to do with it. In our little region we had tried to extirpate the witches, but the more of them we burned the more of the breed rose up in their places.

Once, in a school for girls only ten miles away, the teachers found that the back of one of the girls was all red and inflamed, and they were greatly frightened, believing it to be the Devil's marks. The girl was scared, and begged them not to denounce her, and said it was only fleas; but of course it would not do to let the matter rest there. All the girls were examined, and eleven out of the fifty were badly marked, the rest less so. A commission was appointed, but the eleven only cried for their mothers and would not confess. Then they were shut up, each by herself, in the dark, and put on black bread and water for ten days and nights; and by that time they were haggard and wild, and their eyes were dry and they did not cry any more, but only sat and mumbled, and would not take the food. Then one of them confessed, and said they had often ridden through the air on broomsticks to the witches' Sabbath, and in a bleak place high up in the mountains had danced and drunk and caroused with several hundred other witches and the Evil One, and all had conducted themselves in a scandalous way and had reviled the priests and blasphemed God. That is what she said—not in narrative form, for she was not able to remember any of the details without having them called to her mind one after the other; but the commission did that, for they knew just what questions to ask, they being all written down for the use of witch-commissioners two centuries before. They asked, "Did you do so and so?" and she always said yes, and looked weary and tired, and took no interest in it. And so when the other ten heard that this one confessed, they confessed, too, and answered yes to the questions. Then they were burned at the stake all together, which was just and right; and everybody went from all the countryside to see it. I went, too; but when I saw that one of them was a bonny, sweet girl I used to play with, and looked so pitiful there chained to the stake, and her mother crying over her and devouring her with kisses and clinging around her neck, and saying, "Oh, my God! oh, my God!" it was too dreadful, and I went away.

It was bitter cold weather when Gottfried's grandmother was burned. It was charged that she had cured bad headaches by kneading the person's head and neck with her fingers—as she said—but really by the Devil's help, as everybody knew. They were going to examine her, but she stopped them, and confessed straight off that her power was from the Devil. So they appointed to burn her next morning, early, in our market-square. The officer who was to prepare the fire was there first, and prepared it. She was there next—brought by the constables, who left her and went to fetch another witch. Her family did not come with her. They might be reviled, maybe stoned, if the people were excited. I came, and gave her an apple. She was squatting at the fire, warming herself and waiting; and her old lips and hands were blue with the cold. A stranger came next. He was a traveler, passing through; and he spoke to her gently, and, seeing nobody but me there to hear, said he was sorry for her. And he asked if what she confessed was true, and she said no. He looked surprised and still more sorry then, and asked her:

"Then why did you confess?"

"I am old and very poor," she said, "and I work for my living. There was no way but to confess. If I hadn't they might have set me free. That would ruin me, for no one would forget that I had been suspected of being a witch, and so I would get no more work, and wherever I went they would set the dogs on me. In a little while I would starve. The fire is best; it is soon over. You have been good to me, you two, and I thank you."

She snuggled closer to the fire, and put out her hands to warm them, the snow-flakes descending soft and still on her old gray head and making it white and whiter. The crowd was gathering now, and an egg came flying and struck her in the eye, and broke and ran down her face. There was a laugh at that.

I told Satan all about the eleven girls and the old woman, once, but it did not affect him. He only said it was the human race, and what the human race did was of no consequence. And he said he had seen it made; and it was not made of clay; it was made of mud—part of it was, anyway. I knew what he meant by that—the Moral Sense. He saw the thought in my head, and it tickled him and made him laugh. Then he called a bullock out of a pasture and petted it and talked with it, and said:

"There—he wouldn't drive children mad with hunger and fright and loneliness, and then burn them for confessing to things invented for them which had never happened. And neither would he break the hearts of innocent, poor old women and make them afraid to trust themselves among their own race; and he would not insult them in their death-agony. For he is not besmirched with the Moral Sense, but is as the angels are, and knows no wrong, and never does it."

Lovely as he was, Satan could be cruelly offensive when he chose; and he always chose when the human race was brought to his attention. He always turned up his nose at it, and never had a kind word for it.

Well, as I was saying, we boys doubted if it was a good time for Ursula to be hiring a member of the Narr family. We were right. When the people found it out they were naturally indignant. And, moreover, since Marget and Ursula hadn't enough to eat themselves, where was the money coming from to feed another mouth? That is what they wanted to know; and in order to find out they stopped avoiding Gottfried and began to seek his society and have sociable conversations with him. He was pleased—not thinking any harm and not seeing the trap—and so he talked innocently along, and was no discreeter than a cow.

"Money!" he said; "they've got plenty of it. They pay me two groschen a week, besides my keep. And they live on the fat of the land, I can tell you; the prince himself can't beat their table."

This astonishing statement was conveyed by the astrologer to Father Adolf on a Sunday morning when he was returning from mass. He was deeply moved, and said:

"This must be looked into."

He said there must be witchcraft at the bottom of it, and told the villagers to resume relations with Marget and Ursula in a private and unostentatious way, and keep both eyes open. They were told to keep their own counsel, and not rouse the suspicions of the household. The villagers were at first a bit reluctant to enter such a dreadful place, but the priest said they would be under his protection while there, and no harm could come to them, particularly if they carried a trifle of holy water along and kept their beads and crosses handy. This satisfied them and made them willing to go; envy and malice made the baser sort even eager to go.

And so poor Marget began to have company again, and was as pleased as a cat. She was like 'most anybody else—just human, and happy in her prosperities and not averse from showing them off a little; and she was humanly grateful to have the warm shoulder turned to her and be smiled upon by her friends and the village again; for of all the hard things to bear, to be cut by your neighbors and left in contemptuous solitude is maybe the hardest.

The bars were down, and we could all go there now, and we did—our parents and all—day after day. The cat began to strain herself. She provided the top of everything for those companies, and in abundance—among them many a dish and many a wine which they had not tasted before and which they had not even heard of except at second-hand from the prince's servants. And the tableware was much above ordinary, too.

Marget was troubled at times, and pursued Ursula with questions to an uncomfortable degree; but Ursula stood her ground and stuck to it that it was Providence, and said no word about the cat. Marget knew that nothing was impossible to Providence, but she could not help having doubts that this effort was from there, though she was afraid to say so, lest disaster come of it. Witchcraft occurred to her, but she put the thought aside, for this was before Gottfried joined the household, and she knew Ursula was pious and a bitter hater of witches. By the time Gottfried arrived Providence was established, unshakably intrenched, and getting all the gratitude. The cat made no murmur, but went on composedly improving in style and prodigality by experience.

In any community, big or little, there is always a fair proportion of people who are not malicious or unkind by nature, and who never do unkind things except when they are overmastered by fear, or when their self-interest is greatly in danger, or some such matter as that. Eseldorf had its proportion of such people, and ordinarily their good and gentle influence was felt, but these were not ordinary times—on account of the witch-dread—and so we did not seem to have any gentle and compassionate hearts left, to speak of. Every person was frightened at the unaccountable state of things at Marget's house, not doubting that witchcraft was at the bottom of it, and fright frenzied their reason. Naturally there were some who pitied Marget and Ursula for the danger that was gathering about them, but naturally they did not say so; it would not have been safe. So the others had it all their own way, and there was none to advise the ignorant girl and the foolish woman and warn them to modify their doings. We boys wanted to warn them, but we backed down when it came to the pinch, being afraid. We found that we were not manly enough nor brave enough to do a generous action when there was a chance that it could get us into trouble. Neither of us confessed this poor spirit to the others, but did as other people would have done—dropped the subject and talked about something else. And I knew we all felt mean, eating and drinking Marget's fine things along with those companies of spies, and petting her and complimenting her with the rest, and seeing with self-reproach how foolishly happy she was, and never saying a word to put her on her guard. And, indeed, she was happy, and as proud as a princess, and so grateful to have friends again. And all the time these people were watching with all their eyes and reporting all they saw to Father Adolf.

But he couldn't make head or tail of the situation. There must be an enchanter somewhere on the premises, but who was it? Marget was not seen to do any jugglery, nor was Ursula, nor yet Gottfried; and still the wines and dainties never ran short, and a guest could not call for a thing and not get it. To produce these effects was usual enough with witches and enchanters—that part of it was not new; but to do it without any incantations, or even any rumblings or earthquakes or lightnings or apparitions—that was new, novel, wholly irregular. There was nothing in the books like this. Enchanted things were always unreal. Gold turned to dirt in an unenchanted atmosphere, food withered away and vanished. But this test failed in the present case. The spies brought samples: Father Adolf prayed over them, exorcised them, but it did no good; they remained sound and real, they yielded to natural decay only, and took the usual time to do it.

Father Adolf was not merely puzzled, he was also exasperated; for these evidences very nearly convinced him—privately—that there was no witchcraft in the matter. It did not wholly convince him, for this could be a new kind of witchcraft. There was a way to find out as to this: if this prodigal abundance of provender was not brought in from the outside, but produced on the premises, there was witchcraft, sure.

7

Marget announced a party, and invited forty people; the date for it was seven days away. This was a fine opportunity. Marget's house stood by itself, and it could be easily watched. All the week it was watched night and day. Marget's household went out and in as usual, but they carried nothing in their hands, and neither they nor others brought anything to the house. This was ascertained. Evidently rations for forty people were not being fetched. If they were furnished any sustenance it would have to be made on the premises. It was true that Marget went out with a basket every evening, but the spies ascertained that she always brought it back empty.

The guests arrived at noon and filled the place. Father Adolf followed; also, after a little, the astrologer, without invitation. The spies had informed him that neither at the back nor the front had any parcels been brought in. He entered, and found the eating and drinking going on finely, and everything progressing in a lively and festive way. He glanced around and perceived that many of the cooked delicacies and all of the native and foreign fruits were of a perishable character, and he also recognized that these were fresh and perfect. No apparitions, no incantations, no thunder. That settled it. This was witchcraft. And not only that, but of a new kind—a kind never dreamed of before. It was a prodigious power, an illustrious power; he resolved to discover its secret. The announcement of it would resound throughout the world, penetrate to the remotest lands, paralyze all the nations with amazement—and carry his name with it, and make him renowned forever. It was a wonderful piece of luck, a splendid piece of luck; the glory of it made him dizzy.

All the house made room for him; Marget politely seated him; Ursula ordered Gottfried to bring a special table for him. Then she decked it and furnished it, and asked for his orders.

"Bring me what you will," he said.

The two servants brought supplies from the pantry, together with white wine and red—a bottle of each. The astrologer, who very likely had never seen such delicacies before, poured out a beaker of red wine, drank it off, poured another, then began to eat with a grand appetite.

I was not expecting Satan, for it was more than a week since I had seen or heard of him, but now he came in—I knew it by the feel, though people were in the way and I could not see him. I heard him apologizing for intruding; and he was going away, but Marget urged him to stay, and he thanked her and stayed. She brought him along, introducing him to the girls, and to Meidling, and to some of the elders; and there was quite a rustle of whispers: "It's the young stranger we hear so much about and can't get sight of, he is away so much." "Dear, dear, but he is beautiful—what is his name?" "Philip Traum." "Ah, it fits him!" (You see, "Traum" is German for "Dream.") "What does he do?" "Studying for the ministry, they say." "His face is his fortune—he'll be a cardinal some day." "Where is his home?" "Away down somewhere in the tropics, they say—has a rich uncle down there." And so on. He made his way at once; everybody was anxious to know him and talk with him. Everybody noticed how cool and fresh it was, all of a sudden, and wondered at it, for they could see that the sun was beating down the same as before, outside, and the sky was clear of clouds, but no one guessed the reason, of course.

The astrologer had drunk his second beaker; he poured out a third. He set the bottle down, and by accident overturned it. He seized it before much was spilled, and held it up to the light, saying, "What a pity—it is royal wine." Then his face lighted with joy or triumph, or something, and he said, "Quick! Bring a bowl."

It was brought—a four-quart one. He took up that two-pint bottle and began to pour; went on pouring, the red liquor gurgling and gushing into the white bowl and rising higher and higher up its sides, everybody staring and holding their breath—and presently the bowl was full to the brim.

"Look at the bottle," he said, holding it up; "it is full yet!" I glanced at Satan, and in that moment he vanished. Then Father Adolf rose up, flushed and excited, crossed himself, and began to thunder in his great voice. "This house is bewitched and accursed!" People began to cry and shriek and crowd toward the door. "I summon this detected household to—"

His words were cut off short. His face became red, then purple, but he could not utter another sound. Then I saw Satan, a transparent film, melt into the astrologer's body; then the astrologer put up his hand, and apparently in his own voice said, "Wait—remain where you are." All stopped where they stood. "Bring a funnel!" Ursula brought it, trembling and scared, and he stuck it in the bottle and took up the great bowl and began to pour the wine back, the people gazing and dazed with astonishment, for they knew the bottle was already full before he began. He emptied the whole of the bowl into the bottle, then smiled out over the room, chuckled, and said, indifferently: "It is nothing—anybody can do it! With my powers I can even do much more."

A frightened cry burst out everywhere. "Oh, my God, he is possessed!" and there was a tumultuous rush for the door which swiftly emptied the house of all who did not belong in it except us boys and Meidling. We boys knew the secret, and would have told it if we could. but we couldn't. We were very thankful to Satan for furnishing that good help at the needful time.

Marget was pale, and crying; Meidling looked kind of petrified; Ursula the same; but Gottfried was the worst—he couldn't stand, he was so weak and scared. For he was of a witch family, you know, and it would be bad for him to be suspected. Agnes came loafing in, looking pious and unaware, and wanted to rub up against Ursula and be petted, but Ursula was afraid of her and shrank away from her, but pretending she was not meaning any incivility, for she knew very well it wouldn't answer to have strained relations with that kind of a cat. But we boys took Agnes and petted her, for Satan would not have befriended her if he had not had a good opinion of her, and that was indorsement enough for us. He seemed to trust anything that hadn't the Moral Sense.

Outside, the guests, panic-stricken, scattered in every direction and fled in a pitiable state of terror; and such a tumult as they made with their running and sobbing and shrieking and shouting that soon all the village came flocking from their houses to see what had happened, and they thronged the street and shouldered and jostled one another in excitement and fright; and then Father Adolf appeared, and they fell apart in two walls like the cloven Red Sea, and presently down this lane the astrologer came striding and mumbling, and where he passed the lanes surged back in packed masses, and fell silent with awe, and their eyes stared and their breasts heaved, and several women fainted; and when he was gone by the crowd swarmed together and followed him at a distance, talking excitedly and asking questions and finding out the facts. Finding out the facts and passing them on to others, with improvements—improvements which soon enlarged the bowl of wine to a barrel, and made the one bottle hold it all and yet remain empty to the last.

When the astrologer reached the market-square he went straight to a juggler, fantastically dressed, who was keeping three brass balls in the air, and took them from him and faced around upon the approaching crowd and said: "This poor clown is ignorant of his art. Come forward and see an expert perform."

So saying, he tossed the balls up one after another and set them whirling in a slender bright oval in the air, and added another, then another and another, and soon—no one seeing whence he got them—adding, adding, adding, the oval lengthening all the time, his hands moving so swiftly that they were just a web or a blur and not distinguishable as hands; and such as counted said there were now a hundred balls in the air. The spinning great oval reached up twenty feet in the air and was a shining and glinting and wonderful sight. Then he folded his arms and told the balls to go on spinning without his help—and they did it. After a couple of minutes he said, "There, that will do," and the oval broke and came crashing down, and the balls scattered abroad and rolled every whither. And wherever one of them came the people fell back in dread, and no one would touch it. It made him laugh, and he scoffed at the people and called them cowards and old women. Then he turned and saw the tight-rope, and said foolish people were daily wasting their money to see a clumsy and ignorant varlet degrade that beautiful art; now they should see the work of a master. With that he made a spring into the air and lit firm on his feet on the rope. Then he hopped the whole length of it back and forth on one foot, with his hands clasped over his eyes; and next he began to throw somersaults, both backward and forward, and threw twenty-seven.

The people murmured, for the astrologer was old, and always before had been halting of movement and at times even lame, but he was nimble enough now and went on with his antics in the liveliest manner. Finally he sprang lightly down and walked away, and passed up the road and around the corner and disappeared. Then that great, pale, silent, solid crowd drew a deep breath and looked into one another's faces as if they said: "Was it real? Did you see it, or was it only I—and I was dreaming?" Then they broke into a low murmur of talking, and fell apart in couples, and moved toward their homes, still talking in that awed way, with faces close together and laying a hand on an arm and making other such gestures as people make when they have been deeply impressed by something.

We boys followed behind our fathers, and listened, catching all we could of what they said; and when they sat down in our house and continued their talk they still had us for company. They were in a sad mood, for it was certain, they said, that disaster for the village must follow this awful visitation of witches and devils. Then my father remembered that Father Adolf had been struck dumb at the moment of his denunciation.

"They have not ventured to lay their hands upon an anointed servant of God before," he said; "and how they could have dared it this time I cannot make out, for he wore his crucifix. Isn't it so?"

"Yes," said the others, "we saw it."

"It is serious, friends, it is very serious. Always before, we had a protection. It has failed."

The others shook, as with a sort of chill, and muttered those words over—"It has failed." "God has forsaken us."

"It is true," said Seppi Wohlmeyer's father; "there is nowhere to look for help."

"The people will realize this," said Nikolaus's father, the judge, "and despair will take away their courage and their energies. We have indeed fallen upon evil times."

He sighed, and Wohlmeyer said, in a troubled voice: "The report of it all will go about the country, and our village will be shunned as being under the displeasure of God. The Golden Stag will know hard times."

"True, neighbor," said my father; "all of us will suffer—all in repute, many in estate. And, good God!—"

"What is it?"

"That can come—to finish us!"

"Name it—um Gottes Willen!"

"The Interdict!"

It smote like a thunderclap, and they were like to swoon with the terror of it. Then the dread of this calamity roused their energies, and they stopped brooding and began to consider ways to avert it. They discussed this, that, and the other way, and talked till the afternoon was far spent, then confessed that at present they could arrive at no decision. So they parted sorrowfully, with oppressed hearts which were filled with bodings.

While they were saying their parting words I slipped out and set my course for Marget's house to see what was happening there. I met many people, but none of them greeted me. It ought to have been surprising, but it was not, for they were so distraught with fear and dread that they were not in their right minds, I think; they were white and haggard, and walked like persons in a dream, their eyes open but seeing nothing, their lips moving but uttering nothing, and worriedly clasping and unclasping their hands without knowing it.

At Marget's it was like a funeral. She and Wilhelm sat together on the sofa, but said nothing, and not even holding hands. Both were steeped in gloom, and Marget's eyes were red from the crying she had been doing. She said:

"I have been begging him to go, and come no more, and so save himself alive. I cannot bear to be his murderer. This house is bewitched, and no inmate will escape the fire. But he will not go, and he will be lost with the rest."

Wilhelm said he would not go; if there was danger for her, his place was by her, and there he would remain. Then she began to cry again, and it was all so mournful that I wished I had stayed away. There was a knock, now, and Satan came in, fresh and cheery and beautiful, and brought that winy atmosphere of his and changed the whole thing. He never said a word about what had been happening, nor about the awful fears which were freezing the blood in the hearts of the community, but began to talk and rattle on about all manner of gay and pleasant things: and next about music—an artful stroke which cleared away the remnant of Marget's depression and brought her spirits and her interests broad awake. She had not heard any one talk so well and so knowingly on that subject before, and she was so uplifted by it and so charmed that what she was feeling lit up her face and came out in her words; and Wilhelm noticed it and did not look as pleased as he ought to have done. And next Satan branched off into poetry, and recited some, and did it well, and Marget was charmed again; and again Wilhelm was not as pleased as he ought to have been, and this time Marget noticed it and was remorseful.

I fell asleep to pleasant music that night—the patter of rain upon the panes and the dull growling of distant thunder. Away in the night Satan came and roused me and said: "Come with me. Where shall we go?"

"'Anywhere—so it is with you."

Then there was a fierce glare of sunlight, and he said, "This is China."

That was a grand surprise, and made me sort of drunk with vanity and gladness to think I had come so far—so much, much farther than anybody else in our village, including Bartel Sperling, who had such a great opinion of his travels. We buzzed around over that empire for more than half an hour, and saw the whole of it. It was wonderful, the spectacles we saw; and some were beautiful, others too horrible to think. For instance— However, I may go into that by and by, and also why Satan chose China for this excursion instead of another place; it would interrupt my tale to do it now. Finally we stopped flitting and lit.

We sat upon a mountain commanding a vast landscape of mountain-range and gorge and valley and plain and river, with cities and villages slumbering in the sunlight, and a glimpse of blue sea on the farther verge. It was a tranquil and dreamy picture, beautiful to the eye and restful to the spirit. If we could only make a change like that whenever we wanted to, the world would be easier to live in than it is, for change of scene shifts the mind's burdens to the other shoulder and banishes old, shop-worn wearinesses from mind and body both.

We talked together, and I had the idea of trying to reform Satan and persuade him to lead a better life. I told him about all those things he had been doing, and begged him to be more considerate and stop making people unhappy. I said I knew he did not mean any harm, but that he ought to stop and consider the possible consequences of a thing before launching it in that impulsive and random way of his; then he would not make so much trouble. He was not hurt by this plain speech; he only looked amused and surprised, and said:

"What? I do random things? Indeed, I never do. I stop and consider possible consequences? Where is the need? I know what the consequences are going to be—always."

"Oh, Satan, then how could you do these things?"

"Well, I will tell you, and you must understand if you can. You belong to a singular race. Every man is a suffering-machine and a happiness-machine combined. The two functions work together harmoniously, with a fine and delicate precision, on the give-and-take principle. For every happiness turned out in the one department the other stands ready to modify it with a sorrow or a pain—maybe a dozen. In most cases the man's life is about equally divided between happiness and unhappiness. When this is not the case the unhappiness predominates—always; never the other. Sometimes a man's make and disposition are such that his misery-machine is able to do nearly all the business. Such a man goes through life almost ignorant of what happiness is. Everything he touches, everything he does, brings a misfortune upon him. You have seen such people? To that kind of a person life is not an advantage, is it? It is only a disaster.

Sometimes for an hour's happiness a man's machinery makes him pay years of misery. Don't you know that? It happens every now and then. I will give you a case or two presently. Now the people of your village are nothing to me—you know that, don't you?"

I did not like to speak out too flatly, so I said I had suspected it.

"Well, it is true that they are nothing to me. It is not possible that they should be. The difference between them and me is abysmal, immeasurable. They have no intellect."

"No intellect?"

"Nothing that resembles it. At a future time I will examine what man calls his mind and give you the details of that chaos, then you will see and understand. Men have nothing in common with me— there is no point of contact; they have foolish little feelings and foolish little vanities and impertinences and ambitions; their foolish little life is but a laugh, a sigh, and extinction; and they have no sense. Only the Moral Sense. I will show you what I mean. Here is a red spider, not so big as a pin's head. Can you imagine an elephant being interested in him—caring whether he is happy or isn't, or whether he is wealthy or poor, or whether his sweetheart returns his love or not, or whether his mother is sick or well, or whether he is looked up to in society or not, or whether his enemies will smite him or his friends desert him, or whether his hopes will suffer blight or his political ambitions fail, or whether he shall die in the bosom of his family or neglected and despised in a foreign land? These things can never be important to the elephant; they are nothing to him; he cannot shrink his sympathies to the microscopic size of them. Man is to me as the red spider is to the elephant. The elephant has nothing against the spider—he cannot get down to that remote level; I have nothing against man. The elephant is indifferent; I am indifferent. The elephant would not take the trouble to do the spider an ill turn; if he took the notion he might do him a good turn, if it came in his way and cost nothing. I have done men good service, but no ill turns.

"The elephant lives a century, the red spider a day; in power, intellect, and dignity the one creature is separated from the other by a distance which is simply astronomical. Yet in these, as in all qualities, man is immeasurably further below me than is the wee spider below the elephant.

"Man's mind clumsily and tediously and laboriously patches little trivialities together and gets a result—such as it is. My mind creates!

Do you get the force of that? Creates anything it desires—and in a moment. Creates without material. Creates fluids, solids, colors—anything, everything—out of the airy nothing which is called Thought. A man imagines a silk thread, imagines a machine to make it, imagines a picture, then by weeks of labor embroiders it on canvas with the thread. I think the whole thing, and in a moment it is before you—created.

"I think a poem, music, the record of a game of chess—anything—and it is there. This is the immortal mind—nothing is beyond its reach. Nothing can obstruct my vision; the rocks are transparent to me, and darkness is daylight. I do not need to open a book; I take the whole of its contents into my mind at a single glance, through the cover; and in a million years I could not forget a single word of it, or its place in the volume. Nothing goes on in the skull of man, bird, fish, insect, or other creature which can be hidden from me. I pierce the learned man's brain with a single glance, and the treasures which cost him threescore years to accumulate are mine; he can forget, and he does forget, but I retain.

"Now, then, I perceive by your thoughts that you are understanding me fairly well. Let us proceed. Circumstances might so fall out that the elephant could like the spider—supposing he can see it—but he could not love it. His love is for his own kind—for his equals. An angel's love is sublime, adorable, divine, beyond the imagination of man—infinitely beyond it! But it is limited to his own august order. If it fell upon one of your race for only an instant, it would consume its object to ashes. No, we cannot love men, but we can be harmlessly indifferent to them; we can also like them, sometimes. I like you and the boys, I like Father Peter, and for your sakes I am doing all these things for the villagers."

He saw that I was thinking a sarcasm, and he explained his position.

"I have wrought well for the villagers, though it does not look like it on the surface. Your race never know good fortune from ill. They are always mistaking the one for the other. It is because they cannot see into the future. What I am doing for the villagers will bear good fruit some day; in some cases to themselves; in others, to unborn generations of men. No one will ever know that I was the cause, but it will be none the less true, for all that. Among you boys you have a game: you stand a row of bricks on end a few inches apart; you push a brick, it knocks its neighbor over, the neighbor knocks over the next brick—and so on till all the row is prostrate. That is human life. A child's first act knocks over the initial brick, and the rest will follow inexorably. If you could see into the future, as I can, you would see everything that was going to happen to that creature; for nothing can change the order of its life after the first event has determined it. That is, nothing will change it, because each act unfailingly begets an act, that act begets another, and so on to the end, and the seer can look forward down the line and see just when each act is to have birth, from cradle to grave."

"Does God order the career?"

"Foreordain it? No. The man's circumstances and environment order it. His first act determines the second and all that follow after. But suppose, for argument's sake, that the man should skip one of these acts; an apparently trifling one, for instance; suppose that it had been appointed that on a certain day, at a certain hour and minute and second and fraction of a second he should go to the well, and he didn't go. That man's career would change utterly, from that moment; thence to the grave it would be wholly different from the career which his first act as a child had arranged for him. Indeed, it might be that if he had gone to the well he would have ended his career on a throne, and that omitting to do it would set him upon a career that would lead to beggary and a pauper's grave. For instance: if at any time—say in boyhood—Columbus had skipped the triflingest little link in the chain of acts projected and made inevitable by his first childish act, it would have changed his whole subsequent life, and he would have become a priest and died obscure in an Italian village, and America would not have been discovered for two centuries afterward. I know this. To skip any one of the billion acts in Columbus's chain would have wholly changed his life. I have examined his billion of possible careers, and in only one of them occurs the discovery of America. You people do not suspect that all of your acts are of one size and importance, but it is true; to snatch at an appointed fly is as big with fate for you as is any other appointed act—"

"As the conquering of a continent, for instance?"

"Yes. Now, then, no man ever does drop a link—the thing has never happened! Even when he is trying to make up his mind as to whether he will do a thing or not, that itself is a link, an act, and has its proper place in his chain; and when he finally decides an act,

THE SPECULATIVE FICTION OF MARK TWAIN   223

that also was the thing which he was absolutely certain to do. You see, now, that a man will never drop a link in his chain. He cannot. If he made up his mind to try, that project would itself be an unavoidable link—a thought bound to occur to him at that precise moment, and made certain by the first act of his babyhood."

It seemed so dismal!

"He is a prisoner for life," I said sorrowfully, "and cannot get free."

"No, of himself he cannot get away from the consequences of his first childish act. But I can free him."

I looked up wistfully.

"I have changed the careers of a number of your villagers."

I tried to thank him, but found it difficult, and let it drop.

"I shall make some other changes. You know that little Lisa Brandt?"

"Oh yes, everybody does. My mother says she is so sweet and so lovely that she is not like any other child. She says she will be the pride of the village when she grows up; and its idol, too, just as she is now."

"I shall change her future."

"Make it better?" I asked.

"Yes. And I will change the future of Nikolaus."

I was glad, this time, and said, "I don't need to ask about his case; you will be sure to do generously by him."

"It is my intention."

Straight off I was building that great future of Nicky's in my imagination, and had already made a renowned general of him and hofmeister at the court, when I noticed that Satan was waiting for me to get ready to listen again. I was ashamed of having exposed my cheap imaginings to him, and was expecting some sarcasms, but it did not happen. He proceeded with his subject:

"Nicky's appointed life is sixty-two years."

"That's grand!" I said.

"Lisa's, thirty-six. But, as I told you, I shall change their lives and those ages. Two minutes and a quarter from now Nikolaus will wake out of his sleep and find the rain blowing in. It was appointed that he should turn over and go to sleep again. But I have appointed that he shall get up and close the window first. That trifle will change his career entirely. He will rise in the morning two minutes later than the chain of his life had appointed him to rise. By consequence, thenceforth nothing will ever happen to him in accordance with the details of the old chain." He took out his watch and sat looking at it a few moments, then said: "Nikolaus has risen to close the window. His life is changed, his new career has begun. There will be consequences."

It made me feel creepy; it was uncanny.

"But for this change certain things would happen twelve days from now. For instance, Nikolaus would save Lisa from drowning. He would arrive on the scene at exactly the right moment—four minutes past ten, the long-ago appointed instant of time—and the water would be shoal, the achievement easy and certain. But he will arrive some seconds too late, now; Lisa will have struggled into deeper water. He will do his best, but both will drown."

"Oh, Satan! oh, dear Satan!" I cried, with the tears rising in my eyes, "save them! Don't let it happen. I can't bear to lose Nikolaus, he is my loving playmate and friend; and think of Lisa's poor mother!"

I clung to him and begged and pleaded, but he was not moved. He made me sit down again, and told me I must hear him out.

"I have changed Nikolaus's life, and this has changed Lisa's. If I had not done this, Nikolaus would save Lisa, then he would catch cold from his drenching; one of your race's fantastic and desolating scarlet fevers would follow, with pathetic after-effects; for forty-six years he would lie in his bed a paralytic log, deaf, dumb, blind, and praying night and day for the blessed relief of death. Shall I change his life back?"

"Oh no! Oh, not for the world! In charity and pity leave it as it is."

"It is best so. I could not have changed any other link in his life and done him so good a service. He had a billion possible careers, but not one of them was worth living; they were charged full with miseries and disasters. But for my intervention he would do his brave deed twelve days from now—a deed begun and ended in six minutes—and get for all reward those forty-six years of sorrow and suffering I told you of. It is one of the cases I was thinking of awhile ago when I said that sometimes an act which brings the actor an hour's happiness and self-satisfaction is paid for—or punished—by years of suffering."

I wondered what poor little Lisa's early death would save her from. He answered the thought:

"From ten years of pain and slow recovery from an accident, and then from nineteen years' pollution, shame, depravity, crime, ending with death at the hands of the executioner. Twelve days hence she will die; her mother would save her life if she could. Am I not kinder than her mother?"

"Yes—oh, indeed yes; and wiser."

"Father Peter's case is coming on presently. He will be acquitted, through unassailable proofs of his innocence."

"Why, Satan, how can that be? Do you really think it?"

"Indeed, I know it. His good name will be restored, and the rest of his life will be happy."

"I can believe it. To restore his good name will have that effect."

"His happiness will not proceed from that cause. I shall change his life that day, for his good. He will never know his good name has been restored."

In my mind—and modestly—I asked for particulars, but Satan paid no attention to my thought. Next, my mind wandered to the astrologer, and I wondered where he might be.

"In the moon," said Satan, with a fleeting sound which I believed was a chuckle. "I've got him on the cold side of it, too. He doesn't know where he is, and is not having a pleasant time; still, it is good enough for him, a good place for his star studies. I shall need him presently; then I shall bring him back and possess him again. He has a long and cruel and odious life before him, but I will change that, for I have no feeling against him and am quite willing to do him a kindness. I think I shall get him burned."

He had such strange notions of kindness! But angels are made so, and do not know any better. Their ways are not like our ways; and, besides, human beings are nothing to them; they think they are only freaks. It seems to me odd that he should put the astrologer so far away; he could have dumped him in Germany just as well, where he would be handy.

"Far away?" said Satan. "To me no place is far away; distance does not exist for me. The sun is less than a hundred million miles from here, and the light that is falling upon us has taken eight minutes to come; but I can make that flight, or any other, in a fraction of time so minute that it cannot be measured by a watch. I have but to think the journey, and it is accomplished."

I held out my hand and said, "The light lies upon it; think it into a glass of wine, Satan."

He did it. I drank the wine.

"Break the glass," he said.

I broke it.

"There—you see it is real. The villagers thought the brass balls were magic stuff and as perishable as smoke. They were afraid to touch them. You are a curious lot—your race. But come along; I have business. I will put you to bed." Said and done. Then he was gone; but his voice came back to me through the rain and darkness saying, "Yes, tell Seppi, but no other."

It was the answer to my thought.

8

Sleep would not come. It was not because I was proud of my travels and excited about having been around the big world to China, and feeling contemptuous of Bartel Sperling, "the traveler," as he called himself, and looked down upon us others because he had been to Vienna once and was the only Eseldorf boy who had made such a journey and seen the world's wonders. At another time that would have kept me awake, but it did not affect me now. No, my mind was filled with Nikolaus, my thoughts ran upon him only, and the good days we had seen together at romps and frolics in the woods and the fields and the river in the long summer days, and skating and sliding in the winter when our parents thought we were in school. And now he was going out of this young life, and the summers and winters would come and go, and we others would rove and play as before, but his place would be vacant; we should see him no more. To-morrow he would not suspect, but would be as he had always been, and it would shock me to hear him laugh, and see him do lightsome and frivolous things, for to me he would be a corpse, with waxen hands and dull eyes, and I should see the shroud around his face; and next day he would not suspect, nor the next, and all the time his handful of days would be wasting swiftly away and that awful thing coming nearer and nearer, his fate closing steadily around him and no one knowing it but Seppi and me. Twelve days—only twelve days. It was awful to think of. I noticed that in my thoughts I was not calling him by his familiar names, Nick and Nicky, but was speaking of him by his full name, and reverently, as one speaks of the dead. Also, as incident after incident of our comradeship came thronging into my mind out of the past, I noticed that they were mainly cases where I had wronged him or hurt him, and they rebuked me and reproached me, and my heart was wrung with remorse, just as it is when we remember our unkindnesses to friends who have passed beyond the veil, and we wish we could have them back again, if only for a moment, so that we could go on our knees to them and say, "Have pity, and forgive."

Once when we were nine years old he went a long errand of nearly two miles for the fruiterer, who gave him a splendid big apple for reward, and he was flying home with it, almost beside himself with astonishment and delight, and I met him, and he let me look at the apple, not thinking of treachery, and I ran off with it, eating it as I ran, he following me and begging; and when he overtook me I offered him the core, which was all that was left; and I laughed. Then he turned away, crying, and said he had meant to give it to his little sister. That smote me, for she was slowly getting well of a sickness, and it would have been a proud moment for him, to see her joy and surprise and have her caresses. But I was ashamed to say I was ashamed, and only said something rude and mean, to pretend I did not care, and he made no reply in words, but there was a wounded look in his face as he turned away toward his home which rose before me many times in after years, in the night, and reproached me and made me ashamed again. It had grown dim in my mind, by and by, then it disappeared; but it was back now, and not dim.

Once at school, when we were eleven, I upset my ink and spoiled four copy-books, and was in danger of severe punishment; but I put it upon him, and he got the whipping.

And only last year I had cheated him in a trade, giving him a large fish-hook which was partly broken through for three small sound ones. The first fish he caught broke the hook, but he did not know I was blamable, and he refused to take back one of the small hooks which my conscience forced me to offer him, but said, "A trade is a trade; the hook was bad, but that was not your fault."

No, I could not sleep. These little, shabby wrongs upbraided me and tortured me, and with a pain much sharper than one feels when the wrongs have been done to the living. Nikolaus was living, but no matter; he was to me as one already dead. The wind was still moaning about the eaves, the rain still pattering upon the panes.

In the morning I sought out Seppi and told him. It was down by the river. His lips moved, but he did not say anything, he only looked dazed and stunned, and his face turned very white. He stood like that a few moments, the tears welling into his eyes, then he turned away and I locked my arm in his and we walked along thinking, but not speaking. We crossed the bridge and wandered through the meadows and up among the hills and the woods, and at last the talk came and flowed freely, and it was all about Nikolaus and was a recalling of the life we had lived with him. And every now and then Seppi said, as if to himself:

"Twelve days!—less than twelve days."

We said we must be with him all the time; we must have all of him we could; the days were precious now. Yet we did not go to seek him. It would be like meeting the dead, and we were afraid. We did not say it, but that was what we were feeling. And so it gave us a shock when we turned a curve and came upon Nikolaus face to face. He shouted, gaily:

"Hi-hi! What is the matter? Have you seen a ghost?"

We couldn't speak, but there was no occasion; he was willing to talk for us all, for he had just seen Satan and was in high spirits about it. Satan had told him about our trip to China, and he had begged Satan to take him a journey, and Satan had promised. It was to be a far journey, and wonderlul and beautiful; and Nikolaus had begged him to take us, too, but he said no, he would take us some day, maybe, but not now. Satan would come for him on the 13th, and Nikolaus was already counting the hours, he was so impatient.

That was the fatal day. We were already counting the hours, too.

We wandered many a mile, always following paths which had been our favorites from the days when we were little, and always we talked about the old times. All the blitheness was with Nikolaus; we others could not shake off our depression. Our tone toward Nikolaus was so strangely gentle and tender and yearning that he noticed it, and was pleased; and we were constantly doing him deferential little offices of courtesy, and saying, "Wait, let me do that for you," and that pleased him, too. I gave him seven fish-hooks—all I had—and made him take them; and Seppi gave him his new knife and a humming-top painted red and yellow—atonements for swindles practised upon him formerly, as I learned later, and probably no longer remembered by Nikolaus now. These things touched him, and he could not have believed that we loved him so; and his pride in it and gratefulness for it cut us to the heart, we were so undeserving of them. When we parted at last, he was radiant, and said he had never had such a happy day.

As we walked along homeward, Seppi said, "We always prized him, but never so much as now, when we are going to lose him."

Next day and every day we spent all of our spare time with Nikolaus; and also added to it time which we (and he) stole from work and other duties, and this cost the three of us some sharp scoldings, and some threats of punishment. Every morning two of us woke with a start and a shudder, saying, as the days flew along, "Only ten days left"; "only nine days left"; "only eight"; "only seven." Always it was narrowing. Always Nikolaus was gay and happy, and always puzzled because we were not. He wore his invention to the bone trying to invent ways to cheer us up, but it was only a hollow success; he could see that our jollity had no heart in it, and that the laughs we broke into came up against some obstruction or other and suffered damage and decayed into a sigh. He tried to find out what the matter was, so that he could help us out of our trouble or make it lighter by sharing it with us; so we had to tell many lies to deceive him and appease him.

But the most distressing thing of all was that he was always making plans, and often they went beyond the 13th! Whenever that happened it made us groan in spirit. All his mind was fixed upon finding some way to conquer our depression and cheer us up; and at last, when he had but three days to live, he fell upon the right idea and was jubilant over it—a boys-and-girls' frolic and dance in the woods, up there where we first met Satan, and this was to occur on the 14th. It was ghastly, for that was his funeral day. We couldn't venture to protest; it would only have brought a "Why?" which we could not answer. He wanted us to help him invite his guests, and we did it—one can refuse nothing to a dying friend. But it was dreadful, for really we were inviting them to his funeral.

It was an awful eleven days; and yet, with a lifetime stretching back between to-day and then, they are still a grateful memory to me, and beautiful. In effect they were days of companionship with one's sacred dead, and I have known no comradeship that was so close or so precious. We clung to the hours and the minutes, counting them as they wasted away, and parting with them with that pain and bereavement which a miser feels who sees his hoard filched from him coin by coin by robbers and is helpless to prevent it.

When the evening of the last day came we stayed out too long; Seppi and I were in fault for that; we could not bear to part with Nikolaus; so it was very late when we left him at his door. We lingered near awhile, listening; and that happened which we were fearing. His father gave him the promised punishment, and we heard his shrieks. But we listened only a moment, then hurried away, remorseful for this thing which we had caused. And sorry for the father, too; our thought being, "If he only knew—if he only knew!"

In the morning Nikolaus did not meet us at the appointed place, so we went to his home to see what the matter was. His mother said:

"His father is out of all patience with these goings-on, and will not have any more of it. Half the time when Nick is needed he is not to be found; then it turns out that he has been gadding around with you two. His father gave him a flogging last night. It always grieved me before, and many's the time I have begged him off and saved him, but this time he appealed to me in vain, for I was out of patience myself."

"I wish you had saved him just this one time," I said, my voice trembling a little; "it would ease a pain in your heart to remember it some day."

She was ironing at the time, and her back was partly toward me. She turned about with a startled or wondering look in her face and said, "What do you mean by that?"

I was not prepared, and didn't know anything to say; so it was awkward, for she kept looking at me; but Seppi was alert and spoke up:

"Why, of course it would be pleasant to remember, for the very reason we were out so late was that Nikolaus got to telling how good you are to him, and how he never got whipped when you were by to save him; and he was so full of it, and we were so full of the interest of it, that none of us noticed how late it was getting."

"Did he say that? Did he?" and she put her apron to her eyes.

"You can ask Theodor—he will tell you the same."

"It is a dear, good lad, my Nick," she said. "I am sorry I let him get whipped; I will never do it again. To think—all the time I was sitting here last night, fretting and angry at him, he was loving me and praising me! Dear, dear, if we could only know! Then we shouldn't ever go wrong; but we are only poor, dumb beasts groping around and making mistakes. I sha'n't ever think of last night without a pang."

She was like all the rest; it seemed as if nobody could open a mouth, in these wretched days, without saying something that made us shiver. They were "groping around," and did not know what true, sorrowfully true things they were saying by accident.

Seppi asked if Nikolaus might go out with us.

"I am sorry," she answered, "but he can't. To punish him further, his father doesn't allow him to go out of the house to-day."

We had a great hope! I saw it in Seppi's eyes. We thought, "If he cannot leave the house, he cannot be drowned." Seppi asked, to make sure:

"Must he stay in all day, or only the morning?"

"All day. It's such a pity, too; it's a beautiful day, and he is so unused to being shut up. But he is busy planning his party, and maybe that is company for him. I do hope he isn't too lonesome."

Seppi saw that in her eye which emboldened him to ask if we might go up and help him pass his time.

"And welcome!" she said, right heartily. "Now I call that real friendship, when you might be abroad in the fields and the woods, having a happy time. You are good boys, I'll allow that, though you don't always find satisfactory ways of improving it. Take these cakes—for yourselves—and give him this one, from his mother."

The first thing we noticed when we entered Nikolaus's room was the time—a quarter to 10. Could that be correct? Only such a few minutes to live! I felt a contraction at my heart. Nikolaus jumped up and gave us a glad welcome. He was in good spirits over his plannings for his party and had not been lonesome.

"Sit down," he said, "and look at what I've been doing. And I've finished a kite that you will say is a beauty. It's drying, in the kitchen; I'll fetch it."

He had been spending his penny savings in fanciful trifles of various kinds, to go as prizes in the games, and they were marshaled with fine and showy effect upon the table. He said:

"Examine them at your leisure while I get mother to touch up the kite with her iron if it isn't dry enough yet."

Then he tripped out and went clattering down-stairs, whistling.

We did not look at the things; we couldn't take any interest in anything but the clock. We sat staring at it in silence, listening to the ticking, and every time the minute-hand jumped we nodded recognition—one minute fewer to cover in the race for life or for death. Finally Seppi drew a deep breath and said:

"Two minutes to ten. Seven minutes more and he will pass the death-point. Theodor, he is going to be saved! He's going to—"

"Hush! I'm on needles. Watch the clock and keep still."

Five minutes more. We were panting with the strain and the excitement. Another three minutes, and there was a footstep on the stair.

"Saved!" And we jumped up and faced the door.

The old mother entered, bringing the kite. "Isn't it a beauty?" she said. "And, dear me, how he has slaved over it—ever since daylight, I think, and only finished it awhile before you came." She stood it against the wall, and stepped back to take a view of it. "He drew the pictures his own self, and I think they are very good. The church isn't so very good, I'll have to admit, but look at the bridge—any one can recognize the bridge in a minute. He asked me to bring it up. . . . Dear me! it's seven minutes past ten, and I—"

"But where is he?"

"He? Oh, he'll be here soon; he's gone out a minute."

"Gone out?"

"Yes. Just as he came down-stairs little Lisa's mother came in and said the child had wandered off somewhere, and as she was a little uneasy I told Nikolaus to never mind about his father's orders—go and look her up. . . . Why, how white you two do look! I do believe you are sick. Sit down; I'll fetch something. That cake has disagreed with you. It is a little heavy, but I thought—"

She disappeared without finishing her sentence, and we hurried at once to the back window and looked toward the river. There was a great crowd at the other end of the bridge, and people were flying toward that point from every direction.

"Oh, it is all over—poor Nikolaus! Why, oh, why did she let him get out of the house!"

"Come away," said Seppi, half sobbing, "come quick—we can't bear to meet her; in five minutes she will know."

But we were not to escape. She came upon us at the foot of the stairs, with her cordials in her hands, and made us come in and sit down and take the medicine. Then she watched the effect, and it did not satisfy her; so she made us wait longer, and kept upbraiding herself for giving us the unwholesome cake.

Presently the thing happened which we were dreading. There was a sound of tramping and scraping outside, and a crowd came solemnly in, with heads uncovered, and laid the two drowned bodies on the bed.

"Oh, my God!" that poor mother cried out, and fell on her knees, and put her arms about her dead boy and began to cover the wet face with kisses. "Oh, it was I that sent him, and I have been his death. If I had obeyed, and kept him in the house, this would not have happened. And I am rightly punished; I was cruel to him last night, and him begging me, his own mother, to be his friend."

And so she went on and on, and all the women cried, and pitied her, and tried to comfort her, but she could not forgive herself and could not be comforted, and kept on saying if she had not sent him out he would be alive and well now, and she was the cause of his death.

It shows how foolish people are when they blame themselves for anything they have done. Satan knows, and he said nothing happens that your first act hasn't arranged to happen and made inevitable; and so, of your own motion you can't ever alter the scheme or do a thing that will break a link. Next we heard screams, and Frau Brandt came wildly plowing and plunging through the crowd with her dress in disorder and hair flying loose, and flung herself upon her dead child with moans and kisses and pleadings and endearments; and by and by she rose up almost exhausted with her outpourings of passionate emotion, and clenched her fist and lifted it toward the sky, and her tear-drenched face grew hard and resentful, and she said:

"For nearly two weeks I have had dreams and presentiments and warnings that death was going to strike what was most precious to me, and day and night and night and day I have groveled in the dirt before Him praying Him to have pity on my innocent child and save it from harm—and here is His answer!"

Why, He had saved it from harm—but she did not know.

She wiped the tears from her eyes and cheeks, and stood awhile gazing down at the child and caressing its face and its hair with her hands; then she spoke again in that bitter tone: "But in His hard heart is no compassion. I will never pray again."

She gathered her dead child to her bosom and strode away, the crowd falling back to let her pass, and smitten dumb by the awful words they had heard. Ah, that poor woman! It is as Satan said, we do not know good fortune from bad, and are always mistaking the one for the other. Many a time since I have heard people pray to God to spare the life of sick persons, but I have never done it.

Both funerals took place at the same time in our little church next day. Everybody was there, including the party guests. Satan was there, too; which was proper, for it was on account of his efforts that the funerals had happened. Nikolaus had departed this life without absolution, and a collection was taken up for masses, to get him out of purgatory. Only two-thirds of the required money was gathered, and the parents were going to try to borrow the rest, but Satan furnished it. He told us privately that there was no purgatory, but he had contributed in order that Nikolaus's parents and their friends might be saved from worry and distress. We thought it very good of him, but he said money did not cost him anything.

At the graveyard the body of little Lisa was seized for debt by a carpenter to whom the mother owed fifty groschen for work done the year before. She had never been able to pay this, and was not able now. The carpenter took the corpse home and kept it four days in his cellar, the mother weeping and imploring about his house all the time; then he buried it in his brother's cattle-yard, without religious ceremonies. It drove the mother wild with grief and shame, and she forsook her work and went daily about the town, cursing the carpenter and blaspheming the laws of the emperor and the church, and it was pitiful to see. Seppi asked Satan to interfere, but he said the carpenter and the rest were members of the human race and were acting quite neatly for that species of animal. He would interfere if he found a horse acting in such a way, and we must inform him when we came across that kind of horse doing that kind of human thing, so that he could stop it. We believed this was sarcasm, for of course there wasn't any such horse.

But after a few days we found that we could not abide that poor woman's distress, so we begged Satan to examine her several possible careers, and see if he could not change her, to her profit, to a new one. He said the longest of her careers as they now stood gave her forty-two years to live, and her shortest one twenty-nine, and that both were charged with grief and hunger and cold and pain. The only improvement he could make would be to enable her to skip a certain three minutes from now; and he asked us if he should do it. This was such a short time to decide in that we went to pieces with nervous excitement, and before we could pull ourselves together and ask for particulars he said the time would be up in a few more seconds; so then we gasped out, "Do it!"

"It is done," he said; "she was going around a corner; I have turned her back; it has changed her career."

"Then what will happen, Satan?"

"It is happening now. She is having words with Fischer, the weaver. In his anger Fischer will straightway do what he would not have done but for this accident. He was present when she stood over her child's body and uttered those blasphemies."

"What will he do?"

"He is doing it now—betraying her. In three days she will go to the stake."

We could not speak; we were frozen with horror, for if we had not meddled with her career she would have been spared this awful fate. Satan noticed these thoughts, and said:

"What you are thinking is strictly human-like—that is to say, foolish. The woman is advantaged. Die when she might, she would go to heaven. By this prompt death she gets twenty-nine years more of heaven than she is entitled to, and escapes twenty-nine years of misery here."

A moment before we were bitterly making up our minds that we would ask no more favors of Satan for friends of ours, for he did not seem to know any way to do a person a kindness but by killing him; but the whole aspect of the case was changed now, and we were glad of what we had done and full of happiness in the thought of it.

After a little I began to feel troubled about Fischer, and asked, timidly, "Does this episode change Fischer's life-scheme, Satan?"

"Change it? Why, certainly. And radically. If he had not met Frau Brandt awhile ago he would die next year, thirty-four years of age. Now he will live to be ninety, and have a pretty prosperous and comfortable life of it, as human lives go."

We felt a great joy and pride in what we had done for Fischer, and were expecting Satan to sympathize with this feeling; but he showed no sign and this made us uneasy. We waited for him to speak, but he didn't; so, to assuage our solicitude we had to ask him if there was any defect in Fischer's good luck. Satan considered the question a moment, then said, with some hesitation:

"Well, the fact is, it is a delicate point. Under his several former possible life-careers he was going to heaven."

We were aghast. "Oh, Satan! and under this one—"

"There, don't be so distressed. You were sincerely trying to do him a kindness; let that comfort you."

"Oh, dear, dear, that cannot comfort us. You ought to have told us what we were doing, then we wouldn't have acted so."

But it made no impression on him. He had never felt a pain or a sorrow, and did not know what they were, in any really informing way. He had no knowledge of them except theoretically—that is to say, intellectually. And of course that is no good. One can never get any but a loose and ignorant notion of such things except by experience. We tried our best to make him comprehend the awful thing that had been done and how we were compromised by it, but he couldn't seem to get hold of it. He said he did not think it important where Fischer went to; in heaven he would not be missed, there were "plenty there." We tried to make him see that he was missing the point entirely; that Fischer, and not other people, was the proper one to decide about the importance of it; but it all went for nothing; he said he did not care for Fischer— there were plenty more Fischers.

The next minute Fischer went by on the other side of the way, and it made us sick and faint to see him, remembering the doom that was upon him, and we the cause of it. And how unconscious he was that anything had happened to him! You could see by his elastic step and his alert manner that he was well satisfied with himself for doing that hard turn for poor Frau Brandt. He kept glancing back over his shoulder expectantly. And, sure enough, pretty soon Frau Brandt followed after, in charge of the officers and wearing jingling chains. A mob was in her wake, jeering and shouting, "Blasphemer and heretic!" and some among them were neighbors and friends of her happier days. Some were trying to strike her, and the officers were not taking as much trouble as they might to keep them from it.

"Oh, stop them, Satan!" It was out before we remembered that he could not interrupt them for a moment without changing their whole after-lives. He puffed a little puff toward them with his lips and they began to reel and stagger and grab at the empty air; then they broke apart and fled in every direction, shrieking, as if in intolerable pain. He had crushed a rib of each of them with that little puff. We could not help asking if their life-chart was changed.

"Yes, entirely. Some have gained years, some have lost them. Some few will profit in various ways by the change, but only that few."

We did not ask if we had brought poor Fischer's luck to any of them. We did not wish to know. We fully believed in Satan's desire to do us kindnesses, but we were losing confidence in his judgment. It was at this time that our growing anxiety to have him look over our life-charts and suggest improvements began to fade out and give place to other interests.

For a day or two the whole village was a chattering turmoil over Frau Brandt's case and over the mysterious calamity that had overtaken the mob, and at her trial the place was crowded. She was easily convicted of her blasphemies, for she uttered those terrible words again and said she would not take them back. When warned that she was imperiling her life, she said they could take it in welcome, she did not want it, she would rather live with the professional devils in perdition than with these imitators in the village. They accused her of breaking all those ribs by witchcraft, and asked her if she was not a witch? She answered scornfully:

"No. If I had that power would any of you holy hypocrites be alive five minutes? No; I would strike you all dead. Pronounce your sentence and let me go; I am tired of your society."

So they found her guilty, and she was excommunicated and cut off from the joys of heaven and doomed to the fires of hell; then she was clothed in a coarse robe and delivered to the secular arm, and conducted to the market-place, the bell solemnly tolling the while. We saw her chained to the stake, and saw the first film of blue smoke rise on the still air. Then her hard face softened, and she looked upon the packed crowd in front of her and said, with gentleness:

"We played together once, in long-agone days when we were innocent little creatures. For the sake of that, I forgive you."

We went away then, and did not see the fires consume her, but we heard the shrieks, although we put our fingers in our ears. When they ceased we knew she was in heaven, notwithstanding the excommunication; and we were glad of her death and not sorry that we had brought it about.

One day, a little while after this, Satan appeared again. We were always watching out for him, for life was never very stagnant when he was by. He came upon us at that place in the woods where we had first met him. Being boys, we wanted to be entertained; we asked him to do a show for us.

"Very well," he said; "would you like to see a history of the progress of the human race?—its development of that product which it calls civilization?"

We said we should.

So, with a thought, he turned the place into the Garden of Eden, and we saw Abel praying by his altar; then Cain came walking toward him with his club, and did not seem to see us, and would have stepped on my foot if I had not drawn it in. He spoke to his brother in a language which we did not understand; then he grew violent and threatening, and we knew what was going to happen, and turned away our heads for the moment; but we heard the crash of the blows and heard the shrieks and the groans; then there was silence, and we saw Abel lying in his blood and gasping out his life, and Cain standing over him and looking down at him, vengeful and unrepentant.

Then the vision vanished, and was followed by a long series of unknown wars, murders, and massacres. Next we had the Flood, and the Ark tossing around in the stormy waters, with lofty mountains in the distance showing veiled and dim through the rain. Satan said:

"The progress of your race was not satisfactory. It is to have another chance now."

The scene changed, and we saw Noah overcome with wine.

Next, we had Sodom and Gomorrah, and "the attempt to discover two or three respectable persons there," as Satan described it. Next, Lot and his daughters in the cave.

Next came the Hebraic wars, and we saw the victors massacre the survivors and their cattle, and save the young girls alive and distribute them around.

Next we had Jael; and saw her slip into the tent and drive the nail into the temple of her sleeping guest; and we were so close that when the blood gushed out it trickled in a little, red stream to our feet, and we could have stained our hands in it if we had wanted to.

Next we had Egyptian wars, Greek wars, Roman wars, hideous drenchings of the earth with blood; and we saw the treacheries of the Romans toward the Carthaginians, and the sickening spectacle of the massacre of those brave people. Also we saw Cæsar invade Britain—"not that those barbarians had done him any harm, but because he wanted their land, and desired to confer the blessings of civilization upon their widows and orphans," as Satan explained.

Next, Christianity was born. Then ages of Europe passed in review before us, and we saw Christianity and Civilization march hand in hand through those ages, "leaving famine and death and desolation in their wake, and other signs of the progress of the human race," as Satan observed.

And always we had wars, and more wars, and still other wars—all over Europe, all over the world. "Sometimes in the private interest of royal families," Satan said, "sometimes to crush a weak nation; but never a war started by the aggressor for any clean purpose—there is no such war in the history of the race."

"Now," said Satan, "you have seen your progress down to the present, and you must confess that it is wonderful—in its way. We must now exhibit the future."

He showed us slaughters more terrible in their destruction of life, more devastating in their engines of war, than any we had seen.

"You perceive," he said, "that you have made continual progress. Cain did his murder with a club; the Hebrews did their murders with javelins and swords; the Greeks and Romans added protective armor and the fine arts of military organization and generalship; the Christian has added guns and gunpowder; a few centuries from now he will have so greatly improved the deadly effectiveness of his weapons of slaughter that all men will confess that without Christian civilization war must have remained a poor and trifling thing to the end of time."

Then he began to laugh in the most unfeeling way, and make fun of the human race, although he knew that what he had been saying shamed us and wounded us. No one but an angel could have acted so; but suffering is nothing to them; they do not know what it is, except by hearsay.

More than once Seppi and I had tried in a humble and diffident way to convert him, and as he had remained silent we had taken his silence as a sort of encouragement; necessarily, then, this talk of his was a disappointment to us, for it showed that we had made no deep impression upon him. The thought made us sad, and we knew then how the missionary must feel when he has been cherishing a glad hope and has seen it blighted. We kept our grief to ourselves, knowing that this was not the time to continue our work.

Satan laughed his unkind laugh to a finish; then he said: "It is a remarkable progress. In five or six thousand years five or six high civilizations have risen, flourished, commanded the wonder of the world, then faded out and disappeared; and not one of them except the latest ever invented any sweeping and adequate way to kill people. They all did their best—to kill being the chiefest ambition of the human race and the earliest incident in its history—but only the Christian civilization has scored a triumph to be proud of. Two or three centuries from now it will be recognized that all the competent killers are Christians; then the pagan world will go to school to the Christian—not to acquire his religion, but his guns. The Turk and the Chinaman will buy those to kill missionaries and converts with."

By this time his theater was at work again, and before our eyes nation after nation drifted by, during two or three centuries, a mighty procession, an endless procession, raging, struggling, wallowing through seas of blood, smothered in battle-smoke through which the flags glinted and the red jets from the cannon darted; and always we heard the thunder of the guns and the cries of the dying.

"And what does it amount to?" said Satan, with his evil chuckle. "Nothing at all. You gain nothing; you always come out where you went in. For a million years the race has gone on monotonously propagating itself and monotonously reperforming this dull nonsense—to what end? No wisdom can guess! Who gets a profit out of it? Nobody but a parcel of usurping little monarchs and nobilities who despise you; would feel defiled if you touched them; would shut the door in your face if you proposed to call; whom you slave for, fight for, die for, and are not ashamed of it, but proud; whose existence is a perpetual insult to you and you are afraid to resent it; who are mendicants supported by your alms, yet assume toward you the airs of benefactor toward beggar; who address you in the language of master to slave, and are answered in the language of slave to master; who are worshiped by you with your mouth, while in your heart— if you have one—you despise yourselves for it. The first man was a hypocrite and a coward, qualities which have not yet failed in his line; it is the foundation upon which all civilizations have been built. Drink to their perpetuation! Drink to their augmentation! Drink to—" Then he saw by our faces how much we were hurt, and he cut his sentence short and stopped chuckling, and his manner changed. He said, gently: "No, we will drink one another's health, and let civilization go. The wine which has flown to our hands out of space by desire is earthly, and good enough for that other toast; but throw away the glasses; we will drink this one in wine which has not visited this world before."

We obeyed, and reached up and received the new cups as they descended. They were shapely and beautiful goblets, but they were not made of any material that we were acquainted with. They seemed to be in motion, they seemed to be alive; and certainly the colors in them were in motion. They were very brilliant and sparkling, and of every tint, and they were never still, but flowed to and fro in rich tides which met and broke and flashed out dainty explosions of enchanting color. I think it was most like opals washing about in waves and flashing out their splendid fires. But there is nothing to compare the wine with. We drank it, and felt a strange and witching ecstasy as of heaven go stealing through us, and Seppi's eyes filled and he said worshipingly:

"We shall be there some day, and then—"

He glanced furtively at Satan, and I think he hoped Satan would say, "Yes, you will be there some day," but Satan seemed to be thinking about something else, and said nothing. This made me feel ghastly, for I knew he had heard; nothing, spoken or unspoken, ever escaped him. Poor Seppi looked distressed, and did not finish his remark. The goblets rose and clove their way into the sky, a triplet of radiant sundogs, and disappeared. Why didn't they stay? It seemed a bad sign, and depressed me. Should I ever see mine again? Would Seppi ever see his?

9

It was wonderful, the mastery Satan had over time and distance. For him they did not exist. He called them human inventions, and said they were artificialities. We often went to the most distant parts of the globe with him, and stayed weeks and months, and yet were gone only a fraction of a second, as a rule. You could prove it by the clock. One day when our people were in such awful distress because the witch commission were afraid to proceed against the astrologer and Father Peter's household, or against any, indeed, but the poor and the friendless, they lost patience and took to witch-hunting on their own score, and began to chase a born lady who was known to have the habit of curing people by devilish arts, such as bathing them, washing them, and nourishing them instead of bleeding them and purging them through the ministrations of a barber-surgeon in the proper way. She came flying down, with the howling and cursing mob after her, and tried to take refuge in houses, but the doors were shut in her face. They chased her more than half an hour, we following to see it, and at last she was exhausted and fell, and they caught her. They dragged her to a tree and threw a rope over the limb, and began to make a noose in it, some holding her, meantime, and she crying and begging, and her young daughter looking on and weeping, but afraid to say or do anything.

They hanged the lady, and I threw a stone at her, although in my heart I was sorry for her; but all were throwing stones and each was watching his neighbor, and if I had not done as the others did it would have been noticed and spoken of. Satan burst out laughing.

All that were near by turned upon him, astonished and not pleased. It was an ill time to laugh, for his free and scoffing ways and his supernatural music had brought him under suspicion all over the town and turned many privately against him. The big blacksmith called attention to him now, raising his voice so that all should hear, and said:

"What are you laughing at? Answer! Moreover, please explain to the company why you threw no stone."

"Are you sure I did not throw a stone?"

"Yes. You needn't try to get out of it; I had my eye on you."

"And I—I noticed you!" shouted two others.

"Three witnesses," said Satan: "Mueller, the blacksmith; Klein, the butcher's man; Pfeiffer, the weaver's journeyman. Three very ordinary liars. Are there any more?"

"Never mind whether there are others or not, and never mind about what you consider us—three's enough to settle your matter for you. You'll prove that you threw a stone, or it shall go hard with you."

"That's so!" shouted the crowd, and surged up as closely as they could to the center of interest.

"And first you will answer that other question," cried the blacksmith, pleased with himself for being mouthpiece to the public and hero of the occasion. "What are you laughing at?"

Satan smiled and answered, pleasantly: "To see three cowards stoning a dying lady when they were so near death themselves."

You could see the superstitious crowd shrink and catch their breath, under the sudden shock. The blacksmith, with a show of bravado, said:

"Pooh! What do you know about it?"

"I? Everything. By profession I am a fortune-teller, and I read the hands of you three—and some others—when you lifted them to stone the woman. One of you will die to-morrow week; another of you will die to-night; the third has but five minutes to live—and yonder is the clock!"

It made a sensation. The faces of the crowd blanched, and turned mechanically toward the clock. The butcher and the weaver seemed smitten with an illness, but the blacksmith braced up and said, with spirit:

"It is not long to wait for prediction number one. If it fails, young master, you will not live a whole minute after, I promise you that."

No one said anything; all watched the clock in a deep stillness which was impressive. When four and a half minutes were gone the blacksmith gave a sudden gasp and clapped his hands upon his heart, saying, "Give me breath! Give me room!" and began to sink down. The crowd surged back, no one offering to support him, and he fell lumbering to the ground and was dead. The people stared at him, then at Satan, then at one another; and their lips moved, but no words came. Then Satan said:

"Three saw that I threw no stone. Perhaps there are others; let them speak."

It struck a kind of panic into them, and, although no one answered him, many began to violently accuse one another, saying, "You said he didn't throw," and getting for reply, "It is a lie, and I will make you eat it!" And so in a moment they were in a raging and noisy turmoil, and beating and banging one another; and in the midst was the only indifferent one—the dead lady hanging from her rope, her troubles forgotten, her spirit at peace.

So we walked away, and I was not at ease, but was saying to myself, "He told them he was laughing at them, but it was a lie—he was laughing at me."

That made him laugh again, and he said, "Yes, I was laughing at you, because, in fear of what others might report about you, you stoned the woman when your heart revolted at the act—but I was laughing at the others, too."

"Why?"

"Because their case was yours."

"How is that?"

"Well, there were sixty-eight people there, and sixty-two of them had no more desire to throw a stone than you had."

"Satan!"

"Oh, it's true. I know your race. It is made up of sheep. It is governed by minorities, seldom or never by majorities. It suppresses its feelings and its beliefs and follows the handful that makes the most noise. Sometimes the noisy handful is right, sometimes wrong; but no matter, the crowd follows it. The vast majority of the race, whether savage or civilized, are secretly kind-hearted and shrink from inflicting pain, but in the presence of the aggressive and pitiless minority they don't dare to assert themselves. Think of it! One kind-hearted creature spies upon another, and sees to it that he loyally helps in iniquities which revolt both of them. Speaking as an expert, I know that ninety-nine out of a hundred of your race were strongly against the killing of witches when that foolishness was first agitated by a handful of pious lunatics in the long ago. And I know that even to-day, after ages of transmitted prejudice and silly teaching, only one person in twenty puts any real heart into the harrying of a witch. And yet apparently everybody hates witches and wants them killed. Some day a handful will rise up on the other side and make the most noise—perhaps even a single daring man with a big voice and a determined front will do it—and in a week all the sheep will wheel and follow him, and witch-hunting will come to a sudden end.

"Monarchies, aristocracies, and religions are all based upon that large defect in your race—the individual's distrust of his neighbor, and his desire, for safety's or comfort's sake, to stand well in his neighbor's eye. These institutions will always remain, and always flourish, and always oppress you, affront you, and degrade you, because you will always be and remain slaves of minorities. There was never a country where the majority of the people were in their secret hearts loyal to any of these institutions."

I did not like to hear our race called sheep, and said I did not think they were.

"Still, it is true, lamb," said Satan. "Look at you in war—what mutton you are, and how ridiculous!"

"In war? How?"

"There has never been a just one, never an honorable one—on the part of the instigator of the war. I can see a million years ahead, and this rule will never change in so many as half a dozen instances. The loud little handful—as usual—will shout for the war. The pulpit will—warily and cautiously—object—at first; the great, big, dull bulk of the nation will rub its sleepy eyes and try to make out why there should be a war, and will say, earnestly and indignantly, 'It is unjust and dishonorable, and there is no necessity for it.' Then the handful will shout louder. A few fair men on the other side will argue and reason against the war with speech and pen, and at first will have a hearing and be applauded; but it will not last long; those others will outshout them, and presently the anti-war audiences will thin out and lose popularity. Before long you will see this curious thing: the speakers stoned from the platform, and free speech strangled by hordes of furious men who in their secret hearts are still at one with those stoned speakers—as earlier—but do not dare to say so. And now the whole nation—pulpit and all—will take up the war-cry, and shout itself hoarse, and mob any honest man who ventures to open his mouth; and presently such mouths will cease to open. Next the statesmen will invent cheap lies, putting the blame upon the nation that is attacked, and every man will be glad of those conscience-soothing falsities, and will diligently study them, and refuse to examine any refutations of them; and thus he will by and by convince himself that the war is just, and will thank God for the better sleep he enjoys after this process of grotesque self-deception."

10

Days and days went by now, and no Satan. It was dull without him. But the astrologer, who had returned from his excursion to the moon, went about the village, braving public opinion, and getting a stone in the middle of his back now and then when some witch-hater got a safe chance to throw it and dodge out of sight. Meantime two influences had been working well for Marget. That Satan, who was quite indifferent to her, had stopped going to her house after a visit or two had hurt her pride, and she had set herself the task of banishing him from her heart. Reports of Wilhelm Meidling's dissipation brought to her from time to time by old Ursula had touched her with remorse, jealousy of Satan being the cause of it; and so now, these two matters working upon her together, she was getting a good profit out of the combination—her interest in Satan was steadily cooling, her interest in Wilhelm was steadily waning. All that was needed to complete her conversion was that Wilhelm should brace up and do something that should cause favorable talk and incline the public toward him again.

The opportunity came now. Marget sent and asked him to defend her uncle in the approaching trial, and he was greatly pleased, and stopped drinking and began his preparations with diligence. With more diligence than hope, in fact, for it was not a promising case. He had many interviews in his office with Seppi and me, and threshed out our testimony pretty thoroughly, thinking to find some valuable grains among the chaff, but the harvest was poor, of course.

If Satan would only come! That was my constant thought. He could invent some way to win the case; for he had said it would be won, so he necessarily knew how it could be done. But the days dragged on, and still he did not come. Of course I did not doubt that it would be won, and that Father Peter would be happy for the rest of his life, since Satan had said so; yet I knew I should be much more comfortable if he would come and tell us how to manage it. It was getting high time for Father Peter to have a saving change toward happiness, for by general report he was worn out with his imprisonment and the ignominy that was burdening him, and was like to die of his miseries unless he got relief soon.

At last the trial came on, and the people gathered from all around to witness it; among them many strangers from considerable distances. Yes, everybody was there except the accused. He was too feeble in body for the strain. But Marget was present, and keeping up her hope and her spirit the best she could. The money was present, too. It was emptied on the table, and was handled and caressed and examined by such as were privileged.

The astrologer was put in the witness-box. He had on his best hat and robe for the occasion.

QUESTION You claim that this money is yours?

ANSWER I do.

Q. How did you come by it?

A. I found the bag in the road when I was returning from a journey.

Q. When?

A. More than two years ago.

Q. What did you do with it?

A. I brought it home and hid it in a secret place in my observatory, intending to find the owner if I could.

Q. You endeavored to find him?

A. I made diligent inquiry during several months, but nothing came of it.

Q. And then?

A. I thought it not worth while to look further, and was minded to use the money in finishing the wing of the foundling-asylum connected with the priory and nunnery. So I took it out of its hiding-place and counted it to see if any of it was missing. And then—

Q. Why do you stop? Proceed.

A. I am sorry to have to say this, but just as I had finished and was restoring the bag to its place, I looked up and there stood Father Peter behind me.

Several murmured, "That looks bad," but others answered, "Ah, but he is such a liar!"

Q. That made you uneasy?

A. No; I thought nothing of it at the time, for Father Peter often came to me unannounced to ask for a little help in his need.

Marget blushed crimson at hearing her uncle falsely and impudently charged with begging, especially from one he had always denounced as a fraud, and was going to speak, but remembered herself in time and held her peace.

Q. Proceed.

A. In the end I was afraid to contribute the money to the foundling-asylum, but elected to wait yet another year and continue my inquiries. When I heard of Father Peter's find I was glad, and no suspicion entered my mind; when I came home a day or two later and discovered that my own money was gone I still did not suspect until three circumstances connected with Father Peter's good fortune struck me as being singular coincidences.

Q. Pray name them.

A. Father Peter had found his money in a path—I had found mine in a road. Father Peter's find consisted exclusively of gold ducats—mine also. Father Peter found eleven hundred and seven ducats—I exactly the same.

This closed his evidence, and certainly it made a strong impression on the house; one could see that.

Wilhelm Meidling asked him some questions, then called us boys, and we told our tale. It made the people laugh, and we were ashamed. We were feeling pretty badly, anyhow, because Wilhelm was hopeless, and showed it. He was doing as well as he could, poor young fellow, but nothing was in his favor, and such sympathy as there was was now plainly not with his client. It might be difficult for court and people to believe the astrologer's story, considering his character, but it was almost impossible to believe Father Peter's. We were already feeling badly enough, but when the astrologer's lawyer said he believed he would not ask us any questions—for our story was a little delicate and it would be cruel for him to put any strain upon it—everybody tittered, and it was almost more than we could bear. Then he made a sarcastic little speech, and got so much fun out of our tale, and it seemed so ridiculous and childish and every way impossible and foolish, that it made everybody laugh till the tears came; and at last Marget could not keep up her courage any longer, but broke down and cried, and I was so sorry for her.

Now I noticed something that braced me up. It was Satan standing alongside of Wilhelm! And there was such a contrast!—Satan looked so confident, had such a spirit in his eyes and face, and Wilhelm looked so depressed and despondent. We two were comfortable now, and judged that he would testify and persuade the bench and the people that black was white and white black, or any other color he wanted it. We glanced around to see what the strangers in the house thought of him, for he was beautiful, you know—stunning, in fact—but no one was noticing him; so we knew by that that he was invisible.

The lawyer was saying his last words; and while he was saying them Satan began to melt into Wilhelm. He melted into him and disappeared; and then there was a change, when his spirit began to look out of Wilhelm's eyes.

That lawyer finished quite seriously, and with dignity. He pointed to the money, and said:

"The love of it is the root of all evil. There it lies, the ancient tempter, newly red with the shame of its latest victory—the dishonor of a priest of God and his two poor juvenile helpers in crime. If it could but speak, let us hope that it would be constrained to confess that of all its conquests this was the basest and the most pathetic."

He sat down. Wilhelm rose and said:

"From the testimony of the accuser I gather that he found this money in a road more than two years ago. Correct me, sir, if I misunderstood you."

The astrologer said his understanding of it was correct.

"And the money so found was never out of his hands thenceforth up to a certain definite date—the last day of last year. Correct me, sir, if I am wrong."

The astrologer nodded his head. Wilhelm turned to the bench and said:

"If I prove that this money here was not that money; then it is not his?"

"Certainly not; but this is irregular. If you had such a witness it was your duty to give proper notice of it and have him here to—" He broke off and began to consult with the other judges. Meantime that other lawyer got up excited and began to protest against allowing new witnesses to be brought into the case at this late stage.

The judges decided that his contention was just and must be allowed.

"But this is not a new witness," said Wilhelm. "It has already been partly examined. I speak of the coin."

"The coin? What can the coin say?"

"It can say it is not the coin that the astrologer once possessed. It can say it was not in existence last December. By its date it can say this."

And it was so! There was the greatest excitement in the court while that lawyer and the judges were reaching for coins and examining them and exclaiming. And everybody was full of admiration of Wilhelm's brightness in happening to think of that neat idea. At last order was called and the court said:

"All of the coins but four are of the date of the present year. The court tenders its sincere sympathy to the accused, and its deep regret that he, an innocent man, through an unfortunate mistake, has suffered the undeserved humiliation of imprisonment and trial. The case is dismissed."

So the money could speak, after all, though that lawyer thought it couldn't. The court rose, and almost everybody came forward to shake hands with Marget and congratulate her, and then to shake with Wilhelm and praise him: and Satan had stepped out of Wilhelm and was standing around looking on full of interest, and people walking through him every which way, not knowing he was there. And Wilhelm could not explain why he only thought of the date on the coins at the last moment, instead of earlier; he said it just occurred to him, all of a sudden, like an inspiration, and he brought it right out without any hesitation, for, although he didn't examine the coins, he seemed, somehow, to know it was true. That was honest of him, and like him; another would have pretended he had thought of it earlier, and was keeping it back for a surprise.

He had dulled down a little now; not much, but still you could notice that he hadn't that luminous look in his eyes that he had while Satan was in him. He nearly got it back, though, for a moment when Marget came and praised him and thanked him and couldn't keep him from seeing how proud she was of him. The astrologer went off dissatisfied and cursing, and Solomon Isaacs gathered up the money and carried it away. It was Father Peter's for good and all, now.

Satan was gone. I judged that he had spirited himself away to the jail to tell the prisoner the news; and in this I was right. Marget and the rest of us hurried thither at our best speed, in a great state of rejoicing.

Well, what Satan had done was this: he had appeared before that poor prisoner, exclaiming, "The trial is over, and you stand forever disgraced as a thief—by verdict of the court!"

The shock unseated the old man's reason. When we arrived, ten minutes later, he was parading pompously up and down and delivering commands to this and that and the other constable or jailer, and calling them Grand Chamberlain, and Prince This and Prince That, and Admiral of the Fleet, Field Marshal in Command, and all such fustian, and was as happy as a bird. He thought he was Emperor!

Marget flung herself on his breast and cried, and indeed everybody was moved almost to heartbreak. He recognized Marget, but could not understand why she should cry. He patted her on the shoulder and said:

"Don't do it, dear; remember, there are witnesses, and it is not becoming in the Crown Princess. Tell me your trouble—it shall be mended; there is nothing the Emperor cannot do." Then he looked around and saw old Ursula with her apron to her eyes. He was puzzled at that, and said, "And what is the matter with you?"

Through her sobs she got out words explaining that she was distressed to see him—"so." He reflected over that a moment, then muttered, as if to himself: "A singular old thing, the Dowager Duchess—means well, but is always snuffling and never able to tell what it is about. It is because she doesn't know." His eyes fell on Wilhelm. "Prince of India," he said, "I divine that it is you that the Crown Princess is concerned about. Her tears shall be dried; I will no longer stand between you; she shall share your throne; and between you you shall inherit mine. There, little lady, have I done well? You can smile now—isn't it so?"

He petted Marget and kissed her, and was so contented with himself and with everybody that he could not do enough for us all, but began to give away kingdoms and such things right and left, and the least that any of us got was a principality. And so at last, being persuaded to go home, he marched in imposing state; and when the crowds along the way saw how it gratified him to be hurrahed at, they humored him to the top of his desire, and he responded with condescending bows and gracious smiles, and often stretched out a hand and said, "Bless you, my people!"

As pitiful a sight as ever I saw. And Marget, and old Ursula crying all the way.

On my road home I came upon Satan, and reproached him with deceiving me with that lie. He was not embarrassed, but said, quite simply and composedly:

"Ah, you mistake; it was the truth. I said he would be happy the rest of his days, and he will, for he will always think he is the Emperor, and his pride in it and his joy in it will endure to the end. He is now, and will remain, the one utterly happy person in this empire."

"But the method of it, Satan, the method! Couldn't you have done it without depriving him of his reason?"

It was difficult to irritate Satan, but that accomplished it.

"What an ass you are!" he said. "Are you so unobservant as not to have found out that sanity and happiness are an impossible combination? No sane man can be happy, for to him life is real, and he sees what a fearful thing it is. Only the mad can be happy, and not many of those. The few that imagine themselves kings or gods are happy, the rest are no happier than the sane. Of course, no man is entirely in his right mind at any time, but I have been referring to the extreme cases. I have taken from this man that trumpery thing which the race regards as a Mind; I have replaced his tin life with a silver-gilt fiction; you see the result—and you criticize! I said I would make him permanently happy, and I have done it. I have made him happy by the only means possible to his race—and you are not satisfied!" He heaved a discouraged sigh, and said, "It seems to me that this race is hard to please."

There it was, you see. He didn't seem to know any way to do a person a favor except by killing him or making a lunatic out of him. I apologized, as well as I could; but privately I did not think much of his processes—at that time.

Satan was accustomed to say that our race lived a life of continuous and uninterrupted self-deception. It duped itself from cradle to grave with shams and delusions which it mistook for realities, and this made its entire life a sham. Of the score of fine qualities which it imagined it had and was vain of, it really possessed hardly one. It regarded itself as gold, and was only brass. One day when he was in this vein he mentioned a detail—the sense of humor. I cheered up then, and took issue. I said we possessed it.

"There spoke the race!" he said; "always ready to claim what it hasn't got, and mistake its ounce of brass filings for a ton of gold-dust. You have a mongrel perception of humor, nothing more; a multitude of you possess that. This multitude see the comic side of a thousand low-grade and trivial things—broad incongruities, mainly; grotesqueries, absurdities, evokers of the horse-laugh. The ten thousand high-grade comicalities which exist in the world are sealed from their dull vision. Will a day come when the race will detect the funniness of these juvenilities and laugh at them—and by laughing at them destroy them? For your race, in its poverty, has unquestionably one really effective weapon—laughter. Power, money, persuasion, supplication, persecution—these can lift at a colossal humbug—push it a little—weaken it a little, century by century; but only laughter can blow it to rags and atoms at a blast. Against the assault of laughter nothing can stand. You are always fussing and fighting with your other weapons. Do you ever use that one? No; you leave it lying rusting. As a race, do you ever use it at all? No; you lack sense and the courage."

We were traveling at the time and stopped at a little city in India and looked on while a juggler did his tricks before a group of natives. They were wonderful, but I knew Satan could beat that game, and I begged him to show off a little, and he said he would. He changed himself into a native in turban and breech-cloth, and very considerately conferred on me a temporary knowledge of the language.

The juggler exhibited a seed, covered it with earth in a small flowerpot, then put a rag over the pot; after a minute the rag began to rise; in ten minutes it had risen a foot; then the rag was removed and a little tree was exposed, with leaves upon it and ripe fruit. We ate the fruit, and it was good. But Satan said:

"Why do you cover the pot? Can't you grow the tree in the sunlight?"

"No," said the juggler; "no one can do that."

"You are only an apprentice; you don't know your trade. Give me the seed. I will show you." He took the seed and said, "What shall I raise from it?"

"It is a cherry seed; of course you will raise a cherry."

"Oh no; that is a trifle; any novice can do that. Shall I raise an orange-tree from it?"

"Oh yes!" and the juggler laughed.

"And shall I make it bear other fruits as well as oranges?"

"If God wills!" and they all laughed.

Satan put the seed in the ground, put a handful of dust on it, and said, "Rise!"

A tiny stem shot up and began to grow, and grew so fast that in five minutes it was a great tree, and we were sitting in the shade of it. There was a murmur of wonder, then all looked up and saw a strange and pretty sight, for the branches were heavy with fruits of many kinds and colors—oranges, grapes, bananas, peaches, cherries, apricots, and so on. Baskets were brought, and the unlading of the tree began; and the people crowded around Satan and kissed his hand, and praised him, calling him the prince of jugglers. The news went about the town, and everybody came running to see the wonder—and they remembered to bring baskets, too. But the tree was equal to the occasion; it put out new fruits as fast as any were removed; baskets were filled by the score and by the hundred, but always the supply remained undiminished. At last a foreigner in white linen and sun-helmet arrived, and exclaimed, angrily:

"Away from here! Clear out, you dogs; the tree is on my lands and is my property."

The natives put down their baskets and made humble obeisance. Satan made humble obeisance, too, with his fingers to his forehead, in the native way, and said:

"Please let them have their pleasure for an hour, sir—only that, and no longer. Afterward you may forbid them; and you will still have more fruit than you and the state together can consume in a year."

This made the foreigner very angry, and he cried out, "Who are you, you vagabond, to tell your betters what they may do and what they mayn't!" and he struck Satan with his cane and followed this error with a kick.

The fruits rotted on the branches, and the leaves withered and fell. The foreigner gazed at the bare limbs with the look of one who is surprised, and not gratified. Satan said:

"Take good care of the tree, for its health and yours are bound together. It will never bear again, but if you tend it well it will live long. Water its roots once in each hour every night—and do it yourself; it must not be done by proxy, and to do it in daylight will not answer. If you fail only once in any night, the tree will die, and you likewise. Do not go home to your own country any more—you would not reach there; make no business or pleasure engagements which require you to go outside your gate at night—you cannot afford the risk; do not rent or sell this place—it would be injudicious."

The foreigner was proud and wouldn't beg, but I thought he looked as if he would like to. While he stood gazing at Satan we vanished away and landed in Ceylon.

I was sorry for that man; sorry Satan hadn't been his customary self and killed him or made him a lunatic. It would have been a mercy. Satan overheard the thought, and said:

"I would have done it but for his wife, who has not offended me. She is coming to him presently from their native land, Portugal. She is well, but has not long to live, and has been yearning to see him and persuade him to go back with her next year. She will die without knowing he can't leave that place."

"He won't tell her?"

"He? He will not trust that secret with any one; he will reflect that it could be revealed in sleep, in the hearing of some Portuguese guest's servant some time or other."

"Did none of those natives understand what you said to him?"

"None of them understood, but he will always be afraid that some of them did. That fear will be torture to him, for he has been a harsh master to them. In his dreams he will imagine them chopping his tree down. That will make his days uncomfortable—I have already arranged for his nights."

It grieved me, though not sharply, to see him take such a malicious satisfaction in his plans for this foreigner.

"Does he believe what you told him, Satan?"

"He thought he didn't, but our vanishing helped. The tree, where there had been no tree before—that helped. The insane and uncanny variety of fruits—the sudden withering—all these things are helps. Let him think as he may, reason as he may, one thing is certain, he will water the tree. But between this and night he will begin his changed career with a very natural precaution—for him."

"What is that?"

"He will fetch a priest to cast out the tree's devil. You are such a humorous race—and don't suspect it."

"Will he tell the priest?"

"No. He will say a juggler from Bombay created it, and that he wants the juggler's devil driven out of it, so that it will thrive and be fruitful again. The priest's incantations will fail; then the Portuguese will give up that scheme and get his watering-pot ready."

"But the priest will burn the tree. I know it; he will not allow it to remain."

"Yes, and anywhere in Europe he would burn the man, too. But in India the people are civilized, and these things will not happen. The man will drive the priest away and take care of the tree."

I reflected a little, then said, "Satan, you have given him a hard life, I think."

"Comparatively. It must not be mistaken for a holiday."

We flitted from place to place around the world as we had done before, Satan showing me a hundred wonders, most of them reflecting in some way the weakness and triviality of our race. He did this now every few days—not out of malice—I am sure of that—it only seemed to amuse and interest him, just as a naturalist might be amused and interested by a collection of ants.

11

For as much as a year Satan continued these visits, but at last he came less often, and then for a long time he did not come at all. This always made me lonely and melancholy. I felt that he was losing interest in our tiny world and might at any time abandon his visits entirely. When one day he finally came to me I was over-joyed, but only for a little while. He had come to say good-by, he told me, and for the last time. He had investigations and undertakings in other corners of the universe, he said, that would keep him busy for a longer period than I could wait for his return.

"And you are going away, and will not come back any more?"

"Yes," he said. "We have comraded long together, and it has been pleasant—pleasant for both; but I must go now, and we shall not see each other any more."

"In this life, Satan, but in another? We shall meet in another, surely?"

Then, all tranquilly and soberly, he made the strange answer, *"There is no other."*

A subtle influence blew upon my spirit from his, bringing with it a vague, dim, but blessed and hopeful feeling that the incredible words might be true—even *must* be true.

"Have you never suspected this, Theodor?"

"No. How could I? But if it can only be true—"

"It is true."

A gust of thankfulness rose in my breast, but a doubt checked it before it could issue in words, and I said, "But—but—we have seen that future life—seen it in its actuality, and so—"

"It was a vision—it had no existence."

I could hardly breathe for the great hope that was struggling in me. "A vision?—a vi—"

"Life itself is only a vision, a dream."

It was electrical. By God ! I had had that very thought a thousand times in my musings!

"Nothing exists; all is a dream. God—man—the world—the sun, the moon, the wilderness of stars—a dream, all a dream; they have no existence. *Nothing exists save empty space—and you!"*

"I!"

"And you are not you—you have no body, no blood, no bones, you are but a *thought.* I myself have no existence; I am but a dream—your dream, creature of your imagination. In a moment you will have realized this, then you will banish me from your visions and I shall dissolve into the nothingness out of which you made me. . . .

"I am perishing already—I am failing—I am passing away. In a little while you will be alone in shoreless space, to wander its limitless solitudes without friend or comrade forever—for you will remain a *thought,* the only existent thought, and by your nature inextinguishable, indestructible. But I, your poor servant, have revealed you to yourself and set you free. Dream other dreams, and better!

"Strange! that you should not have suspected years ago—centuries, ages, eons, ago!—for you have existed, companionless, through all the eternities. Strange, indeed, that you should not have suspected that your universe and its contents were only dreams, visions, fiction! Strange, because they are so frankly and hysterically insane—like all dreams: a God who could make good children as easily as bad, yet preferred to make bad ones; who could have made every one of them happy, yet never made a single happy one; who made them prize their bitter life, yet stingily cut it short; who gave his angels eternal happiness unearned, yet required his other children to earn it; who gave his angels painless lives, yet cursed his other children with biting miseries and maladies of mind and body; who mouths justice and invented hell—mouths mercy and invented hell—mouths Golden Rules, and forgiveness multiplied by seventy times seven, and invented hell; who mouths morals to other people and has none himself; who frowns upon crimes, yet commits them all; who created man without invitation, then tries to shuffle the responsibility for man's acts upon man, instead of honorably placing it where it belongs, upon himself; and finally, with altogether divine obtuseness, invites this poor, abused slave to worship him! . . .

"You perceive, *now,* that these things are all impossible except in a dream. You perceive that they are pure and puerile insanities, the silly creations of an imagination that is not conscious of its freaks—in a word, that they are a dream, and you the maker of it. The dream-marks are all present; you should have recognized them earlier.

"It is true, that which I have revealed to you; there is no God, no universe, no human race, no earthly life, no heaven, no hell. It is all a dream—a grotesque and foolish dream. Nothing exists but you. And you are but a *thought*—a vagrant thought, a useless thought, a homeless thought, wandering forlorn among the empty eternities!"

He vanished, and left me appalled; for I knew, and realized, that all he had said was true.